'Hey up, Rachel!'

She turned to see Micky Caradine runn█████████ field. When he reached the top he vaulted o████ ██ █ if he had springs on his feet.

'Where're you off to?' He █████████ over his face as he came up to her. 'Th████ ████████ bobby-dazzler in that outfit.' He gave ███ ████ ██████ ppreciative, and very thorough, all-over inspec███ █████.

Rachel felt a blush cree ██to her cheeks. A smile glowed from her face as she replied, 'I'm having a walk. What are you doing?'

'I've been giving them a hand at the farm. I was on my way home. But I thought it was you.' He walked by her side, his hands stuffed into the pockets of his jeans, his heavy boots crunching the ground. A rabbit suddenly scurried across the path in front of them, and she laughed with pleasure. Micky returned her smile, and there was something in his expression that caused her to blush again.

They walked on in silence for a while. Then Micky looked at her again with appreciation. 'You look a real picture in that,' he said, and something entered his eyes she did not understand.

'Get off with you.' Her nervousness returned. 'You always were the biggest liar in the school,' she said jokingly. It seemed so strange. She knew him so well, and yet she had the feeling she was walking with a stranger.

JANET HASLAM was born and bred in Derbyshire, in the same village on the edge of the Pennines where her ancestors have lived for generations. She now lives in a nearby village with her husband and three children; this is her first novel for Corgi.

RACHEL'S DAUGHTER

Janet Haslam

CORGI BOOKS

RACHEL'S DAUGHTER
A CORGI BOOK 0 552 13976 9

First publication in Great Britain

PRINTING HISTORY
Corgi edition published 1993

Set in 10/11pt Linotype Times by Kestrel Data, Exeter

Corgi Books are published by Transworld Publishers Ltd,
61–63 Uxbridge Road, London W5 5SA, in Australia by
Transworld Publishers (Australia) Pty Ltd, 15–23 Helles Avenue,
Moorebank, NSW 2170, and in New Zealand by Transworld
Publishers (NZ) Ltd, 3 William Pickering Drive, Albany, Auckland.

Made and printed in Great Britain by
Cox & Wyman Ltd., Reading, Berks.

For
Fiona, Duncan and Paula
With Love

Chapter One

1959
'In life, in death, O Lord, abide with me . . .'

Like the rest of the Cooper family, Rachel's voice trailed away as the dying strains of the organ swirled around the high oak rafters of the small chapel. The congregation all stood very still, until the music, seeming to be sucked right back into the large brass pipes, left the chapel in a heavy silence. Several dutifully reverent moments were obeyed, then the quiet was broken by the shuffle of hymn books closing and being placed down on the backs of the old beeswaxed pews.

The preacher began the final blessing and Rachel stood like a statue, very straight, very still, hands clasped tightly before her closed eyes, until the droning monotone came to an end and she felt free to look around the sombre congregation.

Why did everyone look so serious and miserable? she asked herself. God was supposed to be good, giving love and kindness. So why didn't this lot look a bit happier about it? Every week Rachel pondered the mystery. She found it all very confusing . . . and boring.

If her father did not insist the whole family attend regular Sunday worship, she knew she would never set foot inside the place again.

When the preacher was halfway down the aisle, taking his usual laboriously slow journey to the door to bid the worshippers farewell, Micky Caradine dropped his hymn book and made a lot of noise about picking it up again.

Micky's father scuffed his ear. Micky, ever defiant, turned around and pulled a funny face at Rachel . . . and got his ear scuffed a second time.

He was a one, that Micky Caradine. A laugh bubbled inside Rachel, but she kept it hidden. To do something sinful, like

7

actually giving way to mirth in God's house, would have earned her father's displeasure. And that was something to be avoided at all times!

'Good night, Mr Cooper . . . Mrs Cooper.' The preacher shook Daniel and Violet Cooper's hands in turn, then bestowed a benevolent smile over the three members of the Cooper brood, as they trailed in single file through the narrow oak doorway behind their parents.

As Rachel stepped out into the cold night air, she gave a sigh of relief. The night was dark and she glanced at her brother, seeing only the shadows of his face, but knowing he shared her feelings. She was always grateful when chapel was over for another week and they could get back to normal. Not that normal was a particularly pleasing prospect, not in the Cooper household. But at least the rest of the week was not filled with the hypocritical show that was reserved for Sundays.

Daniel Cooper, her father, was the reason Rachel hated chapel and all it stood for. He was, she imagined, the biggest hypocrite of them all. A man who put on an act for the outside world. But let him get behind the closed doors of home and a very different man appeared: a bully of a man who thought his family was there just to serve him; a man who would be obeyed at all times . . . or he saw it his duty to administer punishment of the severest kind.

Rachel and Joseph both bore the scars of their father's rough justice. So far, little Sarah, at only seven, had not yet learned to question his reasoning, which was the greatest sin in the Cooper household.

'Michael Caradine needs taking in hand,' Daniel Cooper announced to anyone who might be listening, as they walked down the frosty path into the darkened street and began the journey home. No-one made any reply. It was not expected. Daniel Cooper always assumed everyone was of the same opinion as himself, no matter what the subject.

They were not allowed to speak to each other as they walked along. Talking on the street was for gossipmongers and slanderers, he declared at regular intervals.

Rachel often wondered what he thought she might say to Sarah on the street that could not be said at home. She knew better than to ask the question. So the two sisters indulged in their usual game, seeing who could blow the biggest breath cloud in the frosty air that nipped at their cheeks and noses. Though even that was done behind their father's back, their heavy breaths blown silently and their giggles stifled behind thick woollen mittens.

The Coopers lived at the end of a row of terraced, grey-stone cottages, halfway up the steep hill which led to the top of the Chevin. Up the top, as all the locals called it. It was one of Rachel's favourite places. When you reached the top, the road ended, giving way to a narrow cart track on which you could walk along the pinnacle of the hills until you reached the next village. You could look down on either side as you walked, getting a bird's eye view of two green, tree-dotted valleys, and when you were coming back, you got a third, of Millbridge, their village, as you reached the brow and began to descend the steep slope.

Rachel loved it up there. She felt that if there really was a heaven it must be like being up the top on a sunny day, with the grass soft beneath your feet and the breeze ruffling your hair. Where the clouds seemed to be so close you could reach out and touch one.

As the family procession turned the corner and began to climb the hill, Billy Bolton, one of Joseph's friends, was crossing the road to go into the Institute where they played billiards.

'Evenin' Joe,' Billy called, and Joseph responded and lifted his hand in acknowledgement. 'Are you coming for a game?' Billy enquired.

'Not at the moment,' Joseph returned. 'Maybe later.'

Daniel Cooper gave a loud snort of disgust and Rachel glanced at her brother, holding her breath as she waited for some sharp retort.

Joseph merely winked at her in return and Rachel breathed again.

Joseph was a man now and would not be put down by their

father, she realized. It pleased her that at last Daniel Cooper had someone to stand up to him. But it also frightened her at times. Their father was so used to setting about his children physically that Rachel feared one day he would lead Joseph to go too far, making him do something he would later regret. Fortunately Joseph had more about him than their father did. All the same, Rachel was thankful her brother would soon be in the army, and out of it.

They were almost home when Millie Stevenson came tripping down the hill. Millie's wide skirt, puffed out by at least two cancan underskirts, flounced around her legs and the high-heeled shoes she was wearing were lethal on the steep incline. Millie was having to cling tightly to her male companion's arm to stop herself falling over: a state which seemed to be causing much hilarity and Millie's giggling laughter filled the night.

'Evenin', Mr Cooper,' Millie chirped as they approached.

'Good evening, Millicent,' Daniel Cooper replied haughtily.

'Good evening,' Violet Cooper said, omitting to add any name and making Rachel wish, that just for once, her mother would have the courage to show her real self. She knew very well that if her father had not been there, her mother would have addressed the girl as Millie. But Daniel Cooper did not approve of overfamiliarity . . . commonness, as he called it.

Rachel called it unfriendly and rude, most of all rude. He was so sure he was better than everybody else around. But his attitude only made him a laughing stock, and made Rachel embarrassed to be his daughter.

As if proving her thoughts had not been too hard, when Millie and her companion had passed by, Daniel Cooper gave a loud sniff of disdain, making clear his feelings. Rachel cringed at her father's arrogance. Millie and her friend might have gone past, but they were still within hearing of her father's bad manners.

But then Millie and the man burst into raucous laughter and, even though Daniel Cooper responded with a second and much louder snort of disgust, Rachel had to smile. She should have known Millie would not be afraid to let him know she thought nothing of his high and mighty ways, she realized, and felt pleased that Millie had responded to his rudeness.

'Harlots,' Daniel Cooper pronounced, peering down his long nose at his two daughters, and reminding them, as he did at regular intervals, 'I would never let such a brazen trollop darken my door.'

'Yes, Father,' Rachel and Sarah replied in unison, as they turned down the cobblestone yard leading to the last tall, dark grey-stone terraced cottage. They knew if they did not reply he would have repeated himself until they showed they had been paying attention.

A single lamp gave little light to their path and they had to pick their way carefully through the clutter of firewood, buckets and brushes that were left lying around. Daniel Cooper gave yet another snort of disgust, at the living conditions of his neighbours. Rachel kept her head down, hoping none of the neighbours were about to hear, and grabbed Sarah's arm to help her along.

Despite his shortcomings, Daniel Cooper was not a mean man where money was concerned. He always expected the house to be neat and tidy and the children well clothed. Rachel would have felt it was a point in his favour, had she not realized it was his own pride he was feeding. But she was grateful for the large fire and the warmth of the comfortable little room, as she slipped off her knitted mittens and thick woollen coat.

Sunday was always a ritual, from getting up in the morning, attending morning service, spending the afternoon in reading or some other quiet pursuit – the Cooper children were never allowed to indulge in noisy pastimes – to evening service followed by the finale: the family conference on the preacher's sermon.

Tonight was to be no different. First they hung their best coats up in their wardrobes. Then the entire family sat round the blazing fire that roared up the chimney of the small front room's brick fireplace.

Daniel Cooper leaned back in his large leather chair and

11

sucked on his pipe. 'What did you learn this evening?' he asked, directing the question at Sarah.

It was always the same. Rachel held her breath, willing her sister to know the reply. He always picked on the youngest first. Rachel felt it was very unfair of him. Then life with Daniel Cooper was always unfair, she reminded herself.

'That you have to help other people,' Sarah eventually, and very timidly, replied.

Rachel breathed a silent sigh of relief.

'Quite right, Sarah. Quite right.' Daniel Cooper nodded in appreciation. 'But what else?' He took his pipe out of his mouth and tapped it against the fire wall. Then he took his tobacco pouch and began to fill the bowl. He was tamping the tobacco and the tension in the room had turned electric, as they all waited for Sarah to continue, before he repeated himself. 'But what else, Sarah? Was there not a moral to the story?'

Oh yes, there was a moral, Rachel thought bitterly, as she watched her sister's face becoming more worried by the moment. The Good Samaritan had been the evening's lesson. Rachel felt her father could take a tip or two from it.

'What if it troubles you to help somebody?' Joseph put in, trying to help his young sister along.

'Be quiet, Joseph,' Daniel Cooper insisted, not raising his voice, but using the unnaturally silent tone that spread dread through Rachel. She knew, when his voice dropped in that ominous fashion, it meant more trouble than had he begun bawling straight away.

'Were you not listening, Sarah?' The menace in his eyes as he fixed the young girl, reached out to Rachel. Even though his gaze was not pointed in her direction, she felt herself go cold inside.

'Yes . . . but . . . I'm sorry, Father . . . I forgot.' Sarah whimpered as she spoke, and visibly shrank into the corner of the old leather sofa.

A tide of anger engulfed Rachel. Oh, how she hated him. She looked to her mother, though knew she would get no help from that direction. Violet Cooper was capable of showing a bit of love when her husband was not around, but it was only a bit, and when he was there she always remained in silent agreement with all he said and did.

At one time it had made Rachel very sad to think their mother did not love them enough. Now it just made her mad, furious in fact, when it was Sarah who was being picked on. Joseph and herself were now big enough to fight back, but Sarah wasn't.

All of a sudden it was too much for Rachel. Not quite realizing what she was doing, she leaped to her feet, rounding her small frame on her father.

'She's only seven! You can't expect her to remember everything.' Temper shivered through her. Her hands, clenched in tight fists, shook with her rage.

For a long moment the air in the room could have been cut with a knife. Daniel Cooper stared at his daughter, the shock of her daring to question him displayed clearly in his bulging eyes and tautly fastened mouth.

Violet Cooper also stared at her daughter, her hand pressed tightly to her chest, as if the shock was too much for her and she was about to have the vapours.

Joseph slowly stood up and moved to his sister's side. Rachel thrust out her arm, holding him back. She had spoken now, by her own doing. She would not get Joseph involved.

The coals in the fire dropped, sending a shower of sparks flying up the chimney. Rachel's gaze shifted momentarily, as the noise made her jump and Daniel Cooper, seeming to be brought back to life by the noise, moved forward.

'We go to chapel to learn the word of God. And learn it we will! *All of us!*' He brought his hand down on the table with a mighty crash that lifted the fruit bowl in the air. 'You are never too young to learn the word of the Good Book,' he insisted, his face darkening, blood rushing to his cheeks. Rachel paled and visibly flinched.

Or have it thrust down your throat, she thought, wishing she had the courage to speak the words, as she reached behind her for the support of the dresser and felt her previous courage leave her as quickly as it had come.

13

'You will both go to your room and write out the entire story of the Good Samaritan . . . and I don't want so much as one word missed out.' His cheeks had turned a vivid red. He thrust his face into Rachel's. 'Not one word!' he hissed, and his spittle sprayed over her face and she shuddered in revulsion. 'Do you hear me?' he demanded, as Rachel turned her head away in disgust.

'Yes . . . yes, Father,' she replied, forcing her voice to show a confidence she was far from feeling, as she waited for the next step: the hand to crack her head around the right way so she was looking at him. He could never bear not seeing the whites of your eyes when he was having a go at you. But at that moment she preferred to be hit than spat at again, and kept her head turned from him.

It was as Daniel Cooper lifted his hand to do what Rachel expected, that Joseph stepped in. He grasped his father's outstretched arm, forcing the older man to look in his face. 'There'll be no more of that,' he said, his voice full of warning, his face full of the years of hate.

Rachel did look around then, suddenly horrified at what she had done. This was what she had feared for a long time, and now she had been the cause of it.

Violet Cooper gasped loudly, and for the second time that evening Daniel Cooper's face displayed utter shock. 'It is my duty to administer punishment to my children,' he insisted, and looked as if he was about to square up to Joseph.

It was Rachel's turn to gasp then. From the cold dread of only moments before, her body was on fire with a fear so warm it felt as if hot water was in her veins.

'No! Joseph!' She thrust herself forward, pushing herself between father and son. She wasn't really sure what she was doing. She was far too small and no match for the two large bodies she was squashed between. But she had to try. Their father was short and stocky, but with powerful arms and legs. Joseph had inherited that strength, but he had also inherited their mother's height and was much taller and had youth on his side. And all Rachel could think was to stop her brother before he proved his strength and did something terrible.

'Get out of it, Rachel.' Joseph would have none of her interference and thrust her away. 'It's about time somebody showed him what it's like to be on the receiving end for a change.'

'No, Joseph. Oh no . . . !' she cried in panic, once more clutching the dresser for support, as she watched her brother draw back his fist and with the other hand grab his father by the collar.

Daniel Cooper visibly paled. 'I . . . I . . .' he began, then words failed him.

Joseph laughed. A loud sarcastic laugh that seemed out of place on his usually gentle mouth. The sound cut into Rachel's chest like a knife. She heard a whimper and was not sure if it came from herself or Sarah, huddled in a frightened ball on the sofa.

'Don't like it, do you?' Joseph's hand remained pulled back. He looked like some ghastly statue, frozen in attack. Only his lips moved, as he said, 'It's another matter when it's you who's going to get hurt.'

Daniel Cooper was actually shaking in his son's grasp. He held his hands up protectively and a strange animal-like sound came from his throat.

Rachel's eyes widened in astonishment. She had never thought to live to see the day when her father would be brought to his knees. Yet, she imagined, if Joseph let go of his collar, that was what her father would do: sink to his knees and beg.

Words failed her. She lifted her hand, as if the action would be enough to stop all this. It took several moments for her to realize what was actually going on.

Joseph did not move. He was not proving his strength by open brutality. He was showing he could do it, if he really wanted to, while his father cringed like a frightened rabbit in his grasp. Actually cringed!

'Let him go, Joseph!' The voice came from across the room.

Rachel's eyes pivoted to her mother. She was unable to conceal her amazement that the woman had actually plucked up the courage to join in, even though she appeared to be joining sides with her husband. Then her mother said, 'Don't do it, Joseph,' and there was a plea in her voice that Rachel suspected was more for her son than for the man she had married.

Or maybe she just wanted to believe their mother would one day come out on their side. It had been a hope she had clung to in the long years of childhood, but she felt so anxious that she was not sure what she was hearing and what she wasn't.

'Don't fret, Mother.' Joseph gave another harsh laugh as he spoke. 'I'm not like him. I don't have to prove my manhood.' He threw his father away, sending him sprawling against the table. 'Look at him!' Joseph's voice was full of scorn, disgust spilled from his gaze and belittled his father. 'He can't take it when he finds someone who'll give it back. But let me warn you . . .' He raised his finger to his father. '. . . I'll not have the girls hit any more. Even when I'm gone in the army. If I come home and find you've as much as raised a finger to them, you'll have me to answer to.'

Daniel Cooper did not reply. Neither did he move. He was still supporting himself on the table, when Joseph said, 'Take Sarah up to bed, Rachel.'

Without waiting to be told again, Rachel grabbed the sobbing Sarah and bustled her up the narrow winding staircase.

'I don't want Joseph to go away,' Sarah sobbed, as they sat on the bed and Rachel rocked her in her arms.

Neither did Rachel. But she knew Joseph had no choice. He would be eighteen in one month and due for National Service. He couldn't have got out of it, even if he had wanted to. Which he didn't. Joseph was looking forward to going in the army.

'He's got to go,' Rachel said, looking down into Sarah's bleak little face. Then she lightened her voice. 'Anyway, things will be different now.' At least she hoped they would. She had never seen her father looking the way he had looked tonight, scared, pathetic. It wasn't something she wanted to see again; not for her father's, but for Joseph's sake.

Eeh, that it had had to come to this, she thought, and

glanced down to find Sarah had cried herself to sleep. If only their father could be more like other men. It was a vain hope, she knew. Her father scorned the village men who made the nightly pilgrimage to the Beehive for a pint or two. He would never have lowered himself. She gave a grim smile. From what she had seen, those men looked a lot happier than her father. It was sad, she thought, as she settled Sarah down in bed, but for all his godliness and piety, Daniel Cooper never looked happy.

It was as Rachel sat at the dressing table uncoiling her long blond plait, that she heard raised voices coming from downstairs. Not again, she thought, feeling her anxiety rising as she sat very still and listened, trying to pick up what was being said. She considered going downstairs to lend support to Joseph. Then decided she would be better keeping out of it. Joseph would not thank her, she told herself. But she really should go down. It wasn't fair to leave Joseph to sort her messes out.

Just then Joseph's voice shouted angrily, 'I'm going. And that's all there is to it!' A moment later the front door slammed and his hurried footsteps tramped down the yard.

Rachel breathed a sigh of relief, the decision taken from her. He was going to spend the evening with Billy at the Institute. She was pleased he had overruled their father, even though it would mean another argument when he got back. At the best of times, Daniel Cooper hated his son frequenting the place, where, in the dimly lit room, the two large green baize billiard tables stood.

Rachel had never been inside the Institute. She had often peeped through the window to see this den of iniquity that so disgusted her father. She had to admit it all looked rather gloomy. Clouds of cigarette smoke swirled in the beams of the two large square lights which hung low over the tables and were the only illumination in the otherwise darkened room. But the Institute with its billiard room and upstairs table tennis room was the only entertainment in the village, apart from the Beehive.

Rachel could just imagine her father's reaction if Joseph

decided to go drinking of a night. She grimaced at her own reflection in the mirror. It did not take much to turn Daniel Cooper's face the colour of beetroot.

As she ran the hairbrush slowly through her long blond hair, she became quietly thoughtful, seeing not her own reflection, but her father in one of his rages. He always looked as if his anger was too much for his stocky body to contain and that at any moment he might explode.

Oh, how she wished he would explode. She had heard of people who had got themselves so worked up they expired, right then and there, falling flat on the floor, one minute alive, the next dead.

It was a terrible thought, she told herself guiltily. It was against all the teachings of Christianity that chapel thrust down your throat. But, even though she stood up and quickly began to undress, she found the thought lingered at the back of her mind.

It was when she had taken off all her clothes and was about to slip her nightdress over her head, that her reflection caught her eye once more. Her gaze rested on the deep scar above her shoulder blade and she ran her finger across the deep indentation, where her father's belt had torn the flesh away from the bone.

Sarah stirred restlessly in the bed and Rachel turned to her and smiled fondly. So far Sarah's little body did not bear any scars from their father's fury, and, if Rachel had anything to do with it, it never would. In that moment she felt her love for her sister grow inside her, expanding with a ferocity that fuelled the hate she had for her father. Despite Joseph's threat, she could not believe her father would not lay his hands on either of them ever again. He was a weak and spineless bully. He would threaten more violence if they told on him. He was a brute.

He was a bastard, she told herself, and pulled her nightdress quickly over her young body and felt a warm flush leaping to her cheeks with the use of the word. Even though she had only thought it, it was an obscenity, a rude word which would have sent her father into a blue funk. She wasn't sure if that

18

was rude either. And she didn't care. In fact, she hoped it was. To Rachel's mind there were not enough rude words in existence to describe her father. He was the worst kind of brute! To confirm the charge she pulled the sleeve of her nightdress aside, looked again at the deep scar on her shoulder, in the perfect position to never be seen. He never left a mark where it would show. They were all well hidden when she was wearing clothes. The upright Daniel Cooper would never have done anything to upset his standing in the local community, nothing that would have shown him up for what he really was.

In that moment Rachel felt more hate for the man who was her father than she had ever felt before. And, feeling weak with the force of her emotions, she sank down on the dressing table stool, dropped her head into her hands, and with all she had inside her, wished her own father to get himself into such a fury that it would kill him . . . and leave them all in peace!

Chapter Two

It was the early hours of the morning before Rachel was to realize the enormity of the evening's last thoughts.

'Wake up, Rachel! Wake up!'

Rachel forced her eyes to open into the half-light coming through the open bedroom door. Joseph was standing over her, his hand on her arm, urgently shaking her awake.

'Come on,' he insisted, the same urgency filling his voice. 'Get up. I've got to get the doctor!'

It was the final word that stirred Rachel into action.

'Doctor! What's . . . what's wrong?' She sat up in bed, the next moment was leaping out, spurred by the troubled look on her brother's face. 'What's wrong? Who's ill?'

Panic shook her voice and she could feel her arms and legs beginning to tremble from something far deeper than the cold air. She pulled her dressing gown quickly round herself. All she could think was that if the doctor was needed at this hour, then it must be serious.

'It's Father. I've taken Mother downstairs. I want you to go and sit with her.'

Downstairs! Rachel looked blankly at her brother. If their father was ill, then why wasn't their mother staying with him? The answer was all too clear. Yet still her lips formed the question, 'Why?'

'Come on, love.' Joseph wrapped his arm around her shoulders.

Terms of endearment and caring actions were frowned on in the Cooper household. Joseph had never put his arm around her before . . . or called her love! That he had now put more dread into Rachel than if he had spoken straight out the awful realization that was slowly forming in her mind.

'What has happened?' she asked, staring numbly into

his face, having the feeling she already knew the answer.

'I think he's gone.' Joseph spoke as gently as he could. 'Mother needs you.' He hesitated and glanced back to the sleeping Sarah. 'Will she wake up?' he asked anxiously.

'No.' Rachel shook her head. 'If she's not awake now, she won't wake up.' Sarah was a heavy sleeper, and at that moment Rachel was thankful for it. She did not know what was going to be waiting for her downstairs but, whatever it was, she wanted Sarah to be spared.

'Come on, then.' Joseph led her out on to the landing.

'Are . . . are you sure?' Rachel glanced briefly at their parents' closed bedroom door, not wanting to imagine the scene that was lying on the other side.

'As sure as I can be,' Joseph replied, and closed the door on the sleeping Sarah before turning back to Rachel. 'As sure as I can be,' he repeated, and for the first time she saw the true colour of his face, like marble in the glare of the landing light's clear globe. She knew then he was sure in his own mind that their father was dead. He just did not want to speak the words.

The memory which Rachel had been trying to push to the back of her mind for the last few, terrible minutes, reared up inside her head. All she could see was herself, sitting at the dressing table. All she could hear was her wish for her father to be dead. She felt faint and grabbed the banister to support herself. Joseph's face blurred, then came back into focus.

'Hold tight, Rachel.' Joseph quickly grabbed hold of her. Had he not, she felt she would have fallen down the stairs. 'Mother needs you. You mustn't let yourself go.'

The urgent plea in her brother's voice brought Rachel back to shaky normality. Yes, she had to be strong, she ordered herself. But Joseph did not know how strong.

'I'm all right now.' She pushed Joseph away and forced her feet to carry her down the stairs to her mother.

It took Joseph thirty-five minutes to get Dr Mellor out of bed and up to the cottage. It seemed to be the longest thirty-five minutes of Rachel's life.

Violet Cooper sat silently, staring at the banked-down fire.

It was cool in the room, but Rachel had neither the sense, nor the inclination, to get the fire going. All she was capable of was sitting in the chair opposite, staring at her mother, the evening's terrible thoughts haunting her.

She had wished her father dead and she had got her wish. It was her fault. She was as guilty of murder as if she had taken a knife and stabbed him with it. She wanted to cry, but her tears were locked away inside, refusing to come out and give release to the emotion that was coiling tightly round her heart.

Her father was dead and she was to blame. She had not liked him, at times she had hated him, but never had she felt love – until now, when it was too late.

It seemed incredible. But love was the only name she could put to it, the strange, overwhelming emotion she had never before experienced for her father. But he *had* been her father. Despite everything she was his flesh and blood and now he was gone. She had a pain deep inside that threatened to tear her in two. A pain for all the things she could have done with him – if only he had loved her. It was a strange feeling, one she could not explain. She could not understand why she should suddenly have wanted to do things with her father. Daniel Cooper had been a man to be avoided as much as possible. But if only he had been different, she kept thinking.

Willing the time on, she looked at the clock. The minute hand seemed to have stopped, frozen at that terrible hour. She looked at her mother, begging her to speak, to ease the burden of guilt pressing on her, to tell her she loved her. A vain, desperate hope, she knew only too well. She could not recall her mother ever speaking those words to her, and now all her mother was doing was sitting like a statue, her face bloodless, her eyes and lips so still that had it not been for the rise and fall of her chest, Rachel could have imagined it was her mother who was dead and not . . .

She lifted her eyes to the ceiling and shivered, wondering how she could have had any loving thoughts towards him. Her father had been possessed of an evil side to his personality. And chapel always said evil people had evil spirits inside them. She shivered again and wished Joseph would hurry back.

The doctor was not there long. After being upstairs for not quite ten minutes, he returned to the front room and plonked his old black leather bag down on the table.

'It was his heart,' he pronounced, as if he was announcing the winner of the Derby – which he had not backed. He scribbled something down on his pad, then peered over his glasses at the silent Violet Cooper. 'I imagine it would have been quick. He would not have known much about it.' When he received no response he turned to Joseph. 'I'll be back later, with the certificate and . . .' He nodded towards Mrs Cooper. '. . . to see if there's anything else you are wanting.'

'Aye.' Joseph glanced bleakly at his mother. 'Yes, Doctor, I think that would be a good idea.'

Rachel felt she was an eavesdropper to some black comedy. Dr Mellor, acting as if this was a normal everyday occurrence, showing not the slightest sympathy. Joseph, now with his hands stuffed in his pockets, staring at the carpet as if he'd lost a pound and found a penny. Herself, wanting to ask the doctor what might have caused it, and feeling as if her tongue had been ripped out. And her mother sitting in the midst of it all as if nothing was happening and no-one else was there.

'You'll see to all the arrangements?' Dr Mellor once more peered over the top of his glasses at Joseph.

Silly old fool, Rachel thought. Who else would see to the arrangements?

Joseph merely nodded, and Dr Mellor walked out and closed the door behind him.

When, in later years, Rachel looked back on the three days between her father's death and his funeral, she found she could remember very little. Her mother remained in the same chair, eating only a fraction of the food she placed in front of her. She spoke very little, and when she did, it was always the same: 'What am I going to do now?' So all the arrangements for the funeral had been left to Joseph and the housework and preparation of the funeral tea were left to Rachel.

Rachel did not mind being thrust in charge of the house. It kept her busy and her mind occupied, preventing her from dwelling too long on her feelings of guilt. What she had minded was that her mother had not only shut herself off from both Joseph and herself, but also Sarah.

Rachel tried to do her best to look after Sarah. But Sarah, being so young, was finding it difficult to understand everything that was going on.

She tried to talk to her mother. But her mother had built a barrier round herself, and seemed not to hear anything that was being said to her.

'Or not want to hear!' Rachel angrily told Joseph, when they were alone in the kitchen.

'Give her time,' Joseph replied, trying to console his sister.

She did give her mother time. Telling herself that Joseph was right, their mother just needed to come to terms with her grief, she let her be for a whole week. It angered her that her mother had chosen to turn her back on her children, leaving her daughter to take her place in the house. She would not have minded looking after her mother, if she had been ill. But Dr Mellor insisted there was nothing wrong with her, and could only put the reaction down to the shock of the suddenness of her husband's death.

Well it had been a shock to them all, Rachel thought, when irritation was getting the better of her, and her mother should have known that and been there to help her children . . . especially Sarah, who needed her more than the others.

She had felt like telling her mother just that on several occasions, putting her anger into words and shocking some life back into her. But she had kept silent, hoping that the following day would bring the change Dr Mellor continually promised.

'Are you going to the Institute?' Rachel looked across the table to Joseph, as they sat quietly after the evening meal. He had not been out for an evening for over a week. She knew he wanted to go, but did not want to leave them alone.

'Well . . .' Joseph looked up, and seemed to be tossing

the idea over inside his head, but not able to make it land the right way up. 'I hadn't thought about it.'

'I think you should.' Rachel pushed her empty plate away. 'We should get back to normal, for our own sakes.'

Normal! She wanted to laugh at her own statement. The Cooper family had never been normal. At least now they had a chance to start life again, this time for real. They no longer had to live under the threat of upsetting their father.

It was a terrible thought, she told herself. She still held herself responsible for her father's death, but could not stop one part of her being relieved he was gone. She had not spoken her feelings to Joseph, she felt they were too evil to reveal, even though she hoped he might share the same relief.

'Perhaps tomorrow.' He glanced at his mother, and Rachel knew he was living on the same dreams that she herself was. Perhaps tomorrow their mother would return to life. Perhaps tomorrow she would be relieved of all the household chores. Perhaps tomorrow would never come!

'Aren't you eating any more of that?' She suddenly glared at Sarah's almost full plate, her voice snapping harder than intended, frustration getting the better of her.

Sarah's bottom lip trembled. 'I'm full,' she whimpered.

Her own thoughtlessness immediately stabbed Rachel. 'I'm sorry,' she was quick to apologize. She rested a comforting hand on Sarah's thin arm. 'Leave it, if you want.' It wasn't Sarah's fault, she reminded herself guiltily.

Joseph levelled his gaze at Rachel. 'Have you had any more thoughts about staying on at school?'

'No!' It was not a subject she wanted to pursue, and she began to pile the dirty plates together, taking her frustration out on the horrible primrose-yellow crockery which her mother loved so much, which she had always hated. 'You know I've already made my mind up about that!' The crockery rattled noisily in her hands, as she slammed the plates around, wishing Joseph would shut up.

Joseph had not been pleased when she told him she was leaving school, halfway through the year that should have ended with her O levels. But it wasn't his decision. Money would be tight, even if she got a job, because she wouldn't be starting off on a big wage. She glanced at her mother, still silent, still frozen. There wouldn't even be a low-paying job, she told herself. At the moment her mother was not capable of looking after herself, never mind a seven year old. And until she was, she had no intention of leaving Sarah in her charge.

'But you'd planned to stay on and get your exams,' Joseph continued, refusing to be put off by his sister's stubborn stance.

'Yes, well, plans have to be changed . . . sometimes!' she added pointedly, not looking at her brother, as she picked up the pile of plates and swept into the kitchen, wanting the subject brought to an end.

But Joseph followed her. 'What about being a teacher?'

'What about looking after Mother and Sarah?' she replied irritably. Training to be a teacher had been what she had lived for. Now it was all gone. She did not need Joseph to point it out to her. 'Who's going to look after them if I'm not here? Sarah's not old enough to look after herself. Surely you don't expect her to come home from school of a dinner time and get a meal for herself *and* Mother.' Bitterness rang through her voice. It wasn't fair, she thought. If only their mother would pull herself together there would be no problems. She wanted to go right back into the front room and shake her mother, making her see what she was doing to them, her children.

Joseph shook his head; that he was worried was plain to see. For the second time in a few minutes, Rachel regretted her thoughtless self-pity.

'Oh, Joseph, I don't mean to snap,' she said, shaking her head in despair, her ponytail bouncing from side to side. 'Can't you see the position I'm in? If I tried to go back to school it would be no good. I'd be forever worrying what was happening here. I'd not be able to concentrate on anything.'

'Mother will get right,' Joseph assured, but Rachel could tell from his voice that he did not really believe himself. He was of the same mind as she was, and something told her it was going to be a long time before her mother was right again – if ever she was!

'Perhaps, perhaps not,' she replied wearily. 'But for the present I have to get my priorities right.' She stared hopelessly at Joseph, then she shoved him aside. 'And right now my priorities are to get the washing-up done. So get out of my way.'

She was drying the pots when Joseph came back into the kitchen. 'I think I will go down for a game.'

'Good.' Her smile was relieved. She was pleased he had finally made the decision.

'Will you be all right?' He looked concerned.

'Course we will. Get yourself off and stop worrying. We'll have to get used to not having you around soon, won't we?' As soon as she had spoken, Rachel wished the words back, for a shadow covered Joseph's face.

'Why did it have to happen now? Just when I'm to go in the army!' He thumped one hand against the other in frustration.

Rachel wanted to tell him she was pleased it had happened now. That he could go away knowing he was leaving them safe and in peace. But even though she thought those things, and could see Joseph was being torn in two with concern, she was still of the opinion the words were not suitable to pass her lips.

'Come on now.' She put the tea towel down and forced herself to look happy. 'You've been looking forward to joining up. You've always wanted to get in the army.'

'Aye, like you've always wanted to be a teacher,' he responded dryly.

'Yes, well!' She turned away from the pointed look he was levelling at her. 'Some things can be changed, some can't. You're going in the army and that's that. We'll be fine here. You've got nothing to worry about us for. And anyway, I thought you were going to the Institute? If you don't hurry up, Billy will have so much chalk on his cue you won't stand a chance.'

Joseph smiled at his sister's attempt at humour. Then,

something he had never done before, he pulled her into his arms and gave her a big hug.

Rachel, who had always longed for someone to take her in their arms and hold her – not even her mother had ever held her that way – was so taken by surprise, that she was suddenly overcome. The emotion she had been holding in check for the past week found release, and clinging to Joseph for all she was worth, she sobbed into the fabric of his shirt.

It was several minutes before Joseph finally spoke. 'Come on. Everything will be all right. Life's always been hard, but it won't be half as hard as it has been. Will it?' He looked down into her eyes with brotherly concern.

Rachel shook her head. No, it would not be as hard. And now one of them had actually said it, spoken the words that revealed the relief they were both secretly feeling. She felt her heart lightening. In that one moment she felt as if a great weight had been lifted from her. Her father had, at times, been inhuman. But she was only human, and she could not help the way she was feeling. It was only natural she should feel relief, after living in the tense atmosphere her father's presence had created. It was nothing to be ashamed of, she told herself.

'Eeh, what do I look like?' She pushed Joseph away, realizing she was keeping him from the game she had urged him to go to. 'I'll have to go and get Sarah ready for bed in a minute. I don't want her to see me like this.'

'Here, use this.' Joseph handed her the tea towel, the corner wet where he had run it under the cold tap.

'Thanks.' She smiled fondly, grateful she had a brother like him, amazed he had turned out so gentle and caring after all the beatings he had endured. 'Now get yourself off to the Institute.' She flapped her hand at him.

For a moment Joseph looked uncertain.

'Go on. Get yourself off. You know you want to.'

He grinned sheepishly. 'Aye, I do.' Still looking hesitant he turned to go, then turned back.

Rachel gave him a nod of dismissal.

'I won't be late back,' was his parting comment.

It was as Rachel was tucking Sarah up in bed, that Sarah asked, 'Will Mother be better to fetch me from school?' Her face crumpled. 'I don't want to stop for school dinners,' she said, very close to tears.

Rachel smiled, though it was touched with sadness as she looked down on the worried little face. 'Don't you go fretting now.' She brushed her hand over her sister's golden hair. Once before Sarah had attempted to stay at school all day. It had been a disaster, causing sleepless nights and, on one occasion, a wet bed. The few remaining doubts that Rachel possessed about whether she was doing the right or wrong thing in leaving school were wiped away. 'You'll not have to stop for school dinners. I'm not going back to school unless Mother's well enough to look after you. So I'll be here for you just the way Mother . . .' She pulled herself up short. She had been about to say the way Mother *was*! As if it was their mother who was dead. 'I'll be here for you,' she quickly amended, hoping that her fears that her mother had, in a way, died, were not going to come true.

Soothed by Rachel's reassurance, Sarah sat up in bed and threw her arms around her sister's neck. 'Thank you, Rachel. I love you.'

Even a seven year old! Rachel thought, tears misting her eyes, as she sat down on the bed and wrapped her arms around Sarah, and realized how much they had missed by living under their father's strict rule.

It was too much. First Joseph, now Sarah speaking her feelings. For the second time that evening Rachel began to cry. 'I love you too,' she sobbed, only pulling herself together when she realized her tears were about to undo all the good work of her reassurances, and set Sarah off.

'Come on now, back down,' she urged, gently pushing Sarah on to the pillow. 'And don't go fretting about anything. We'll be fine.' What did it matter if you couldn't get the job you wanted? she asked herself, as she tucked the blanket in and straightened the quilt. There were plenty more jobs, and the happiness on Sarah's face, when she realized she was not going to be deserted, was worth ten.

29

'Night night. God bless,' she said, as she walked to the door and switched off the light.

'Night night, mind the bugs don't bite,' Sarah replied with a giggle.

Rachel smiled. It was what Sarah always said, but usually whispered so that their father would not hear. 'Yes,' she replied, making no attempt to conceal her own amusement. 'And they will if you don't get to sleep,' she insisted, making Sarah giggle again.

Freedom! Rachel thought, smiling as she pulled the door to within a couple of inches of being closed. Then she made her way downstairs, thinking, if only their mother would get right everything would be perfect.

'Would you like a cup of tea?' Rachel looked hopefully at her mother, willing some response out of the silence. She had spoken the moment she stepped down the last stair, in the hope that the suddenness might stir her mother, take her off guard, or something.

Her mother made no reply. Her gaze remained fixed on the blazing fire, and Rachel's heart sank.

'How about a glass of sherry? It will do you good. Pick you up.' Her mother was not a drinker, but she enjoyed a glass of sherry on special occasions. Rachel was willing to try anything that might put the life back into her.

But her mother only shook her head: a slow, spiritless action that tore Rachel in two.

'Eeh, Mother.' In despair she fell to her knees at her mother's side and grasped the hand that lay limply on her knee. The cool lifeless flesh was a shock to her own warm skin and, for the third time that evening, she was close to tears.

'Speak to me,' she pleaded, as she looked up into her mother's blank face. 'It's all over now. We have to go on living.' Why was she having to say these things? she wondered bitterly. It should be her mother who was doing the reassuring.

For a moment she wanted to scream. It wasn't fair. She had her life in front of her and it was all being spoiled. 'Get yourself right, Mother,' she begged, anger spurring her words. 'Then I can go back to school. I can be a teacher!'

But her mother would not get herself right, and Rachel wondered, as she looked on the bleak form, how she could even think she might. She would not even get herself out of the chair and get herself a cup of tea. She had to have someone to take her to the toilet. It was as if she had gone back to childhood. Rachel could not understand why. She did not want to believe her mother had loved her cruel husband more than she loved her children. But it was the only conclusion she could come to.

For several minutes she stayed there, clinging to her mother, trying to will some of her own energy into the lifeless limbs. Then, slowly, her mother turned. But the emptiness of her gaze put an end to Rachel's short belief that she had succeeded in rousing some response. Her mother's eyes looked right through her, and Rachel trembled.

'Help me to bed,' Violet Cooper finally said, with the same lack of emotion in her voice.

Nevertheless Rachel saw a meagre hope and jumped to her feet, only too eager to agree. It was the first time her mother had gone to bed since the night her husband died. It was the first sign of improvement, Rachel told herself, taking her mother's arm and helping her to her feet.

But the lifting of Rachel's spirits did not last. As if she was a child, her mother stood by the bed and allowed Rachel to undress her, put her nightdress on for her, then help her into bed.

There was no response, when Rachel said, 'Good night.' And, as she switched off the light and closed the door behind her, her spirits wilted completely. She had the awful feeling this was to be her life from now on.

She was not sure how she could know it. But from somewhere deep inside herself came the depressing realization that her mother was not going to get better. It was not a new thought, but previously she had been able to push it away. Now there seemed to be something very definite about it. It seemed as if her dreams had been buried along with her father.

31

At fifteen she had become mother to Sarah and nurse to her mother. Any dreams she might have had about examinations and teaching had to be thrown out of the window.

It was the price she was having to pay for her sinful wish to have her father dead, she told herself, as she made her way quietly down the narrow staircase and into the cosy little room which had suddenly taken on the appearance of a prison.

Chapter Three

The following morning Rachel tried to sound cheerful, as she came out of her bedroom to meet Joseph coming down from the garret. All the cottages on the yard were three storeys high and Joseph had the large top room for his own.

'Morning, love.' Joseph sounded equally bright.

Rachel smiled. She liked the way he had taken to calling her 'love'. It strengthened the decision she had come to while lying awake in the dark, to make them all snap out of the doldrums. She had stared into the darkness, listening to Sarah's slow rhythmic breathing. It had been such a peaceful, contented sound and Rachel had found confidence in it. Life was going to be different, she told herself, but that did not necessarily mean bad. It was, after all, the fresh start she had longed for, and she would be a fool if she messed it up by getting depressed about what might have been.

She had heard the mill clock strike three before finally falling to sleep and the lack of rest showed in her face.

'Are you all right?' Joseph asked, looking concerned.

'Fine,' Rachel replied breezily, and hurried down the stairs before Joseph had time to prolong the conversation.

While she prepared the breakfast, Joseph got the fire going and filled the coal scuttle so she did not have to keep running out to the coal house at regular intervals.

'Will there be anything you need getting before you go away?' she asked, looking up from the cheese sandwiches she was preparing for Joseph's lunch-time snap. A lump came to her throat with the thought of Joseph's imminent departure. She kept it hidden. The last thing she wanted was for him to feel bad about leaving them. They would manage, she told herself. She was determined they would manage.

Joseph looked up from the plate of eggs and bacon he was

demolishing. 'No.' He shook his head as he struggled to get his mouth around a large bit of bacon. When the bacon was reduced in size, he said, 'I've got most things I'll be needing. All you need worry about is a bit of last minute washing.'

'That's no problem,' Rachel replied, then returned to the unfinished snap and fell silent. She was going to miss Joseph, she realized, allowing herself a moment of secret self-pity.

'Did she say anything?' Joseph lifted his eyes to the ceiling and the bedroom where their mother lay.

Rachel shook her head and the sadness she had forbidden clouded her eyes. 'Help me up to bed!' It wasn't much and, in the cold light of day, seemed even less than she had imagined last night. 'But it's a start,' she added, forcing her voice to lighten. 'It's a move in the right direction. The doctor said time was the only cure.'

'Aye, but how much time?' Joseph sighed heavily. 'You can't throw your own life away. Can't you think of . . .'

'*No!*' Rachel was adamant, and cut her brother off mid-speech. She knew what he had been about to say: bringing the matter of school back to light. 'I've made the decision and there's no going back.' She placed the cheese sandwiches on to a piece of greaseproof paper, folded them into a packet and pushed it across the table at him. 'We're going forward from today. Not just me, all of us. I don't want to hear any more discussions on what might have been.' For a long moment she favoured him with a determined stare.

'But you've got your life in front of you, Rachel,' he pointed out seriously. He placed his knife and fork down on the empty plate and pushed it across the table. 'I've got the feeling Mother's going to be awkward from now on.'

Awkward! That had not been the way she had seen it. But the end result was the same. She leaned her hands on the table and looked at Joseph. 'I think you're right,' she agreed, slowly nodding her head in acceptance. 'I think I'll be in charge of the house from now on. So I have to make my plans with that thought in mind, don't I?' she added pointedly.

'What plans? What will you be able to do with Sarah and all this round your neck?' His hands swept the air.

'Sarah will never be round my neck,' she retorted fiercely. She loved Sarah more than anything in the world. Sarah would always be a pleasure, never a burden. 'And I haven't had time to think properly, not yet. But I will. Something will turn up.'

'I hope you're right, love.' Joseph pushed his chair back and stood up. A deep frown furrowed his brow. 'But always remember you have a right to your own life.' He picked up his snap and pushed it into his jacket pocket. 'See you later,' he said, as he went out of the door.

Picking up Joseph's dirty plate and mug, Rachel took them into the kitchen. Through the window she could see him walking along the yard. His navy-blue boiler suit was clean and pressed the way he liked it, with the same care as if it had been his best suit. A metal ruler poked out of the long side pocket and she could imagine the clinking of the pencils and small screwdrivers he always had at hand in his breast pocket. He was a good-looking chap, she thought, pride putting a smile on her face. His blond hair, the same colour as her own, was always clean and as neat as his clothes. And he walked so proud. Several of the village girls were already running after him. When he got his army uniform there would be no holding them back.

When he reached the end of the yard he turned down the hill, towards the mill where he was at present working as a mechanic. Rachel turned her attention back to his dirty dishes in the washing-up bowl and gave a deep sigh. When her brother walked out of the cottage to go in the army she could not see him ever coming back. If he did not stay in the army, which she thought he would, he would find a girl and marry and set up his own home.

Rachel hoped he would. She hoped with all her heart that her brother would be happy. But oh, how she was going to miss him!

Forbidding herself to think any further about it, she turned quickly from the sink and put more bacon in the frying pan. Then she called Sarah down for breakfast.

She had hoped that calling Sarah might provoke some action from both bedrooms, and had deliberately called loudly.

But her mother's door remained closed and Sarah was Rachel's only company at the table.

Rachel was at least pleased to see Sarah seemed to have made a change for the better. She gobbled up all her bacon and eggs without any prompting, and only stopped chattering when her mouth was too full to speak.

Rachel hoped it might be a good omen, a sign that things were picking up and that her mother would be the next. She glanced at her mother's breakfast, keeping warm under the blue flame of the grill. It annoyed her to see good food going to waste. But she would not take it up. She wanted her mother to get right again and mollycoddling wouldn't help. If she wanted any breakfast she would have to come downstairs for it, she told herself, and turned her attention back to Sarah.

But Violet Cooper did not come downstairs, either to eat her breakfast or sit silently in the chair. And at the last minute, Rachel was forced to give in.

Sarah was standing at the door, her blond plaits peeping out from beneath the hood of her navy-blue gaberdine raincoat. The little red satchel, filled with an assortment of chewed crayons, matched the red wellington boots and woolly mittens. Rachel smiled at the picture her sister made, as she slipped into her own gaberdine coat; the old school coat she no longer needed. Then she was about to push Sarah through the door, when she stopped.

'Wait a minute!' she said, sounding exasperated. If she didn't take her mother's breakfast up it would get thrown away. And it was important her mother should eat. If she didn't she'd never get right.

Her mother was lying with her eyes closed, as Rachel entered the dimly lit room, carefully balancing the breakfast tray on one arm. Her mother made no move and for a moment Rachel stared at her. She had the feeling she was not asleep, as she moved forwards and put the tray down on the oak bedside cabinet. Then she stood back and looked at her again.

'I brought your breakfast,' she said after a few moments. There was no reply, so she opened the curtains and walked out.

There had been a heavy frost and the hill was slippery. The walls glistened and a thick coating of hoar stretched all the way up one side of the mill chimney. The hill was always treacherous in such conditions and Rachel held tightly to Sarah, as they picked their way carefully down the steep slope.

'Can Sally come and play with me now?' Sarah asked, just as they were trying to navigate a particularly nasty patch of ice.

'No she can't!' Rachel snapped. She understood what Sarah meant by 'now'. Their father would never have allowed friends round to the cottage and *now* he was gone Sarah obviously thought all that was going to change.

Sarah's little face crumpled. 'Why not?' she enquired plaintively.

'Oh!' Rachel stopped and grabbed hold of the wall to support herself. 'I'm sorry.' She had done it again, taken her frustration out on Sarah. 'I'm tired, and it's making me snappy.' What with the ice, and her mother's silence was playing on her mind. She looked down into Sarah's watering eyes and felt her heart tearing in two. Sarah was the last person she should be getting at. 'Of course Sally can come and play.' Sarah had made a very obvious improvement this morning, it was time she did the same, and made the effort to begin the new life she kept telling herself she now had.

'Tomorrow?' Sarah's face brightened hopefully.

'Maybe. We'll see how Mother is first though.'

The little girl seemed placated and a smile remained on her face all the way to school. Then she was laughing and giggling as she met up with Sally and two more friends, and only stopped to give Rachel the briefest of waves before going through the door.

Happy she has not got to stop for school dinners, Rachel thought, and smiled to herself as she passed the Institute and the Beehive, before walking back up the hill. She was pleased she had got at least one problem sorted out. And only wished that her mother's problems would be so easy to deal with.

'Mornin', Rachel. How's your mam?'

Rachel smiled as the short, well-padded figure of Polly

Webster waddled towards her. She was dressed in a bright green coat with a huge fur collar and a pair of battered old walking boots. The boots had belonged to her late husband and Polly had taken to wearing them for several years now. Whenever the hill was covered in ice or snow the boots appeared, after she had discovered the thick rubber treads prevented her from slipping.

'Is she getting on all right?' Polly continued.

'Not too bad, thanks Polly.' Rachel felt no embarrassment in calling the elderly lady by her first name. Despite her age, which Rachel judged to be well into her sixties, Polly Webster was Polly to everyone, old and young alike, and stubbornly refused to answer if addressed as Mrs Webster.

'Well now, that's a good thing,' Polly replied thoughtfully. '*If* it's right!' Polly's kindly old eyes fixed on Rachel.

Rachel dropped her gaze, and reminded herself that Polly was a shrewd one. She should have known she would see right through her. Some said she was too wise. Her father had called Polly a witch. Then her father hadn't had a good word to say about anybody. Besides, Rachel didn't care for what people said. She knew Polly was one of the kindest people she had ever known.

'She isn't too good,' she corrected, and gave Polly a thin smile. 'But the doctor said she'll be all right, given a bit of time.' Her mind filled with the earlier image of her mother's refusal to speak, and she knew she was trying to convince herself as much as Polly.

Suddenly her head dropped on to her chest, tears pressed at her eyes and the emotion she had hidden from Sarah threatened to choke her. It was several moments before she could speak. 'I don't think she is going to get right, ever again,' she finally gasped, as she fought against the humiliation of crying in the street. Not here, she ordered herself. Not where everyone could see.

Her pride finally won, and she was able to lift her head and meet Polly's concerned gaze, and say, 'But we'll manage. It means I've had to leave school. But we'll manage.'

Polly tut-tutted. Then she placed her hand on Rachel's

shoulder and looked her straight in the eyes. 'Course you'll manage! Perhaps I shouldn't be saying this, not just now. But you know me, always says what needs to be said. Your mam's weak, always has been. I expected something like this to happen. But you're not weak, lass. You're like your granddad Cooper, and he was a fine man. It was a crying shame he got killed in the trenches. Your dad would have been very different if he'd had him around when he was growing up.'

Rachel gave a little smile. It was not the first time Polly had told her she came from good stock. Her grandfather had been shot in 1917 and, if Polly had never told her, Rachel would have known nothing about him. It was a subject her father had never raised, except to say his father had died for his country. Her grandmother had always found her son's children a nuisance, and Rachel could never recall the irascible old woman stringing more than two words together to any of them, and now she was also dead.

They were a strange family, Rachel thought, as she stared into Polly's eyes and felt a gentle comfort seeming to flow from Polly into herself.

She gave a little laugh. 'I feel weak now,' she said, disputing any claim to strength.

'That's only natural, and it's no sin. You'll get over it,' Polly assured, and her old eyes began to twinkle. 'Just you remember, lass, there's a rainbow with a pot of gold waiting for everybody. You just have to go out and find it!'

Rachel couldn't see any rainbows at the moment. Neither could she imagine any waiting over the horizon. But Polly meant well. 'At least I've got our Sarah,' she said. Sarah was a rainbow of sorts, and better than any pot of gold.

'You see, lass, you're already looking for the good bits. Keep it up. And if you want any help you know where to find me.'

Polly waddled off across the road, her boots gripping the slippery surface as if she was a mountain goat. Rachel stood for a moment watching her go. She felt a comforting warmth spreading down her arm from the place where Polly had rested her hand. It was a pleasant feeling, and seemed to be having an uplifting effect on her. It made her wonder if Polly really did have some magical power. She smiled, thinking what her father would have said if he had found her having such sinful thoughts.

Evil! Blasphemous!

She could just hear his pious declarations. But she no longer cared what he might or might not have thought, and turned to continue up the hill with the smile still on her face. She supposed that was another sin, disrespectful to her father. But he was gone now. He could no longer vent his wrath on her. From now on she would think and do what she wanted to think and do. It was a nice thought. It felt good.

The first thing Rachel did when she reached home was to go up to her mother. She was still feeling happy after talking to Polly and she experienced a stab of disappointment when she found her mother was still in bed. She had had the feeling suddenly everything was going to be all right and she would find her mother was up and back to normal.

That was not to be. Her mother's eyes were now open, but the glare she gave her daughter was as cold as the fat congealed around the untouched bacon and eggs still lying on the tray.

'Shall I help you get dressed?' Rachel asked, forcing herself to sound hopeful, even though she felt she was wasting her time. Her mother's expression had changed, but not for the better. The vacant stare, which had been fixed on her face since her husband's death, had gone. In its place was a stubborn scowl and, when she spoke, her words echoed with bitterness.

'I'll not be getting up,' she announced, and there was such an obdurate quality to her voice that a shiver ran over Rachel's flesh.

She had never heard her mother sound so harsh. For years she had been the meek little wife, pathetic in her unresisting tolerance of her husband's cruelty. Now Rachel was seeing another side and it frightened her. Frightened her more than her father's temper had ever frightened her.

'You can't stop in bed all day,' she said, attempting

persuasion by common sense. 'There's nothing wrong with you. The doctor says it's only shock. You'll get over it.'

'Shock! Bah! What does he know? My legs have gone.'

Rachel was stunned by her mother's words. 'How can you know that?' she finally asked. She was certain she had not ventured out of the bed. Then, refusing to show any alarm at her new condition, Rachel went over to the tall oak drawers to get some clean underwear for her to put on. She was determined to make her make the effort.

Violet Cooper had very different ideas. 'I know!' she snapped nastily. 'They're my legs and I can feel them from where I am!'

'Well, if you can feel them they're not gone. Are they?' Rachel dropped the underwear on the bed, rested her hands on her hips, and matched her mother's mutinous stare. Being soft had got her nowhere, she realized. And now she could see it was well past time to get tough.

'If you think I'm going to be running up and down stairs all day for you, you can think again. I'm already doing your job. How do you think Sarah feels? Knowing her mother can't be bothered to look after her!'

The small hope that her words might load guilt on her mother was soon gone.

'What do I care?' she snarled, and narrowed her eyes to hard little slits. 'I never wanted any of you! Born out of sin, that's what you all are!'

It was a moment before Rachel could speak. The vile words had put only one conclusion into her head. But that seemed unthinkable of her highly religious parents.

'But . . . but you were married,' she finally found voice to say. 'In the chapel!' Her father had always gone on about the family's religious ceremonies.

'Oh, yes, we were married. But you wait, my girl. You'll find out what that means. Marriage!' The word was a witch-like screech, and Rachel took a step backwards. 'It's just a way of making men's fornication legal. You'll find out. Just you wait and see!'

She was unhinged, Rachel told herself, as her mother's

voice rose in a frenzy of hate. It was the only conclusion she could reach. This was more than a mere reaction to shock. Her father's death had tipped her mother over the edge, turning her into something Rachel did not recognize, and did not want to recognize.

'Stop saying such horrible things,' Rachel insisted, before sweeping the breakfast tray into her hands and hurrying to the door. She would not hang around and provide an audience for her mother's spite. If she had hated her husband so much, it made it doubly damning that she had stood back and allowed his cruelty to go on.

Rachel was in the middle of mopping the linoleum on the kitchen floor, when the mill clock struck ten. She paused, leaning heavily on the stave as she wrung the mop in the bucket. She wondered what Sarah was doing. But the thoughts of simple arithmetic and matchstick drawings would not take her mind off her mother's rantings. It confused Rachel. If her mother had hated the physical side of marriage so much, she should have been over the moon that it was all over. Or so Rachel thought. But if nothing else, it took away any doubts about the future. From what she had seen that morning, she doubted there was much chance of her mother getting better. She really was now in control of everything. The thought made her shiver, as she began sweeping the mop across the floor once more.

Her legs gone! Rachel only hoped they were and that she would stay put in the bedroom. The last thing she wanted was for Sarah to hear such talk.

She was emptying the bucket down the sink, when the banging began on the ceiling. Now what? She put the bucket down and stared at the ceiling. It was only realizing that if she did not get upstairs quickly the ceiling would come down, that made her move.

'I want the pot!' Violet Cooper demanded, the bitterness on her face making her almost unrecognizable.

Rachel had the feeling a screw turned inside her, locking away any remaining feelings she had for her mother. She glanced at the walking stick, propped against the bed, and felt

42

the screw tighten further. The stick had been in the closet, put there by Rachel herself. To get it, her mother had taken at least four steps from the bed, then had to climb the steps into the closet to reach the stick.

'Well, you know where it is.' Rachel's voice trembled with anger. She looked steadily at her mother. 'And if you don't get yourself out of bed to use it, you'll lie in your own mess. For I'll not come and change your sheets!' Without waiting for any reply, she turned and walked out. It was too late for her mother to demand care and attention from her. She would give her the same as she had been given throughout her childhood. That amounted to seeing she was clothed and fed. Love had never come into it.

As Rachel closed the stairfoot door behind her and walked through the front room to the kitchen, she could not find it in her heart to feel any sympathy for the spiteful figure she had left behind in the bedroom.

Chapter Four

The seasons changed, winter into spring, spring into summer. For Rachel life fell into a pattern of looking after her mother and always being there for Sarah. Joseph had been in the army for seven months and she had got accustomed to not having him around. She still missed him, missed having someone to fall back on in her weaker moments, missed having someone who she felt shared her own problems.

Her mother had not come out of the bedroom since the night Rachel had taken her up to bed. She was not displeased with the arrangement. There were days when her mother was not fit to be with other people. Days when her screaming and carrying on became almost unbearable. When she threw her food all over the bed, the floor, and even Rachel, insisting that she was trying to poison her. There were days when she refused to get herself out of bed to use the pot.

When her mother was in that frame of mind, Rachel wanted her to be shut away from the world, and she didn't care how much running up and down stairs she had to do, so long as no-one else witnessed her at her worst.

Then there were the other days, when she was quiet and unresisting. When she ate everything Rachel put in front of her and even, at times, got out of bed to spend some time sitting in a chair by the window.

Although in one way she preferred her mother at those times, the state of apathy and the silence that seemed to go on and on and seemed inhuman caused Rachel more worry than when she was being screamed at and made the target for numerous cups of tea and meat pies. There was something so lifeless about the condition, as if she had died inside and was just waiting for her outer shell to follow where the rest of her had gone.

There were also times when Rachel felt that she, herself, must also be mad, trying to keep her mother at home. Dr Mellor had tried several times to persuade her to have her mother hospitalized: for her own sake more than her mother's.

Rachel always refused, vigorously denying any suggestion that she was not capable of looking after her mother. Nevertheless there were days when she was too much for her and she had to admit it to herself, but she would never have made the same admission to anyone else. She was too afraid that if she did and her mother was taken away, it might be considered she was too young to keep the house on. And, worse than the house, Sarah! Rachel was terrified Sarah would be taken away and put in a home, and she was prepared to do anything to stop that happening.

Fortunately her father, though not a rich man, had had a bit put by and they had enough to live on for the present, so long as they were careful. And Joseph always put a cheque inside his letters to help them along, which took away any immediate pressure on Rachel to find work because they needed the money. So she made the willing choice to continue to nurse her demented mother in the hope that Sarah would lead as normal a life as was possible under the circumstances.

'What does he say? Is he coming home?'

Rachel grinned at Sarah. 'Give me a chance to get it open.' Her fingers trembled with excitement as she struggled to get the airmail envelope open. She took the cheque out first and placed it on the table. Then she opened the two sheets of flimsy writing paper. Joseph had been stationed in Germany for four months and, though Rachel wrote to him every week, they only got one back a month from him. She had been expecting this one to arrive for several days now.

Even though his letters were few and far between, they were always long. He had plenty to say and Rachel loved hearing from him and knowing he was all right.

'He sends his love and a big kiss to you,' she told Sarah, making her giggle with pleasure.

'Is he coming home?'

Rachel quickly scanned each side of the paper. 'Not that I

45

can see. But he's well and happy,' she said, and sat down at the table, returned to the beginning and began to read out loud to Sarah.

'Germany sounds nice,' she said, after reading a long passage on a trip to Bavaria he had taken with some friends. 'He likes it there and . . .' Her heart suddenly skipped a beat and her voice faded away.

'What is it?' Sarah demanded, displaying her frustration that Rachel had stopped reading.

For a moment she could not speak and was only able to stare into Sarah's disapproving frown. 'He's . . . he's got himself a girlfriend,' she finally managed to utter.

'Is she a Germany?' Sarah asked, unperturbed.

'German,' she corrected absently. 'The people are called Germans. And, yes, she is . . . Ulrika . . . That's her name.' It was something she had never contemplated: Joseph finding himself a German girl. She felt the blood drain from her face as she read the passage over again to herself, just to make sure she had got her facts right.

There was no mistake and, from the way Joseph wrote about her, he seemed serious about this Ulrika – too serious for Rachel's comfort.

What would happen if they got married? she asked herself, staring at the letter as if reading, not seeing one word, her mind frozen on the disturbing piece of news. Would Ulrika come to live in England? Would she expect Joseph to set up home in Germany? She recalled how Jacky Warren had married a German girl he had met while he was over there. She had come back to England with him. But it hadn't worked out. The girl had found it very difficult to settle down. She had felt the English people still remembered the war too clearly and were unfriendly towards her because of it. In the end Jacky had been forced to return to Germany with her.

It was not fair, Rachel silently raged. Joseph could not do this to her. She felt as if the roof was suddenly falling around her head. She glanced at Sarah, waiting patiently for her to resume reading. She looked back to the letter, but could not find her voice. She felt Joseph had let her down. She had known one day he would find a girl to marry. But it should have been an English girl, preferably one from the village who would not want to set up home too far away. And Joseph loved Germany. His letters were always full of how much he loved the place. It would not take much to make him stay there!

'Go on!' Sarah insisted irritably, having put up with the silence for too long.

'What?' Rachel looked absently at Sarah. 'Oh, yes,' she said, pulling herself together and forcing herself to read the remaining pages before Sarah began to riot. But her mind was not on what she was reading, and when she finished she quietly folded the letter, put it back in the envelope and placed it on the shelf. Then she got out the ironing board and began to work her anger out on the large pile of freshly laundered clothes in the washing basket.

It had been arranged that Sarah was to go on a picnic that afternoon with her friend Sally. Mrs Ryde, Sally's mother, called for Sarah at two o'clock.

As Rachel watched them going off down the yard, loaded with sandwiches, biscuits and bottles of pop, a feeling of relief swept over her. She needed some time to herself, to come to terms with Joseph's news. As they turned down the hill, she closed the door, knowing what she was going to do.

Fortunately it was one of her mother's quiet days and when Rachel took her a cup of tea and a plate of scones and biscuits, she just looked from Rachel to the plate, then closed her eyes.

Rachel was well aware that meant her mother did not want to be bothered. Nevertheless, she said, 'I'm going out for a bit.' She thought it only right she should let her mother know she would not be around. 'Our Sarah's gone out with Sally,' she added, then walked out. She knew there was no point waiting for a reply. And besides, she wasn't interested whether her mother had anything to say on the subject or not. She was going out on her own, not to do the shopping, not to meet Sarah, just for herself. It seemed a long time since she had done anything just for herself.

She changed out of her old blue dress and put on a new dirndl skirt with a matching blouse. She had made the outfit herself, the material purchased from five pounds Joseph had sent her for her sixteenth birthday, with a message to get herself something nice. The skirt was pale pink with a border of large bright pink and purple flowers around the hem. The sleeveless blouse was plain and the exact match to the pale pink of the skirt. It was the first really grown-up outfit she had owned, and she felt pleased with herself when she put it on. There had been enough money left over to buy a pair of white leather ballerina pumps to complete the outfit. She felt suddenly grown up as she slipped the pumps on to her bare feet and admired her reflection in the mirror.

Although Rachel was pleased with what she saw, she was looking only at the clothes. The skirt and blouse fitted perfectly. She was a good seamstress. Mrs Morris, her old needlework teacher, had always been full of praise for her work, and it came easy to her. She'd never had to struggle with fiddly bits, awkward pleats, getting the zips straight, or neat button holes.

What Rachel did not see was the young woman beneath the dress. The way the pale pink complemented her golden hair, or the pretty face beneath the high bouncing ponytail: a style her father would never have allowed her to wear. Neither did she notice the way her body had changed and that it was not only the outfit that turned her into an attractive young woman.

Smiling with the pleasure of her efforts, she twirled round to see the skirt billow out. She had almost given in to the desire to buy a cancan underskirt. She never went anywhere to wear one, she had told herself, and decided the shoes would be a more sensible purchase. She was glad she had made that decision, as she looked at her feet and realized her old black shoes would have looked very out of place.

At the end of the yard Rachel turned up the hill. It was a beautiful late August day and the villagers were taking the chance to get out in the fresh air. There seemed to be people everywhere, some industriously in their gardens; others leaning over walls to chat to neighbours; some, like Rachel, taking a stroll in the sun.

'Where're you off to?' Polly Webster called, as she walked past her open door.

'Up the top for a breath of fresh air,' she replied, laughing as Polly's head peeped nosily around the door frame. 'Fancy coming with me?' she joked, knowing she could not have walked up the steep incline to the very top, also knowing she would not take offence.

Polly let out a great gust of laughter. 'Eeh, lass, you'd have to get Johnny Waldren's milk cart to pull me up on. And his horse is dead.' She gave another gust of laughter and Rachel laughed again, feeling Polly's infectious attitude to life rubbing off on her.

It was strange how easy it was to laugh when Polly was around, she thought. There never seemed to be much laughter in her life at other times.

'Come and have a cuppa on your way back,' Polly invited, and with a wave Rachel accepted and went on her way.

Popping into Polly's for a chat and a cup of tea had become one of the few pleasures she had in life. Polly had become a true friend, always ready to give advice when it was needed, or a shoulder to cry on when she was low. If it had not been for Polly, she didn't know how she would have coped with her mother, and she would always be grateful to the old lady for her kindness.

The hill got steeper towards the top and her steps slowed. The sun beat down on her neck and she felt perspiration run down her back, and when the road came to an end she breathed a sigh of relief. Wiping the moisture from her neck she gazed fondly on the sight she loved: the wavy line of the cart track as it stretched a path across the top of the green hills.

She breathed deeply, enjoying the smell of the fresh mown grass coming from the golf links down the left-hand side of the hill. To the right was a farm with fields full of cows and sheep, and in the distance the large beech wood. At the bottom of the valley lay the railway, river and the road, but the climber only got the odd glimpse of those from the top.

It had been a long time since she had been up there alone. It had been her favourite haunt before her father died, before she was burdened with responsibility. She sighed, feeling her commitments weighing heavy. She loved Sarah and would do anything to stop them being parted. But there were times, increasing of late, when she wished she had a bit more time to herself. To be young. To be sixteen and do all the things a normal sixteen year old could do; dancing and going to the pictures.

She walked for a while, enjoying the freedom. Then she sat on the wall and looked down the green valley. Peacefulness seemed to stretch out before her, going on for ever. The only activity was the birds swooping in the clear blue sky. The world was still, at rest. But Rachel's mind would not join it. She smiled grimly, wondering why she should contemplate a social life of her own. She would never have been allowed to indulge in such sinful pastimes as dancing and going to the pictures if her father had still been there. Despite everything life was more tolerable without him. She might be in a prison of sorts, but she preferred it to the one she had escaped from. At least now it was a prison she had entered with some free will. Sarah would not be a child for ever. If only Joseph . . .

Anger returned with thoughts of her brother. She jumped down from the wall and began walking again, needing the exercise to work off her temper. She felt Joseph had let her down, yet knew she was being unfair to him. He was entitled to his own life. There was no point them both missing out on the pleasures of life. But the news had been so unexpected. The morning's letter had wiped away the crutch she had been leaning on. She had known he could not leave the army. But had somehow felt safe knowing he was there for her. It was his responsibilities that had taken him away, she had told herself. Or he would have been there with her. Someone else had made the decision that her brother should do National Service, doing his bit for the country. Putting the blame for her brother's absence on someone else's shoulders had helped Rachel.

Now she felt she had lost him. He was not there for her

any more. He was there for someone else . . . someone called Ulrika . . . a girl who belonged to a foreign country.

Misery engulfed Rachel, tears pressed at her eyes and she sank down on the grassy bank, feeling the frustration of the long months of all work and no play tearing at her.

It wasn't fair, she told herself, allowing self-pity to consume her. Joseph was free, enjoying himself. While she was left to cook food that was thrown at her, put up with the endless abuse and wash soiled sheets. She didn't even have the chance to sneak a night out on her own.

A nosy dog came sniffing round her legs and prompted her back to reality. She looked up, anxious not to be seen in that state. The owners were still some way down the track. She jumped up, blew her nose and wiped her eyes, tickled the dog under the chin and began to walk along the path once more, thankful that no-one had come by and caught her feeling sorry for herself.

It was nothing but self-pity, she told herself, with an anger that was directed inwards. It was neither use nor ornament to anybody.

The couple with the dog passed the time of day as they passed Rachel and she forced herself to smile as she responded, even though she was furious with herself for allowing the moment's weakness to come to the surface. She was usually more resilient, getting over such times with a brisk round of housework, taking her frustration out on the hoover or washing machine.

At least she did have a hoover and washing machine to take it out on, she told herself, realizing she did have things to be thankful for. Most of her neighbours in the yard still thrashed away with a brush and dustpan and a dolly peg in a tub.

Heaven forbid! Rachel grimaced at the thought of having to fight with a dolly peg every Monday morning. The next time she was feeling sorry for herself, she would remind herself that life could have been worse.

Rachel was still wearing a smile, when she was brought up short by an unseen voice.

'Hey up, Rachel!'

She turned to see Micky Caradine running up the field. When he reached the top he vaulted over the wall as if he had springs on his feet.

'Where're you off to?' He was grinning all over his face as he came up to her. 'They looks a right bobby-dazzler in that outfit.' He gave her a very appreciative, and very thorough, all-over inspection.

Rachel felt a blush creep into her cheeks. She had never experienced male compliments before; only from Joseph, and a brother did not count. She liked it; a smile glowed from her face, as she replied, 'I'm having a walk. What are you doing?'

'I've been giving them a hand at the farm. I was on my way home. But I thought it was you. I saw you sitting on the wall back there.'

Rachel felt her colour heighten. She hoped he had not seen her crying. He couldn't have done, she reassured herself. Her tears had been spilled sitting on the grass below the wall. He would not have been able to see her from the other side.

Her confidence restored by reasoning, when he invited himself along, she was happy to agree.

'I haven't seen you at chapel lately?' he said, as he walked by her side, his hands stuffed into the pockets of his jeans, his heavy boots crunching the ground.

'I don't go any more,' she replied shortly. It was not a topic she particularly wanted. Chapel returned her to a time she would rather forget. There had been plenty of requests to return to regular worship. But she would not go.

A rabbit suddenly scurried across the path in front of them and she laughed with pleasure. And was pleased its appearance put an end to the subject of chapel, when Micky said, 'I think we're frightening the natives.' But not so happy, when he added, 'I should have brought the gun.'

She scowled at him. 'Not with me, you shouldn't!' she warned.

Micky laughed. 'You always were soft,' he said, his laughter turning into a cheeky smile.

Rachel felt a blush coming on again and quickly changed

the subject. 'Polly tells me you've got set on at the Railway.'

Micky beamed with pleasure. 'It was what I wanted. The Railway or Rolls-Royce.'

She felt a stab of envy for something she had missed out on, and realized her feelings must have shown, when he frowned. 'It's a pity how things turned out for you,' he said.

'That's the way of things.' She shrugged the matter off and forced herself to smile. Micky was only a few months older than herself. But he had seen the extra year at school through and had come away with all the examination passes needed to get into engineering. He had got exactly what he wanted.

'I'm pleased you got it,' she said, forcing her self-pity away. He had always been a rogue, always getting himself into trouble. But she had always had a soft spot for him and had often found herself bailing him out of a tight corner. She imagined it was because he was so different from her, full of confidence, never afraid of speaking his mind.

Micky returned her smile, and there was something in his expression that caused her to blush again.

'When do you start your new job?' she quickly asked, feeling self-conscious and dropping her gaze to the ground.

'At the beginning of next month.'

Rachel nodded, but continued to stare at the ground, fearing he would think her foolish. There she was, all dressed up in her new clothes, yet acting like a child and not able to understand why. She didn't speak until she almost stepped on a beetle, then only a gasp of horror.

'Do you remember when I put that one on Miss Bland's chair?' Micky asked, and Rachel hoped his laughter was at the memory, and not her own silly reaction.

'Yes, I do!' She could remember only too well. The English mistress had walked into the room to find the huge creature sitting waiting for her. She had been furious and instructed all the boys to empty their pockets. She had been looking for a matchbox, or something similar which the beetle had been carried in. Micky had been sitting behind her at the time and he had shoved an empty cigarette packet into her hand. Fortunately the window next to her had been open and, when

53

Miss Bland was not looking, she had dropped the packet out of the window. She could still recall the shiver of revulsion when she had peeped out and watched a second large beetle escape from the packet and crawl away over the grass.

'You didn't half give me an earbashing at playtime,' he reminded her, making her laugh.

She recalled how furious she had been with him. Not for almost getting her into trouble with Miss Bland, but for putting the beetle into her hand, even if it had been inside the cigarette packet.

'You deserved it,' she insisted, her own laughter increasing, as she recalled the horror on Miss Bland's face as she had pulled her chair out and almost sat down on the poor creature.

Rachel's self-consciousness disappeared in her amusement and she felt her old self again with him. And when he reached out and took hold of her hand, her initial surprise soon evaporated and she allowed her hand to remain in his as they walked along.

They walked in silence for a while. Then Micky looked at her again with appreciation. 'You look a real picture in that,' he said, and something entered his eyes that she did not understand.

Her nervousness returned. 'I made it myself,' she said, only able to think he was referring to her clothes.

'You'd look good in a sack bag,' he replied, the strange look growing in his eyes and adding to her unease.

'Get off with you.' She felt her cheeks turning to crimson again. 'You always were the biggest liar in the school,' she said jokingly, not knowing what else to say. It seemed so strange. She knew him so well that she would not have thought it possible to feel embarrassed in his company. Yet she had the feeling she was walking with a stranger. She glanced nervously at her watch. 'I think I should be going back now,' she said, not really sure why she had said it. One half of her wanted to keep walking with her hand in his. The other half was frightened of that same feeling and was relieved when he agreed without hesitation.

Micky did most of the talking as they walked back. He was

a great talker, never short of a subject and Rachel only found it necessary to nod and put in the odd word every now and again.

Now they were on the way home her anxieties had gone, and she found she liked being with him and enjoyed his company: someone of her own age, who she felt a kind of kinship with. It was also nice to be walking hand in hand with a boy. It was an experience she had never imagined she would get the chance of, being unable to go out in the evenings, which was courting time.

Courting! It seemed a strange word. Was that what Micky was doing . . . courting her? She did not think it was appropriate to ask the question, it would have caused her too much embarrassment. So she remained silent, taking the occasional furtive glance at his face when she thought he wasn't looking.

He was tall and well made, and good looking with his mop of brown curls and tanned skin from the times he worked at the farm. Good looking, in a roguish sort of way. Which fitted his character perfectly, she thought, a smile growing on her face and happiness spreading warmly inside her.

When they reached the end of the yard and were about to part company, he suddenly leaned forward and planted a quick kiss on her cheek. Then he quickly turned away and walked off down the hill, whistling merrily, his hands stuffed back in his pockets once more.

Rachel pressed her hand to her cheek, covering the place where she could still feel the kiss. I'm sorry, Joseph, she apologized silently, and vowed to never let self-pity get the better of her again. She could not blame Joseph any more, not now she knew how it felt to walk hand in hand and be kissed.

With a strange excitement bubbling inside her, she turned into the yard, forcing her feet to walk, when really they wanted to skip.

It was not until Polly Webster appeared at the door, that Rachel remembered she should have been calling in on her way back home.

'That cup of tea's stewed by now,' she announced, and waddled into the kitchen and sank down on a chair with a relieved sigh. Her cheeks were as red as the checks on her dress and she flapped a handkerchief in front of her face. 'This heat will be the death of me!'

Rachel's happiness instantly vanished. 'Oh, Polly! I'm sorry . . . I forgot . . . I . . .' She stopped the apology there. She did not know what to say. Micky had said nothing to make her believe he wanted to see her again. She would look a bit silly if she said she was Micky Caradine's girlfriend, and he never showed his face again.

But Polly finished Rachel's sentence for her. 'Had other things on your mind,' she said.

She blushed, realizing Polly must have seen her with Micky, walking down the hill, hand in hand!

'I hope you know what you're about?' Polly continued bluntly. 'He's trouble, is that one.' She watched Rachel steadily for a long moment. Then she folded her arms, the action hitching her ample bosom higher. 'I don't want to see you get hurt,' she declared meaningfully.

'Oh, Micky's all right.' Rachel was quick to leap to his defence. All the same, she quickly set about putting the kettle on, so she did not have to look into Polly's shrewd eyes.

'We'll have that cuppa now,' she said, hoping Polly would drop the subject.

For a time Polly took the hint. They were both sitting at the table, drinking the tea, before she began again.

'Micky Caradine isn't for the likes of you, Rachel. He's too cute, too crafty by half. And you aren't very worldly wise, are you?' She looked pointedly at her.

Rachel shook her head. She had to agree with the last. She wasn't very knowledgeable about life, her upbringing had been too sheltered. But she knew how a baby was made, and she knew those were the things you must not do until you were married. And besides, Micky was no stranger, she knew him well enough. She was the first to admit he was a bit of a devil, that only added to his charm. She couldn't believe there was any real harm in him.

'I'm not just an interfering old woman,' Polly continued. 'I'm telling you for your own good. Your mam should be doing this. But, well she isn't, and that leaves only me to poke my nose in.'

Rachel smiled fondly. She placed her hand on Polly's old arm. 'I never think you're poking your nose in. I don't know what I would have done without you these last months.' If only she had had parents like Polly and Walter Webster, she thought. Life would have been very much different. Not so rich in wealth, but what they lacked in money they more than made up for in love. It seemed strange, and rather ironic, that two such ideal people as Polly and her late husband had never been blessed with children of their own.

Polly patted Rachel's hand. 'It costs nothing to give a bit of help, lass. But the rewards are great.'

Rachel's smile tightened. She could not see what reward Polly might gain from listening to her own self-pitying bleatings. But listen she had, on the many occasions she had felt low and run to her for support. Not once had Polly told her off for moaning. She had always been ready to listen until she had got it all off her chest. Then she would give her all the advice she was looking for, before turning the conversation round with some silly tale or amusing anecdote, until laughter put tears in their eyes.

There were tears in Rachel's eyes now, as she said, 'I'll never be able to thank you enough.'

'Get off with you!' Polly gave one of her great gusts of laughter. 'If you only gave to receive you'd end up very disappointed. All I want from you is to see you happy. And I can't see that with the likes of Micky Caradine! So just you mind my words, lass. He's trouble with a capital *T*, and you'd be best to keep away from him.' Polly hesitated, and rubbed her rheumatic knees as if they had started playing her up. 'I can see *trouble* brewing if you mess with him!' she added meaningfully.

Rachel didn't know what to say. She could understand Polly's anxiety, but she knew Micky far better than Polly did. They had gone through school together and shared the same classes. 'He's all right, really he is,' she said, attempting to reassure her old friend.

Polly sighed, more in despair, than from the heat. 'Aye, well just you be careful,' she warned, just as the mill clock chimed out five o'clock. 'I'll be getting off. It's tea time,' she said, and heaved her short, round body slowly from the chair. 'Remember what I've said!' She paused and gave Rachel a pointed look, before turning to go.

'I will,' Rachel replied with an air of defeat, as she got up and followed Polly to the door. But, as she watched the old lady waddle down the yard, calling cheery greetings to everyone she passed, she thought the advice was no longer necessary. Her state of high excitement had gone, washed away by Polly's warning. She felt she had been silly to imagine Micky would place any more significance on the afternoon than a walk in the sun. She couldn't see him coming round to knock on the door. He knew she was always tied up with her mother and Sarah.

She turned back into the kitchen with the sad realization that the afternoon had been the exception, rather than a rule. Micky had just taken advantage of the situation.

Chapter Five

Over the following week Rachel came to believe she *had* placed more importance on the meeting with Micky than Micky himself had. He had made no attempt to see her again and, although she told herself she was being silly and trying to make something out of nothing, she was disappointed he had not been around. He liked her, she felt sure he liked her. The strange expression when he had looked at her must have had some meaning, she thought.

She wished she were more experienced in such matters, more like some of the girls she had been at school with; those who had been going out with boyfriends while they were still at school.

It would have helped having someone her own age to talk to. But never having been allowed to bring friends home, she had no-one she was close to. The only person she had to discuss things with was Polly . . . and Polly had made it quite clear what she thought of Micky. So she kept the subject to herself in Polly's company.

Neither had she been able to tell Joseph about Micky in her weekly letter. Despite everything, she still felt let down by her brother. She had tried to sound happy about his new relationship and asked several questions about Ulrika. But the subject of Micky Caradine had not touched the paper.

It worried her to think she could not tell Joseph about Micky. She had always been close to him and they had never kept secrets before. She wondered if it was because she suspected he would object the way Polly did. Then she told herself it was because Micky had not shown up again and she hadn't told him because there was nothing to tell. If, and when, there was something to relate, she would be only too pleased to tell her brother everything. Before the subject could cause her further worry, she had sealed the envelope and taken it straight to the post office.

'I've got a tummy ache,' Sarah whined, holding her stomach and taking on an exaggeratedly pained expression.

'It'll go off if you eat your breakfast,' Rachel replied, and put a plate of scrambled eggs on toast in front of her sister. 'It's just excitement,' she added, taking no notice of the further groans as she turned back to the gas stove and began to prepare her mother's breakfast. It was always the same on the first day of school term. The rest of the time Sarah loved school and was only too eager to get there. But the first day after a holiday there was always a complaint of tummy ache, headache or earache.

She stuck two slices of bread under the grill and stood waiting for it to toast. She kept her back turned on Sarah, determined not to listen to any more whines, and looked down at her dull navy-blue dress. She wished she could afford some material to make something different to wear around the house. She was sick of wearing the dull clothes her father had insisted on.

As she was spooning scrambled egg on to her mother's plate, Sarah began to whine again. She looked at her sternly. 'I want to see you eating that when I come down,' she said, and picked up her mother's tray and manoeuvred it through the door.

'I don't want it!' Sarah declared petulantly, but Rachel made no reply and carried on through the front room to the stairs. She had found ignoring Sarah's moans got the quickest results. If you tried to cajole her out of it she stuck her heels in and became more obstinate. If she thought you weren't taking any notice she gave up.

As she went carefully up the narrow winding stairway, she turned her attention to her mother and wondered what mood she would find her in today. She hoped she had not got two awkward customers on her hands. One at a time was more than enough to cope with, she told herself, as she shouldered the door open and walked in, only to feel her heart sink.

Her mother was propped up on the pillows with her arms folded tightly across her thin chest. Her mouth was pinched into a bitter line and her eyes, drawn angrily together, caused two deep furrows to reach up her brow. Rachel could almost feel the air of hostility and quickly crossed the room and put the tray down on the bedside cabinet, having no desire to prolong her stay. 'Breakfast,' she said simply, and turned to leave.

'Where're you going?' her mother hissed.

Rachel paused, calming her temper before turning back to face her mother. 'Sarah has to go to school. You know that.' She kept her voice even, refusing to show any emotion that might goad her into one of her fits.

Violet Cooper glanced at the tray, disgust curling her nose. 'I *don't* want eggs!' She sounded like a spoiled child. 'You give me eggs every day. I'm sick of eggs!'

Rachel did not point out that on a previous occasion she had insisted she wanted only eggs for breakfast.

'What would you like?' she asked carefully.

'Bacon and sausage and tomatoes!'

It was a demand and Rachel bristled. She feared her voice would let her down, or she would say something she would regret, and it was several moments before she felt composed enough to reply. 'We don't have any bacon. You can have sausage and tomatoes. But you'll have to wait till Sarah has gone to school,' she added firmly.

'Wait!' her mother screeched. 'Wait! Wait! Wait!' Her voice rose until she was cackling like a witch and Rachel wanted to cover her ears.

She glared at the unrecognizable woman in the bed, and her eyes filled with a coldness that spoke far greater than words.

'Who do you think you are to tell me to wait?' her mother demanded, the words spitting like fire from her lips.

The person who is stopping them locking you up, Rachel thought bitterly, and her voice was as cold as ice, as she said, 'Sarah has to be at school in twenty minutes. I'll cook you some sausages . . . *When I get back!*' Then she turned and

61

walked out. She was not worried if the arrangement was not to her mother's liking. If it didn't suit her she could get up and get her own breakfast, she thought angrily, and hurried down the stairs with a flow of obscenities following her.

When she got back to the kitchen it was to find a belligerent Sarah sitting with her arms folded, the way her mother had been, her breakfast lying untouched.

It was the last straw. Her frustration exploded and she snapped. 'Get that eaten this minute!' she shouted, raising her voice to Sarah in a way she had never done before.

Sarah's startled eyes pivoted to her sister's stormy face, and her lips trembled.

'Get it eaten!' Rachel repeated angrily. 'Or you'll go to school without anything!'

'But I've got tummy ache,' Sarah pleaded and tears filled her eyes.

'I don't care what hurts!' She had had enough whimperings and demandings this morning to last her a week, and her face hardened as a tear rolled down Sarah's cheek. 'And you can stop that!' she warned. 'It's always the same after a holiday. There's nothing wrong with you and you're going to school whether you like it or not!' Resting her hands on her hips she stood over Sarah and waited.

Sarah slowly picked up her fork and began to eat. She had taken four laborious mouthfuls between sobs, before Rachel came to her senses.

'Oh, Sarah!' she cried, and dropped on to a chair and buried her face in her hands. She was doing it again. Taking her anger out on Sarah when it should have been her mother she was getting at. 'I didn't mean it.' She reached out and pulled her sister into her arms, and tears filled her own eyes. 'I'm feeling a bit down. I didn't intend to snap at you.' What with her mother and Joseph, and Micky raising her hopes only to dash them down again. It was all too much. Everything seemed to be against her.

She looked into Sarah's sad little face and smiled tightly, and Sarah slipped on to her knee and wrapped her arms around her neck. Rachel tugged fondly on one of her sister's long blond plaits and knew how wrong she had been. Sarah was her saviour in all this. She was always ready to return the love given to her and was the last person she should be snapping at.

'I'm sorry, love,' she whispered into the top of Sarah's hair, and they clung to each other and cried together.

'Eeh, come on,' Rachel finally said, realizing time was passing by and the mill clock would soon be striking nine. 'This is no good. You'll be late for school. Are you going to eat your eggs? Or do you want some bread and jam?'

Sarah looked into her eyes and attempted an eight year old's smile of encouragement. 'I'll help you do the washing and everythng, if I don't go to school,' she offered with hopeful innocence.

Rachel smiled and wiped the tears from her sister's cheeks. 'Get off with you!' she teased. It had been a good try, touching in its innocence, but the intentions had been sincere. 'One of us has got to end up brainy, and it isn't going to be me.' She lifted Sarah off her knee and straightened her clean white blouse and tartan kilt. 'Now get your face washed and get something inside you. Or you'll be late and I'll have a lot of explaining to do to Miss Hickingbottom.'

The thoughts of the teacher's reaction to late arrival spurred Sarah. She needed no more prompting and hurried into the tiny bathroom, which was the converted larder at the back of the kitchen.

'Here, don't forget this!' Rachel had to thrust Sarah's PE bag at her, when it was almost overlooked in her eagerness to run off and meet her friends at the school door.

It was good to see. Rachel shook her head and smiled as she walked back up the hill. Sarah's happy nature prevented her from dwelling on any upsets for too long, and her stupid burst of anger, thankfully now forgotten, must not happen again. Her sister's pleasant nature was something to be proud of. It was also a miracle, after living with their father for her first years, and she felt it her duty to make sure nothing changed Sarah.

Since taking charge of her sister's welfare, she had gone

out of her way to let her bring friends home to play. Their father had never allowed any of them to bring their friends to the cottage, or to go out playing after school. And she knew only too well that most of the village children were of the opinion she thought she was too good for the likes of them. She could not blame them. It was, after all, the impression her father had tried to cultivate: an image that he was on a different level to most of the villagers.

It hurt her to think she had missed out on so much because of her father's attitude. It made her determined Sarah was not going to suffer in the same way; even though there were times when it was awkward to have someone at the cottage, if her mother was having one of her noisy times.

Fortunately Sarah had now got accustomed to hearing her mother rant and rave and took no notice. Which seemed to rub off on any friends she had playing with her.

Rachel smiled, recalling one occasion when Sally had asked, 'What's the matter with your mum?'

'Ignore her,' Sarah had replied. 'She gets bad dreams.'

The two little girls had gone on playing as if nothing was out of the ordinary, her mother's screeching carrying on in the background.

She had been so proud of Sarah then, of the way she had accepted her mother's illness. She had always kept Sarah away from the bedroom when things were at their worst. But the noise her mother made was impossible to hide and she had often worried if it might be affecting Sarah. She had tried to explain it was the illness and their mother didn't know what she was doing. But she had never thought about 'bad dreams' and was proud of Sarah's inventiveness in finding a solution that was acceptable to herself and to other children.

As soon as she reached home she put an apron over her dress. She wondered briefly why she was trying to protect the old rag. Because you can't afford a new one, she reminded herself, and dropped three sausages into the frying pan. The sausages began to sizzle and she opened a can of tomatoes and put them in a saucepan, and hoped her efforts were going to pacify her mother.

Her mother had been better of late, the quieter, more subdued days had increased in number. But Rachel held no hopes that her condition was improving and the violent attacks would stop. Dr Mellor had told her it had gone on too long for any permanent change for the better.

When Rachel returned to the bedroom with the second breakfast, she found her mother's temper had not decreased. If anything it had got worse.

'Where've you been?' she demanded nastily.

Rachel did not reply. The unwarranted attack on Sarah leaped to her mind and she had the feeling words would choke her.

The first tray was still sitting on the cabinet, so she placed the second tray across her mother's lap, before picking up the first one. Then she turned away from her mother's hostile glare, wanting to go before she told her exactly what she thought of her.

'Where do you think you're going?' she demanded, before Rachel had taken two steps forward.

Rachel paused and turned slowly back to face her mother, her expression blank, showing none of the emotions whirling round inside her body like a tornado. 'I'm taking this downstairs to wash up while you eat your breakfast.' She spoke slowly and precisely, the way she would have done to a child.

'Don't take that tone with me, madam!' she snapped, her nose curling in disgust as she looked down on the tray in her lap. 'What's this?' she demanded.

Rachel sighed audibly. 'Your breakfast. You asked for sausages and tomatoes,' she pointed out stiffly, her endurance being stretched to breaking point.

'And bacon! I wanted bacon as well. Where's the bacon?'

Rachel heard the cup and saucer on the tray in her hands rattle, as her arms began to tremble with the fury she was trying so hard to subdue. Giving vent to her own feelings would only make her mother twice as bad. 'I told you we did not have any bacon,' she replied, feeling the tremble of her limbs also affecting her voice.

'You'd have had bacon if Joseph was here,' her mother spat hatefully. 'You'd have had bacon for him. *Wouldn't you?*' The tiny slits of her eyes fixed her daughter. Rachel wished she had taken the first tray down earlier, and that her hands were free to snatch the fresh breakfast from her mother's lap and make her go without.

'We still have bacon . . . some days. We just don't happen to have any today. Now, are you going to eat it, *or not*?' On the last, Rachel's voice took on a threatening tone, much like her mother's. It was the last time she would pander to her mother's awkward whims, she told herself. If she did not eat what was put in front of her, she could go without.

Violet Cooper's response to her daughter's obvious change of attitude, happened so quickly, Rachel did not have time to move. Before she knew what was happening, her mother had flung the tray through the air and she was covered in food and hot tea. The flying tray knocked the tray from her hands and a red and yellow stain ran down her dress, a sausage stuck in the band of her apron and her shoes and feet were spattered with food and surrounded by broken crockery.

For several moments Rachel stood frozen, glaring at the hateful sneer of satisfaction on her mother's face. She dare not move. If she did, she had the feeling she might have put her hands around her mother's neck and strangled the life out of her.

Then her mother began to laugh, in the high-pitched cackle that sounded so much like a witch. It was the final straw. Only half aware of what she was doing, Rachel leapt at her mother. She grabbed her by the shoulders and began to shake her. But the laughter only increased and she shook her more and more, harder and harder, as the evil sound coming from her lips filled the room and seemed to echo inside her head. In the next moment her hand swung back and she had every intention of hitting the silly sneer from her mother's face.

The abrupt silence, the almost joyful anticipation suddenly filling the eyes which stared goadingly at her, brought Rachel back to sanity. With a shudder of revulsion, she realized her mother was waiting, wanting her to strike. Disgust curled painfully inside her stomach: not only for the pathetic creature her mother had turned into, but for what she was making herself change into. Even so, it was a few moments before she could steady her rapid breathing and gain enough sense to lower her hand.

'I should have you locked up,' she said, turning away and beginning to clear the mess from the floor, before her mother had time to say anything that might make her change her mind and see the act through. Slapping her mother would be a sin, but she feared that one day she would be provoked so much that she would not be able to stop herself.

It was not long before Violet Cooper was cackling again and hurling obscenities at Rachel. She kept her head down and refused to be drawn into further argument. Her mother was well and truly mad, she told herself, and felt ice run down her spine, as she imagined the long years of nursing that stretched before her. For no matter how bad her mother became, she was not going to allow anything to happen that would make Dr Mellor insist on putting her away and risk losing the cottage and Sarah. In a few years she might consider it. When she was older and felt secure that her taking responsibility for Sarah would not raise any eyebrows. But until that time came she would keep up the pretence and insist her mother was not too much for her. She could, and would, put up with anything, so long as she could keep Sarah at home.

With one tray balanced on the other and all the rubbish scooped on to the top, she stood up. She did not look at her mother and was at the door before she stopped, turned coldly, and said, 'You're an evil old woman and you'll get your just deserts one day!'

'Not from the likes of you, I won't,' her mother hissed back. But Rachel had already walked out. She had no intention of standing around to listen to anything she might want to say. She could go without anything to eat, she thought angrily. She was not going back to her until dinner time. Her mother could stew in her own juice and the carpet could stain.

When she reached the kitchen, she marched straight outside

and tipped the debris from the tray into the dustbin. She was about to put the lid back on, when she was taken by surprise to see Micky striding down the yard. His hands were stuffed inside the pockets of brown corduroy trousers that looked scruffy enough to belong to him, but his check shirt and winkle-picker shoes looked new and too smart for him.

She was about to ask him where he was going, because, for Micky, he was dressed up. Then she remembered her own clothes, and the mucky mess all down the front, and when he called, 'Hello there,' with a grin filling his face, she could not respond.

She had wanted so much to see him. But not just then. Not with her dress covered with her mother's breakfast and splashes all over her face.

'What you been doing? Having a smashing time?' he joked, his grin broadening as he stopped and peered at the broken crockery in the bin, then at Rachel's dress.

'I tripped over carrying Mother's tray upstairs,' she said shortly, annoyed that he should find it so funny and finding no disgrace in the lie. She didn't want him, or anyone else, knowing just how bad her mother really was. She had no doubts that the neighbours must have heard some of the rantings. But Polly was the only person who knew what she really had to put up with, and she had every intention of keeping it that way.

'Anyway, what are you doing here?' she enquired, finally gaining enough sense to put the dustbin lid back on. Then she held the trays in front of her and hurried to the safety of the doorway, before any neighbours appeared to see the state she was in. 'I thought you should be at work by now?' she said, turning to him.

'I am. But I get a day release for Tech and it doesn't start till next week. So I came to see if you wanted to go for a walk?' He leaned against the door frame, hands still in pockets, and grinned down at her.

'A walk!' She could not conceal her surprise, or her happiness. But the next moment she was remembering the pile of washing waiting to be done. 'I can't . . . I . . .'

'Aw, come on, Rachel! Your Sarah's at school. We've got till dinner time.' Micky looked downcast.

She did not need much persuading. Sarah was at school, she thought. This was the only time she had to herself. For a few moments she pondered the rights and wrongs of leaving the housework to go off and enjoy herself.

Would it be so wrong? Just this once, she asked herself, attempting to lay the remaining doubts. She wanted to go – for herself. But . . . ? The memory of the episode with her mother provided the final spur.

'Give me a minute to get changed,' she said, putting the smile back on to Micky's face. Then she hurried into the kitchen and dropped the dirty trays on to the table, where they could stay until she came back. She gave her face and legs a quick wash to get rid of all the splashes and hurried upstairs. Grabbing the previously worn dirndl skirt and blouse from the wardrobe, she threw them on.

Excitement bubbled inside her as she rushed around, for once the sixteen year old with little to worry her. It had not occurred to her that she could make time for herself during the day, while Sarah was out at school, and she thought Micky was very clever to have thought of it. In all the haste she did not give herself the time to stop and consider where her actions might be leading her.

Rachel breathed a sigh of relief as they passed Polly's cottage and the door was closed. In the hot weather Polly's door was always left open if she was in. So she must be out, Rachel reasoned, and hoped her old friend would not return before she had come back down the hill with Micky. Then she told herself to stop worrying about Polly. There was nothing wrong in going for a walk. The washing and cleaning would get done when she got back. She turned her attention to Micky's incessant chatter, but couldn't stop herself glancing over her shoulder to make sure Polly was not there.

They had reached the top of the hill and left the cottages behind, before Rachel relaxed. Micky took hold of her hand as they began to walk along the dusty track, and she smiled, enjoying the feeling. She had forgotten how nice it felt to walk hand in hand with him. It made her feel older, more important, as if she really mattered to him. She knew she mattered to Sarah, but this was different. Micky had had no obligations to come and take her out. He had chosen to do so because he wanted to.

The sun bathed the hills in a glow which seemed to have an almost magical quality for Rachel. High above her head a skylark trilled out its beautiful song. Down on the golf links a group of women were enjoying a game. One of the players had lost her ball in the rough below the wall edging the track and was causing much laughter from her colleagues as she searched for it.

Rachel would have gone to help, but Micky pulled her away. 'Let's go down the fields and walk back along the road,' he suggested.

Rachel willingly allowed him to lead her to the wall. There was no footpath through the fields, but it was common practice to jump over the wall and make a circular tour back to the village. The farmer made no objections, so long as you kept to the edge of the fields and did not upset the livestock.

When they reached the wall he helped her up. 'Hang on and I'll help you down,' he said, before vaulting up on to the wall himself and dropping down into the long grass on the other side.

'Come on.' He held his arms up and she slipped from the wall into his grasp. He held her for a moment and she looked up into his face, nervous anticipation rendering her dumb. It was not long before his arms slipped all the way round her waist and he pulled her close.

Rachel had expected him to kiss her on the lips. It had been a dream she had cultivated since their previous walk and his chaste peck on the cheek. But when his lips touched hers the feeling was nothing like she had imagined it would be. His lips felt cool and wet and there was a forcefulness about him that she did not like. He pulled her closer, squashing her to him. She could feel something hard pressing into her. It was not a pleasant feeling and she was relieved when he obeyed her mumbled protests and let her go.

A funny half-smile twisted his lips, as he looked down at her. 'What's up? Haven't you ever been kissed before?'

Rachel felt foolish. Colour rushed to her cheeks and she looked down at the ground.

'You haven't, have you?' he persisted knowingly.

She could not look at him. He must think her a real child, she thought, wishing the ground to open and swallow her up, as her humiliation grew.

'It doesn't matter. I'll teach you,' he said, with a confidence that frightened her. Then he wrapped his arm round her shoulders and led her down the field. 'Don't you worry. I'll teach you everything you need to know.'

Rachel was not sure she wanted to know anything any more. Anxiety was taking over from the humiliation. There was something so self-assured about his manner, as if he knew he had got her right where he wanted her.

Suddenly she wanted to turn around and go home the way they had come. But if they did that it would mean having to climb the wall again. That would put her in the same position as before, and she wanted to avoid anything that would cause him to hold her tightly again. Though it was the longer distance, all the fields had gates and she felt the way they were going was perhaps the safest, after all.

They had reached the second field, before she was to reconsider her thinking.

This was by no means the safest route, she realized anxiously, as Micky suddenly stopped and pulled her round to face him.

'Let your mouth open this time,' he said, and made to kiss her again.

Rachel acted instantly, turning her head away, out of his reach. The action did little to boost her confidence. All she could see before her was the closeness of the dense beech wood, inhabited by foxes, rabbits and squirrels, and no-one to come to her aid. To the other side she knew there was the farm, but the length of three fields away, and she had not seen any of the farm hands working in the fields. Down below was the road, but it was out of sight from that point. And they had

71

walked too far down for the ladies of the golf team on the other side of the hill to hear if she called out. Fear rose goose bumps along her flesh and she tried to push his hands off her arms.

'Come on,' he urged, an urgency in his voice that added to her fear. 'It'll be all right. I'll show you what to do.'

'No you won't, Micky Caradine!' she insisted, realizing her only defence was herself. She pushed her hands hard against his chest and tried to back away. Polly had been right. He was trouble! Why hadn't she listened to Polly? she wondered too late.

His arms moved round her. 'Stop it! Stop it right now!' she demanded, lifting her hands and trying to knock his arms away. 'No!' she screamed, as he jerked her to him and his head came down. She pushed against his chest with renewed vigour and turned her face away in the nick of time. His wet lips landed on her cheek and a shiver of revulsion ran through her.

The next instant she lashed out, striking him a sharp blow across the chin and driving her clenched fist hard into his chest. Stunned, he reeled backwards.

She saw her chance, took it, and ran for freedom. But she did not get far. A fallen tree branch lay hidden in the long grass. She tripped over it and went sprawling to the ground. Before she could scramble to her feet he was on top of her.

'*Stop it! Stop it!*' she screamed, as she felt his hands pull her blouse free of her skirt. As his hand pushed her bra aside and grasped her breast, she clawed at his head, pulled his hair, and tried to bring her knee up into his groin.

'You stop it, you silly little cat,' he growled, as he forced her hands above her head and pinned them down with only one of his, leaving the other free to molest her body.

Rachel tried to bite him. She tried to kick him. But his legs were much stronger and he soon had her legs in the position he wanted, her body imprisoned beneath his own.

Even when she came to realize she was no match, she continued to fight with all she had. But he was by far the stronger and made easy work of her. So easy, that for years afterwards she nursed the feeling she had not put up enough fight, that she had allowed him to rob her too easily of a most precious part of herself.

'There, that wasn't so bad, was it.' He grinned down at her, as he pushed himself up and began to fasten his trousers. 'First time always hurts a bit. Next time will be better.'

There won't be a next time, she thought bitterly, and numbly pushed her skirt down and tucked her blouse back into the waistband. As she pushed herself up from the ground, she saw her pants lying where he had thrown them. She swept them up and stuffed them in her pocket. She would not put them on with him there, watching. Then she turned away and walked down the field, leaving him standing there.

She did not want him to follow her. She could not look at him. Revulsion curled her stomach and it was only pride that stopped her being sick right there in the field. She felt filthy, as if she would never be clean again. Sinful! Born out of sin, her mother had said. Well now she could understand what her mother had been saying. Micky had been like an animal. The memory of his loud grunting echoed in her head. She clasped her hands over her ears, trying to shut it out. It stayed, and she began to run. Faster and faster, trying to get away from the noise, from all that had happened to her. Through one field after another, as if the devil was after her. Her lungs were bursting but she did not stop. She forced herself on, as if the burning in her chest would scorch away the vileness she could feel clinging to her, outside and inside. Vileness that began with the taste of Micky's wet mouth on her lips and ended in a cold repulsive stickiness at her thighs.

She had never thought she would ever hate anyone as much as she had hated her father. But she had been wrong. As she ran through the grass, feeling the warmth of a sun that seemed to mock her distress by its brightness, she hated Micky Caradine as much, if not more, than the man who had sired her, and with a vengeance that ran like molten lead inside her veins.

She could not remember if she passed anyone as she ran along the road and up the hill. Her mind was too frozen on the appalling act that had been committed against her. When she reached home she burst through the door and straight through the kitchen to the bathroom.

She turned both taps full on and ripped off her clothes. Not waiting for the bath to fill, she sat in the shallow water and, shivering, watched numbly as the water level rose up the sides.

When the bath was half-full, she turned off the cold tap and let the hot tap complete the job. Steam rose in a thick obliterating cloud around her and the water was almost scalding her skin. She wanted it that way. She wanted the memory of Micky Caradine to go up in the steam that filled the room and dripped from the walls. She wanted the water's heat to sterilize her body and make her clean again.

Taking the scrubbing brush she scrubbed every inch of her skin, until it was raw and painful. She had to get it off, she told herself. Every particle of Micky Caradine had to be removed from her body and washed down the drain. Which was the only fitting place for him. She even used the hard brush on her lips, where she could still feel the repugnant touch of his mouth and tongue. She had to be clean, untouched. But it was too late, she realized, and her head flopped against the side of the bath in despair. He *had* touched her. He *had* forcefully entered her body and taken away her virginity. Now she was no better than the harlots her father had taken such pleasure in condemning.

She gagged and knew the feeling of nausea was about to erupt. She just managed to get out of the bath and throw herself over the toilet before her stomach contents evacuated all over the white china.

Straightening up with a groan she gazed numbly at the faint outline of her reflection in the misted mirror. Quickly her hand wiped the steam away. She had to see, face what she had turned into. The hot water had turned her skin a vivid pink. It reminded her of the tomatoes her mother had thrown at her earlier. Scratchy red lines, some bleeding, showed the course the scrubbing brush had taken and grey areas of bruising were beginning to show the strength of Micky's brutality.

But the damage to her body was nothing in comparison to

74

the damage of her mind. She had been robbed of her innocence in the most obscene way she could have imagined. Micky had taken a part of her, leaving her empty on the inside, yet cloaked in a tight band of hate on the outside. She hated what she saw, her body, the thing that made her a woman. She looked down at the floor, at the crumpled skirt and blouse: the outfit she had loved so much, the first clothes she had had which made her feel grown up – a woman!

Well she never wanted to feel like a woman again, she told herself with bitterness and anger, and picked up the skirt and held it in her fingers as if it had become deadly poison. 'Only a harlot, a whore, would wear clothes such as that,' she said savagely, quoting her father. Knowing, if he had still been alive, he would have been only too ready to cast the first stone.

Tears began to creep slowly from her eyes. She looked once again on her mottled body, hair hanging wetly down her back, eyes still wide with shock. Her father had been right, she thought. People did judge you by the clothes you wore. If she had been dressed in her usual dull clothes, Micky would never have looked at her. It had been her own fault. 'A right bobby-dazzler' that was what he had called her. It had been the brightly coloured clothes that had caught his eye and put the silly smile on his face.

She dropped the skirt back to the floor and wrapped herself in a towel. Then she went to the kitchen and fetched a brown paper carrier bag, stuffed the contaminated clothes inside and folded the top tightly so she could no longer see them. Then she left the bag on the kitchen floor and ran upstairs, thankful that at least her mother was now quiet.

It did not take her long to throw on her old grey school skirt and a dull blue blouse. Much more fitting, she thought, as she glanced briefly at the plain ensemble before hurrying downstairs. She had ten minutes before Sarah needed collecting from school, and she had an urgent job to do.

Picking up the carrier bag and a box of matches, she hurried out to the dustbin. She placed the lid on the ground and dropped the carrier bag into the bin on top of the broken crockery from earlier, but she did not really notice the mess from her mother's frenzy. All she wanted to see were the flames, and bitterness tightened her lips as she touched a lighted match to the brown paper and stood back. The flames, slow at first, suddenly leaped up, but she found no release in watching the objects of her disgust drift skywards in the cloud of grey. It would take more than a puff of smoke to rid her mind of the horrors.

It only took a few minutes for the bag and its contents to burn away. She stood for a little while longer to make sure every scrap had disintegrated. She wanted nothing left, not one remnant to remind her of her own wanton stupidity.

When she was satisfied it had all gone, she turned away from the smouldering dustbin and walked along the yard. Her heart was leaden and her feet felt like clay. The bath had done little to cleanse her spirit and she had the feeling, had Sarah not been waiting for her, she might have walked right past the school and on to the river. Although she did not think that even the River Derwent had enough water to wash away her sin.

Chapter Six

'Oh Polly!' Rachel looked at the old lady in despair, for a moment unable to finish what she had to say. 'I'm going to have a baby,' she finally managed in a small voice. Her chin fell on to her chest. She could not look at Polly, but she had had to tell someone.

Throughout the autumn and over Christmas she had tried to deny what was happening to her. It could not be true, she told herself. God would not expect her to love and care for a child conceived in such disgusting circumstances. Besides, she had enough to do with her mother and Sarah without having another body to look after.

'I don't know what to do,' she whispered, still unable to look Polly in the face.

But the retribution, the I-told-you-so, she was expecting, did not come. Polly took her arm and pressed her down into one of her old, overstuffed armchairs. Then she pulled a straight-back chair up close and sat down.

'And what makes you so certain of that?' she asked, and her voice was so soft and gentle that Rachel wanted to cry. She had been foolish and did not deserve concern. In that moment she would have preferred Polly to shout and punish her.

'What makes you so certain?' Polly repeated, just as gently.

'I haven't had a period since last August,' she whispered. Five months. Inside her she had a baby that was halfway to being born. Her voice rose in bitterness, as she added, 'It's punishment! God's punishing me!' But she didn't tell Polly what He was punishing her for . . . wishing her father into his grave.

'You can stop that right now!' Polly warned firmly, and hitched her arms under her bosom and took on a look of determination, which at another time would have made Rachel smile. 'That was your dad's way of talking and I'll not be hearing it from you. God is good. He doesn't go round dishing out punishment like your father's fire and brimstone way of thinking. I'll have no more talk of punishment in my house. So let's get back to the matter in hand.' She hitched her bosom higher and the gentleness returned to her voice, as she enquired, 'And have you done what's necessary to make a baby?'

Rachel nodded and the tears she had been trying to hold back began to fall on her tightly clenched fists lying in her lap. Polly's concern was tearing at the strangling emotions she had kept to herself for the longest five months of her life. No matter what Polly said, she could only believe God was punishing her for her sins. And He was doing it the most terrible way. Making her grow and nurture the seed planted in such sinfulness, until it was a child that would be a constant reminder. Every day she would have to look at it and remember.

'Was it Micky?' Polly asked, having to repeat herself before Rachel plucked up the courage to nod again.

'And what's he got to say about it?'

Rachel looked up then. Her watery eyes were wide with amazement, and for several seconds she could only stare into Polly's concerned gaze. 'He doesn't know,' she finally gasped. He had not taken it upon himself to make any further visits and she was not going out of her way to find him. She wanted nothing to do with him. The disgrace of being an unmarried mother was far more preferable to marriage with Micky Caradine.

'Well, if he's the father, don't you think it's about time you told him?'

'*No!*' Rachel replied with determination. And with a rush of anger swept the tears from her cheeks with her hands. 'I don't want him or his baby!' The insistence of her words glared coolly from her eyes. 'It seems I've got one, whether I like it or not. But I'll not have the both of them!' She shook her head, the repulsion of the idea clear on her face. If that was what marriage was all about it was something she coul do without.

'Well, now!' Polly leaned forward and looked closely into her face. 'It seems we've got a pretty kettle of fish here.' For a time she watched Rachel steadily, and the sorrow in the old eyes filled Rachel with guilt. She had let Polly down by ignoring her warnings about Micky. But she was not throwing it back in her face. She wished she would. She felt she deserved it for her stupidity. Thinking she knew better than Polly! Better than the wisest person in the village! Her tears welled up again. 'I'm sorry, Polly,' she sobbed, as her head fell into her hands. 'I'm so sorry.'

Polly let her cry for several minutes. Then she took hold of her hands and pulled them from her face. 'I know you're full up, lass,' she said, as Rachel finally looked up at her. 'But crying isn't doing any good now. You've got to face the facts and get it sorted out. Think what you're going to do.'

Rachel looked confused. 'What is there to do?' She was going to have a baby and, as far as she could see, that was all there was to it. Events had been taken out of her hands. It would just happen now. It was all a matter of time.

'First you have to see the doctor to make sure. Although from what you've already told me I don't think there's much doubt.' Polly sighed heavily and leaned back in the chair. She looked suddenly very old and Rachel felt guilty for causing so much trouble. 'Then you have to decide if you're going to keep it or have it adopted.' There was another way. But she doubted Rachel knew about it and she herself could never have condoned it. In any shape or form murder was murder, so she wasn't going to put the idea into her head.

'Adoption!' Rachel looked interested. She had not thought of that. Then she had not thought clearly about anything since first coming to realize her condition. 'How . . . How do you go about arranging it?'

'Let's not jump the gun, lass,' Polly said, trying to slow down Rachel's eagerness. 'Before you come to that decision you have to be sure it's what *you* want! After all's said and done, it's your baby we're talking about. It's part of you and it's not easy to give part of you away. So don't go thinking it is.' She pushed herself up from the chair with a breathy sigh. 'Now let's have a cup of tea and talk about it properly.'

Before Polly had returned with the tea, Rachel's mind was made up. Adoption was the perfect solution, she told herself, as she stared at the highly polished brass ornaments that cluttered Polly's mantelpiece and listened to the gentle rhythmic tick of the old grandfather clock in the corner. It would be much kinder to give the baby up to someone who would give it the love she would never be able to feel. It would always remind her of Micky. Besides, even if she had wanted the baby, she was not in a position to look after one. With Sarah and her mother she would never be able to manage the demands of a baby.

'What'd we do without tea?' Polly laughed as she waddled from the kitchen with two cups and saucers in her hands.

The laughter took the concern from her face, and Rachel smiled, glad to see her old friend had returned to her usual self again. 'We'd have to drink coffee,' she said, finding her own mood now lifted enough to make the joke. She knew how much Polly hated coffee.

Polly gave a snort of disgust. 'I'd turn to ale first,' she said, making Rachel laugh. It was a thin, watery sound. But it was a sound she had not thought to hear from herself again, and she thanked God for letting Polly be there for her. She pulled herself up sharply, taking stock of the thought. She had actually thanked God! The laughter slipped from her face, to be replaced by a tight smile of gratitude.

'Now what you thinking?' Polly peered suspiciously at her new expression.

Rachel shook her head in wonder and gratitude. 'I'm just counting my blessings.'

Polly frowned. 'You're not going all religious on me again, are you?'

She shook her head again. 'I think I just learnt my lesson there.' She suddenly wondered why she had listened to her father for so long. If God really was so plentiful with his punishment, surely all her father's whores and harlots would have been struck by lightning long before now.

Polly put the cup of tea into her hand and flopped back on to the chair with her own. Rachel looked at the mismatched china cup and saucer, red roses on the cup and blue lavender on the saucer, and she smiled fondly. Her mother would never have stooped so low as to offer a cup and saucer that were not made for each other. In fact everyone in the room would have been drinking from identical china. It had been nothing but show. In her own way her mother had been as bad as their father. And look where it had got them! One gone, and the other would be better off gone as well.

'Now we've got to think this out properly.' Polly put her cup and saucer on the table and dragged Rachel back to the present. 'You've got to weigh up all the alternatives and come up with what's right for yourself.'

Rachel knew Polly would object if she let it be known she had already made the decision, so she nodded in agreement and began to drink her tea. Polly meant well. But how could she think of herself, no matter what the subject. Her life was not her own to do with as she liked. Sarah was the most important part, and Sarah would always come first and far above some unknown baby which had never been wanted in the first place.

The trip to Dr Mellor's surgery confirmed what Rachel already knew. She was pregnant. There was no shock in the confirmation. Since talking to Polly she was sure of the road she was going to take, the only one open to her.

At first Dr Mellor had been uncertain of the wisdom of her immediate insistence that the baby was to be adopted. There was plenty of time before the final decision had to be made, he said, as he peered over his black-rimmed glasses and looked as disapproving of the situation as she had expected him to look.

But she had been immovable as she sat in the dingy little room, trying not to think what was in the dusty, murky, coloured bottles that cluttered the shelf behind his head. She wanted the matter settled in her own mind. There had to be no danger of the birth arriving without any adoptive parents being found.

Finally, Dr Mellor had agreed to set the wheels in motion and, as Rachel got up to leave, pushed his glasses up his nose and leaned back in his chair with a snort of disgust that reminded her of her father. Which only made her hold her head a little bit higher as she walked out.

Fortunately she suffered no sickness during the pregnancy and, until the final month, when tiredness began to wear her down, showed little signs of the coming birth and was able to carry on as usual.

No-one except Dr Mellor and Polly knew of her condition. Although she felt sure some of the eagle-eyed neighbours must have noticed her increased weight and come to their own conclusions. But she had never spoken to any of them much, except to pass the time of day. So she kept up the aloofness. No-one was given the chance to ask any prying questions about why she had taken to wearing her mother's dresses; which hung loosely on her narrow shoulders and camouflaged the growing bulge of her stomach.

She went out as little as possible. All the shopping was done at the little grocery store next to the school, which fortunately sold just about everything. And for the final three months, when she felt everyone would know, just by looking at her, she never went further than the bottom of the hill.

It was only for a few months, she told herself, on the days she found her mind wanting to be free and take her down the steps that passed the large sombre mill. Then on over the river by the bridge that gave the village its name of Millbridge.

But the self-imposed imprisonment did have a good side. She found it gave her plenty of time to think, and she began to drag herself out of her despondency with plans for the future. The main plan being to get herself working. She wasn't sure how she could fit a job round her mother and Sarah. But there had to be something she could do, she thought. Her life revolved around doing things for other people. She could see now that it had only been wanting something just for herself, that had made her go with Micky. Well she would never fall into that trap again. She would find something, no matter how small, that was just for herself. If she did, she was sure she would feel better about life, and not such a dogsbody.

The weekly letter she wrote to Joseph was still the high spot of her week. She told him how Sarah was getting on at school, how the insecure little girl he had left behind had turned into a happy outgoing child with many friends. Rachel was now grateful he had found himself a German girlfriend, who kept him from coming home when he had leave. She had never found the courage to tell him about her condition, even though he had almost come home at Easter. A letter had arrived, throwing her into panic. He said that although Ulrika's parents had invited him to spend his leave with them, he felt it was time he paid a visit home.

Rachel had been quick to reply. It would be rude to refuse Ulrika's parents' offer, she told him. Then suggested if he could get leave at Christmas, that would be a nice time to see him. It would, she had written, make Christmas more special for Sarah. But more importantly, if she could put him off until the end of the year, he need never know about the baby.

She felt it best that her brother was kept in the dark. If he found out, his first question would be regarding the father, and she was afraid he would take it upon himself to seek retribution. That would stir up trouble and her condition would become general knowledge; which was the last thing she wanted. So Joseph did not come home, and Rachel turned her anxieties to Sarah.

She wished she could have explained everything to Sarah. She was worried what affect her sudden disappearance might have on her young sister. It was out of the question for the baby to be born at home, with her mother there, and she had had to agree to going into hospital.

Polly had once again become her saviour, offering to move into the cottage to take charge of Sarah and her mother while Rachel was away. And she had also provided an excuse for her sudden disappearance: appendicitis. Under the circumstances a lie was better than the truth, she said, and Rachel had readily agreed. In any case, Sarah was too young to be told the truth. She didn't even seem to have noticed Rachel's changing shape, or reluctance to leave the cottage. So with everything planned to the last detail, Rachel sat back to wait the birth, and the return of freedom.

Three days after Rachel's seventeenth birthday, and two weeks before she was due, Rachel's daughter arrived in the world. It was an easy birth. But Rachel felt no gratitude to the new little being for making a quick entrance, and when the midwife offered her the tiny bundle wrapped in a pink· blanket, she turned away. She did not want to see the child, the product of her sin, the cause of so much pain and so many sleepless nights.

For the two days spent in the maternity ward, Rachel wrapped herself in a cocoon of isolation. She spoke only when addressed directly by one of the nurses, and completely ignored all the other new mums who were only too ready to cuddle their babies.

It was a great relief when she was told at lunch time on the second day that she could go home, and she was almost finished packing her case, when the staff nurse came up to her.

'Are you sure you don't want to look at her? Just once?' the nurse asked, smoothing down her starched white apron as she spoke.

How many times had she been asked that same question? The answer had always been the same. No! She did not want the child. Why couldn't they understand? Why couldn't they accept that she knew what she was doing? 'No,' she repeated yet again, and tossed her toilet bag on top of her nightdress and snapped the case lid shut. 'No! I . . . don't . . . I . . . do not want to see her!' But she had hesitated just long enough for the nurse to see she was not clear in her mind.

'But if you don't take a look at her, you might always wonder what she was like,' the nurse pointed out carefully.

The nurse had struck the right spot. Rachel had already begun to wonder what her daughter looked like. She didn't even know if she was properly formed. She had been conceived in such an obscene way it seemed reasonable to expect she had given birth to a monster. It seemed an odd thought to have, about a baby you did not care for. But it was a thought that had begun to torment her, as she lay in the stiff white hospital sheets, watching all the other new mums happily tending their perfect offspring.

For several long moments she chewed uncertainly at her lip. Then slowly turned to the nurse. 'Perhaps,' she began. 'Just this once!' she added pointedly, as she watched a smile of victory spread over the nurse's shiny scrubbed face. She was not changing her mind. The situation at home made it impossible for her to take the child with her. So one look was not going to alter anything. She only wanted to make sure she had not spawned a monster.

She stood glued to the spot, trying to convince herself she was doing the right thing. But the nurse turned away, giving her no time to go back on the decision, and was halfway down the large ward before she realized she was supposed to be following her.

As she stepped through the nursery door for the first time, her stomach churned. It had blue walls with pink blinds at the windows. Rows of transparent cots lined the walls, the occupants covered with pink or blue blankets. Rachel looked all around, anywhere but at the cot the nurse was standing by. She felt her throat go dry as the nurse lifted the pink blanket and picked up a tiny bundle wrapped tightly in a white sheet. Sweat began to run down her palms and she wiped her hands nervously on her skirt as the nurse carefully unwrapped the sheet and held her daughter out for Rachel to see.

'She's beautiful,' the nurse said, as Rachel stood frozen to the spot. She had expected her feelings to be extreme when she looked on the baby that had been forced on her by violence. But the reality was far more numbing than the imagination. The nurse was right. The baby was beautiful. Perfect, she thought, as she dragged her eyes from the shock of the tiny face to make a mental inventory: two arms, legs and feet; ten tiny fingers and toes. Nothing was missing. The tiny little body in the oversized nappy was perfect. But nothing was so perfect as the crumpled pink face with the dark blue eyes that seemed to be focused unsteadily on a point over Rachel's shoulder.

'No!' She shook her head, trying to deny what was in front of her. There was not one spark of Micky in the child's face, not the tiniest bit of evidence to show who the father was. The face she was looking at was a perfect duplication of one she had seen before, nine years before. Baby Cooper, as the arm band identified her, was an exact copy of her Aunt Sarah at the same age.

Suddenly she turned and hurried from the nursery. She had to get away and she cared nothing for the startled look the nurse gave her. It *was* Micky's child, she told herself, as she almost ran down the ward to the bed that had been her home for the past days. *It was! It was!* She did not want it! Would not have it!

When she reached her bed, she pulled herself together. If she made too much fuss they would assume she was changing her mind. They would try and pressure her into taking the baby home. Before anyone had time to make that suggestion, she put on her coat and picked up her small battered case. Then without waiting for the ward sister to give her permission, showed herself out of the hospital to the nearest bus stop.

'I told you to get a taxi!' Polly scolded, looking concerned as Rachel walked through the cottage door.

Rachel managed a weak smile, but felt more like crying. It was so good to be home and to have left it all behind. It was the past now and she wasn't going to allow herself to think about it any more. The decision had been made and there was no going back.

'I felt all right at the hospital,' she said. Physically if not mentally. 'I thought I'd be fine on the bus. It was only the hill that got to me, anyway.'

'You silly little, madam,' Polly continued to scold, as she took the case from out of her hand, helped her off with her coat and steered her into the front room and down on to the worn leather sofa. 'Now you stay put while I put the kettle on,' she ordered, before waddling hurriedly back into the kitchen.

Rachel smiled. Polly and her cups of tea. Now she knew she really was home. Her smile deepened. It was all she was capable of, she felt so exhausted. She let her eyes wander slowly round the small neat room, acquainting herself with all the familiarity. The old leather sofa and twin chairs and all her mother's china ornaments were in exactly the same place they had always been. The room had been that way for as long as she could remember.

Since she was a baby, she thought. Now she was a woman. Had just given birth to a baby of her own; a baby that would never see this room, never know its mother. The constant tick of the clock on the dresser suddenly grew inside her head, louder and louder, until she felt dizzy and wanted to scream at it to stop. A strange feeling, almost of fear, settled over her, and when she looked around the room all she could see was a baby's face – her baby's face!

Anxiety overtook her weariness and she jumped up from the sofa and hurried to the kitchen, to Polly. She needed to be with someone, needed the closeness of another human being to still the whirlpool of doubt spinning inside her head.

When she walked through the kitchen door, Polly was just pouring the boiling water into the teapot. 'I thought I told you to stay put.' She peered accusingly through the rising steam. Then looked concerned, as Rachel pulled out a chair and flopped down at the small scrub-top table as if a great weight was pressing her down.

'I didn't want to be on my own.' Rachel gave a tight smile, as she admitted her moment's disconcerting weakness.

'Are you all right?' Polly's kindly old eyes made a thorough study of her face, before she turned away to put the kettle down on the gas stove. 'Perhaps you should go to bed,' she suggested, as she pulled another chair out and sat down alongside her at the table.

'No. I'm all right, really I am,' Rachel assured her, leaning on the table and resting her chin in her hands. 'They wanted me to keep the baby,' she said flatly.

'Well, that's the way of things,' Polly replied, as she poured milk into two cups.

Rachel stared at her old friend and suddenly wanted to cry again. She wanted to be told she had done the right thing. But Polly remained silent. 'I didn't want her,' she continued, trying to prompt some reaction from the old lady. 'I couldn't have looked after her. I've done what's best for her. She'll have a much happier life with two parents who will love her. I'd never be able to love her.' It all spilled out as Polly sat quietly and listened. 'They will love her . . . Won't they?' she finally asked.

'Yes,' Polly replied gently, nodding her old head wisely. 'They'll love her. Whoever she goes to will be a couple who have been wanting a baby and can't get one of their own. So you've no fear that she'll be loved and wanted.'

'But you don't think I should have given her away?' Her voice was flat and her eyes pleaded with her old friend to be given the right answer.

But Polly was too wise. She knew Rachel had to come to terms with what she had done by herself. Whitewashing over wouldn't help her, and would only put off her recovery until a later date, when she finally realized it had been her own doing.

'That's your decision, lass,' she pointed out gently. 'Nobody can tell you what you should or shouldn't do on a matter like this.'

Rachel toyed with a teaspoon on the table. Polly was right, she realized, her spirits dropping. She knew what Polly was saying: it had had to be her own decision. But if only she had not looked at the baby! If only the baby had not looked like Sarah. If only! If only!

'But whatever you do, lass,' Polly said, and rested her hand on Rachel's arm. 'You can rely on me to be here to help you. Should you need it.'

'Thank you.' She put her hand on top of Polly's. She had once before thanked God for giving her Polly, and she thanked him again. The old lady was always right and never short on offers of help.

As her hand rested against Polly's wrinkled skin, she suddenly felt her strength renewed, the way she always seemed to feel better when she touched her. 'It's all behind me now,' she suddenly said. 'I'm going forward from now on. And I won't be making any more mistakes.'

'I'm glad to be hearing it.' Polly sat back and gave the tea a stir. 'It's a wise man who learns from his mistakes.'

Rachel smiled. She might not be a wise man but she could be a wise woman, she thought, as she ran a finger in circles round a wood knot in the table top, and considered Polly's words. Perhaps it was too soon to be completely wise. But she felt like a woman now. If nothing else, the last few months had made her grow up. She had learned a lot and, in the learning had left the insecure girl behind her. The thought turned her mind to another insecure girl, the one she had left behind at the hospital. She quickly pushed the thought away. She had done the right thing, she told herself. The baby would go to a home with two parents who would love her and be able to give her far more than she could.

'I'll never be able to thank you enough for all you've done for me.' She looked up at Polly and spoke suddenly, turning her mind away from the depressing thoughts. 'I don't know what I'd have done without you.'

'Get off with you!' Polly gave a great gust of laughter and hitched her arms under her matronly bosom. 'Fine world it'd be if you couldn't help a body . . .'

'And if you only gave to receive you'd end up very disappointed.' Rachel laughed as she finished her friend's well-used saying for her. 'Well, that's a good thing. Because I don't have much to give you,' she joked, feeling a lightness of spirit she had not felt for a long time.

Polly chuckled and began to pour the tea. Then she fell serious. 'Did you ever tell Micky?' she asked.

'No.' Rachel shook her head. Polly had not raised the question of Micky since the first time she had told her of the baby. In one way she could understand her way of thinking

89

that he should be told. But Polly did not know the full story, did not know he had forced himself on her . . . And she had no intention of telling her. It was too humiliating.

'You'll be pleased to know he's gone,' Polly said, and pushed Rachel's cup of tea at her. 'He's got the Railway to transfer him to York.'

'To live?' Rachel could not stop herself looking surprised. She wondered if he had run away because he had found out about the baby, but there was no bitterness with the thought. If he had, he had done her a favour. If he hadn't, he had still done her a favour. Whichever it was, a great wave of relief was rushing through her.

'Aye. Much better job. So his mam says.' Polly lifted her eyes to the ceiling in disbelief. 'Any roads, it's a blessing for you.'

'Yes it is,' she said meaningfully, and felt she wanted to laugh. He was gone. She wouldn't have to worry about coming face to face with him again. Suddenly she had the feeling her luck was changing. 'I'm going to start working,' she announced, taking Polly aback. 'I've been thinking I should find myself something to do. I need something to occupy me.'

Polly gave a huff of disbelief and hitched her bosom a couple of inches higher, the way she always did when her thoughts were becoming intense. 'I'd have thought you had enough to do as it is!'

Rachel grimaced affectionately. She had known Polly would be against the idea. But it was one she had considered for long enough now, and she had every intention of seeing it through.

'I need something for myself,' she explained.

'You're right there, lass,' Polly agreed. 'You've got to think about yourself a bit more. But are you ready to row straight into a job? What about your mam? I'd always come over and see to her for you. But there'd still be a lot of work when you got home.'

'I've thought it all through and there won't be any need for you to worry. I'm going to work from home. I'm taking up dressmaking. I'll be here all the time for Sarah and Mother.

90

I don't expect to get off to a fast start. But if I get one or two customers it will get me going. It's something I can build on when Sarah's older.' The final answer to what she could do had not come to her until she was in the hospital. She had been lying in bed listening to the woman in the next bed telling a visitor how she would be needing a whole new wardrobe of clothes, now she was thin again. It had struck her how much some women spent on clothes: women whose husbands had good jobs. And she was good at sewing and always enjoyed making things for herself and Sarah. It suddenly seemed the perfect solution and she had decided right there and then that dressmaking was to be her chosen profession.

'It seems like a good idea,' Polly said, but looked only half-convinced. 'Then most ideas seem good until you put them into practice. Myself, I don't want to see you wear yourself out.'

'I won't.' She smiled fondly at the old lady's concern. 'But it's time I started to think about making something of my-self.'

Polly levelled her a steady gaze. Then she broke into a smile that took years from her old wrinkled face. Her eyes twinkling, she said, 'You'll make something of yourself, lass. Never fear that you won't. You'll find your rainbow, and your pot of gold.'

Polly and her sayings, Rachel thought fondly.

'Maybe I will, maybe I won't,' she replied. 'But if I don't it won't be for lack of trying.' Micky Caradine might have pushed her down to the bottom of the deepest pit, but in doing so he had returned the courage she had let slip in the months since her father's death. She might only be seventeen and leading the life of a much older woman, but things could be a lot worse. Today she had walked out of the maternity ward and turned her back on her mistakes. From now on she was going forward.

'You're special, lass,' Polly continued knowledgeably. 'And special people always find their gold. Just you believe me.'

'Oh Polly!' Rachel laughed and shook her head. 'How can you be so sure?'

'I can feel it in my water,' Polly replied, making her laugh again.

Then she stopped and gave a sigh, half in amusement, half in regret. 'I wouldn't have thought special people got themselves into the mess I've just been in.'

'You'll see,' Polly replied confidently. 'Everything has its reasons. And its price. Just remember my words, lass, and you'll live to see the day when you can say old Polly was right. Now, let's get this tea drunk before it's cold enough to form icicles.'

Rachel picked up her cup with a smile. For once she could not believe Polly knew what she was talking about. But she did hope that some of her philosophical attitude to life might rub off on her.

Chapter Seven

1964

At midday on Saturday 29 February, the old mill clock struck twelve for the last time. It was the end of an era. The prominent village landmark, whose chimes had dutifully marked out the hours of the day and night for the villagers, was to be taken down. The old mill was to be flattened and the clock was to spend the rest of its days at the industrial museum in Derby.

The whole village was suffering from a state of bereavement, feeling the loss as deeply as they would that of a close friend. Nothing was going to be the same, was the comment on everyone's lips.

'What will they put there?' Sarah asked, looking far too serious for a twelve year old.

Rachel shook her head. She stared at the clock face, both fingers pointing upwards, frozen in the moment of doom. 'I don't know,' she said. 'I don't think they have any plans. The building is unsafe and has to come down.'

'Will we be poor now?'

'No!' Rachel laughingly replied. The village was full of doom and gloom at the demise of the ancient building and some of it had rubbed off on Sarah. 'All my best customers have husbands working in Derby. We won't go short. Neither will many of the villagers. The old mill had only been used for storage for a long time now, and they've no intention of pulling the new mill down.' She looked up at the tall red-brick chimney looming over their heads. She wondered how, if the occasion should ever arise, they would get the giant chimney down with all the cottages clustered so closely around the bottom. The village would start a civil war if they ever decided that had to go, she thought, and smiled as she urged Sarah away.

'Come on,' she said, her mind turning to more important matters. 'We've got to get this dress round to Mrs Morrell. She wants it for tonight.'

Rachel's dressmaking venture had got off to a fine start. One week after placing an advertisement in the post office window, she had received two orders. During the second week Mrs Morrell had placed an order for two dresses. She was a lady from the other side of the village, where all the houses were large and considered to be posh by the cottage-dwelling villagers from their side of the river. Mrs Morrell had been so impressed by the results of her work that she had told her friends. The following weeks had proved hectic but very profitable. Now she had a long list of regular clients and a business that was going from strength to strength.

'I wish we lived in a house like that,' Sarah said, gazing longingly at the first big stone house, as they went over the bridge and turned the corner to walk down the road that ran alongside the river.

'What are you complaining about?' Rachel scolded teasingly. 'Here am I working my fingers to the bone and you're ungrateful.'

Sarah laughed and threaded her arm affectionately through her sister's. 'No I'm not,' she assured her. 'But it would be nice to live somewhere like this and be able to feel important.'

'Get off with you.' Rachel laughed, but she understood what Sarah was saying. Having the ladies of Mulberry Bush Lane for customers was very nice and gave a constant supply of orders. But she did get fed up at times: having the feeling that certain of them looked down on her, as if she was a servant.

'One day,' she said, only half-joking, and looked on the row of grand houses and the determination, which for some time she had felt growing inside her, took a surge. 'Just you wait. One day we'll be stepping out of one of those doors and it'll be our own. Then you can stick your nose right up in the air.' She clipped her finger under Sarah's nose to lift it higher, and Sarah pranced down the road like a very fine lady.

They were still giggling when they reached the Morrells' gate.

'Hello, Rachel!' The tall form of David Morrell straightened up from the flower bed he was weeding. He came towards them, trowel in hand. 'You're looking happy today.' His eyes twinkled from beneath his blond hair, as he smiled down at them, and Rachel felt her cheeks redden. He was always so nice. A real gentleman.

'Just our Sarah telling silly jokes,' she said, feeling her colour heighten further. She hoped he had not seen Sarah cavorting down the lane. He always addresssed her as an equal and she did not want him to think they were being disrespectful.

He grinned at Sarah. Then nodded to the large flat cardboard box Rachel had under her arm. 'You got it done then?'

'Have I ever let you down?' she teased offendedly, then laughed as amusement filled his eyes.

'I won't show you in,' he said, and glanced down at his muddy wellington boots, just as his wife, Judith, opened the door and greeted Rachel.

'It's beautiful!' Judith exclaimed in appreciation. 'You've done me proud. Then you always do.' She turned slowly around, admiring her reflection in the full length mirror of the bedroom, where she had taken Rachel to try on the finished garment.

Judith's dark hair was the perfect contrast to the delicate cream silk, Rachel thought. She smiled inwardly, telling herself Judith would look stunning that evening when they entertained the American guests, business clients from David's company, Rolls-Royce.

For a moment she felt very envious of Judith Morrell. Then she reminded herself of the true facts. Her smile was tight as she instructed Judith to make another twirl, while she inspected the dress for imperfections. Judith was a very beautiful woman. She had a perfect size ten figure, a dressmaker's dream. Her face looked ten years younger than her thirty-eight years. She had a lovely home, a husband who adored her, and a lifestyle many would envy. It was only when she moved, as she did now for Rachel's continuing inspection, that you could tell anything was wrong. The slight limp had become more pronounced over the past year. Rachel had also noticed that she had now begun to drop things which had seemed firm in her hand.

There was no cure for the multiple sclerosis from which Judith suffered. Rachel thought it was a crying shame that such nice people should be made to suffer so badly.

Money could not buy you everything, she told herself, and asked Judith to stand still while she gave a critical eye to the straightness of the hem.

'Does it feel right?' she questioned seriously, knowing no matter how good a garment looked, if it did not feel right on the wearer it was no good.

Judith laughed. 'You've never made anything that didn't feel as comfortable as a kid glove. Let me go and show David?' she begged, displaying the excitement of a five year old.

Rachel gave her permission and Judith turned for the door, her eagerness accentuating her awkwardness. For a moment Rachel watched her unsteady gait, and wondered how she could get so much pleasure out of something so simple, with the terrible illness hanging over her head. It made her feel guilty for her own moments of self-pity.

When they reached the lounge, David and Sarah were sitting drinking coffee and talking about school. David immediately looked up as his wife entered, and the love that filled his eyes, and the smile that gently curved his lips, seemed so special, and tugged at something deep inside Rachel's chest.

It did not happen very often, the full realization of what Micky had done to her. But when it did it was sharp and deep, and always at a moment such as this. When some small action made her aware of how much had been taken from her.

She would never get married. She never allowed herself to think of going out with anyone because she would never let anyone touch her again. The very idea of sex was repugnant to her and she could not believe she would ever find a man who she would be willing to allow get close to her. Even so, when she witnessed a tiny action of love as simple as the expression in David's eyes, she knew Micky had robbed her of far more than her virginity. He had taken away the basic need inside her to be loved and to be able to return love.

'Sit down and have a coffee while I go and take this off,' Judith instructed Rachel, before slowly and awkwardly making for the door.

It was painful to watch, Rachel thought, a heaviness pressing at her chest, as she sank into the luxuriously deep upholstered chair and took the china cup and saucer David handed to her. Even perfect lives had their crosses to bear, she thought sadly staring pensively out of the large picture window at the beautiful view of the river and the weir so close by.

'How's your mother getting on?' David asked, drawing her attention back to the room.

'Not so bad,' she replied automatically. Then she remembered he had been to the cottage often enough with his wife to know how things really stood. She smiled crookedly, and amended, 'She hasn't been too good this past week.'

Usually Rachel went out to her customers, never allowing them to be in the cottage for more than the few minutes it took to arrange an appointment. But Judith was always popping in with some fabric she had just brought and wanted making up straight away. She assumed Judith never wanted to waste a minute of what time she had left to her, and so she always went out of her way to do whatever she wanted.

'Have you never considered having your mother put in hospital?' David asked. 'No-one would blame you. You've done more for her than most people would ever contemplate.'

David was the only person, other than Polly, who could get Rachel talking. She was comfortable with him, and her voice was easy, as she said, 'I won't say it's never crossed my mind. But I've managed her at home for five years. I don't think it would do her any good to be moved now.'

Over the years her mother had improved slightly. She no longer made any vicious attacks on her and her manner had become quiet and subdued, almost submissive, Rachel felt at times. There were still a few noisy periods for her to cope with, but now they were mainly concerning her own salvation, calling on God to forgive her sins. There had even been a few occasions when she was normal enough to thank Rachel for all she had done for her. So she was firmly convinced it was now too late to think of having her mother locked away.

'Don't you ever feel life is passing you by?' David persisted.

For a moment Rachel looked surprised. Then she shook her head. 'I'm doing far better than I could ever have imagined. I don't feel I'm missing anything.'

'What about boyfriends? You're always so tied up with work and looking after your mother you don't seem to have any social life.'

'Perhaps I don't want any social life!' She was immediately on the defensive and spoke more sharply than intended.

'I wasn't trying to pry,' David replied, and she was relieved to hear his voice unaffected by her brusqueness.

'I'm doing exactly what I want to do. I'm happy as I am,' she said, making a conscious effort to speak in a normal voice. She put her cup and saucer down on the coffee table, hoping the action might conceal the flush of embarrassment rushing to her cheeks. 'I make a very comfortable living out of sewing,' she continued, keeping her eyes fixed on the discarded cup and saucer. 'It fits perfectly with my home life . . . For now.'

'For now?' David questioned interestedly. 'Does that mean you have exciting plans for the future?'

Rachel paused uncertainly. She had never spoken of her dreams to anyone – not even Polly. But they were nothing to be ashamed of, and she was sure David was not the type of person to laugh and ridicule her.

'I intend to open my own shop,' she said, only half-confident she had been right to speak her hopes.

David looked impressed and her tension eased.

'It won't be for a long time,' she said. 'I don't have the money yet and there's still mother to think about.' She felt heat filling her cheeks once more, thinking it seemed as if she was saying her mother had to die before she could realize her dreams, and quickly explained, 'If I had the money I could pay someone to look after her during the day. But I don't . . . Not yet.'

'That sounds like a fine idea,' David said, in full agreement with her. 'You have the talent and more than enough determination to get it going.'

Rachel felt her cheeks going hot again, though this time with pleasure.

'Would you still make things to order or just make things to sell in the shop?' David asked.

'Both,' she replied, enthusiasm bubbling in her voice. 'If someone came with a specific order I would do it. But I'd like to design my own range as well.'

David nodded appreciatively. 'You intend to be exclusive then, top of the market range?'

'Oh yes,' she replied very determinedly. She had thought it all out very carefully. The three years dressmaking experience had taught her where the real money was: ladies such as Judith, who lived in places like Mulberry Bush Lane; who wanted to look their best and would pay that bit extra to ensure they never turned up at some important function to find another woman wearing the same outfit.

As they walked home, Rachel felt light of heart. Telling David of her aspirations seemed to have made them more real, as if they were no longer a tiny seed of hope deep inside herself but a real goal, something that was definitely going to happen, rather than a might be.

'Here!' she said, taking her purse and picking out the two half-crowns of change David had given her when he paid for the making of his wife's dress. 'Get yourself some sweets.' She dropped the coins into her sister's hand.

'Five shillings!' Sarah looked down at the coins, then stared at her as if she had gone mad. The most she usually gave her was two shillings, and more normally only one shilling.

'Yes. I'm feeling lucky today. Don't look so surprised or I might change my mind.' She laughed at her sister, and looked across the grey water careering over the weir to the still and silent mill clock waiting its demise. It was the end of an era, she told herself. But there was no reason to assume that should be bad. Maybe the new era would be far better than the last. David had said she had enough determination, and she did have, determination to do anything she wanted to do.

It was strange, she thought, but she could not recall having the same driving force when she was younger. She wondered briefly if Micky's treatment of her had anything to do with it. Had he instilled her with a need to win and prove she was something more than the bit of dirt he had used? Perhaps she should thank him? She cast the thought away as being ridiculous and turned her mind to more pleasant topics.

'You're not going to spend it all on chocolate, are you?' she asked, having second thoughts about giving Sarah such a great sum of money all at once.

When they reached home they went first into the front room. Sarah immediately took off her coat and hung it on the hook behind the door. Rachel gave the fire a poke to get it going before taking her own coat off and hanging it up. Then she went to the kitchen to make her mother a cup of tea.

Rachel was halfway through the kitchen door, when she came up short. Her heart leaped upwards with an alarming jolt. Someone had been in the kitchen. The tea towel was lying on the floor, too far away from the hook on the wall to have fallen there of its own accord. She could clearly remember hanging it on the hook herself, just before going out. Nervously she looked around the room. Goose bumps rose on her flesh and a feeling of sickness made her clasp her hands over her stomach. They had been burgled, she told herself, not wanting to believe. But someone had been there while they had been away. A strange feeling filled the room. She could feel it like a tangible presence wrapping around her, touching her.

Almost of their own accord her eyes leaped to the red and black chinese tea caddy where she kept the money. The caddy was still there and a quick inspection proved the contents untouched.

But what . . . ? She looked round, dazed and unable to

understand. Her gaze followed the line of tins and bottles packed on the high shelf. They were all there, nothing had gone. She turned away, looked round the kitchen once more, nothing was missing, only the tea towel had been moved.

No it wasn't, she thought, spinning back to the shelf, not really sure where the sudden thought had come from. But . . . !

Her gaze leaped at the shelf once more. The old Quality Street tin they used as a first-aid box was in the wrong place. No! she begged, as the terrible thought entered her mind.

Ice trickled down her spine as she grabbed the tin and pulled the lid off, flinging it to the floor in her haste. What was in her mind was unthinkable. Her mother had not set foot out of the bedroom in five years!

As she picked up the aspirin bottle she knew the unthinkable had happened. The bottle, which had been almost full, was now empty.

The tin and its entire contents followed the lid, crashing to the floor as she flew out of the kitchen.

'Get Doctor Mellor! Tell him it's urgent,' was all she had time to shout at the startled Sarah, as she dashed through the front room. Then, flinging the stair-foot door so wide it crashed into the wall, raced up the stairs faster than she had ever done before.

'Mum! Oh Mum!' Her mother was breathing, but only just. Her skin looked grey and her lips had an ominous bluey purple hue. Rachel could only stand looking at the wasted body and closed eyes. She felt so helpless. She should be doing something, she told herself, yet did not know what. She fell to her knees at the side of the bed and clasped her mother's hands, feeling her own trembling as she tried to will life back into her.

'No! No! Don't let this happen!' she begged, calling on God's help. 'Why?' she asked, looking at her mother's silent face. 'Why did you get up? Why now? Why did you have to get up when we weren't here? Why? Why? Why?'

But her mother could not respond. The tablets had taken quick effect on her already weakened body. She had slipped past the point of no return and Rachel's pleas were spoken into an empty room!

When Dr Mellor arrived, puffing and panting, with his glasses halfway down his nose after running up the stairs with a frightened Sarah behind him, Rachel was sitting in the chair by the window. He looked at her with a question in his eyes and she could only shake her head in despair.

'It's too late,' she finally and quietly said.

Sarah began to sob loudly, but Rachel did not hear. She was numbed beyond imagination by her mother's death. Over the years she had felt hate for her mother, irritation that she would not make herself do more, which she had never doubted she could have done, if she had wanted to. She had felt sympathy at times, seeing the pathetic creature her mother had turned into. But it had been a long time since she had felt recognizable love. Yet now she was being torn in two with a sorrow that was blinding. She saw nothing of Dr Mellor going to the bed to check that her diagnosis was correct. All she could see was her mother's face, almost beautiful in its peacefulness. And she knew, despite everything her mother had put her through, she had still loved her, still wanted that bond between mother and daughter to remain firm. Her mother had been in no fit state to keep up that bond. So she had reversed the roles, keeping the maternal love flowing in their unsteady relationship for the past years.

She sat like a statue. Even when Sarah threw herself into her arms, she did not respond.

Dr Mellor peered over his glasses and frowned deeply. 'Go and get old Polly,' he instructed, pulling Sarah away and pushing her to the door. Then he took Rachel by the arm and led her downstairs. She followed blindly. She didn't want to go, didn't want to leave her mother, but she had neither the voice nor the will to object.

'Now then, lass. What's to be done with you?' Polly said, as she pulled a chair up in front of her and sat down. 'Talk to me, lass,' she urged, and placed her cool hand on her arm.

The action startled Rachel. The flesh touching her was so cool – like her mother's had been. But her mother was upstairs,

102

where they had left her. She blinked, and found herself looking into Polly's concerned face. She looked deep into Polly's eyes, matching concern for concern. 'Are you all right, Polly?' she asked, fear vibrating her voice.

'Course I am, lass,' Polly confirmed, and Rachel felt weak with relief. 'It's you we're bothering about. You wouldn't say anything.' Polly gave her arm a comforting rub.

Rachel suddenly returned to reality. Sarah was gazing at her with a worried tear-stained face. Polly's kindly old eyes were scrutinizing her with the concern only Polly's eyes were capable of. Dr Mellor was looking suddenly relieved, his dour expression brightening with the hint of a smile.

'Whatever came over me?' she asked, rubbing her head as if trying to put some sense back into it. 'Mother's . . .' She hesitated for a moment, wondering if it had all been a bad dream. But no! She could not hide from the truth. 'Mother's dead . . . Isn't she?'

The question needed no reply. The tone of her voice clearly expressed her grasp of the truth.

Polly nodded her head. 'Aye, lass, she is.'

Dr Mellor shuffled nervously in the background, then moved forward. 'Yes, she's dead, Rachel,' he repeated Polly's confirmation. 'But I don't know how. From the look of her I'd say she took something . . . Some tablets. But how did she get tablets?' he asked, his tone suddenly serious.

A look of shock passed over Rachel's face. 'You . . .' she began, unable to form the unthinkable question. 'You can't think I gave her something to kill her?' she finally managed to gasp out in disbelief.

'Course he doesn't!' Polly quickly put in, casting the doctor a warning glare.

'Now, Rachel,' Dr Mellor placed a hand on her shoulder. 'Don't let any of us go jumping to conclusions. I have to find out the cause of death. There will have to be an autopsy, no matter what. But if you can throw any light on the matter it will help us to know what we're looking for.'

Rachel looked from the doctor to Polly, then back to the doctor. He thought she had killed her own mother, she told herself. 'Aspirins!' she snapped angrily. Then her voice became wooden, as she added, 'She took a bottle of aspirins. She came downstairs while we were out and took the bottle full. There was nothing wrong with her legs,' she added, her voice rising as she suddenly realized she was defending herself. 'You know that!' She looked fiercely at Dr Mellor. 'You know she stayed in the bedroom because she chose to stay in the bedroom . . . Until today.' Her voice died on the last and she dropped her head into her hands, unable to take any more.

Sarah, after standing silently in the background, suddenly came to life. She rushed to her sister's side. 'Leave her alone,' she screamed. 'She didn't do anything. Go away,' she sobbed. 'You're horrible to think such things!'

'Now, now, little lass,' Polly said, pulling Sarah away from Rachel and holding the sobbing twelve year old in her arms. She looked sternly at Dr Mellor. 'Shouldn't you be getting off to make arrangements?' she suggested pointedly. 'You can't leave her in the house with these two.'

'Will you stay?' the doctor asked.

'Course I'll stay!' Polly snapped.

The shortness of the response gave Rachel the distinct impression Polly had only just stopped herself from tagging 'you silly old fool' on the end. And she lifted her face from her hands with the wild desire to laugh out loud. Fortunately the sight of the sobbing Sarah in Polly's arms reminded her she had nothing to laugh about, and put an end to the out of place humour. Leaping up she wrapped her arms around both Sarah and Polly together, dropped her face against the back of Sarah's neck and gave way to the grief that was tearing at her soul.

The funeral went ahead four days later. Dr Mellor seemed to have satisfied himself that she was in no way responsible for her mother's death, and he never brought up the subject again.

Rachel did wonder if Polly might have had something to do with his change of heart. Polly firmly denied it. 'Don't give him the time of day, unless it's necessary,' she insisted, dismissing the subject with a flapping hand when she asked her right out if she had been getting at Dr Mellor.

Although Rachel did not mind if Polly had interfered – she knew in her own heart she was blameless – she would have liked to have known if Dr Mellor had come to the same conclusion for himself, or had his arm twisted; which she knew Polly was more than capable of.

It no longer mattered she told herself, as they left the cemetery. It was all over now, another part of her life brought to a close. The end of an era, she had thought that very day, while looking on the old mill clock in its final hours, never realizing how significant the moment was going to be for her. She wondered if her mother had planned it that way. If, after a unspectacular life, she had tried to give herself a spectacular death: one people would remember. The thought made her sad.

'I wish they'd go,' she said, and cast a look of despair at Polly, already doing the washing up.

'Sit yourself down, leave them to get on with it themselves for a bit,' Polly ordered.

Rachel didn't need telling twice. She sat down at the kitchen table and rested her chin on her hands. 'I'm glad we had it at chapel,' she said. It had been the first time she had been back inside the chapel since the night of her father's death. She had relented for her mother's sake, feeling she would have wanted her final service in the chapel she had visited so regularly, before her illness.

'You did the right thing, lass,' Polly confirmed.

Rachel smiled at her. Then suddenly frowned. 'You shouldn't be doing that,' she said, only then realizing Polly was doing her job for her. 'Sarah will help me. When they've all gone,' she added despondently. She had been surprised how many people had turned up to pay their last respects. It had pleased her to see the tiny chapel bursting at the seams. But now she wanted her mother's friends to go and to be left alone.

'I like to be busy,' Polly replied, and plunged another pile of plates into the water. 'Besides, it might give some of them a hint that we're ready to clear up.'

'Oh Polly,' Rachel found herself laughing. Without thinking she got up and went to the old lady, wrapping her arms around her neck. For a moment she rested her face against the back of her shoulder. 'What ever would I do without you?' she asked.

'You'd have to do the washing-up, for a start,' Polly replied dryly. She peered over her shoulder into her face. 'And you're not dressed for it. So get away before you get soap on your clothes.'

Rachel tightened her arms in a brief hug, then turned away. She glanced down at the charcoal grey suit she had made specially for the occasion. With its straight skirt and short box jacket it was the first femininely elegant outfit she had worn. Since the day of Micky's attack she had hidden her body beneath shapeless, dull, pleated skirts and equally dull blouses and cardigans. Today she had felt she wanted to look her best for her mother.

'Does it look all right?' she asked, suddenly afraid it might not have been very fitting to have new clothes for a funeral.

'It looks grand,' Polly confirmed. 'It's about time you started to dress yourself up a bit.'

Rachel grimaced. It had been pure chance that she had the material, suitably dark, purchased initially to make some new school skirts for Sarah. She was not sure what had prompted her to make the suit. It had been the second night after her mother's death, while she had been tossing and turning in search of sleep that would not come, that she had got up in the small hours, knowing she had to do something to take her mind off things. The material had been laid out on the table, the scissors poised to make the first cuts for Sarah's skirts, when she suddenly stopped herself. All her clothes were dull and suitable for a funeral, she had told herself, but from somewhere came the strange urge to have something special, something that would match up to the Sunday best her mother had always provided for her when she was a child. The Cooper children had always been the best dressed children in the chapel, and she felt her mother would have wanted her to keep up that record.

It all seemed rather silly now, she thought. Wearing a fancy outfit, as if her mother could have seen her. 'I feel strange,' she said, standing like a statue in the middle of the kitchen.

'What? Ill?' Polly turned around with concern on her face and soap on her hands.

Rachel shook her head. 'No. Empty. Odd. Not how I would have expected to feel at my mother's funeral. I just want to get back to normal.' Normal! What was normal? Running up and down the stairs for her mother? Washing dirty sheets every day? Was that the normal she craved?

It seemed impossible to imagine, but at that moment the answer was yes. She would gladly have gone on doing all those things if only her mother was back with her. It would have been impossible to have stayed in every minute of the day to make sure her mother was all right. Yet she felt she should have done that, that she should have been there when her mother had needed her the most. She felt she was responsible for her mother's death, responsible by neglect.

'You'll soon get back into the run of things,' Polly assured, turning back to the sink and plunging her hands back into the water. 'You can get on with your own life now, lass. You've got nothing to regret. You did your best for her.'

Rachel smiled tightly. It was funny how Polly always seemed to know what you were thinking and was able to provide answers to the questions you did not ask.

'Will you carry on sewing? Or will you get yourself another job now?'

'I'll continue sewing,' she replied without hesitation. 'It's doing well and I've got plans for the future.'

'Oh yes!' Polly peered round suspiciously. 'And do these *plans* concern anything other than working your fingers to the bone?'

'I enjoy what I do. And I have every intention of making a success of my life.'

Polly nodded sagely. 'Aye, I can see that,' she said dryly. Then, before Rachel could reply, put in, 'Go and collect some

107

more dirty pots from in there.' She nodded pointedly at the front room. 'And give your Joseph a hint that it's time to get rid of them.'

Some hours later Rachel drew the curtains on the starlit frosty night. The front room felt cold and she poked the glowing coals, watching the star-like sparks shoot up the blackened chimney. She sat down in her mother's chair and found herself wondering if the sparks would go all the way up the chimney and through the darkened sky to heaven and her mother. She hoped her mother was in heaven, that she had at last found the peace that had eluded her on earth.

'Penny for them,' Joseph said from their father's old chair on the opposite side of the fireplace.

Rachel shook her head. 'They're not worth a halfpenny.' She smiled at her brother with a fondness that was touched with sadness. She looked across to Sarah, sitting at the table with her head buried in a book. It was so long since they had sat there that way, like a family again. If only it could have been a happier occasion that had brought them together. Funerals! she thought. If nothing else they brought families back together, even if it was only for a short time.

'Have you set a date for the wedding?' she asked, turning her attention back to Joseph.

'We had talked about May. But perhaps we should leave it a bit longer.'

Rachel stared into the leaping flames of the fire, her lips tightly compressed as she held back the words she wanted to say. Joseph had announced his engagement to Ulrika in a letter that arrived along with his Christmas card. She had long before accepted the fact that she had lost her brother to a foreign girl and a foreign land. And in response had written two letters: one congratulating Joseph, the other welcoming Ulrika to the family. Other than a brief thank you conveyed in Joseph's next letter, she had received nothing from her soon to be sister-in-law.

At the time the lack had not unduly concerned her; perhaps the girl could not write in English, she had offered in the girl's defence. That was, until yesterday, when Joseph had turned up for their mother's funeral – alone.

Of course Ulrika had never met their mother. But now that she was officially Joseph's fiancée, Rachel felt it only proper that she should have accompanied him to England for his mother's funeral.

'What's the point of putting it off?' she asked, forcing her voice to deny the coolness she was feeling. What was done was done and life had to go on. No-one realized that better than her. She had been telling it to herself for years.

'I don't know if it would be right.' Joseph spoke quietly and he did not look at her. 'I wouldn't want anything to spoil the day for Ulrika.' He finally found the courage to look his sister in the eye.

'It's three months away,' she returned, and concealed a shudder as, for the first time, she saw traits of their father in her brother: a self-centred obsession with their own needs. Ulrika was the only thought in Joseph's mind. Consideration for his mother's memory did not enter into any decision to prolong the wedding date.

'Besides,' she added shortly, suddenly having no care for her brother's feelings, 'Ulrika never knew Mother. The marriage will be in another country, totally separate from here.' Her strong brother, the young man she had looked up to, loved and respected so much, had turned into a weak man. She had seen it in that brief moment he had not been able to meet her eyes, and she knew, no matter what she thought or said, the marriage would go ahead in May. Ulrika would make sure of that.

Joseph returned to Germany the following day and left the cottage just before ten o'clock. The army had only granted him a short pass, he said.

Rachel was sceptical. She knew the army was always willing to grant compassionate leave under these circumstances. But she remained silent, not speaking her thoughts as she watched him walk away down the hill.

She looked at the recently acquired sergeant's stripes, displayed proudly on his sleeve. But she could not smile. The man who was walking down the hill was a million miles from the one she had watched before, in his navy-blue boiler suit. She was saying goodbye to a stranger, she thought sadly. Her brother had been lost to her a long time ago.

Chapter Eight

In the beginning, Rachel felt guilty of the extra time she now had to pursue her career. Time which before had been taken up by running about attending to her mother. Fortunately, she found peace of mind in her work, and the regrets over her mother's death were soon diminished, as she strove for the perfection she always insisted upon. Quality was her trademark and her fame was spreading fast, passed on by satisfied customers to friends and relatives. Her clientele was spread throughout the surrounding villages, and she even had two ladies who travelled from Derby to see her.

Now that her mother was no longer there, Rachel worked only from home. She had rearranged the house, turning the front room into her sewing and fitting room. The chairs and sofa had been taken upstairs and her mother's old bedroom was now the sitting room. The table had stayed downstairs, because that was needed for cutting out the material and the paper for her patterns. But their meals were now eaten at the small kitchen table. It was plenty big enough for two, Rachel had insisted, when Sarah's nose had wrinkled up in disapproval.

To appease Sarah, who had the impression her home was being turned into a factory, Rachel had Joseph's garret bedroom decorated. She found just the right colour pink carpet at just the right price, and made matching curtains and bedspread, turning the room into the perfect place for the young lady Sarah was fast becoming. The expense had meant dipping into the money being saved to purchase her longed-for shop. But she was more than compensated by the pleasure on Sarah's young face when she first saw the finished room all in pink and white and all her own.

The move also benefited Rachel. She now had the old

shared bedroom all to herself. It was somewhere she could be alone with her dreams, where she could relax and let her mind create the designs which would one day fill her shop – or rather boutique, as it was now becoming fashionable to call the small, exclusive dress shops such as her own was going to be.

'Can I bring Carol round after school?' Sarah asked. 'She's got some material and wants a suit making for their Margaret's wedding.'

Rachel looked up from the sewing machine to her sister, standing halfway through the door, seeming to have re-membered at the last minute.

'Margaret's wedding!' she repeated incredulously. She sighed loudly. She was well aware, as was the entire village, that Margaret Land was to be married at the weekend – in four days time. 'How long has Carol known of Margaret's wedding?' she asked irritably, knowing the answer. Rachel now understood why Sarah had left saying anything until the last moment. Margaret's wedding had been planned for months. The wedding of the year, some of the villagers were sarcastically naming it, feeling Margaret was stepping out of her class because she was marrying some university lecturer from Bristol and the wedding was to be a top hat and tails do.

It was always the same with Sarah's friends. If they wanted something making they wanted it yesterday. She did not mind getting rushed orders from her real customers, but Sarah's friends never expected to be charged the full price.

'Well . . . ?' Sarah shrugged her shoulders and added a hopeful smile.

Rachel sighed again, knowing she had been won over. 'Tell her she can come. But I'm making no promises it will be ready for Saturday!'

Sarah broke into a grin. 'Thanks sis,' she called, and ran off down the yard.

You're a soft touch, she told herself, and turned back to the sewing machine. She already had two dresses to finish before Friday.

She had been working for some time, when the door opened. 'You there?' Polly called, and came waddling into the room, puffing and panting. 'Do you want any shopping?'

Rachel frowned at her. 'What are you going shopping for? You know Sarah will do it after school.' She was becoming concerned for the old lady. Recently she was looking older and was struggling more with her breath than she used to do.

'I want a bit of fresh air in my lungs,' she said.

Rachel shook her head in despair as Polly flopped on to one of the straight-backed chairs left in the room, and gave a great gasp. The weight of her enormous bosom seemed to be fighting the rise and fall of the lungs she was concerned about. Rachel felt her worry increase.

'Well, have a rest before you go any further,' she insisted, knowing she would never talk her out of it altogether.

'Stop fretting.' Polly was twice as insistent. 'I'll stop on my way back and have a cuppa with you . . . If you've not got anybody here,' she added dryly. 'Which'll be a wonder!'

'It's all good for profits,' Rachel replied glibly, knowing what was coming next. Polly made it very obvious she did not approve of her single-minded life style, and she put the half-finished dress down on the sewing machine, turned in her chair to face her friend, and prepared herself for a lecture – which did not come.

'What are you wearing to the party?' Polly asked.

Rachel grimaced. She did not want to go to the party. It was being held after Margaret Land's formal wedding reception and almost everybody in the village had been invited. She had tried to find some excuse. But Polly had made it clear, if she had to, she would drag her there by the hair.

'My grey suit. *If* I go.'

'*If you go!*' Polly repeated. 'Of course you'll go. Sarah's going. Besides, I need you to take me. I might enjoy myself and need carrying home.'

Rachel looked disbelieving. There was no chance of Polly needing to be carried home. Alcohol had never been one of her vices, and never would be.

'Haven't you got anything better than a funeral suit?' Polly stated bluntly. 'What's that you're making there?' She peered at the heap of cornflower blue fabric draped over the sewing machine.

'That isn't mine and you know it.'

'Maybe I do. I also know it's time you brightened yourself up. It's not natural for a girl of your age to go around in mourning all the time.'

'I'm not in mourning, Polly. These are my usual clothes.' She glanced at her navy-blue dress, respectable, but dull.

'I know that as well. And it's still not natural at your age. You should be enjoying yourself. Not always have your nose pressed into that machine, making fancy clothes for other folk.'

'It's what I want to do. And I don't want fancy clothes. If I did, I would make them,' she added pointedly.

'You mean you don't want to make yourself look nice for fear any of the lads take a fancy to you.'

'Yes, Polly!' she stressed meaningfully. 'You know why I do it. So please let the matter drop.'

'You've got to face it sometime,' Polly persisted. Her voice had gentled and there was a sadness in the old eyes which stabbed at Rachel. Polly genuinely believed she was thinking of her welfare and she did not know how to convince her she was wrong. One hundred pleading Pollys could not have changed her mind. Not once in the years since Micky's attack had she felt a natural yearning pulling her towards any young man.

'Perhaps I will, one day. When I meet the right person,' she said, having no belief in her words, but hoping they might placate Polly.

'*Meet the right person!*' Polly gave a disgusted huff. 'How will you meet anybody if you never go anywhere?'

'Maybe he'll be at the party on Saturday night,' Rachel replied dryly. She turned back to the sewing machine, dismissing the subject. How many times would she have to tell Polly before she gave up and let her be. Unfortunately, she could not think of a number high enough. Polly would never give up. She saw it as her duty not to give up. She was

114

of the old school, who believed a woman could never be really happy unless she was tied to some man.

'Well I'll be off. I can see you're busy,' Polly said, taking the hint and heaving herself out of the chair.

'I'm sorry.' Rachel felt guilty and looked apologetic. 'It's just . . . Oh I'm so fed up with hearing about the blessed wedding!'

Polly nodded understandingly. 'Well, there's probably more to that than meets the eye,' she pronounced meaningfully. Margaret Land was a year younger than Rachel and, from the looks of it, had done all right by herself. It was times like this when she could have cheerfully strangled Micky Caradine for what he had done. He had turned Rachel into an old woman. It wasn't right. But she had built a wall around that part of her life. She had to knock it down herself and until she did there was not much anyone else could do.

'Do you want anything bringing?' Polly repeated the enquiry she had arrived with, as she waddled to the door, still puffing and panting.

'Bring a packet of biscuits and we'll have them with that tea,' Rachel called, knowing she had been out of turn with her and wanting to make it clear she was still welcome. 'And make them chocolate. I feel like spoiling myself.'

Polly shook her head as she went through the door. Chocolate biscuits! Spoiling herself! It made you want to cry.

The party was well under way when Rachel and Polly arrived at the hut, so named because it was a large wooden building. It was surrounded by tennis courts and a bowling green and was the sports and social club for the mill. There was a small stage at the far end, though Rachel could never remember it being used for live entertainment. The church and chapel bazaars and Christmas parties were the room's usual functions. She could not recall anyone ever holding a wedding there before. Trust Margaret to be different, she thought, and steered Polly over to an empty table in the corner.

The record player on the stage was blasting out 'Please Please Me'. Rachel made her way to the bar, her eyes searching the crowd of youngsters on the dance floor for Sarah, who had come down earlier with Sally and her parents. She eventually found her sister, bouncing around the dance floor to the rhythm of the hectic beat. Her blond hair was shining like gold in the bright overhead lighting put up for the day and Rachel smiled, happy to see her enjoying herself.

'Hello, Rachel.'

She had almost bumped into David Morrell, loaded with a tray of drinks. Laughing she made her apologies and moved aside to give him a wide berth.

'Shall we be seeing you tripping the light fantastic?' he asked, balancing the tray expertly on one arm.

'Oh no!' Rachel shook her head vigorously. She had never danced in her life and wouldn't know where to begin. And she had no intention of finding out. The modern dancing fashion might be standing apart from your partner, but there was still too much intimacy in the actions for her liking. 'I forgot to bring myself a partner,' she joked, hoping light-heartedness would put an end to the subject far quicker than any revelations that she did not want to do it.

David laughed. 'I don't see that being a problem in your case. And while your card's still empty put my name down. I'm sure it will soon get filled up.'

David walked away leaving her to stare bewilderedly at his departing back. Then she hurried to the bar; wishing she had not bumped into him; wishing she had never given in to Polly's bullying insistence that she should come; wishing she had had the courage to just say no to everyone.

She would not dance with him, she told herself, as she made her way back through the crowd, an overfull glass of bitter lemon balanced precariously in each hand. Polly had made her come to the party, but no-one else was going to make her do anything she didn't want to do, she thought mutinously.

When she reached Polly, she put the drinks on the table and sat down, hoping her angry frown was not noticeable. She hadn't been there long, when Margaret came over.

'You look beautiful,' she said sincerely. It was true. In the ballerina-length Nottingham lace wedding dress, Margaret

116

looked like a fairy princess. The short veil worn for the ceremony had been removed from her head and her dark curls gleamed with health and vitality. She glowed with happiness from head to foot and Rachel felt a stab of envy. Then she reminded herself of what Margaret had let herself in for that night, and told herself no dress was worth that. She wondered if Margaret had any ideas about what was to come, but decided, if she had, she would not have looked so happy.

'I'm glad you came, Rachel,' Margaret said. 'You should get yourself out more often.'

'I'm doing what I want,' she replied, her voice tightening noticeably. Did everyone in the village have the idea she was to be pitied and saved from herself? The thought annoyed her. She wished she lived in the town, where no-one concerned themselves about anyone else.

'Our Carol loves that suit you've made for her,' Margaret said. 'Makes her look really grown up.'

The subject of her work returned the smile to Rachel's face. She looked automatically towards the dance floor. But it wasn't Carol Land, in the lime-green suit she had sat up most of Thursday night to get finished, that her eyes settled on. The group of girls, who had previously been alone on the dance floor, had been joined by a number of boys. Her heart skipped a beat. Sarah was dancing with Alan Caradine – Micky's brother.

'How's your Joseph getting on?' Margaret asked.

Ice trickled down Rachel's spine and it was a moment before she realized Margaret was waiting for her reply. 'Oh . . . all right . . . He's getting married next month.' She tried to look at Margaret, but found her gaze drawn back to the dance floor.

'In Germany?' Margaret enquired.

'Yes.' She nodded her head too quickly. They're only dancing, she told herself, but could not shake off the sudden sickness lying heavy in her stomach.

'Will you be going over for the wedding?'

'No,' she replied bluntly. Then, realizing Margaret was looking surprised, quickly went on, 'Finances won't run to it.

117

And all Ulrika's family will be there. We won't be missed.'
No, they would not be missed, she repeated to herself. Not
even by Joseph. Her brother was as foreign to her now as if
he himself had been a German.

'Where are you going for your honeymoon?' she suddenly
asked, knowing it was a big secret and hoping the enquiry
might make Margaret go away and leave her free to go and
sort Sarah out.

It worked. 'Away!' Margaret gushed, and quickly moved
on to the next table.

Rachel immediately stood up determined to go and get
Sarah away from the dance floor.

Polly's hand reached out, grabbing her wrist and pulling
her back. 'Leave it be,' she said calmly, making it obvious
she knew what was in her mind. 'They're only kids. There's
no harm in it.'

Rachel flopped back into the chair. 'I can't let it go on,'
she said anxiously. 'What would happen if . . . ?'

'Now then,' Polly ordered sternly. 'Sarah's only twelve and
Alan's not much older. Don't start marrying them off already!'

'I'm not,' Rachel quickly denied. But she knew in her heart
Polly was right. When she looked at her sister dancing with
Micky's brother, she did not see two schoolchildren enjoying
innocent fun. She saw a long involved relationship before her
eyes. A relationship she had never, in her wildest moments,
contemplated; a relationship she would never be able to
endure.

'But what if . . . ?'

'What if nothing,' Polly cut in sharply. 'Sarah's got to mix
with lads for her own good. If you'd had more freedom you'd
never have got sucked in by the first one that came along.'

For a moment she could only stare at Polly. Sucked in! If
only she could tell her the truth.

'Face facts, lass,' Polly continued. 'If you hadn't led such
a sheltered life you'd have known what's what and wouldn't
have been led astray so easy. Let the girl have her fun. If you
try to bend her you'll only make trouble for yourself.'

Rachel looked back to the dance floor. Polly was right –

as usual! But oh how she wished it could have been another boy Sarah was dancing with . . . Any other boy at all.

'I'm sure it must be time for our dance.'

She jerked her head around to find David hovering over her. She had been too lost in her worries to notice him approaching. For a moment she was stuck for words. It was his expectant expression that finally made her find her voice, and she stammered, 'Oh . . . I'm . . . I'm not very good at dancing. I'd really rather not.'

David smiled with a knowingness that sent colour flooding to her cheeks. 'Come on with you,' he insisted. 'We all have to begin somewhere. I won't expect you to win medals.'

'No,' she shook her head vigorously. She couldn't do it. It would be too embarrassing.

'Get off with you,' Polly chipped in.

Rachel favoured Polly with a cool glare. But the determined look she was given in return made her realize she was fighting a losing battle. She had the choice of either getting up and going peacefully with David, or having to suffer the embarrassment of Polly treating her like a two year old.

With reluctance she forced herself out of the chair. David stood back to allow her through and she led the way to the dance floor, butterflies of apprehension going wild inside her stomach.

Fortunately the modern dancing was not difficult. You just stood there and shook yourself about and she soon found the rhythm by watching the closest members of the crowd and copying them.

They had been dancing for some time before she finally plucked up courage to look up into David's face. Then she wished she had not. The smile in his eyes gave her the uncomfortable feeling he could see all the insecurities in her head – and knew the reason why.

'How is Judith?' she asked, finding a confidence of voice, as she tried to pretend they were back home in the sewing room. Just passing the time while Judith tried on the latest edition to her wardrobe.

'Not too bad. Her legs don't seem to have got any worse

for some time now. But I'm afraid she is dropping things more regularly. Margaret looks nice. Did you make her dress?'

Rachel shook her head, a tiny smile played on her lips. Margaret thought her marriage was lifting her into a higher class, but she still had a lot to learn. She would never have considered having a 'home-made' dress for her wedding, thinking such clothes were cheap. She pictured Judith Morrell in the elegant navy-and-white spotted dress and jacket she was at present wearing. She looked like a real lady!

'I don't have to ask the same of your own outfit,' David said, passing an appreciative glance over her grey suit and causing flames to leap into her cheeks. 'Your work always seems to have your hallmark stamped all over it. You have certainly been blessed with the fingers of a tailoress.'

'You'll make my head swell so much I'll not get through the door,' she joked, hoping he could not hear the self-consciousness in her voice. She was growing more uneasy by the minute and she wished the record would stop and she could escape.

Half her wish was granted. The record came to an end. But the next moment Elvis Presley's voice filled the room and the tempo changed to a sultry ballad. Couples joined together and before she knew what was happening, David had taken her hand and was pulling her closer.

'I don't think I can do this,' she quickly said, feeling panic rising. It was the first time a man had held her. The first time she had been close to a man since . . . !

'Then I'll teach you. Just follow me.'

She tried to smile, but it was tight and forced. She could feel his arms holding her, his legs forcing hers into the right steps. She began to tremble and was sure he must also feel it.

'Relax,' he said, proving her right and causing the trembling to increase. He smiled down into her face and his eyes were filled with far too much understanding for her comfort.

She told herself it was impossible, yet could not rid herself of the fear that David knew everything about her. When he

120

spoke, he doubled that fear, and she felt her whole body go tense with apprehension.

'I'm no threat to you, Rachel,' he said gently. 'I'm a happily married man and my wife is here watching. There's nothing wrong in what we're doing.' He gave her a crooked smile. 'So let yourself relax and enjoy it.'

Her smile conveyed her nervousness. Did the whole village know what Micky had done to her? No-one had ever spoken of the baby, even when she was at her largest. She had never allowed anyone to come too close, or get into any conversation other than the single syllable kind. But she did not doubt that her condition had been noticed. Well it might be common knowledge that she had an illegitimate child somewhere, but no-one could know how that child was conceived . . . Or by whom, she told herself. She felt a certain safety in the knowledge that her secret was still safe, and forced herself to relax a little in his arms. It was only David, she told herself. But David was still a man and she was extremely grateful when the music drifted away.

'Thank you, David,' she quickly said, making it clear their dancing had also come to an end.

'Come and have a word with Judith,' he invited, and moved to take her arm to escort her across the room. Then changed his mind and let his arm drop to his side and Rachel to walk freely: an action that doubled her embarrassment and made her realize how stupid she must have appeared.

As they wound their way through the crowded room Rachel could see Polly had been joined at her table by the Misses Dewhurst – two elderly sisters who spent most of their lives being shocked by the goings on of the world, and who coped with all the traumas by sipping copious amounts of sweet sherry.

Leaving David, she made a detour to Polly. 'I'm going to have a word with Judith. Do you want to come?' she asked, offering the old lady an escape.

'No, lass. Leave me be. Go and enjoy yourself.'

'Will it be your turn next, Rachel?' Lizzie, the younger of the two sisters questioned nosily.

For a moment she did not know what to say. It was the sort of personal question she would never have asked. 'Oh no,' she finally gasped. 'I'm far too busy to think about getting married.'

'Haven't you got yourself a chap, then?' Agnes, the older and more blunt sister, put in. 'You'll have to watch out, or you'll be on the shelf.'

Rachel felt her face redden.

'Rachel won't ever be on the shelf,' Polly asserted, bristling with indignation. 'She's pursuing her career before she saddles herself with any man. What was your two's excuse?'

Oh Polly! Rachel cringed. 'Come on over to Judith,' she urged, fearing that the three old ladies might start throwing things if they were left together too long.

'I'm right here,' Polly insisted stubbornly. 'Get yourself off.'

'Yes,' Lizzie Dewhurst agreed. 'You young ones don't want to be stuck with us old ones.'

In some bewilderment, Rachel left the table. Then she heard the conversation behind her turn to the fact that, due to the First World War, young men were very scarce when the Misses Dewhurst had been in their prime. And she had to smile.

'Everything all right?' David questioned, as she approached the table where Judith and the women were sitting with the men standing round.

'I think so,' she said, casting a quick glance back to see if they had actually begun acting out the First World War. All was calm, and she sat herself down between Judith and Lucy Sharratt.

With the women Rachel felt immediately at ease, on safe ground. She hoped David did not notice the change in her and, if he did, did not take it too personally.

'Has he worn you out?' Judith asked. 'David likes dancing.' She gave a resigned shrug. 'Unfortunately I am now blessed with two left feet.' Her smile brightening, she added, 'Still, that's better than none.'

Rachel smiled and said she had enjoyed it, and the little white lie seemed to gain more importance in the light of

Judith's joking acceptance of her condition. What was wrong with her? she asked herself. If she was in Judith's position, living in the knowledge that one day her life would be cut short, then she would really have something to complain about.

With all women together the conversation naturally turned to fashion. Lucy Sharratt had her own hairdressing salon and Rachel was very interested in her views on running your own business.

'Do you intend to have your own shop?' Lucy asked.

'I hope to,' Rachel replied defensively. She was not prepared to admit it was her life-long dream.

'Of course she will,' David butted in from behind, making Rachel blush and Judith scold her husband for his interference.

Fortunately Sarah chose that moment to come looking for her sister.

'Having a good time?' Rachel tried to look happy, but her eyes busily scanned the background to see if Alan Caradine was hanging around. He wasn't and she relaxed a little.

'It's great,' Sarah replied enthusiastically. Her face was flushed from all the exertion and her eyes sparkled with something Rachel both envied and feared.

Her little sister was growing up, she realized sadly, and there was nothing she could do about it.

'Can I go to the pictures?' Sarah asked.

'What?' Rachel's shock was evident. 'Well . . . When . . . who with?' She tried to gather herself, but wasn't sure she succeeded.

'Next Saturday. The Ritz is having a special night. They're showing *Summer Holiday* and *The Young Ones* together. Can I go? Please, sis! I've got enough money to pay for myself.'

The last comment stabbed Rachel. Was she really so mean she would not give Sarah the money to go the pictures? she asked herself. No, she replied very definitely, that was not the problem. 'Who are you going with?' she repeated, frowning as her fears seemed to be descending on her.

'All of us. Please, sis. We're all going together. I'll be left out if you don't let me.'

Despite Sarah's pleadings, Rachel still wanted to say no. But Polly's warning rang loudly in her head. Sarah was no longer the small child who would do everything she was told. She was not yet old enough to take responsibility for her own life, but it would not be long before she was. If she did not loose the lead gradually, then Sarah would one day snap it for herself.

'All right,' she agreed, keeping her reluctance hidden. She did want Sarah to be more worldly wise when she was thrust into adult life than she herself had been. The thought of history repeating itself was not very pleasant.

For the rest of the evening Rachel found it difficult to take her eyes off Sarah for one moment. She had danced with several of the other young boys now, but Alan seemed to be the most popular choice.

Rachel lost the art of conversation. Her stomach felt heavy and she had the feeling if she took one more sip of bitter lemon she would be sick all over the table. Making her excuses to Judith and David, she returned to sit silently with Polly and the Misses Dewhurst. Fortunately, the latter were so full of sherry that they talked incessantly and did not seem to notice her lack of response to their questions.

'Sarah wants to go to the pictures next week,' she said, as she was about to leave Polly at the door of her cottage. They had left Sarah at the end of the yard, to run home while she helped Polly up the hill.

'And what did you say?' Polly asked carefully, leaning with her hand on the cottage wall to regain her breath after the walk up the hill.

'I said yes.' Her voice was flat with the doubt she could not shake off. 'They're all going. All those that were there tonight.' Which included Alan Caradine.

'Well then, you've nothing to worry about.'

'But she is only twelve.'

Polly gave a loud snort. 'We used to go to the twopenny rush when we were nine, and it never did us any harm.'

Rachel grimaced and nodded her head in slow acceptance. 'Yes . . . I know . . . but . . .'

'But nothing,' Polly cut in. 'If she's going with all her pals she'll not come to much harm. You should try it yourself, and find out!'

Ignoring Polly's last gibe, Rachel took the large key from her hand and unlocked the door. 'Get yourself inside. I'll see you tomorrow.'

'Good night, lass,' was Polly's parting comment, as Rachel turned away and crossed the road. She walked down the hill with a feeling of impending doom. At the end of the yard she stopped and looked up at the street lamp, watching the moths flinging themselves in a frenzy at the glass. They would rather batter themselves to death than give up, she thought, as one particularly large specimen hit the glass with a thud and fell to the ground, fluttered aimlessly for a few seconds, then was still.

Silly creatures, she thought. Then wondered if she was not a little like the moths herself. Would she never be able to give up protecting Sarah? She wished Sarah could stay a child, in ignorance of the real meaning of life.

The thought led her mind on and, for the first time, she wondered what her daughter was like. She would be three in a couple of months time, growing into a little girl. She had often found the image of a tiny baby creeping into her mind, but she had never before considered her daughter to be growing, never allowed her mind to move on in time from the baby in the hospital nursery.

The thought of her daughter changing without her knowing it was painful to her. She turned quickly away from the lamp, as if the physical action would also turn her mind in another direction.

It didn't work, and she hurried down the yard suddenly eager to reach the security and the welcoming glow of the lights of home, and the company of Sarah.

Chapter Nine

Rachel slept badly on Friday night, Sarah's imminent trip to the pictures plaguing her mind. It was almost four o'clock before she finally got to sleep, then she overslept, not waking up until ten minutes past nine.

She was in the process of dragging herself downstairs, thanking the heavens that it was Saturday and there was no school for Sarah, when there was a knock at the door.

Oh no! she thought. The last thing she needed was to meet someone in her present condition. 'Who is it?' she called. She was still in her nightclothes and had no intention of opening the door to just anybody.

'It's Lucy . . . Lucy Sharratt!'

Rachel lifted her eyes to the ceiling in despair. She could just picture Lucy standing there, make-up freshly applied, not a hair out of place. She pulled her old dressing gown tightly round herself and dragged her fingers through her dishevelled hair. Then she turned the key, pulled the bolt and peered round the door, making sure Lucy's husband was not with her before opening it wide.

Lucy was alone. She looked somewhat sheepish. 'I'm sorry it's so early. But Geoff has just found out he has to go to Barbados in ten days. I'm going with him.' She smiled pleadingly. 'I was hoping you could make a few things for me to take.'

Rachel smiled. She wondered how many 'a few' would turn out to be. She kept her thoughts to herself; at least Lucy had the good grace to look a little embarrassed.

'Come in,' she invited. 'You'll have to excuse me – I overslept.' She felt fuzzy from the lack of sleep, and Lucy's bright, chirpy chatter was doing nothing to clear her head.

She went straight to the kitchen and poured a glass of milk

and lit the grill. The gas popped to life and, as she blew out the match and dropped it in the bin, she turned to Lucy. 'Sit down and tell me what you want while I make some toast.' She stuck a slice of bread under the grill. 'I can't think straight before I've had breakfast,' she said. Allowing one of her clients into the kitchen was something she would never do under normal circumstances. But this morning she was past caring.

'You're not going down with something?'

'No.' She shook her head, and wished she hadn't when she felt the stirrings of a headache. 'Just tired,' she said, and smiled to herself. She was well aware Lucy was more concerned about not getting her new clothes on time, than any real consideration for her health. 'I didn't sleep much last night. Do you know exactly what you want?' she added, turning the conversation back to business as she took the toast from the grill.

Lucy handed her a sheet of paper containing the list of required items. 'I haven't got the material yet. I thought it best to find out if you could do them all first. If you can I'll go and pick something up. I can be back here by lunch time.'

Rachel's eyes ran slowly down the list: two pairs of shorts, two beach sarongs, one skirt, one pair of slacks, one cocktail dress. The dress would be the biggest job; Lucy liked her evening wear to be highly decorated, with fancy braiding and sequins which had to be hand sewn and that took a great deal of time. The rest were all simple and would not take long. 'I can do those for you,' she said, and handed the paper back to Lucy. 'You're lucky the wedding is over.' She stared at the toast and decided she no longer wanted it. Then she thought of the weeks prior to Margaret's wedding. They had been the busiest she had ever known. She smiled to herself. It seemed incredible, but she had made over two hundred pounds clear profit out of the wedding. She only hoped the rush would not be followed by a lull which made her have to dip into the money put into the special bank account. She had pledged never to touch it until the day she needed it to pay for her longed-for shop. The balance stood at nine hundred and twenty-five pounds, not enough to start a business, but a small fortune to her. And with people like Lucy Sharratt around she would soon get there, she thought, suddenly forgetting her annoyance that Lucy had caught her only half-awake.

'Have you ever thought of having your hair cut?' Lucy asked.

Rachel shook her head and her hand went embarrassedly to the tangled mess hanging round her shoulders.

'I'd do it for you myself – if you wanted it doing . . .' Lucy offered.

She still shook her head. Since her marriage, Lucy had run her hairdressing business from a distance, and spent most of her time running around the world with her husband. Rachel was well aware the offer was a privilege granted to only a chosen few. It pleased her, but she still declined. She preferred her hair long, so she could roll it up into a bun and have done with it.

'I might be out at dinner time.' Rachel turned the conversation back to business. 'I'm taking Sarah for a pair of shoes. She wants them for tonight. She's going to the pictures.'

Despite her misgivings, Sarah's offer to pay for herself had stabbed her. She was careful with money, would have been the first to admit it, but she hoped Sarah did not look on her thrift as meanness. Plagued by guilt she had made Sarah a new dress and had promised her a new pair of shoes to go with it.

'Peter and Hilary are going too,' Lucy said. 'Will it be all right if I call in with the material when I take them? Do you want me to give Sarah a lift as well?'

Rachel hesitated for a moment. It would have saved her a lot of worry, knowing Sarah was being taken to the door and brought back to the door. Sarah might not want to go with Lucy's son and daughter, she told herself. She must not interfere, she thought, wanting desperately to do so.

'You can bring the material then, but don't worry about Sarah. She's going with a group of friends and I'm not sure what the arrangements are.'

When Lucy had gone she wished she had said yes to her.

Sarah could have had a lift and met her friends at the pictures, she reasoned.

But when Sarah came downstairs, bubbling with excitement about the coming evening, she had not got the heart to dampen her enthusiasm by suggesting she change her plans.

'You look a picture!' Rachel glowed with pride as she looked at her sister. The red dress, with pleated skirt and white lace Peter Pan collar, was perfect against the blond hair which hung in a neat pigtail down her back.

Sarah glowed with equal happiness. 'Thanks sis,' she said meaningfully, and admired the red patent leather shoes for close on the hundredth time.

'You'll wear them out with looking.' Rachel laughed. The shoes had been a real extravagance. But the pleasure on Sarah's face made every penny of the £1 19s 6d worthwhile.

'Just you behave yourself,' she warned, a shadow falling over her face.

'Oh sis!' Sarah's face crumpled into a grimace, but Rachel was saved from further protest by the arrival of Carol Land.

'You ready?' Carol called.

Sarah rushed to the door with Rachel in close pursuit.

'Have you got your purse safe? Have you got a hanky? Have you . . . ?'

'*Rachel!*' Sarah looked pleading.

It had been a long time since she had heard her sister use her full name. The severity of it pulled her up short. 'Sorry,' she apologized, embarrassed that she was embarrassing Sarah. 'I just want you to have a good time.'

'We will,' Sarah and Carol chorused together. Then they hurried along the yard, leaving Rachel at the door.

She waited there until they had turned the corner and were out of sight. Then she ran along the yard to watch them walk down the hill to where the entire group was beginning to congregate outside the school, before going to catch the bus.

Alan Caradine was there. She could clearly see him. She felt uneasiness begin in her stomach. Stop it, she ordered

129

herself, wanting to take her eyes away from the boy, but unable to do so. He did not seem to be taking any notice of Sarah's arrival. But he was there!

'I've got a box of cream cakes here that will go off if they're not eaten.'

Rachel swung round at Polly's voice. She was standing right behind her, a white cardboard box in her hands. 'Then why did you buy a box full just for yourself?' she asked sceptically.

'I was feeling hungry.'

'If I didn't know you better, Polly Webster, I'd say you'd been spying on me.' She looked disapproving, but it was good-natured. Knowing how anxious she was about the evening, she had expected Polly to pop in and offer some moral support.

'You can learn a lot by spying,' Polly asserted knowledgeably. 'Are you coming to get the plates out? Or do I have to do it myself?'

'You do it,' she instructed, turning her attention once more to the bottom of the hill. 'I want to see them go.'

Polly tut-tutted and waddled off down the yard.

Rachel stayed to watch, until the last of the group had vanished down the road in the direction of the bus stop.

'Well, what did you see?' Polly questioned dryly, when Rachel finally walked into the kitchen.

'They went for the bus.'

Polly stopped arranging the cream cakes and set her with a telling expression. 'I could have told you that without standing gawping.'

'I was not gawping!' Rachel retaliated, feeling offended and making no attempt to conceal it. She had every right to be concerned about Sarah.

'Then what was you doing?' Polly enquired, as she lifted the plate and displayed the cakes in front of her. 'Spying?' She exaggerated the last to make her point.

It forced a smile from Rachel. 'All right. You win. I was gawping. Aren't those cakes ready yet?' She picked up the parcel of material Lucy Sharratt had dropped off earlier and

130

swept through to the front room, leaving Polly's chuntering response behind.

The cream cakes had long been consumed. Rachel gazed thoughtfully into the small black-leaded fireplace in the new upstairs sitting room.

'Penny for them,' Polly said.

She smiled, recalling other occasions when Joseph had said the same thing. When they had still been young. It seemed so long ago now, the time when she would never have believed anything could have split them – brother and sister. The thought disturbed her. It had happened so easily, without her consent, without her doing. She could not bear to think that one day she might lose Sarah in a similar way.

'When I was small and had to walk past the mill, I used to run. The sound of the clicking frames frightened me. I don't know why.' She gave an embarrassed shrug, not knowing why she was telling Polly this. But there was only interest in Polly's gaze, no mocking of her childish fears, and so she went on. 'The noise was always there. It sounded as if the frames were about to break through the walls. The school once took us to look round the mill and I thought if I see what is making the noise I won't be frightened any more. It didn't help. I had nightmares afterwards, seeing myself dragged into the thread and wound up tightly on one of the big bobbins.'

'That's nothing to be ashamed of,' Polly replied gently, looking concerned now, as well as interested. It had been a long time since Rachel had opened herself up in this way, long before her mother's death. She hoped it might lead to the unfolding of the tightly held secrets of Micky's attack. She was certain in her own mind it had been an attack, rather than a willing exercise on Rachel's part. But Rachel would never say, never speak of it or the baby it had produced. And the longer she kept it bottled up inside the more poisonous it would become. 'We're all frightened of something . . . At one time or another. But what made you think of it now?'

'I'm frightened now,' Rachel admitted.

'What about – Sarah?'

131

She nodded slowly and turned to face her old friend. 'What will I do if I lose her?'

'You'll carry on, lass,' Polly replied without any hesitation. 'You've got to accept that one day Sarah will be grown up. She'll find herself a husband and you'll be happy for her. You wouldn't want her to go through life being lonely now, would you?'

For a moment Rachel could not reply. Memories of Micky flooded her mind, hateful, repugnant memories. 'But having a husband,' she finally began, hesitantly, unsurely, 'means you have to . . . have to . . .' She could not say any more. Her mother's rantings on male fornication joined the memories of Micky, and her body recoiled from the mere thoughts.

'Have to do what?' Polly questioned matter of factly. 'Go to bed with them?'

Rachel felt a hot flush leap into her cheeks. She wished she had never begun the conversation.

'If you love a man there's nothing wrong in that.' Polly leaned forward and gazed at her pointedly. 'And that's what makes the difference. You'll find out for yourself. One day!' She added the last more in hope than certainty. Rachel had a long way to go before she could see her allowing any man to get near to her.

'That's not what my mother said.' Her voice was flat and she turned back to stare bleakly into the fire, feeling hopeless.

'And what had she to say on the matter?' Polly enquired.

Rachel did not reply. But Polly could guess. She had witnessed enough of Violet Cooper's ravings to know the way the woman's mind had worked. She shook her head sadly. Not only had Rachel got Micky to shake off, she also had to rid her mind of the crazy advice of her sick mother.

'Your mother was mad,' she asserted, speaking bluntly, feeling the moment called for it. 'She didn't know what she was doing or saying. Did she ever say anything like it before she was ill?'

Rachel shook her head. 'No . . . but . . .' It was in anger or madness that the truth often came out.

'No buts about it,' Polly scolded firmly. 'Sarah will be

right. So long as you don't go sticking your own fears on to her.'

'I'd never do that,' Rachel replied quickly, the suggestion putting more fire into her eyes than Polly had seen all evening. 'I've never told her . . . anything. And I never will.' She glanced at the clock. 'She should be home in half an hour,' she said.

'Aye, she should,' Polly agreed dryly, knowing the subject had been brought to a close. Unsatisfactorily.

In fact it was only twenty minutes later when Sarah came bouncing through the door.

'It was great,' she declared, the beam on her face echoing the sentiment.

'You're early.' Rachel's face displayed the relief she was feeling at the return of her sister.

'We didn't have to wait for the bus. Carol's dad fetched us in the Land-rover.'

'All of you?' Rachel's imagination tried to picture twelve large children squashed into the back of Mr Land's scruffy Land-rover, usually used for carting around the building materials of his trade. She hoped he had washed it out first.

'Can I take a drink to bed?' Sarah asked, glancing at the clock to see it was well past her bedtime.

'Yes, and some biscuits if you want,' she said, and watched her sister go happily out of the room. Please, God, don't ever let anything spoil her happiness, she silently begged.

'Well, now that she's home, I'll make for my own bed,' Polly announced, and struggled out of the easy chair.

'I'll walk with you.' Rachel jumped up to help her to her feet, feeling more love for the old lady who was no relation than she had ever done for both her parents put together.

Polly clung to her arm as they walked slowly up the hill to her cottage. The effort was fast becoming too much for her, Rachel sadly realized. 'Life's never easy, is it?' she said, giving her arm an affectionate squeeze.

'You're not going all philosophical on me, are you?' Polly's shrewd old eyes peered into the shadows the single street lamp cast over Rachel's features.

She gave a little laugh. 'I thought that was what you wanted me to be?'

'Maybe, lass. Maybe,' Polly managed to reply. Then the exertion of walking up the steep slope caused her so much puffing and panting that speech was impossible. And Rachel fell silent in sympathy.

As they reached the cottage door an owl hooted from a branch of Polly's apple tree. 'My little friend's there,' she said, leaning on the wall to gain her breath, as Rachel unlocked the door and let her in. 'Keeps me company through the night, he does.'

Rachel smiled, and silently thanked the owl. 'I'm glad somebody is making sure you don't get up to mischief,' she teased and handed the key back to her.

'Would that I could,' Polly replied, and managed to find enough breath to give one of her great gusts of laughter.

It warmed Rachel to hear the old familiar sound that seemed to be happening less often of late. And there was a smile on her face as she turned away and crossed the road.

But Polly's laughter vanished as she stood illuminated in the light from her doorway and watched her go until she had reached the end of the yard.

As she closed the door a great sadness filled her. She hoped she had enough time left to be able to see the day Rachel was really happy.

Chapter Ten

Joseph and Ulrika married, as planned, at the end of May. Rachel and Sarah received an invitation. Rachel returned a polite refusal along with a wedding present: a silver cigarette box, which, after she had purchased it, seemed rather ostentatious. Not knowing what they had got and what they had not got, she had been at a loss to choose something more useful. Joseph smoked, she told herself, hoping he had not given up the habit, as she carefully wrapped the valuable gift in tissue paper before a final covering of thick brown paper.

The summer had been a long and hot one, when clothes had been an encumbrance. Shorts and skirts with T-shirts had become the everyday wear. No-one wanted to be bothered with fancy clothes or hot formal wear and Rachel found trade dropping off.

She put the spare time she found on her hands to good use. Beginning with the upstairs sitting room, she started to decorate the house. Then she worked through to her own bedroom, down the stairs into the sewing room, and on to the kitchen.

'Can't you ever sit still?' Polly asked dryly, looking on from a chair in the doorway. Rachel was perched on the ladder, slapping paint on the kitchen ceiling, and getting most of it on herself.

'I want to get it all done before I start getting a rush of customers,' she replied, straining to reach right into the corner. Once the kitchen was finished there was only the tiny bathroom. She had never imagined she would get the whole house done. It wasn't before time. It had badly needed brightening up, she told herself to justify the expense. Not that it had cost a fortune. Cheap paint cleaned the place up

135

just as well as expensive. But even the cheapest had put a frown on her face. With less money coming in she could see her beloved shop slipping further into the future.

Although the warm weather continued well into October, thoughts of the coming winter turned minds to warmer clothing. Business picked up, slowly at first, then, in the month before Christmas, returned full throttle.

'You're up to your neck in it again!' Polly's voice held a mild rebuke. Though Rachel knew she had intended it to be more severe.

Ignoring the gibe, she replied to Polly's earlier suggestion of a trip to town. 'Anyway, why do you want to go to Derby for a new coat? I'll make you one. Tell me what colour you want and I'll get the material myself.' Rachel stopped and studied the turquoise and purple rainbow stripes of the material she had just lain out for cutting. 'This is going to be the devil's own job to match up,' she said, speaking more to herself than to Polly.

Polly tutted loudly. 'And you think you've got time to be making things for the likes of me!'

Rachel favoured her with a telling stare. Polly knew if she wanted something making it would be given first priority. She studied her old friend for a moment. Her gaze softened. She had aged in the last months. The hot weather had not done her much good and Rachel was becoming more and more worried about her. She did too much. But wouldn't be told. Now she wanted Rachel to take her into town to buy a new coat, when she had at least six good ones hanging in her wardrobe.

'You'll have to wait until next week,' she said, having no intention of letting her make the tiring journey. She would get some material herself, she knew well enough what Polly liked, and have it made up before she knew what was happening.

'As long as it's before Christmas,' Polly said, at the same time as there was a knock on the door. 'I'll get it on my way out,' she said, and pushed herself up from the chair and gave

136

her painful knees a rub. 'It'll be a customer and you'll want me out of the way.'

As Polly went out, she let David Morrell in.

'Hello, David!' Rachel said, sounding surprised that he was on his own. 'I've not seen you for a while.' She noticed he looked pale and drawn. 'Are you all right? How's Judith?' she asked anxiously.

David hesitated a moment. 'She's not too good.'

The tone of his voice gave her the impression Judith was worse than 'not too good'.

'That's why I'm here,' he explained. 'I know you don't come out to customers any more. But would you make an exception? A couple of months ago Judith stumbled at a friend's house and broke some valuable china. Now she won't go anywhere. She's very low. I thought some new clothes might cheer her up.'

'Of course I will,' she readily agreed. He looked so distraught and her heart went out to him. The Morrells had been such good friends to her she would do anything for them. 'But there's nothing here that she can hurt. Maybe if you could persuade her to come it would help get back her confidence.'

David could only shake his head, and the sadness surrounding him reached out to touch Rachel. A large lump came to her throat. 'Sit down,' she said, dropping the cutting-out scissors on to the blue and purple material, which suddenly seemed too bright and gay for the moment. Had the fabric not been pure silk and worth a fortune, she felt she might have screwed it into a ball and stuffed it in a drawer, out of sight. 'Polly's just made a pot of tea. Would you like a cup?' she asked. Tea and sympathy, she told herself, was supposed to be the cure for all.

David nodded his head. 'Please,' he replied wearily, and Rachel hurried to the kitchen, well aware that he was on the verge of cracking up.

'Has Judith got worse?' she asked gently, bringing a chair up to his side and sitting down. 'Or was it just the accident?' She could understand how Judith must be feeling. Her own

137

house was filled with beautiful things that she treasured dearly. The poor woman would be so embarrassed that she had destroyed someone else's treasured belongings. Life was so unfair, she thought, looking at David's distraught features and feeling his pain as if it was her own.

'She has deteriorated,' he said sadly. 'But . . . the accident . . .' His voice trailed away, his chin fell on to his chest and he began to sob.

At first Rachel did not know what to do. She had never seen a man cry before, and he was sobbing like a baby. She wished Polly had stayed. She would have known exactly what to do. She always knew how to handle a crisis.

Keep calm, she ordered herself, recalling that Polly always remained calm and unruffled and took charge. But how did you take charge? she wondered anxiously. Then noticed the cup and saucer jiggling unsteadily in his hand and took it from him.

'I'm sorry, Rachel.' He lifted his head to apologize and the misery on his face cut through her. 'I didn't intend to embarrass you. I've never been like this before.'

Rachel smiled reassuringly. 'If you're feeling like a good cry, have it now. You don't want to upset Judith by doing it in front of her,' she said, wondering just where the words and the wisdom were coming from – surely not herself!

He gave her a tight smile and pulled a cleanly folded white handkerchief from his pocket and wiped his eyes. Then he shook his head in disbelief. 'I don't know what came over me. What must you think?'

Rachel knew exactly what had come over him. The same thing that had come over her often enough when she had been looking after her mother, the strain of feeling hopeless and impotent. But she didn't tell him that. Instead she said, 'I think you're a very caring person.' Then she got up and put both cups of tea down on the table, sweeping the silk fabric to one side with a brush of the hand. What did fancy material matter at a moment like this, she thought, turning back to him as he pulled a packet of cigarettes and a silver lighter from his pocket.

He stuck the cigarette into his mouth, paused, then took it out again. 'Do you mind?' he asked, looking up at her.

She shook her head. 'Go ahead,' she said, a smile pulling at her lips. Always the gentleman, she thought, moving back to sit beside him once more.

He took a long thoughtful draw on the cigarette, forcing the smoke deeply and noisily into his lungs, then he exhaled with equal slowness.

Rachel waited silently, feeling that he had something more he wanted to say.

Finally, he began. 'Have you got over the shock of your mother's death?' he asked.

'Yes,' she replied guardedly. She was not sure this was the type of subject he needed right now. 'Do you want your tea back?' she asked, and jumped up to get it without waiting for his reply.

'I don't want to upset you.' He smiled bleakly into her eyes as he took the cup and saucer from her. 'Did your mother ever talk about it with you?'

She sat down slowly, looking blank. He could not mean . . . ?

'Killing herself?' David provided the proof that her unthinkable thought had been correct.

She felt colour flooding her cheeks. 'I didn't do it.' Her response was sharp, spurred by the stab of guilt she always felt when thinking of how her mother died. How, if she had been here, it would not have happened. 'Doctor Mellor thought I did it. But I didn't.' She was babbling, but could not stop herself. 'I don't know why she chose that day to leave the bedroom. She'd never done it before.'

David reached out and placed his hand on her arm. 'I'm not accusing you,' he said gently. 'I never, for one moment, thought you had had anything to do with it.' The concern in his voice brought tears to her eyes. 'It's just that we've both been in similar circumstances. And I need someone to talk to.'

'I'm sorry.' She blinked back her tears, feeling guilty for letting her own emotion show, when it was David who needed comfort. Then, suddenly becoming aware of his hand and realizing he was touching her, she withdrew her arm as if burnt.

'I'm sorry too.' He glanced apologetically at the place on her arm where his hand had rested. 'I didn't mean to touch you.' A shadow passed over his face as he spoke the last.

'What did you want to talk about?' she quickly asked, feeling her cheeks redden and wanting to get back to the main subject as rapidly as possible.

'I . . .' he sighed loudly. 'I don't know how to begin.' He took a long pensive draw on his cigarette, seeming to steel himself for what he had to say. When he finally spoke it was all of a sudden and very quickly. 'Judith wants me to promise that when she becomes totally helpless I will help her kill herself.'

'Oh . . . !' It was all Rachel could utter.

'Did your mother ever suggest . . . ?'

'No!' She cut him off before he could finish. 'If she had ever spoken in that way I would never have left her.' She pulled herself up. Apology put a grimace on her face, as she realized what she was saying. Her words could have been construed as a charge of negligence on David's part for leaving Judith to go there. 'I . . .' she began.

'No.' He stopped her with a shake of his head and his hand moved, as if he was going to place it on her arm again.

But then he dropped it back into his lap, as if having second thoughts and Rachel felt very guilty. She gave herself a mental kick for her previous recoil from his touch. He would never hurt her, she told herself. But she could not find the courage to place her own hand on his arm, and offer him the comfort he needed.

'I could never do it.' He looked straight into her eyes and she could see how heavily the decision was weighing on him. 'But I have to ask myself if I'm right to think that way. Am I being selfish? In Judith's position, would I want to die?'

'Oh, David!' She felt as if the same great weight was lying in the bottom of her stomach. How could Judith place him in this position? But, as she asked herself the question, she knew

140

the answer. She would, herself, prefer death to the lingering infirmity that Judith was to be sentenced to. Being unable to perform even the most personal of tasks for herself was too horrible to contemplate. Judith was fully aware that was most probably to be her lot when the illness reached the final stages. She would be helpless, totally dependent. Oh yes, she could understand Judith's request. But she could find no answer for David.

'Maybe she will change her mind when the time comes.' She felt no confidence in the suggestion. 'It shouldn't happen for a while yet . . . Should it?' she added uncertainly, seeing the gloom behind his eyes deepen. 'Should it?' she repeated, when he remained ominously silent.

'I don't know,' he finally replied, lifting his shoulders in defeat. 'There's no telling. Some days she seems better, others worse. That's the way it is. You never really know.' He stubbed his cigarette out in her father's old pipe ashtray that, for some reason Rachel could never explain, had remained on the mantelshelf since his death. Then he swallowed the rest of his tea. 'I'm sorry to have burdened you with this. It was not my intention.'

Rachel's smile did not touch her eyes. She felt his burden as if it was her own. Yet was pleased to do so. There was sweet little could be done for Judith, but she could help David by listening to him and showing him he was not alone in the world. She hoped it would be later rather than sooner, but whichever it turned out to be, there was going to come a time when he would need all the friends he could get.

'You needed to get it off your chest,' she said. She hoped she had been as much use to him as Polly had been to her in the past similar circumstances. She'd have gone mad if she hadn't had Polly to run to. 'And don't be frightened to come again . . . If you want another talk,' she offered, wanting to make it clear that he had not embarrassed her and she would always be willing to listen.

'Thank you,' he said meaningfully. Then for several moments stared into the bottom of his empty cup. 'How's the idea for the shop going?' he suddenly asked, meeting Rachel's concerned gaze with what she could clearly see was forced enthusiasm.

'Many more summers like the last one and it will never become anything more than an idea.' She turned easily to her favourite subject, relieved that he had chosen the change of subject for himself, his worries, for the moment, pushed aside.

It was the night of the school Christmas party. Saturday night trips to the pictures had now become a regular outing for Sarah. Even so, Rachel had never got used to not having her sister at home during the evening, and each Saturday was a nightmare for her.

'Mr Ryde *is* bringing you home?' she checked, for somewhere close on the tenth time.

Sarah laughed. 'Yes, I shall be quite safe. Stop fretting. After all, we will be at school, with *teachers* spoiling the fun.' Her nose curled up with disapproval and Rachel found herself smiling. 'I'm a big girl now,' she assured, and wrapped her arms around her sister's neck. 'I know what's right and wrong. And I'd never do anything silly.'

A big girl! Yes, and that was the problem, Rachel thought. At thirteen, Sarah was already two inches taller than she was. When she was all dressed up she looked more like an eighteen year old.

She pushed Sarah away and looked her up and down and frowned seriously. 'It's my fault, isn't it?' she said, and her concern deepened. 'I should not let you wear such fashionable clothes.' The straight-skirted dress in hues of purple and pink made Sarah look quite the young lady. Too much of a young lady for Rachel's liking. She wondered why she had allowed herself to be talked into making such a tightly fitting skirt for her young sister.

Then she knew the answer. 'Everyone is wearing them. You would not want me to be the odd one out!' Sarah insisted. The way she had insisted, over and over again, until Rachel had given in and agreed to make her own pattern.

'I'm not wearing them,' Rachel pointed out, and looked down at her own grey pleated skirt and navy-blue jumper. She suddenly felt very plain and dowdy. But that was how she wanted to feel. Wasn't it? she asked herself, finding, oddly, no answer was immediately forthcoming.

'Well you should,' Sarah replied very knowledgeably, and went to the mirror to inspect her hair for the eighth time. Rachel sighed. It was always the same and tonight she had kept count, just to prove she was not imagining it.

'I don't know what your customers think of you sometimes,' Sarah continued, as she fiddled with the large curls that curved a semicircle on her cheeks. It was a new short style she had just acquired, also against Rachel's better judgement. 'You make all those fabulous clothes, yet your own look as if they've come out of the rag-bag.'

'Thank you,' Rachel replied dryly and turned away. She wondered if it was perhaps time to tell Sarah the truth. No! she quickly told herself. There was no point in filling her head with such rubbish. Besides, she had no wish to live through the agonies again. They were better left locked away at the back of her mind. Where they didn't hurt so much.

'I forgot to tell you,' she suddenly said, turning her mind to pleasanter things. 'There was a letter from Joseph this morning. He's sent some money for Christmas presents.'

'How much?' Sarah turned eagerly from the mirror, her appearance suddenly forgotten.

'Five pounds,' Rachel replied flatly. There were times when Sarah had a mercenary streak that was very unbecoming.

Sarah clapped her hands together with joy. 'I can buy those shoes I've seen in Barley's.'

'Barley's!' Rachel could not conceal her disbelief. Barley's was one of the most expensive shops in town. 'What happened to Hallam's?' she asked dryly. Sarah really was getting ideas above her station and, more worryingly, above her purse.

'Oh don't be so stuffy,' Sarah snapped. Then she stared at Rachel. 'Do you always have to do this?'

'What?' Rachel looked puzzled.

'Whenever I'm going out you just stand around . . . Watching me! It's as if you think I'm going to run out the door with the family silver stuck up my dress.'

Rachel was saved from answering by the sound of a car horn. 'That'll be Sally,' Sarah said, and was out of the door before Rachel could blink.

What am I doing wrong? she asked herself despairingly, as she sat down at the sewing machine and picked up Polly's coat. It was almost finished and she wanted to get the finishing touches done and get it over to Polly, before the visit to Derby was brought into conversation again.

Was she doing anything wrong? she wondered, as she threaded the correct colour cotton on to the machine. Was Sarah just a natural thirteen year old? She pondered the thought for some time. Life under their father's rule had been so restricted that she had no real experience of her own to call back on. She did know that was not what she wanted for Sarah: no friends, no social life, no knowledge of the real world. She wanted Sarah to have friends, both male and female. If there was ever a Micky Caradine in Sarah's life, she wanted Sarah to know what to do and not be so innocently trusting as she had been.

The train of her thoughts began to take her down a path she did not want to follow. Black memories rose in her mind. The sewing machine went faster and faster, as she tried to force her concentration on the buttonholes of Polly's coat and away from Micky's attack.

She fumbled with the needle and the thread, as she fixed the large brown buttons in place and found the image of a baby filling her mind. No! she thought angrily. She did not want to remember her daughter. But she could not stop herself wondering if she was happy. Did her parents love her? Were they good to her? It was too late to worry, she told herself, and stuck the needle through the plastic hole with such force that it went right through and into her finger on the other side.

'Ouch!' She sucked at her finger and felt tears of self-pity sting her eyes. It's Christmas, she told herself. Everyone was happy at Christmas. But she was not convinced by her own words and, as she broke the thread on the final button, she felt her gloom deepening and knew she had to go and see Polly and get away from her own depressing company.

She was halfway across the road, with Polly's new coat neatly folded in a bag, when she stopped, having a sudden thought. It was Christmas! At least it would be in three days time. It was a time to enjoy yourself. Polly was always bringing cakes and biscuits over to her. Her little treats, as she called them. It was about time she did something to return the favour.

Pulling her grey duffel coat tightly around herself to combat the cold, she turned down the hill. She went past the end of the yard and down to the bottom, to the Beehive, which was across the road from the school. Polly liked a bottle of bitter lemon and a bag of crisps. And she was going to get them for her, she told herself, feeling almost proud that she dare do something so brazen as walk into a public house. She smiled to herself, thinking what her father's reaction would have been to such a suggestion. But when she looked up at the frosty stars clustered round the top of the mill chimney, they looked too beautiful to have anything to do with him. So she refrained from trying to taunt his memory by directing the question to heaven, and hurried on down the hill.

She felt strange going into the pub. The noisy smoky atmosphere was something she had never experienced and there was a strange smell, which she could only assume was the beer. Neither had she experienced all the male faces that turned in her direction as she walked through the door.

'Hello, Rachel.' Millie Stevenson was the barmaid and her enthusiastic greeting diminished Rachel's unease. Leaving the group of men crowding the other end of the bar, Millie came straight to her aid. 'You're a stranger in here,' she said pleasantly. 'What can I do for you?'

Rachel smiled her thanks to Millie. One of her father's harlots, she thought, knowing which one she would choose every time. 'Two bottles of bitter lemon and two bags of crisps, please, Millie.' She gave the order quickly, wanting to get served and get out. She knew most of the men in the bar but had never received the attention from any of them that she was now getting.

'Aren't you stopping for one?' Jedadiah Flint, at ninety-five and still going strong, the oldest resident in Millbridge, looked up from the game of dominoes he was involved in. 'Let me treat you!'

'No, thank you, Mr Flint. It's very kind of you. But I don't have the time. Polly's waiting for me,' she replied politely, adding the little white lie to make her quick departure more plausible. She felt colour creeping into her cheeks and was not sure if it was the lie or the situation that was bothering her the most.

'There you are, Rachel.' Millie placed two packets of crisps beside the two bottles on the bar, as Rachel went to open her purse.

'No,' Millie said, refusing the money. 'It's seen to. You're being treated.' She pointed to the far end of the bar and Rachel's astonished gaze followed her finger. It only took an instant for her to realize the embarrassment she had been feeling was nothing compared to what was now running hot and violent in her veins and turning her cheeks the colour of beetroot.

Micky Caradine grinned and lifted his pint to his lips. 'Cheers, Rachel,' he said, with his usual cocky self-confidence, and took a long swallow.

It was a moment before she could collect herself enough to do anything and she only stared at him. Then, hoping the tremor in her hands was not obvious, she carefully placed a bottle of bitter lemon in each of her coat pockets, picked up the crisps and looked him straight in the eye. 'Thank you, Micky. Happy Christmas,' she said, and turned and walked out with her back straight and her head held high.

She hurried up the hill so fast she did not give herself time to think. Several times she almost stumbled as her feet met with the patches of frost that were quickly gathering beneath the stone walls. But she did not slow down and when she reached the safety of Polly's cottage she sank into one of her old armchairs and crumbled into a shaking jelly.

'Whatever's the matter?' Polly asked, frozen with her back bent and the poker in her hand. She had just been poking the fire, when Rachel's hasty arrival had taken her by surprise.

146

'He's back.' Rachel sat up straight in the chair, pinning her wide, disbelieving eyes on the old lady. She couldn't really believe she had done it: looked him in the eye; spoken to him!

'Who?' Polly asked, finally putting the poker back in its brass stand by the fireplace and turning to her. 'Who's back?' she repeated. But from the look in Rachel's eyes she felt she knew the answer.

'Micky Caradine.' The name slipped from her tongue like a nasty taste. 'He's back. I've just seen him. In the Beehive.'

Polly looked shocked. 'Whatever were you doing in the Beehive?'

She produced the bitter lemon from her pockets. 'He's brought us a drink.'

'Well you can chuck it down the lavie,' Polly quickly asserted, and folded her arms and lifted her bosom in a manner that meant business.

Rachel had been about to agree. Then she suddenly stopped herself. Seeing Micky had been the moment she had long been dreading. She had known she would bump into him, sooner or later. Well she had done it! And she had managed to hold her head up. He had not shamed her and she would never let him shame her again. She was older and wiser now and any fears she had harboured about him had just been wiped away. She still hated him, and always would. But he was no longer the ogre of her mind. Suddenly he was no more than the pathetic little creature he really was. And he was not going to do her, or Polly, out of their drink.

'No!' she said, with a determination that made Polly look askance. 'We'll drink them!' She had fetched the drink for Polly's enjoyment and *he* was not going to spoil it.

Polly was bemused as she sank into the other armchair. She was not unhappy with the unexpected reaction, but totally bemused.

Rachel fetched two glasses and opened the bottles. 'Happy Christmas, Polly.' She lifted her glass to her, and smiled at the way the shrewd old eyes were watching her, carefully assessing if she had finally flipped. 'It's going to be a good one.' She felt good right through. She had just cleared a hurdle she never thought she would be able to approach. Maybe Sarah was right, she thought. Perhaps she should brighten herself up a bit. 'Oh, I've brought you an early present.' She pushed the bag across to Polly.

'You only wanted to do me out of an outing!' Polly grumbled, as she turned slowly around in the new coat for Rachel to examine her work.

Rachel smiled. The look on Polly's face was enough to tell her she was as pleased as punch with the coat. She pursed her lips and cupped her chin. 'You don't think it's a bit bright for you?' She turned a critical eye to the loud brown and gold check, not something she would have worn herself, but knowing it was exactly what her old friend liked.

'No, it isn't!' she was quick to disagree. 'I want something with a bit of life to it. There's plenty of chance to wear dull when you're in your shroud. They never make them fancy. And you're a long time dead!'

Rachel laughed. 'I'll make a special order for you. Purple with gold braid. You'll look like an Egyptian queen.'

Polly gave a great gust of laughter. 'A mummy who was never a mummy!' She laughed until tears rolled down her cheeks and she flopped down into the chair so hard she almost knocked the stuffing out of it; which only made her laugh more.

'Do you ever think of your own little one?' Polly asked, after a long moment of contemplation brought on by her joke about lack of motherhood.

'Don't spoil the evening,' Rachel said, even though her own thoughts had been turned the same way.

'I was just thinking if you had accepted Micky, you might be able to accept you had a daughter.' She knew Rachel had only taken the first step of a long journey. But there was no harm in trying to hurry her along a bit.

'Maybe.' Rachel leaned back in the chair and stared into the dancing firelight. 'I've always accepted I had a daughter. It's not something you can miss happening,' she added dryly.

'Do you ever regret giving her away?'

'No,' she replied, too quickly. She glanced nervously at Polly, hoping she had not noticed. 'I could never have kept her. She would have reminded me.'

'Perhaps.' Polly rocked back and forth with her hands on her knees. The maternal instinct was a strange thing, she thought. Women could love children born to them by men they hated and despised. But now was not the time to make that point to Rachel. Coming face to face with Micky had released a small amount of the torment she kept hidden away. But she was not ready to let go completely. It saddened her. She often had the fear she would never be ready.

The logs on the fire settled noisily and Polly leaned forwards and threw another one on. Then she sat back and watched Rachel, sitting there all silent, outwardly calm and relaxed. Only she knew that the inside was a very different matter. It was a heavy burden for her to hold. Not for the first time, she hoped she would live to see the day when Rachel, the young woman she had grown to love as she would have loved her own daughter, would find happiness.

On Christmas Eve, Rachel packed the oyster satin nightdress and négligé set she had made for Judith. It was her Christmas present. A bit extravagant, but she considered the money well spent if it brightened Judith's life up a bit.

After David's visit she had made a call on Judith, but no amount of persuasion could make her agree to any new clothes. She never went out any more, she firmly asserted. Besides, she had a wardrobe full of things she would never get to wear again.

It had been a depressing day for Rachel. She had never thought to see Judith, who usually coped so well with her illness, so low.

'It wasn't fair,' she had said to Polly, when she called round on her way home, needing cheering up.

'It's the way of things. Rich or poor, we all end up the same,' Polly said. She had been sitting in front of the fire, polishing her extensive collection of brassware, with a patchwork blanket over her knees that made her look suddenly so very old, and Rachel had wanted to cry.

As she turned down Mulberry Bush Lane with Judith's gaily wrapped present tucked under her arm, Rachel stopped and peered over the wall at the river. The water was in full spate, charging flatly over the falls so that anyone who did not know it was there would have missed the weir. The air was bitingly cold and she huddled into her new coat. She glanced down at the thick, light-fawn wool, and tried to tell herself she felt right in it. It had been made on a whim, after taking Sarah's charge of being a rag-bag to heart. There was nothing startling or flashy about it, she had continually told herself, as she hurriedly made the coat up, before she could change her mind and make something for Sarah. She had even added some light cream fabric to the sleeves, so that when the wide cuffs were turned back they made a nice contrast. It was loose fitting and perfectly respectable, she assured herself, as she hitched Judith's present higher under her arm and set off walking again. But she felt very noticeable wearing it.

As she walked through the Morrells' gate, she hoped Judith would not be offended by the rather sexy design of the nightdress and négligé. It was what the old Judith would have gone straight for, she assured herself. But she was not sure any of the old Judith still remained. She sighed despondently and hoped this had not been a big mistake. Nightwear had seemed like a good idea at the time. Judith didn't have to go out to wear a nightdress, she had reasoned, after Judith's adamant refusal to have anything new.

You're here. It's too late to change your mind, she told herself, held her breath and rang the bell.

When David opened the door she immediately thought how much better he looked than the last time she had seen him. He still looked tired, but there was more colour in his cheeks.

'Rachel!' He looked surprised to see her standing there.

'I've brought a present for Judith,' she said. 'It's all right. It isn't a ball gown,' she quickly added, when his eyes dropped doubtfully to the parcel which, although wrapped in Christmas paper, was clearly one of her dress boxes. She felt her heart sink.

'Come in.' He stood back to let her through. Rachel didn't speak. She suddenly had the feeling that it *had* been a mistake.

When she walked into the lounge to Judith, Rachel could see the reason for David's rosy cheeks. There was a half-empty bottle of whisky on the table and an almost empty bottle of gin. Several empty tonic bottles littered the floor and a large ashtray was overflowing with cigarette ends.

'What a lovely surprise.' Judith's words were slightly slurred. Rachel could not be sure if it was from the alcohol or her illness. 'We don't get many visitors nowadays. I think I embarrass them.'

It *was* the drink! Without waiting for an invitation Rachel sat down on the long cream leather settee. 'The water's high,' she said, just for something to say. And, to give herself something other than the pathetic figure of Judith to look at, stared out of the large picture window at the grey column of water thundering past at dizzying speed.

'Do you want a drink?' David asked, only then coming into the room.

'No thanks,' she declined, having no intention of giving either of them the excuse to join her. She wondered why he had not come straight into the room with her. Then she saw his eyes drop to the present, his expression one of almost dread. It was her gift, she realized, that was causing him a considerable amount of concern.

'A Christmas present for you.' She quickly handed the parcel to Judith, before David's attitude made her turn and run, the parcel still under her arm.

At first Judith seemed reluctant to remove the wrapping. It should not be opened until Christmas Day, she made her excuse.

Rachel had the feeling if she did not see it opened for herself, it would never get opened. It took several attempts at persuasion on her part, before Judith finally relented and her shaky hands began to untie the red ribbon.

David sat stiff and silent in his chair. Rachel could almost feel the tension coming from him. It annoyed her. She wanted to scream at him to calm down . . . for Judith's sake.

'It's beautiful!' The look in Judith's eyes was all the proof Rachel needed that her choice had been the right one. Tears filled Judith's eyes as she tried to thank her, then failed.

'Well, you don't have to go out to wear it,' she said, feeling honesty was needed. Pushing Judith's problem under the carpet had never been their problem before. Now that was what seemed to have happened. They had lost the determination to enjoy what was left to them. They had changed. The house had changed. It was like a morgue, as if they were both sitting waiting for the final hour.

'As it's Christmas Eve I'll let you wear it tonight,' she said, making a joke of the words. These two needed livening up, she realized, and she was determined to do it. 'I'm sure David has something special for you tomorrow,' she added, as Judith wiped her tears and gave her a watery smile of gratitude.

She glanced teasingly at David. 'You must have something hidden under the bed,' she said, and was relieved to see his expression had lightened considerably.

He grinned at her, and the old David returned.

'That's better,' she said quietly and meaningfully. 'You both had faces fit to turn cream sour when I came in.'

Judith sighed heavily, as she stroked her hand almost lovingly across the oyster satin nightdress. Then she looked at Rachel. 'We're not used to spending Christmas alone,' she said, the sadness in her voice wiping the smile from Rachel's face.

'Aren't you seeing anyone tomorrow?' She could not believe all their so-called friends had deserted them on Christmas Day.

'It will be a nice change. Just the two of us,' David put in, rather too quickly. Rachel could see he did not believe himself.

It was a spur of the moment decision. 'Why don't you come and spend the day with us?' she asked. 'There'll only be myself and Sarah and Polly. So come and make it a party.' If she had stopped to think before speaking, Rachel would never have opened her mouth, thinking it would have

152

embarrassed Judith to refuse. Now she was glad she had spoken. The more she thought about it, the more sensible it seemed. And she wasn't taking no for an answer.

'But . . .' Judith began.

'No buts!' Rachel cut in. 'We don't have anything grand like turkey. But we have a capon big enough to go round. Sarah will be over the moon. She always says we should have more people for Christmas dinner. So I'll see you anytime before twelve o'clock. We'll push the boat out and have a sherry before we eat.'

David was struck silent. So was Judith. For several moments they stared dumbly at each other, both seeming to be waiting for the other to speak first.

It was Judith who broke the spell. She suddenly laughed, and taking her cue, David also began to laugh.

'Why don't we?' Judith asked, still looking at her husband for approval.

'Why don't we?' he echoed eagerly, and turned to Rachel with a look of wonder on his face. She smiled, knowing he was thanking her for making his wife smile again.

'Well, now that's settled, I'd better go and start making preparations.' She was about to get up from the settee and leave before Judith had a change of heart.

'Just a minute,' David said, stopping her. For a moment Rachel's heart sank. She had the impression it was he who was going to spoil the arrangements, and not Judith. But then he continued, 'We have a large turkey. Why don't you take that?' And she almost let out a sigh of relief as he leapt from the chair and vanished into the kitchen before she had time to speak.

'Good heavens!' Rachel laughed when she saw the turkey. 'I hope it will go in the oven!' It was eighteen pounds and larger than anything she had ever seen.

The turkey, along with a large plum pudding, an equally large chocolate log, and a ten-pound ham, were too heavy for Rachel to carry home, so David gave her a lift in his car.

'Thanks,' he said, turning to her as they pulled up at the end of the yard, gratitude spilling from his eyes.

'Do you think she will come?' Rachel looked concerned. She had bamboozled Judith into accepting. It was more than possible she would change her mind when she had time to think.

'If she doesn't she won't get any dinner – or tea!' He glanced meaningfully at the two large brown paper carrier bags she was clutching on her knee.

She laughed. Parting with their food had been a deliberate ploy on his part. He was as eager to see Judith happy again as she was. It made the sombre mood of her arrival at Mulberry Bush Lane difficult to explain. But they were out of it now. And she had every intention of keeping them out of it. For another day, at least, she told herself, as she climbed out of the car and dragged the two heavy bags with her.

'See you in the morning,' she called, as he turned the car around and drove off down the hill. She was unable to acknowledge his wave because of the carrier bags bursting at the seams.

As she walked down the yard and had to struggle round a load of logs her next-door neighbour had had delivered the previous day, she sent up a silent prayer that Judith would not change her mind. Then she sent up a second prayer that the turkey *would* go in the oven!

Chapter Eleven

The turkey had gone into the oven, but with little room to spare on either side and just enough space to squeeze a pan of roasting potatoes underneath. At twelve-thirty the large bird was ready and the sizzling potatoes golden brown. The kitchen was filled with steam from the four saucepans boiling away on the gas rings, and Rachel was red faced and sweating from her efforts of trying to get everything ready at the same time.

She glanced at the clock and the panic which had been steadily growing since eleven o'clock reached fever pitch. Where were they? she asked herself, as she picked up a spoon to give the apple sauce yet another stir. Then changed her mind and turned the flame beneath the saucepan off, before the sauce turned to caramel.

Her frustration exploding, she rushed into the front room, brandishing the tablespoon like a weapon. The old table had been converted back to its original use and was already laid for dinner with her mother's best bone-handled cutlery and the cut-glass cruet set that only came out on special occasions. The sewing machine and all her equipment had been pushed into a corner and hidden by the tapestry screen customers changed behind. Everything was ready. Except the guests were not here.

'They're not coming,' she gasped anxiously, the tablespoon making erratic circles in the air.

'Is it spoiling?' Polly turned from the fireplace, where she had been reading the array of Christmas cards on the mantel. She was more concerned for the state of Rachel's nerves than the condition of the food.

'No. But it soon will be!' She stuck the spoon under her arm and feverishly attempted to push a stray wisp of hair back into her ponytail. She'd been too busy all morning to fix it into its usual bun. And all for nothing, she thought defeatedly.

'Well stop fretting,' Polly ordered firmly. 'There's still time. Come and sit down. I'll take over.' She flapped her hand towards a chair as she waddled across the room. 'I can do the rest.'

'No you won't!' Rachel was adamant. Polly was not doing a thing today, she wasn't going to let her. She contemplated calling Sarah down from her bedroom, but was reluctant, knowing summoning her sister before she was ready to appear would mean an afternoon of sulking. 'Perhaps I'll go to the end of the yard and see if I can see any sign of them,' she said, more to turn her mind away from her sister, who was getting more difficult to control by the day, than from any hopes she might find Judith and David coming up the hill.

'There's no need. They're here.' Polly nodded towards the window as a shadow passed by.

Rachel did not wait to feel her relief. She rushed to the door and could not stop it showing as she greeted Judith, clinging tightly to David's arm.

'I hope we haven't kept you waiting,' Judith said, as Rachel stood back and David guided her to one of the two easy chairs and helped her into it.

Rachel and Sarah had lugged the two chairs down from their mother's old bedroom the previous evening. The old sofa had proved too heavy and too large for the narrow, awkwardly winding staircase and, recalling the struggle they had had to get it up there in the first place, they had given up. Rachel was happy so long as there were two comfortable chairs for Polly and Judith. She could manage with a straight-back chair, and David and Sarah would have to, she decided, feeling as if her arms were about to drop off when the last chair finally reached the front room.

'I had a spot of bother getting dressed,' Judith explained, when she was comfortably seated.

'Don't worry, I planned everything for one o'clock. You're just in time,' Rachel lied. She could see Judith was nervous and didn't want to make her worse by the addition of guilt. Then, remembering the almost ruined dinner, quickly hurried back to the kitchen, hoping it had not all been a big mistake.

'I hope we've not caused problems,' David said, as he came into the kitchen, just as Rachel was struggling to lift the turkey from the roasting pan to a large willow pattern meat platter. 'Here, let me help,' he offered, rushing to her assistance and Rachel stepped back, only too ready to relinquish the heavy bird, which looked as if its legs were about to drop off from over cooking.

'Is Judith all right?' she asked, and stood looking concerned, too anxious at that moment to make herself do anything else in preparation of the dinner. Judith had not wanted to come, she thought, and just knew everything was going to go wrong.

'I think so . . . now . . . but . . .' He paused as he manoeuvred the turkey through the air, suspended on a fish slice and the carving fork, then let it down very gently and with a sigh of relief. He turned to Rachel. 'She's frightened of having an accident or doing something silly. I told her worrying about it would make it happen. Which I suppose was the wrong thing to say.' He looked guilt-ridden and hopeless at the same time.

Rachel bit her lip. She didn't know what to say. For a moment all she could think of was her mother's treasured best china. She had thought of using the everyday set, but had decided that would have looked too obvious and made Judith feel uncomfortable.

'She'll be all right,' she assured David, trying to assure herself at the same time.

David smiled, but not very convincingly. 'Need any more help?' he asked.

'No.' Rachel took the fish slice and carving fork from his hands. 'You can take the turkey through. I'll be with you in a minute . . . And shout our Sarah down. She's stuck in her bedroom.' As usual, she thought.

All the food was laid out and Polly, Judith and Rachel were seated round the table with David carving the turkey, before Sarah finally appeared.

Rachel looked up as the stairfoot door opened. Knowing

her sister had only been messing around in her bedroom, a habit she had taken to of late, she was about to make some comment on her late arrival. But the sight of Sarah took the words right out of her mouth and she could only stare at her, frozen in shock.

Sarah was wearing make-up: pale pink lipstick that made her look ill and dark black lines above her eyes that swept up and out at the corners and gave the impression of a cat. Her dress was black, straight cut with a hem that ended well above her knees, and the sharply pointed revers of the neck plunged far too deeply for Rachel's liking. In horror her gaze slipped slowly down to her sister's black-stockinged legs and on to the black patent leather sling-back shoes with heels at least two inches high. She opened her mouth to speak, but no words would come. She wanted to tell Sarah to get straight back upstairs and get them off: the dress, the shoes, the make-up; everything that turned her into a thirteen-year-old harlot.

Harlot! Dear God she was turning into her father. But she couldn't think of another word that more aptly described her sister's appearance.

'Hello, Sarah,' David said, as she tottered round the table, making it obvious she was not accustomed to such high heels. 'That looks smart.' As Sarah passed behind him, he gave Rachel a knowing wink.

Rachel grimaced inwardly, yet her face remained blank. She did not know whether to thank David for making the obvious attempt at lightening the tension, or to scream at Sarah for causing it in the first place.

'Is it new?' David continued, as Sarah pulled her chair out and sat down.

'Yes,' she replied, and made Rachel want to die, when she smiled up at him in a provocative manner.

What had she done wrong? she asked herself. Where had her little sister gone? There was no trace of a thirteen year old in the Sarah who sat across the table, flirting with a man old enough to be her father.

She looked to Polly in despair, and saw her own thoughts mirrored in the shrewd old eyes. Polly did not speak. She merely gave the slightest incline of her head and Rachel knew the message was in the silence. This was not the time to speak out, Polly was saying.

'Who wants the parson's nose?' David's voice once more cut through the silence and returned Rachel to the moment.

'I thought that was the carver's privilege,' Judith teased, as he spiked the delicacy on the fork and offered it around.

Rachel forced herself to laugh. She had invited Judith and David to get them out of the miseries, not the other way around. Now, because of Sarah, they were the ones having to play host. Well, Sarah was not going to spoil the day for her, or the others, she told herself determinedly. There would be plenty of time to sort her out – later.

David and Judith had brought two bottles of wine with them and by the time Rachel was on her second glass, she was feeling warm and glowing and relaxed. The problem of Sarah had diminished in size and she was enjoying herself in a way she could never remember doing before.

She smiled, watching Polly, her face flushed from the one glass of wine she had agreed to take in honour of the occasion, regaling them with stories of life in the good old days. David was laughing so much he had tears running from his eyes.

It was good to see, she thought happily. Far better than the tears she had seen him shed before. Judith was also looking happy. She had refused any wine, settling for a glass of mineral water to accompany her dinner. Nevertheless, she seemed to have forgotten the tension that had held her stiffly when she arrived.

Sarah was the only problem that marred an otherwise perfect meal. She looked at her sister and the smile slipped from her face. Sarah was knocking the wine back with little effort, and she had been chipping into the conversations with the confidence of someone many years older.

Well you wanted her to be confident, she reminded herself, and took a slow and thoughtful swallow of the sparkling white wine David had brought. It tasted sweet and the bubbles fizzed on her tongue. It was an uplifting feeling, one she could get used to, she thought, the smile returning to her face. And she pushed Sarah to the back of her mind, not allowing her silliness to upset what was turning out to be one of her best ideas in a long time.

'That was a superb meal.' David leaned back in his chair and patted his perfectly flat stomach. 'I think these trousers need letting out a couple of inches.'

'Not today,' Rachel was quick to reply, and laughed. 'It's a holiday for everyone . . . And that includes me.'

'That makes a change,' Polly put in dryly. 'One day's holiday a year – now that's really something.'

Rachel gave her a good-natured scowl. 'Polly thinks I work too hard,' she said, addressing the other members of the table. I should drink more often, she thought. At any other time she would have been embarrassed that Polly had made her comments in front of other people.

'Did you know the Sharratts are leaving?' Using both hands, Judith carefully put her glass of water down on the table before continuing. 'They're going to live in Barbados. Lucy showed me some photographs of the house. It's beautiful. Close to the sea and they have their own swimming pool.'

'A swimming pool!' For a moment Sarah was an innocent thirteen year old, her eyes expressing the disbelief that anyone could really have their own pool.

'Yes. And the sea and the sky looked so blue. They've invited us out for a holiday, once they're settled in. But . . .' Judith's voice diminished, her enthusiasm lapsed in the realization that it was a dream she would never see come true.

David reached out and gave her hand an affectionate squeeze. He smiled into her eyes, but his smile was tight and echoed his wife's sadness.

Rachel felt a lump come to her throat. It was so unfair, she thought. They were so close. They had everything – except peace of mind! 'Go and make the coffee,' she quickly instructed Sarah. It had been more of an order than she intended, as she fought to keep her own emotions hidden from view.

At first Sarah did not move. 'Why me?' she finally questioned, her voice mulishly obstinate.

'Because I made the dinner. You're perfectly capable of making coffee.' Rachel's tone hardened. She levelled her sister a look that said do it, or else!

For a moment Sarah's face reflected surprise. Rachel refused to soften. She had never spoken to her sister in that way before. And that was probably the cause of the present problem, she told herself, as Sarah got up and teetered unsteadily out of the room.

'And take those shoes off before you come back,' she called after her. 'Or you'll spill the lot.'

Polly gave Rachel an encouraging nod.

'It's just her age,' Judith offered, but Rachel wasn't convinced.

'Lucy Sharratt's shop will be coming on the market.' David turned to Rachel. 'It would be ideal for you.'

Rachel suddenly forgot her errant sister. Lucy's hairdressing salon was in Belper, not Derby, as she had planned her shop to be. But it was a busy little town and the shop was in the middle of the main street. It would have been a good start . . . if she had the money!

'I don't have the funds yet,' she stated flatly. Even if the summer had not been disastrous, she would not have had enough money for a place like Lucy's. It was a depressing thought. It made her wonder if she would ever have enough money. Every year prices went up by far more than she was saving. It was impossible for her to work any more hours, she already worked every minute God sent her.

'Why don't you look into a loan?' David suggested.

Polly snorted in disgust. 'And that means more work to pay off your debts! You'll kill yourself with work!'

Rachel grimaced at Polly.

'Not necessarily,' David said. 'The shop has a large flat above it. It brings in a good weekly rent. Which would help to cover any repayments.'

Rachel was suddenly interested again. Borrowing the money had never occurred to her because she knew nothing about the subject. 'I wouldn't know how to go about getting

161

a loan.' She leaned on the table, giving David all her attention. 'Do you think I could get one?'

'Being young and unmarried you'd need someone to stand surety,' he said.

'What do you mean?' She frowned, feeling she was already out of her depth.

'Someone to be your guarantor,' he explained. 'Who would agree to pick up the tab if you could not keep up the repayments.'

That was it then. She slumped back in the chair, her enthusiasm crashing. There was no-one who would do that for her. 'It will have to wait a bit longer.' She gave a sigh of regret. It would have been nice. But it was out of the question. She suddenly grinned at Polly, who had been sitting quietly taking it all in but giving off an air of disapproval. 'You can relax,' she teased. 'I'm not taking over Brindley's just yet.'

They were still laughing when Sarah came padding back into the room on stockinged feet. 'What have I missed?' she enquired irritably, and plonked the tray of full coffee cups down roughly on the table.

Rachel glared at her.

'Your sister getting ideas above her station,' Polly said. 'It's about time she realized there was more to life than work.'

'Work is all I want,' Rachel replied with determination and a harshness to her voice put there by Sarah's pettish attitude. Then, realizing the way she had spoken had turned all the eyes in the room on her, began to fiddle with the coffee cups and distributed them round the table with more haste than was necessary.

While they drank the coffee, David lit up a large cigar and Polly almost swooned.

'King Edwards!' she said. 'They're grand!' She took a deep breath, savouring the rich aroma. 'It takes me back to when my Walter was alive. He liked a King Edward on special occasions.' She smiled reflectively, and Rachel knew she was, for the moment, lost in her own private world of memories.

A fond smile grew on Rachel's lips. She was pleased to see her old friend happy. But then she caught the look that passed between Judith and David: a very special kind of smile that spoke far more than words ever could. Her own smile vanished. She felt a pang deep inside herself, one she could not explain. There were times when she felt so lonely. She had her dreams, she told herself. They were all she needed. They had almost come true today; if only she could have afforded Lucy's shop. But it didn't matter. One day she would have a business that she and Sarah could be proud of. And when that happened nothing else would matter.

'I think it's time to open the presents.' Judith's voice brought Rachel back to the moment, just as David was placing a large parcel in front of her. Then he handed two smaller ones to Sarah and Polly.

Oh no. Rachel felt embarrassed. They had provided nearly all the food and brought presents as well. She jumped up and went to the cupboard, grateful she had had the forethought to wrap two small boxes of sweets, so she had something to give each of her guests when she gave Polly her gift. But they didn't look much and she placed them on the table feeling rather guilty.

Sarah had no such feelings of unease. She tore into her present with a lack of decorum that once more turned her back into a child. 'It's great!' she gasped, gazing excitedly at the gold charm bracelet with four charms: a heart, four-leaf clover, little bell that tinkled, and an S for Sarah.

Polly had a bottle of lavender water and some matching soap from Judith and David. Rachel had made her a hat out of the same material as her coat, which she immediately tried on.

Polly's present to Sarah was a matching fountain pen and propelling pencil. Rachel glared at her, to no avail, when Sarah pushed the pen set aside with the briefest of thanks, and returned her attention to the gold bracelet now dangling from her wrist. Fortunately Polly was too tied up in front of the mirror to notice. She was busily dabbing lavender water behind her ears and admiring the new gold-and-brown-checked hat which looked absolutely atrocious with the lilac and green dress she was wearing. But she didn't seem to notice anything wrong with the colour scheme and waddled grandly round the room for all to see, with the hat perched cockily on her head.

'Aren't you going to open yours?' David asked, and Rachel looked down at her own two parcels, knowing she could not ignore them any longer. She didn't want to open them. Sarah's bracelet was obviously gold, the real thing, not some cheap imitation, and she felt embarrassed at the cost of such a gift. She suspected her own would be of the same value, if not more, and the elegant dark green foil with a gold bow did nothing to ease her mind. The parcel looked expensive even before she had opened it.

Polly's parcel looked typically Polly. The wrapping paper was covered in Santas and Christmas trees and bells and reindeer. But she knew her old friend well enough to suspect the nature of its contents.

'It'll be Easter if you don't hurry up,' Polly scolded good naturedly, before Rachel began. She opened Polly's first. 'It's lovely,' she said, hoping she sounded sincere. The pale blue jumper, in delicate lace knit with a large floppy collar, was lovely. It was pretty and feminine. But she'd never wear it!

She knew it had been a deliberate choice. She looked up to find Polly looking right back at her, the shrewd old eyes seeming even more shrewd than usual. A light of defiance touched Rachel's eyes. Polly and her interfering, she thought rebelliously. Well, she could buy her all the feminine clothes she wanted but she couldn't make her wear them!

'It's just your colour,' Polly said, knowing exactly what was going through her mind.

Rachel forced herself to smile, put the jumper down and turned to the second present. When she got it open she had the feeling a conspiracy was going on.

'Thank you,' she said, but failed to keep the stiffness out of her voice. 'It's lovely. But you shouldn't . . .'

'It's just what you need,' Polly put in, glee lighting her eyes as Rachel held the cream jersey dress up in front of her. 'Now you know it's not just me who thinks you should brighten yourself up.'

'Oh . . . We didn't mean . . .' Judith looked uneasy. 'It's . . . We thought you never seem to have time to make anything for yourself.'

Rachel smiled her thanks, wanted to kill Polly for embarrassing Judith and David, and carefully folded the dress up again. It was a beautiful dress, elegant, like the ones she made for other people. But not for herself. The long straight sleeves and high round neck made the dress perfectly respectable. But the close fitting design would cling to the figure. It was the kind of dress that was seductive by its simplicity and she would never feel right wearing it.

She felt intensely guilty, as if she was ungrateful, especially as David must have rushed into town at the last minute to get the presents. But she could not alter the principle that ran deep inside her, too deep and too lasting to be cut away because it had been scorched into her soul by fear.

'I chose the colour to go with your coat,' David said. 'If it isn't the right size you can take it back and change it.'

Rachel hoped the smile she gave him looked sincere. She wondered why she had allowed Sarah's rag-bag remark to prompt her to make the new coat she had worn only once; when she went to see Judith yesterday. Her old duffel coat suited her much better, she thought, and folded the dress carefully and put it back in its bag.

'It looks perfect,' Sarah chipped in, equalling Polly's enthusiasm. 'Go and try it on.'

'I'll try it later,' she said. 'I'm sure it will be fine.' But as she spoke her mind was already planning on taking the dress back. She could get something else, something in navy blue or grey. Maybe she could get two skirts for it. 'Come on, Sarah, let's clear away.' She put the dress and Polly's jumper on the dresser and began to pile the dirty cups and saucers on to the tray. Then she dragged an unwilling Sarah into the kitchen and hoped the subject of the Christmas presents would be forgotten by the time she returned to the front room.

They were halfway through the washing up, when David came in. 'I'll take over for you,' he said, taking the tea towel out of Sarah's hand.

165

'No you won't!' Rachel flashed her sister a don't you dare stare. But Sarah was not letting the chance pass. She was out of the kitchen before Rachel could blink.

'I don't know what's got into her.' She sighed heavily, feeling the problem of her sister weighing heavy on her shoulders. 'She was always so good. It all started with Margaret Land's wedding!'

'She's just finding her feet,' he said, offering reassurance as he began to wipe a wine glass. 'It isn't strange, at that age.'

'But she can't go around dressed like that!'

'No,' he agreed thoughtfully. 'But I think if you talk to her like an adult, rather than get angry, she will see reason.'

Rachel wasn't sure he knew what he was talking about. She had never shouted at Sarah. There had never been any need – before!

'Would you seriously like Lucy's shop?' he suddenly asked.

'Yes,' she replied without hesitation. She paused for a moment, staring out of the window. It was a bright sunny day, too warm for the season. It looked more like spring in the gardens across the yard. The weather had warmed up. Teasing, she thought, just like David's suggestion, giving her hope that had ended as quickly as it had begun. She sighed. 'It's a year too early.' She plunged a pile of plates into the washing-up foam. 'This time next year, and I might have been able to manage it.'

'Why don't you think of a loan?'

She gave a dry laugh. 'Who would back me?' she asked, making the question sound as unreasonable as she felt it was.

'If the price was right. I would.'

Rachel almost dropped a plate. She looked stunned as she turned to him. 'You would?' she asked, not sure she had heard correctly.

'Yes,' he replied confidently. 'If I could afford it. We'd have to find out the facts and figures first. And . . . ! I'd expect a small favour in return.'

'What?' she asked guardedly, suddenly wondering if she had misread him after all. If he wanted her to . . . ?

'Let Judith be a part of it,' he said, stopping her thoughts before she turned him completely into another Micky Caradine.

She didn't know if she wanted to laugh or cry for her unchivalrous thoughts. She felt herself blushing furiously, as if she had actually put them into words and he was aware of her unwarranted suspicions on his character.

'I know she wouldn't be able to do much. But there's nothing wrong with her brain. She could sit behind the counter and take the money . . . or . . . or wrap the dresses up.' His face fell. 'Perhaps she would drop them,' he added flatly.

'No . . . no . . . of course Judith can be part of it,' Rachel quickly assured him. 'There'll be something she can do.' She could understand his reasons and agreed with them, even though he had not spoken them. Letting Judith have something to do might renew her interest in life. If they could persuade her to do it! She wasn't so convinced Judith would agree. But if David was willing to have a go, then so was she, and she wasn't going to say anything that would make him think it had been a silly idea and take the offer back.

For several seconds she returned excitedly to the washing up. Then her spirits wilted. 'But . . . but what if I made a hash of it? If I lost money then you'd lose your money, as well.' The suggestion was silly, she told herself flatly. She could never put David in that position.

'No I wouldn't. So long as I could cover the loan if you couldn't pay. If that should happen we'd still have the shop to sell and that way I'd recoup my money.'

He made it sound so simple. Was it really that straight-forward? She thought for a minute, then another, then another, before she finally asked, 'Is that right?'

'Of course it is. I'm not about to throw my money away. In any case, it will never happen. I've got complete faith in you.'

It was another minute before she turned to him, her face serious. 'Would you do that?' She felt as if she was dreaming. She wanted to pinch herself, yet if it was a dream didn't want to wake up.

'I've said it, haven't I? Are we partners?'

167

'What if Judith won't agree?'

'Then I shall be a sleeping partner in a very lucrative business. So . . . Are we partners?'

A smile broke slowly over her face, until she was grinning with pure delight. 'Yes,' she agreed. 'If the price is right!'

'I'll have a word with Lucy tomorrow,' he said. 'Once we've found out how much she wants for it we can begin doing some sums. If it's within your limits I'm sure she'll be only too pleased to make a deal with you and save herself the trouble of putting it on the market.'

'Do you think she would?' she asked, suddenly feeling nervous, seeing her shop being taken from her by someone who could pay a higher price.

'I'm sure she will. She owes me a few favours.' He stopped wiping the plate in his hands, and looked suddenly serious. 'I'll tell Judith tonight. So I'd rather you didn't say anything when we go back in there.'

Rachel smiled fondly. 'Of course I won't.' It was only natural he wanted to tell his wife himself and she would respect that wish.

'Come on you two!' Polly stuck her head round the front room door. 'The Queen's on in a minute.'

'Time to stand to attention,' Rachel joked, and pulled the tea towel out of his hand. Polly never missed the Queen's speech and she thought it was a sin for anyone else to do so.

As she sat in front of the television, Rachel felt too happy to listen, even to Her Majesty's once a year speech. It was strange how easily she got on with David, she thought. He had become such a good friend that she never thought about him being a man, one of the deadly breed to be avoided at all costs, except for the one unchivalrous moment of earlier, she reminded herself, and almost blushed all over again. It really was time she stopped judging them all by Micky, she told herself. She gave a little sigh, doubting she would ever be able to really trust a man. Today had proved it. David was always nice, he never looked at her with anything but kindness in his eyes, and yet she had still been able to think there was

168

something improper when he said he wanted a favour. She gave another little sigh and looked at him, sitting on the other side of the table, puffing away on another cigar. She wished he could have been her father. How different life would have been.

'Where did you get that dress?' Rachel looked steadily at Sarah. She was firm, but had ordered herself not to lose her temper, even though she felt like raising the roof.

It was late in the evening and the first time they had been alone together. David and Judith had just left and had taken Polly home when they went. It had been a lovely day, apart from Sarah. 'Well?' she prompted, feeling her voice hardening, as Sarah stared at her in belligerent silence.

'I got it with Joseph's money,' she finally replied, her voice short and clipped.

'I thought you were getting shoes?' Rachel glanced blandly at the high heels now back on her feet. 'Are those they?'

'No!' Sarah snapped. 'These were cheaper and meant I could afford the dress as well.'

'I see.' Rachel paused, feeling her restraint withering. 'Don't you think they are a little too old for you?' Anger sparked in Sarah's eyes and Rachel knew she was going to need all her self-control to remain calm.

'*No*! I do not.' Sarah rested her hands on her hips and glared at her sister.

'Well I do!' Rachel countered, facing a Sarah she had never seen before, and one she didn't much like. It had all happened so suddenly. Sarah had taken to spending more time alone in her bedroom of late. She had even made it quite clear that Rachel was not welcome any more in the pink and white room at the top of the house. Rachel had not minded that. She had assumed Sarah wanted some privacy and had found nothing strange about it. But suddenly she saw it as Sarah distancing herself from her and it frightened her.

She was less firm, as she said, 'There will be plenty of time to wear things like that when you are older. They don't look very nice on someone your age. They look . . .' She had been about to say cheap. She amended herself, and finished, '. . . rather silly.'

'Just because you want to go round looking like a granny doesn't mean everyone else does.' There was such animosity in Sarah's voice and Rachel took a step back, stung by the words.

'I wear what suits me,' she returned lamely.

'What suits you!' Sarah scoffed, the scorn on her face turning her features into a parody of her youthful prettiness. 'You're twenty and you look forty. And it isn't just me that thinks so. Why do you think Polly gave you that jumper? Why do you think David and Judith gave you that dress? Don't you think they were trying to tell you something?'

'I don't think that is any of your business,' Rachel countered coolly, her anger returned in the face of Sarah's insults.

'And what I wear is none of your business,' Sarah flung back hotly. Then cut Rachel to the quick, when she said, 'I'm fed up with having to do what you say. You're only my sister, for God's sake!'

'Don't swear!' Rachel insisted with equal fire. 'I may only be your sister, but I'm the one who clothes and feeds you. I think that gives me the right to some say in the matter.' Her voice rose higher and higher, she could no longer keep her temper and she didn't care. Sarah needed telling a few home truths. 'And I will not have you going around looking like that . . . It's cheap!' Oh dear, she was beginning to sound like her father. She cast the thought aside. It had to be said. 'What do you think people will say about you if you go around dressed like that?'

'People!' Sarah screamed. 'What do I care about people?'

'What about Polly, and David and Judith? What impression do you think you've created with them?'

'*They're old!*' Sarah's nose curled up with distaste and Rachel felt something snap inside her. 'I don't care what old people think! And you're old, just like them. All you care about is sewing, sewing, sewing! You don't have any fun!'

For the first time in her life Rachel wanted to hit her sister. She thought of the gold bracelet hanging from her arm. She had been only too ready to accept that from *old* people, people she didn't care about.

'Get upstairs this minute!' she demanded fiercely, wanting Sarah out of the way before she lost control and did what she wanted to do: slapping her so hard it would knock some sense into her hard, mercenary head. 'Get those clothes off and that muck off your face. And don't let me catch you wearing any of them again! I'll have no sister of mine going around like a little tramp!' It had been more than she had intended to say. But she could not have stopped herself, anger throbbed through her in a way she had not experienced since the night her father had died.

Tears glistened in Sarah's eyes. Rachel could see she was using all her will power to stop them falling. And suddenly she looked like the Sarah of years ago: when their father had been yelling at her and she had held back her tears for fear of his reaction if she began to cry. Rachel's heart immediately softened. She wanted to pull her sister into her arms and hold her and be close – as they used to be close. But she hesitated a moment too long.

'All my friends wear make-up,' Sarah insisted. 'You want me to look like a baby. You don't want me to grow up.' Her tears won control and black channels of eyeliner rapidly streaked her cheeks, adding to the bleak misery of her screwed up features.

Rachel stepped forward, but it was too late. Sarah had already turned away. Before she could wrap her arms around her, Sarah was racing upstairs, her noisy sobs increasing with each step she took.

Rachel flopped into an easy chair, a great boulder of misery pressing her down. What had happened to cause such a gulf between them? Sarah had been such a happy, lovable little girl.

She thought back over the years, searching for something, anything that might give a clue to Sarah's present behaviour. There was nothing. Her memories of Sarah were always the same: happy, laughing. Even when their father had been alive and she had been frightened in his presence, when he was not around she had been far more relaxed than either herself or Joseph.

She wondered if the obvious tension had affected Sarah in some unseen way. It hadn't affected Joseph and herself, she thought, then suddenly stopped herself. Or had it? she asked, and pictured Joseph walking away down the hill the last time he had been home. He had been different. She couldn't put her finger on what it had been, but he had seemed strange, not happy, as if a weight was on his shoulders.

And she could never have said she herself was normal. But that had been more Micky's doing. Hadn't it?

She sighed despondently. If only her father could have been different, she thought. If he had been a man she could have modelled other men on . . .

What was the point? She tugged at the band in her ponytail and freed her hair. It was all hypothetical. Water under the bridge. If it was possible to go back and rectify your mistakes the whole world would be travelling backwards.

She gave a thin smile. She was beginning to think in Pollyisms. Her smile vanished, memories of her own mistakes bringing to mind the misty image of a little girl.

I wonder what she'd had for Christmas? she thought. She hoped it was something nice.

She forced herself from the chair as if her body had become lead. You'd have made a terrible mother, she told herself. She wasn't capable of looking after one child, two would have been a disaster.

Shaking her hair out so it fell around her shoulders like a golden cape, she went to the door, turned the key and pulled the bolt. Then went up to bed, her steps as heavy as her mind.

At the bedroom door she hesitated and considered going up the second flight of stairs to Sarah's room. Leave it till morning, she told herself. They would both be in better condition to act rationally after a good night's sleep. There had already been far too much said tonight.

172

Chapter Twelve

On Boxing Day the atmosphere in the cottage at the end of the yard was very tense. Rachel had not had a good night and got up early to find Sarah was already downstairs and preparing breakfast. It had never happened before. Rachel was always the one to get breakfast for her sister to stumble down to and she hoped it heralded a change for the better and that her argument of the previous night had been taken to heart. Sarah was at least dressed more normally, she thought gratefully, as she looked at her blue woollen slacks and white polo neck jumper.

Unfortunately, Rachel's hopes were short lived. Sarah made a hasty apology, then said she realized she owed a lot to Rachel, but she really could not expect her to do everything the way she liked. They were two different people, she continued, speaking in a manner that chilled Rachel. She was speaking in a way that would have been more fitting had she been the elder and Rachel the adolescent in need of guidance.

'You are still a schoolgirl,' Rachel pointed out firmly. 'And until you have a job and can look after yourself I am responsible for you. Whether you like it or not!'

'I don't want to fall out again.' Sarah lifted her chin defiantly and glared at her sister.

'Neither do I!' Rachel responded with equal force. 'I don't want you to be miserable. I don't want to stop you having fun. But I draw the line at dressing up as if you're twenty.'

'It's what everyone is wearing,' Sarah insisted petulantly.

Rachel was unmoved. 'Well you are not. Not until you're older and can cope with . . .' She pulled herself up short. What had she been about to say? Can cope with the problems brought on by dressing in an alluring manner, making yourself look attractive and available to the opposite sex.

She rubbed her head, as if the action would remove the unwanted thoughts from her mind. She had not dressed provocatively when Micky had attacked her. Her clothes had been ordinary, nice, she had felt good in them, but they had been in no way suggestive. There had been nothing in her appearance or manner that had echoed, even in the slightest, the previous day's image of Sarah tottering into the room on her high heels, looking like Lolita.

So much for that theory, she told herself, and looked down at her severe navy-blue dress, buttoned to the neck. It suddenly reminded her of a nun's habit. Her father would have been proud of her, she told herself, realizing Micky had done more to force her into her father's pious ways than her father had ever succeeded in doing. Was it any wonder she and Sarah were growing apart? She trying to make herself totally invisible and Sarah trying to be noticed. She sighed, understanding now why Sarah fought against all she did and said.

'I don't want you to get hurt,' she said, guilt tempering her anger. She reached out and gave her sister's arm an affectionate squeeze. But there was no reciprocating warmth and the sadness in her eyes deepened.

'For God's sake,' Sarah snapped. 'What's wrong with you?'

She recoiled her hand in shock. 'Don't blaspheme, Sarah,' she insisted. 'It isn't very ladylike. And I won't have it in this house!'

Sarah carried on as if she had not spoken. 'I know you had mother to look after, and before that father stopping you living. But you're free now. You can go out and do what you want. I won't stop you. You act like you're already an old maid.'

'I don't want that kind of life.' Rachel's voice hardened with the offence of Sarah's last words. She had thought that maybe a time would come when she could tell Sarah about Micky, explain everything, and in doing so help Sarah to be wiser. But the little sister she could have talked to was no longer there.

First Joseph. Now Sarah. Was it something in herself, she wondered, that made the people she loved turn away from her?

'Unless you dress to my liking I shall not let you go out of the door.' She did not speak in anger, but with a sternness that brooked no refusal and brought shock to Sarah's mulish expression.

'You can't stop me,' she continued to challenge, after a long moment of silence.

'Oh yes I can.' Rachel was determined now. It was too late to shilly-shally about. She had obviously been too soft and was now paying the consequences. 'And if you don't do as you're told I shall have you put in a home.' It chilled her to speak the words that she had worked so long and hard to prevent. She could never have done it. She just hoped Sarah did not realize that and would take the threat to heart.

It was a sulky Sarah who washed the breakfast pots. But when she had finished, Rachel was pleased to find she did not vanish into the privacy of her bedroom. Although, by the end of the day, the constant skirting round each other like tigers in a cage was so wearing she wished Sarah would make herself scarce and give her some peace.

It was the second day of the new year when David knocked on the door.

'I've spoken to Lucy,' he said, as he walked into the front room, once more reverted to the functional sewing room. 'And Judith's quite interested – I think,' he added uncertainly, as he turned to Rachel.

She grimaced. 'But not over the moon?'

'I think she will be if you can find something she can do. I'm sure she wants to. But she's nervous.'

Rachel nodded thoughtfully, as he took off his sheepskin coat and hung it on the corner of the customer's changing screen. 'And what did Lucy have to say?' she asked, hoping it was good.

'She wants four thousand five hundred for it. But if you want it and it saves her the trouble of estate agents, she's happy to drop it by two hundred and fifty.'

Rachel grimaced again. 'It's a lot of money.' Her spirits

wilted. It would take for ever to pay off, she thought. Maybe she should forget it.

'Don't look so glum.' David tried to force a smile out of her. He succeeded, but it was very thin. 'Let's work it all out on paper before you give up. I'm sure we can knock her down to four thousand.'

She did smile then, at the way David had read her mind. Not for the first time, she realized, recalling dancing with him at Margaret Land's wedding. He had known then that she was stiff and uncertain because he was a man. She blushed with the memory and quickly moved the clutter of bobbins and pins from the table, before pulling the chairs up for them to sit on.

'See . . . It isn't so bad.' David pushed the writing pad across the table to Rachel.

For almost two hours they had been doing calculation after calculation. Rachel studied the paper carefully, checking over David's sums. Not that she thought he was not capable, she wanted to be sure in her own mind she was not biting off more than she could chew.

'It all looks reasonable. On paper.' Her voice betrayed her doubt. Cold feet, she told herself, because of David. If she had been playing with her own money she would not have given it a second thought. 'What happens if I have another slump, like last summer?'

'Stop worrying. Business is always risky. If you're not prepared to take the gamble you should not be getting involved.' His smile was reassuring. 'People will always need clothes,' he pointed out, pulled a packet of cigarettes from his pocket, asked permission, and lit up. 'And you can always go into beachwear.'

'Why didn't I think of that?' Her determination had returned. If David was not showing any concern for his money, then why should she? He was content he was not going to lose out on the deal. And he wasn't! She would make sure of that, she told herself, just as the stairfoot door opened and Sarah appeared.

'Where are you going?' Rachel immediately enquired.

looking hard at her sister, realizing she was trying to make a quick exit under cover of David's presence.

'To Sally's,' was the brief reply.

'Not in those shoes.' Rachel pointedly dropped her gaze to the high-heeled shoes of Christmas Day. A red pleated skirt protruded from beneath Sarah's navy-blue anorak and, apart from the shoes, she was dressed to Rachel's liking. She was relieved to see her words had not fallen completely on deaf ears. But those shoes had to go.

Sarah looked downcast for a moment. 'Can I take them to Sally's, if I wear another pair to go in?'

'No!' Rachel's tone brooked no refusal. Sarah was presenting her with a challenge. It was obvious she had not thought she would make any comment in front of David. But Rachel realized whatever happened now would point the way for the future. She had to stand firm or Sarah would use every trick in the book to get her own way. 'You're much too young to be wearing high heels. You'll end up with bandy legs.' She wasn't sure if it was true or not. She had heard it said before and it seemed appropriate to the moment.

Sarah looked belligerent, was about to say something, changed her mind and went back up the stairs. She reappeared within minutes and stood purposefully for Rachel's inspection. 'These all right?' she asked stiffly. Rachel nodded her approval at the sensible flat black shoes and Sarah vanished with only the briefest of goodbyes.

'Back to business,' she said, and gave the writing pad a quick last glance. 'When can we settle things with Lucy?' she asked, wanting to get it all done.

'A.S.A.P.' David replied, but Rachel did not miss the uncertainty in his voice.

'What's wrong?' she asked, suddenly nervous and looking concerned.

'Do you think you will be able to manage a full-time business as well as Sarah?'

She stared silently at the table. The same thought *had* crossed her own mind. She had responsibilities to Sarah, but she also had responsibilities to herself. She had worked long and hard for this. Sarah was not being deserted in favour of the shop, she would be a part of it. And she could help, which might not be a bad thing.

'I'll manage,' she finally said, her voice filled with the confidence that the shop was as right for Sarah as it was for herself.

David stubbed his cigarette out, slowly and deliberately. It was a long moment, before he said, 'Shall I see Lucy?'

Rachel felt a sigh of relief well up inside her. For an awful moment she had thought he was going to back out. Earlier she would have been willing to back down, but not now. Now she could really see her shop was within her grasp and she would move heaven and earth to get it.

'No,' she replied. If she was going to be a businesswoman she might as well start now. 'I'll see Lucy myself.'

'Fine.' He looked impressed and she felt a glow of pride. She had thought he might disapprove of her going to see Lucy alone. His confidence inspired her. She was at a turning point in her life, she thought happily. The only way was up and that was the direction she was going.

'Don't forget to knock Lucy down to four thousand,' was his parting comment, as he left her feeling that nothing could go wrong, ever again.

Rachel leaned back in the big chair, the hypnotic tick of Polly's grandfather clock lulling her into dreamy reverie. She could see it all in her mind's eye: The Boutique – that was to be its name.

The sound of soft snoring made her suddenly look up. Polly's head had flopped back against the crocheted anti-macassar, eyes closed, mouth open. Rachel frowned. It was not like Polly to drop to sleep when she had company.

She wondered if she had bored her, yet she knew in her heart, despite all her chunterings about too much work, Polly was as excited about the plans for the shop as she was herself. It was not hearing about David's earlier visit that had sent Polly to sleep. It was a tiredness that went right through to her old bones. It worried Rachel. She found herself contemplating life without Polly to run to when things went wrong. It was a numbing prospect. Yet it would happen. One day. Not yet, she begged, please don't let it happen yet.

Polly stirred and rubbed her head, as if trying to get rid of an annoying pain. 'I must have dropped off for a minute,' she said, putting a smile on Rachel's face. She had been gone to the world for over half an hour.

'I must be getting back,' Rachel pushed herself out of the chair. She didn't really want to leave the comfort she always found in Polly's front room with its clutter of brass ornaments and crocheted mats. Neither did she want to leave Polly just then. The tiredness in her eyes made her look very old, and ill. But Sarah would be back and wanting her tea.

'Aye, lass. You be running along,' Polly said.

Rachel did not move. 'Are you all right?' she finally asked. She knew there was nothing worse than telling someone they looked ill when they felt fine. She had not wanted to upset Polly, but she was concerned.

'As right as I'll ever be.' Polly flapped her hand at her. 'Get yourself off. Sarah will be waiting.' Her hand went back to her temple and she grimaced.

'Why don't you get Doctor Mellor to give you a check-up?' she suggested, suddenly very worried. It wasn't like Polly to be ill, she always shrugged aches and pains away.

'What for?' Polly's voice rose in disbelief. 'There's nothing he can do for me. It's called old age, lass. They haven't got a pill for it. Stop your fussing and get home.'

Rachel felt helpless, and guilty. She had been so excited about her own plans she had not noticed Polly's condition. 'I'll pop round later,' she said, as much for her own peace of mind as Polly's.'

'No you won't.' Polly was quick to object and seemed to liven up considerably. She peered at her with a warning glare. 'I'm quite all right. And I shall be watching *Coronation Street* and not wanting any interruptions.'

Rachel smiled. She did not point out that *Coronation Street* was only on for half an hour. She knew that was Polly's way of saying stop fussing.

'All right, I'll see you tomorrow,' she agreed, not wanting to offend her old friend by treating her like a child. But, even though she smiled as she walked out of the door, she was worried. Polly was too fiercely independent for her own good, and when she wasn't feeling at her best her independence was at its most powerful.

It was a dark night and, as she crossed the road, she stopped to look up at the sky filled with stars but no moon. She repeated her plea that nothing should happen to Polly. It was a selfish plea, she realized. If everything went well with Lucy, she knew she was going to need Polly's down-to-earth advice and her ear to bend when things were not going to plan.

'Trying to find a lucky one? Or are you counting them?'

The momentary shock of finding Micky Caradine standing next to her, was soon washed away by his infuriatingly confident grin. He was wearing a black leather biker's jacket and his hair hung long and lank in his neck. She thought it suited him. It made him look what he was – a thug!

She flashed him a warning glare, filled with the anger of memories so easy to recall. Then she walked quickly down the hill and away from him.

'Got nothing to say to me?' He caught up by her side and tossed a dry laugh into the cool night air.

Oh yes, she thought, she had plenty to say. But he wasn't worth the waste of breath. She wouldn't give him so much as one minute of her time.

As they reached the end of the yard he skipped in front of her and barred her way. 'I thought we could go for a drink?'

Rachel stopped short, her mouth dropping open. He thought what? Had he no shame? What a stupid question, she told herself. He had no shame, no honour, no pride, no morals, no guts – no anything!

'I've got myself a car now,' he persisted, the cold hate of her glare having no affect on his thick skin.

She had the almost uncontrollable urge to slap his face, knocking the cocky smirk from his hated features. But that would cause her to touch him.

180

'Not if you were the last man alive,' she ground through clenched teeth. 'You've got a nerve even daring to speak to me.'

He gave a mocking laugh and lifted his hand, would have touched her cheek, if she had not swiped him away, the horror of being touched by him giving her the ability. It also provided her with more physical strength than she had imagined she possessed and the blow sent him reeling backwards into the lamp-post.

For a moment he looked stunned. It pleased her to realize her unexpected force had surprised him. She was no longer the naïve girl, the trusting puppy he had led so easily by the hand, and the sooner he understood that the better.

'Now get out of my way,' she demanded. 'I'm going home!'

He did not move and she was forced to walk round him.

'One day,' he called sneeringly after her, 'you'll wake up and find you're a dried-up old maid.'

Rachel stopped, turned slowly around. 'Well, if I do it will be by my own choosing. And if I don't it will be because I've found myself a *man*. But I can't see any of those around here!' The hate that had festered deep inside her far too long hardened her voice. Almost tangible arrows of ice flew through the darkness to the pathetic figure he made beneath the street lamp.

The hard man, she thought, looking at the leather jacket and shiny, buckled winkle-picker shoes. He really thought he was something. Disgust curled her lips in a mocking smile. Without speaking another word she turned and walked down the dark yard, leaving him unexpectedly silent.

There would be no more Micky Caradines in her life, she thought, as she circled the pile of logs that had been lying in front of her neighbour's door since before Christmas. She was pleased she had met him that way and been forced to come face to face with her hatred. He was nothing, she realized, beneath contempt. The dread of finding herself alone with him had proved nothing more than a wild fantasy. She had not been afraid. In fact she had been more afraid when she bumped into him in the Beehive, with other people around. All she had felt tonight was anger, such a powerful anger that she had found the words to wipe the silly smile from his face.

As she opened the cottage door and stepped inside, she had the pleasant feeling she had just closed a door on a part of her life she did not need. But when she looked into the kitchen and saw Sarah standing there, her mind suddenly filled with the image of a little girl – one who looked very much like Sarah.

Chapter Thirteen

For three months Rachel worked from dawn to dusk, then often into the night as well. Every available space in the cottage was filled with garments to stock the new shop.

The Sharratts were not leaving for Barbados until May, so Lucy was in no hurry to get rid of her business and a completion date for the sale was jointly decided for the beginning of April. The delay suited Rachel. It gave her time to make ample stock, while at the same time keeping some money coming in by continuing to supply her regular customers.

The childish excitement she had felt at the beginning had turned into a determined obsession. She threw herself totally into the project and found she thrived on the challenge. She began to enjoy seeking out the best suppliers and haggling to beat the prices down for her large orders. She had turned into the businesswoman David had thought her to be, as he told her on the many occasions they talked through new ideas, or sat together to go over the accounts and make sure everything was going to plan.

David was proving to be the perfect partner. He was always there to listen and offer advice if it was asked for, but he never poked his nose in and tried to tell Rachel what to do. He supplied the names of joiners and decorators needed to convert the hairdressing salon into a dress shop, but always allowed her to make the arrangements and give the orders, unless she specifically asked him to do it for her.

Rachel gave the workmen one month to complete the work and planned the opening for May 1st, it being a Saturday, the busiest shopping day of the week.

There were only two hiccups during the conversion. The first was when one of the joiners hammered through a water pipe, the fault not being found until the following day, when the place was flooded. Fortunately that was in the early days and there had been plenty of time to dry the shop out, helped along by the addition of several industrial heaters that David had provided.

The second was when Rachel went to inspect the finished decorations and, instead of finding pale Wedgwood blue paint on the walls, found something closely resembling air force grey. A few quick, very strong words to the foreman had soon put it right. And with exactly one week to go before opening, the conversion was complete, the shop ready to have its racks and shelves filled with stock.

Sarah had got very excited about the new shop and seemed to have settled down again. Rachel had not been given further occasions to pull her up on her clothes and, of her own accord, Sarah had taken on more of the housework to leave Rachel free to her sewing. She had even begun to help with the sewing, taking on the fiddly task of fixing the buttons and fastenings and tacking pieces together ready for her to machine.

'Sarah's got the gift,' Rachel said one evening, as she inspected the buttons her sister had fixed neatly to the jacket she was about to put on the ironing board.

'It's in the blood, lass,' Polly said, putting the *Derby Evening Telegraph* down and peering over the top of her reading glasses.

'I don't remember my mother ever doing any sewing.' She laid the jacket on the ironing board and straightened it out. Then she paused and looked at her old friend. It was good to see her back to her old self and she was thankful whatever had been ailing her seemed to have passed by. She hoped it would stay that way and picked up the iron and carefully brushed it across the lapels of the jacket. 'My mother hated having to sew a button on,' she said, returning to the previous subject.

Polly shook her head and removed her glasses. 'It was your Great Aunt Martha. Your dad's aunt. She took in sewing.'

Rachel stopped and looked up. 'I didn't know that.' She

sounded surprised. Then wondered why she should find anything odd about not knowing a member of her father's family. He had never spoken about his family. She could vaguely recall the dour old lady who had been her grandmother. She had died when Rachel was six. Her grandfather had been killed in the war and she had never known him. 'I didn't even know he had an aunt,' she said, and returned to the ironing.

'He had two,' Polly said, folding her arms and heaving her bosom upwards, her manner looking suitable to the important information she was about to relate.

Rachel smiled. 'Two?' she questioned pointedly, knowing her old friend could not wait to tell her their life story.

'Aye. Clara, the other one, went to be a housekeeper at one of the big houses in Holbrook. Of course, he never had much to do with either of them.'

Of course! Rachel's smile broadened. A housekeeper! She could just imagine her father's reaction to having a relative who was one of the serving classes. And he wouldn't consider a seamstress much better. It would have been considered a more genteel profession than a housekeeper, but to her father it would still have been taking in other people's work.

'Did they have any families of their own?' She stopped ironing again, suddenly excited by the prospect of having relatives somewhere, some unknown cousins who might prove to be normal people. It would have been nice to think they existed.

Polly shook her head. 'Neither of them married. Although,' she paused thoughtfully, 'I seem to recall a bit of scandal to do with Clara. It was said she'd had a baby, and it was the man's from the big house. It wasn't uncommon in those days. Always covered up though. You'll never find the truth.'

'Oh well.' Rachel sighed, and lifted the jacket up, gave it a thorough inspection, then hung it up on the stairfoot door. The gift of sewing had come from Great Aunt Martha, she told herself, and reached for one of the last two dresses needing pressing before being taken to the shop. As she laid the dress out, she gave an inward grimace. She also had something in common with great Aunt Clara. It hardly seemed like a gift. But it was nice to know she had not been the first to let the Cooper family name down.

'David's bringing the car later, to take me to the shop with these last few things,' she said, turning her mind to more important matters. 'Do you want to come with us and have a look?' Polly had not seen the shop and Rachel was eager for her to take a look. It was the first real thing she had done without Polly's constant advice and help, although once Polly had learned David was backing her and she was not doing it all alone, she had been encouraging her all the way. But until Polly had seen the shop, Rachel felt her approval was not complete. And Polly's approval was something she needed.

'No. I'll come when you open up. It's only two days away now. I can wait that long.' Polly perched her glasses back on her nose and returned to the newspaper.

Rachel hung the dress up with the jacket and placed the second dress on the ironing board. Two days, she thought. Even after all the work it still seemed like a dream. It was a dream, she told herself, a dream come true—thanks to David. She wondered what her father would have thought about her setting up in business. Would he have been pleased? Would he have been able to find a little pride in his hard heart for his daughter's accomplishments? She gave a sigh. She doubted it. He always found fault with everything.

The racks were full of dresses and suits bearing the exclusive blue and silver Boutique label. The back room was piled with tissue paper, paper bags and large substantial carriers. Everything was ready. All she needed now was customers, Rachel told herself, feeling her pulse racing with the alarming dread that no-one would come through the door.

At nine o'clock promptly she turned the door sign from closed to open. At exactly one minute past nine the electricity went off.

'Oh no! There's a power cut!' she wailed, turning to David in horror.

He hurried to the door and looked across at the shops across

186

the road. 'They've got power over there,' he said, and dashed outside to look at the shops on either side of The Boutique.

'No! Please no!' Rachel begged, imagining a hundred and one things the workmen had inadvertently done.

David hurried back into the shop and confirmed her worst fears. 'They're on on both sides. It must be us.' He raced through the shop and vanished into the small back room.

Rachel looked round in despair. She wanted to run after him, but knew if she did she would only get in his way. And breathing her panic over him wouldn't help.

'Don't worry.' Judith looked up from the chair positioned behind the till on the small glass counter. It had taken a lot of persuasion, but she finally overcame her insecurities and agreed to help in the shop. For as long as she possibly could, she had made clear. Rachel had worried she would back out at the last minute, but the excitement of all the preparation had worked wonders for her. And she had thrown herself into the stocking up with a vitality even she had never thought to see in herself again.

'You always get teething troubles,' she continued. 'How on earth did you find time to make that suit on top of everything else?' She passed an admiring glance over Rachel.

Rachel grimaced. 'Does it look all right?' she asked, knowing Judith was trying to take her mind off the electricity, and trying to show willing. She had made the suit specially for the opening. It was her usual navy blue and it buttoned up to the neck. But the skirt was straight and, though not exactly tight, much smarter than her usual baggy creations. The jacket was short and fitted snugly to her waist and she had even put gold buttons down the front and on the pockets.

She glanced down, tugged at the jacket and nervously smoothed the skirt over her thighs. It was time she smartened herself up, she had told herself, when she had been deciding what to wear for the special occasion. Her argument with Sarah had opened her eyes and made her realize the clothes she had been wearing had had nothing to do with Micky's attack. She had thought of Judith and certain of her other customers, of the elegant suits and dresses she made for them. She had to admit they always looked feminine. But they never looked sexy in a tarty way. She sighed. The suit looked very businesslike, she told herself, assuring herself of the fact by glancing in one of the long wall mirrors.

'It looks wonderful!' Judith declared. 'You should find the time to make yourself more outfits like it.' Then, in her innocence, wiped away all Rachel's courage, by adding, 'You're a very beautiful woman. You should take advantage of it. Not hide it away.'

Rachel felt herself blushing as she turned to the mirror again, this time taking a hard look and feeling her insecurities overwhelm her. Her blond hair was screwed into its usual knot on top of her head, making her small frame look taller. The jacket hugged her waist and accentuated her breasts and the slender heeled shoes made her legs shapely. Beautiful! She couldn't see that. But a woman . . . Yes! Her eyes seemed to widen as she looked at herself and they suddenly reflected the long-hidden fear. She turned quickly away. Her gaze had reminded her too much of the time she had stood in the bathroom, searching her body to see what Micky had done to her. It was not a memory she wanted at any time, but especially not then, at the opening of her shop, the beginning of her new life.

'No-one will be able to see!' She lifted her hands and looked around in despair, leaping to the more pressing problem to escape her own mind. It was an exaggeration. The day was bright and sunny and it was only towards the back of the shop that the light faded. 'They'll think we're still closed!' She spun around as David knocked a tin of buttons to the ground in the back room. The clattering rain of plastic and metal sent a convulsive shudder through her taut nerves and she gave a loud groan.

'Calm down. David will fix it,' Judith assured.

But Rachel could not calm down. It was all going wrong. And it had to work. For herself. For David. If the shop failed she was letting everyone down.

'I'll go and see how he's getting on,' she suddenly said,

and hurried down the shop, needing the physical activity of actually doing something.

She reached the back room just as the lights came on.

'It was only the fuse,' David said, as he stretched his tall form upright from kneeling in front of the fuse box, and almost bumped his head on the shelf filled with tissue paper and plastic bags.

'Where's the crowd?' Sarah called, as she came bouncing through the door, loaded with milk, tea and sugar, the only items Rachel had forgotten.

Rachel was too busy feeling relieved about the electricity to respond.

'They'll be here soon,' David replied confidently, and Rachel hoped he was right as he went to the front window and looked out. 'The street is beginning to fill up now.' Rachel joined him and they both looked up and down the street at the steadily growing number of people passing by. 'You don't need me any more, so I'll be going,' he said, glancing at his watch.

Rachel looked uncertain. It had been agreed he would not stay at the shop. Having a man hanging round would frighten the customers away, he had said when they were making preparations. She had agreed with him then, thinking his reasons were because he would have felt embarrassed hanging around in a ladies dress shop. Now she felt it might be better to have him around. 'What if the lights go out again?' she asked, trying to think of any reason to keep him there. When it concerned the shop David had become Polly, her crutch to lean on.

'There's plenty of fuse wire back there. Get Sarah to go and buy a torch just in case.'

'All right,' she reluctantly agreed. She was being insecure and she knew it. It was not a very good side to be showing the man who had trusted her enough to put his money behind her, she realized, and forced a confident smile to her lips. 'Don't forget lunch,' she reminded jokingly, as he kissed Judith goodbye and went to the door. 'Or Polly,' she added. Polly was making sandwiches for them and David was

189

bringing her back with him at lunch time. They could have got something from the coffee bar at the bottom of the street, but Polly had wanted to do it and she had wanted her to feel a part of everything.

As David closed the door his expression said, Would I? And Rachel suddenly found herself smiling for real.

At nine thirty-five the bell on the door heralded the first customer. After that it never seemed to stop ringing for more than a few minutes at a time. A constant flow of customers filled the little shop. Some only came to look around the new establishment, but a good many went out carrying the large Wedgwood blue carrier bags with 'The Boutique' emblazoned across the front in silver lettering.

By the time David returned with Polly and her basket of sandwiches, all three members of staff were ready for a break to catch their breath.

They were in the midday lull, so Rachel stayed in the shop while David went into the back room with Judith and Sarah to have lunch.

'We've done well.' Pride glowed from her face.

'I'm glad to hear it, lass,' Polly said, as she flopped down on one of the two blue velvet chairs. She had had a good nose round and a grumble that there was nothing on the racks that she had not already seen at the cottage.

Rachel's smile broadened and she looked fondly on her old friend. She looked as pleased as punch and sat there as if she owned the place. It made Rachel wonder if she was also going around with a slightly silly smile on her face. Her earlier anxieties had been forgotten in her eagerness to serve her customers and she had to admit the look on Polly's face resembled the feeling she had inside.

The door bell pinged and two ladies came in. Polly immediately took on a grander appearance. She'd have made a good duchess, Rachel thought, and would have laughed, had it not have seemed rude in front of customers.

The two ladies departed, each carrying a large bag. They had both bought two dresses.

'That's the type of customer I want,' she confirmed with

feeling, and walked round to the front of the counter with a look of self-satisfaction. 'I think it's going to work, Polly. I know it's early days. But I think it's going to work.'

'It'll work, lass. Don't you fear. You've put your heart and soul into this. It won't let you down.'

Rachel smiled at her. If putting your heart and soul into something ensured success, then she was on to a winner. Everything she had in that department had gone into her work, and always would. She would never have anything that was more important to her, nothing that would take her mind off her clothes – her creations, her babies. Her eyes clouded with memory and she stared out into the street that was beginning to fill once more with the afternoon rush.

No, she ordered herself, and spun round to look at the dresses hanging on the rails, the suits stylishly displayed on mannequins, the two satin and lace nightdress and négligé sets pinned to the wall; made on an afterthought to see if there was a market for luxurious nightwear. *These* were her babies, the only ones she would ever have, the only ones she wanted.

The ping of the door bell brought her spinning round and she was grateful for the diversion to drag her away from her moroseness.

The afternoon went even better than the morning. She could not believe how much money they had taken, as she hurried across to the bank at the end of the day. In one day! she thought, smiling to herself. Of course every day was not going to be the same. The week days would just tick over. But if they did half as well every Saturday she would have no complaints.

As soon as they got home, Rachel took off the navy-blue suit and hung it in the wardrobe next to the cream dress David and Judith had given her at Christmas. She had not had the heart to take it back and change it, and had half-contemplated wearing it to the shop. It would have been a nice gesture to David and Judith, she had thought. But, although the dress had fitted like a glove, she had felt wrong in it: a little too feminine for her liking.

She ran her hand down the soft cream jersey and grimaced.

Then closed the wardrobe door, at the same time closing a door in her mind that seemed to be opening more and more of late. She could not understand why. But one part of her now wanted to put the dress on. The other part was terrified of what the dress turned her into.

Slipping into her old grey skirt and baggy jumper, she pushed the thoughts from her mind. They were not necessary, she told herself. Her life was all mapped out now, clearer than it had ever been. On Monday she would get up, put on her smart navy-blue suit, and go to work – just like a real businessman!

'You're not working tonight!' Sarah looked astonished when she found Rachel at the sewing machine. 'How can you? I'm shattered.' She stuck a ham salad by the side of the machine and flopped down on the floor with her own plate. 'Are you going to manage the shop by yourself during the week?'

'It won't be busy,' Rachel replied, without looking up. 'Saturday will be the busiest. And you and Judith will be there then.' Judith was to work every Saturday. But during the week she would just pop in when she felt like it. It was an arrangement that suited Rachel. She didn't want Judith wearing herself out and could see no real need for two of them to be there during the week. Even though she had set herself up with a new sewing machine in the shop's back room, she was confident she would be able to continue sewing and look after the customers.

'I could leave school.' Sarah looked hopeful.

'No you could not.' Rachel shot her sister a warning look. She could stop any ideas on that line. 'It's against the law. And even if it wasn't I wouldn't let you!'

Sarah pouted and stuck a large lettuce leaf in her mouth with her fingers.

Rachel wondered why it was you always wanted what you couldn't have. She would have given anything to stay on at school. Now she was giving Sarah that chance and she was making it very clear she was leaving at the first possible moment.

'I can work in the shop when I leave school. Can't I?'

'Yes,' Rachel gave a sigh of resignation and carried on sewing. 'If that's what you really want.' She wanted Sarah to have the chance to do what she wanted. If she wanted to work in the shop, why should she complain.

'It's what I want,' Sarah replied confidently. 'Maybe I could make some things, as well?'

Rachel looked impressed and nodded in agreement. Her little sister was growing up, and not for the worse this time, she thought. She smiled as she ran the needle down a long side seam. In some ways they were so different. Sarah had all the confidence. But she had all the determination. Maybe they'd make a good team, in the long run.

'Are you going out tonight?' she asked.

'To Sally's.' Sarah jumped up as if the thought had suddenly renewed her lost strength.

Half an hour later she was ready to go. She looked at Rachel, bent over the sewing machine, and shook her head in disbelief. 'You've got tomorrow,' she pointed out, as she was about to leave.

'Have a nice time,' Rachel called, without looking up from the sewing machine, the ham salad lying untouched by her side.

Chapter Fourteen

1967

'I won't hear of it!' Rachel shouted, in the manner that had become usual in the limited conversations she and Sarah now had.

'It's too late. I've already told the teachers I'm not stopping on.' Sarah tossed her long blond hair over her shoulders, her eyes unrepentantly peering from beneath her heavy fringe.

'I'll go and see the teachers for myself.' Rachel threw down the half-finished nightdress and glared at her sister. She did not need this, she told herself. The fashion show was only days away. Sarah knew that. She could have been a bit more considerate!

'You will not,' Sarah countered. 'I'm leaving school in two weeks time – whether you like it or not. If you won't let me work at the shop I'll get a job somewhere else!'

'Doing what? You'll have no qualifications. It's only for one year! Just get a few O levels and then see how you feel.' Sarah was bright, very bright, if only she would apply herself. All her teachers had said the same thing. The problem was Sarah would not apply herself. Rachel sighed in frustration. She had been a fool to let her see there was a job ready and waiting for her at the shop. It gave her no reason to push herself beyond the least possible schoolwork she could get away with.

It's your own fault, she told herself. She had no real objections to Sarah working in the shop. She just wished she would get a few exams behind her first, in case she found she didn't like it and wanted to change course. She should have made that clear right at the beginning, when she first told Sarah she could have the job. Now she was in a cleft stick. In the two years since opening, the shop had gone from strength to strength. But, unfortunately, Judith had deteriorated and was now confined to a wheelchair and no longer able to help, and Rachel had had to take on a part-time assistant. Even so, she was finding it difficult to keep up with all the work and it was obvious to Sarah that she was needed.

'I'm not staying on. School bores me. It's for kids.' Sarah dug her heels in and looked unrepentant.

And that was the problem, Rachel thought. Sarah was too old for her years. She thought she knew it all. Rachel sighed again and looked down at the crumpled heap of black satin lying on the floor where she had thrown it in temper. She had to get on. She had no time for silly arguments. 'Let's leave it for now,' she suggested, playing for time. 'We'll both think about it and discuss it again. Tomorrow.'

Sarah smiled grimly. 'There's nothing to discuss. And if you could drag yourself away from work for five minutes to take a look at the real me, you'd know that for yourself,' she insisted, and slammed out of the door.

Rachel watched sadly as her sister hurried past the window, head held high, her long-legged stride carrying her gracefully away. With a sigh she turned away and dropped her head into her hands, feeling a great need to cry and wash away the heaviness inside her. Her sister was a woman. At fifteen Sarah was more woman than she was at twenty-three. It was not just her height, which was now six inches more than her own meagre five feet three inches. There was nothing gangling in Sarah's appearance. She was confident and graceful and beautiful – too beautiful!

It frightened Rachel. All the advice, all the warnings she had intended to give her sister! It was too late now. They couldn't talk any more, only row. If she broached a subject, Sarah would fly off the handle, accuse her of being old-fashioned, a fuddy-duddy, out of touch. If Sarah tried to attempt a conversation, it was always the wrong time for her and she would snap back, her mind wrapped up in the sewing she was doing.

Sweeping the black satin up from the floor, she finished attaching the last piece of lace to the nightdress bodice, only to realize she had fixed it on inside out. The nightdress hit the floor for the second time. What was wrong with her? She never made mistakes! Furious with herself, she leapt up from the sewing machine, paced the room a couple of times, then hurried out of the door, needing someone to talk to.

Polly was in what had now become her usual position: sitting in a chair by the window. When she saw Rachel coming across the road, she waved, and her old face lit up in a welcoming smile. Rachel reciprocated and hurried to her door.

'How you feeling?' she asked, as she walked into the cosy front room. She studied her old friend's face for a moment, looking for signs of the pale weariness that seemed increasingly to be affecting her of late. Polly never got out of the cottage any more, her legs had finally limited her to hobbling about the confines of her own home.

'Not so bad, lass,' she replied brightly, and took the crocheted blanket from her knees and draped it over the little table by her side. She didn't like keeping it on in company. She thought it made her look like an invalid, which she'd never accept she almost was. 'Is something up?' she asked.

Rachel grinned. Every morning she looked in before going to the shop, to make sure Polly was all right. And every evening she always made time to spend an hour with her. She might have known her shrewd old friend would guess there was something troubling her, turning up in the middle of Sunday afternoon.

'No more than usual,' she replied heavily, and sank into one of the big armchairs.

Polly shuffled herself and her chair round to face her. 'Sarah?' she asked, shaking her head sadly.

'She's adamant she's leaving school. Won't listen to reason.' Rachel rubbed her forehead tiredly and let her head drop back against the crocheted antimacassar.

'Why don't you want her to leave school?' A frown wrinkled Polly's old brow and her eyes became intense little slits. Rachel sighed. She knew that expression well enough. And she had thought Polly would be on her side!

'If she doesn't like working in the shop she'll need

something behind her to get a decent job,' she said, and folded her arms, feeling defeated. 'She's clever enough, when she wants to be. It's such a waste.'

'She already knows what it's like working there,' Polly pointed out evenly. Then added suspicion to her voice. 'Is there something wrong with her working in the shop?'

'Well . . . no. But I think she's taking the easy way out.'

'Easy!' Polly gave a great gust of laughter. Rachel smiled. It had been a long time since she had heard the famous laugh. 'I don't see anything easy in all the work you put in,' Polly continued, after catching her breath.

'But it is *my* shop!' Rachel replied, much too quickly.

'Aye,' Polly returned knowledgeably. 'And you've hit the nail on the head there, lass. It's yours and woe betide anybody that tries to interfere. Are you sure you're not just frightened Sarah might try to take over?'

Rachel looked put out. 'I don't know what you mean!'

'It's a good boss that knows how to delegate. A bad boss thinks nobody can do it better than themselves. Let Sarah work for you. Let her learn enough to be able to take over running the shop and you concentrate on making the stuff. You said yourself she's clever enough.'

Rachel felt cornered. She looked dubious, as she said, 'And what happens if we fall out and she throws a paddy? Do you think I could trust her under those circumstances?'

'If you let her have enough control to make her feel needed, I think you'll find a very different Sarah underneath.'

'Let her have control!' she gasped, jumping out of the chair with the need to pace the floor. Her irritation increased when she found Polly's clutter of furniture hindering her path. 'It's too ridiculous,' she snapped. 'How can you even suggest it?'

'You cut her out,' Polly said, taking no notice of Rachel's ill humour. 'You cut everybody out, when it comes to your blessed frocks.'

Her words reminded Rachel of Sarah's earlier condemnation of not taking time to look at her properly.

'Let Sarah be a part of it,' Polly continued. 'She wants to

be. You'll have to admit, sooner or later, that you need help, and you should be able to trust your own flesh and blood better than a stranger.'

Rachel stared at Polly for a long time. 'Am I being selfish?' she finally asked.

'Not selfish, lass. Just determined to prove something to yourself. I can understand that. *I* know why!' She laid emphasis on the last. 'But you've done it now. You're successful and it's about time you stopped fighting Micky's ghost.'

Rachel flopped back into the chair, her hands clenched tightly before her in the tension brought on by Polly's last words. 'Is that what I'm doing?' she asked, her voice and expression bleak.

'Aye, lass, it is.' All of a sudden Polly sounded very old and weary. 'I've always known it. I hoped you'd come to realize it for yourself . . . before now. But you haven't. So somebody's got to tell you, for your own good. Nobody can work the way you work and not pay for it.'

'But I feel fine,' she insisted. It was not an argument she was eager to accept, especially the part about Micky. If Polly was right it meant he had done some good. That was something she would never allow herself to believe.

'In body you might feel all right,' Polly persisted, knowing Rachel would not be easily swayed. 'But what about in mind? Why do you think you've been so short tempered with Sarah. You'll end up having a nervous breakdown, or worse still, like your mother!'

Rachel went cold on the thought. 'But Sarah's only fifteen,' she protested.

'Stop judging Sarah on yourself,' Polly said firmly. 'She's a lot different to how you were at that age.'

Rachel could not dispute that. In fact they were so different there were times when she found it hard to believe they came from the same parentage.

'Maybe you're right,' she reluctantly agreed, but doubt echoed in her frown.

'I'm right, lass,' Polly confirmed, weariness suddenly

slurring her words. 'There are times when I wish I wasn't. But I know you too well.'

Rachel smiled tightly into the old eyes. 'And *I* know you too well, Polly Webster. You're tired. I'm wearing you out and that *is* being selfish.'

'You haven't got a selfish bone in your body,' she quickly denied. 'If you had you'd never have looked after me the way you've always done.' She smiled, her wrinkled old face lighting with affection, and Rachel's heart tightened with love.

'You'll find your rainbow and its pot of gold,' Polly continued, her voice getting weaker by the moment. 'Just trust old Polly.'

Rachel's smile was filled with the emotion that swelled inside her body for her old friend. She recalled the time, so long ago now, when Polly had first told her of the gold at the bottom of the rainbow. Waiting for special people! She had not felt special then and she did not feel any more special now. 'Maybe I've already found it,' she said quietly. The Boutique had gone better than she could ever have imagined, ever have hoped. She was presenting her first fashion show at the end of next week. What more could she ask for!

'No you haven't,' Polly stated, and seemed to revive herself. Though Rachel wasn't sure she was completely aware of what she was saying, when she went on, 'You don't know the half of it. You'll get a surprise one day. A big surprise. When you're least expecting it.' Her voice drifted away and her head lolled sideways.

Rachel smiled sadly. Poor old Polly, she thought fondly. She had become a prisoner in her own home. The only entertainment she had was the television and watching people walk up and down the hill. She got up from the chair and put the blanket back over Polly's knees. Then she quietly let herself out. As she crossed the road she pondered the unfairness of life. Polly, slowly being drawn to the inevitable end. Judith, her vitality stolen from her and reduced to dependence on a wheelchair. And the likes of Micky Caradine, now thankfully living in Derby so she did not have to set eyes on him too often, careering around in a flashy sports car and living the life of Reilly. It didn't seem right. But, as Polly would have said, it was the way of things.

By the time Sarah arrived home, Rachel was ready for her. The little kitchen table was set for two, the kettle was on the boil and a pan of spaghetti and a pan of bolognese sauce simmered on the gas rings. Rachel wasn't too keen on the meal, but it was Sarah's favourite, and it was cooked to perfection.

'What's this?' Sarah's surprise quickly turned to suspicion.

'I want to talk to you. Sit down.' Rachel flapped her hand at the table. Then turned away to dish up. 'We seem to have lost the art of talking. Properly, not shouting and screaming at each other.' After much deliberation she had realized there was something in what Polly had said. Sarah remained silent. Rachel hoped they had not drifted too far apart to ever get back together again. Sarah's face was not very encouraging. She could see her sister was of the opinion she was about to get another lecture.

'We need spoons,' Sarah suddenly said.

'What?' Rachel, about to sit down, stopped herself halfway. It had not been what she was expecting and for a moment was at a loss to know what she was talking about.

'We need spoons,' Sarah repeated stiffly. 'For the spaghetti. You've given us knives!' She finally put in the full explanation.

'Oh yes.' The penny dropped and Rachel picked up the knives and exchanged them for spoons. Then she sat down, silently thoughtful, her mind revolving over the right way to begin.

'I'm not going back on my decision about school,' Sarah asserted, getting the first say.

'I might not be asking you to.' Rachel attempted to reclaim the upper hand.

'*Might!* What exactly does that mean? If you're thinking of offering me conditions, you can forget it. I won't have them.'

Rachel gave a silent sigh. She had had everything planned to perfection and had lost control already. Sarah just would

200

not listen. She was not interested in anything she had to say. She suddenly began to doubt Polly's wisdom. It was in frustration when she hit out, 'I could be getting on with the mountain of work I have, instead of sitting here trying to talk sense into your silly head.'

'Well, don't let me stop you,' Sarah blazed. She stood up so quickly her chair toppled backwards. 'Don't let anything come between you and your precious creations.' She tossed her head with haughty contempt and stalked out of the room. But not before Rachel had seen the glisten of tears in her eyes.

In an instant she was up and running after her, suddenly fearing this was their last chance, if they did not heal the rift now, they never would. She caught Sarah at the foot of the stairs. 'I'm sorry,' she gasped, feeling her own emotion about to choke her. She grabbed Sarah's arm to stop her going up the stairs.

Sarah tried to brush her hand away.

'Don't turn your back on me,' Rachel begged. She wondered what she was saying. Why shouldn't her sister turn her back on her? *She* had turned her back on her, making the shop and her sewing more important. She could see it all now. Every word Polly had spoken had been the truth. She had been so wrapped up in her own problems she had never taken the time to care for Sarah properly. In her heart she had cared, but she had never let it come out of her heart, never let it show to the person who meant the most to her, because she was fuelled with a burning obsession to be someone. Someone who commanded respect. Someone with authority. Not because she wanted the world's approval, but because she wanted to be in a position to look down on Micky Caradine. She wanted to make him fear her as much as she had feared him. Make him squirm every time he thought about her, because she was a somebody and somebodies were not the kind of people you took into a field and treated like dirt. Polly had been right about that, as well.

'What's the point, Rachel?' Sarah's eyes were wide with the tears she stubbornly refused to let fall.

A tight band closed around Rachel's heart. She had

201

alienated her own sister so much that she would not show her true misery in front of her. It was all an act, the hardness, the confident indifference, put on to keep her real feelings hidden away, where they could not be hurt. Sarah was acting the same way as she herself did over Micky Caradine, putting on a front. It was a chilling realization. It tore Rachel in two.

'I want to talk to you,' she quickly said, feeling her whole world slipping away from her grasp. 'I've been doing a lot of thinking. I've been wrong. I know that now. But give me a chance to put things right. You can leave school with my blessing. And you can work in the shop.' She was blabbering at the end, the words tumbling out as she raced to get everything said before Sarah finally turned her back and walked away. Which she expected her to do, and could not have blamed her.

Silence followed. It was several moments before Rachel realized Sarah's cool scorn had turned to an expression of quiet interest.

It was Sarah who finally spoke. 'You'll let me work in the shop?' she questioned uncertainly.

'Yes.' Rachel's voice held all the certainty for both of them. 'And no more hassle about staying at school.'

'Promise?'

'Promise,' Rachel repeated.

A smile pushed Sarah's tears completely away. 'I'll not let you down.' Her voice, full of childish enthusiasm, reminded Rachel of the Sarah she thought she had lost.

Rachel smiled then, her emotion coiled tightly inside her. 'I know you won't,' she said, and Sarah moved forward and wrapped her in a big hug. It was so good to feel the closeness of another human being, a closeness that was sadly lacking in Rachel's life, that it was her undoing. Tears began to spill down her cheeks. 'Look what you're doing to me?' She shoved Sarah away and dashed her hands across her cheeks. 'That spaghetti will be cold by now.'

Sarah laughed. 'I'll warm it up. We can discuss the terms for my new job while we're waiting.' She hesitated, looked uncertain. 'Unless you have to get back to sewing?' she added carefully.

Rachel shook her head. 'No. I'm doing no more sewing tonight. I think I've learned a lesson today, the hard way.'

Sarah frowned and Rachel pushed her towards the kitchen. 'I thought you were going to get the spaghetti warmed up?' she said, having no intentions of going into the details of the lesson she had learned. 'And what are these terms we have to discuss?'

'Oh,' Sarah shrugged and grinned. 'You know – like what the wages will be.' She ducked through the door a moment before Rachel could catch her a playful tap on the shoulder.

After that it was a lovely evening. Sarah did not go out to meet her friends and Rachel did not pick up a piece of material all night. They sat in the upstairs sitting room and talked the night away.

Just like old times, Rachel thought, as she switched off the light and climbed into bed. She wondered why Polly had not put her straight before today. It was not like Polly to hold back on her opinions, no matter how delicate the subject.

A small chink had been left in the curtains and a bright star peeped through. She lay still, watching the star, feeling it was looking back at her. It was a good omen, she told herself. Like Polly's rainbows with hidden pots of gold. She smiled into the darkness, recalling Polly's prophecy of a big surprise. She wondered if it was true that Polly had powers beyond the bounds of normal understanding. They had never talked about it. Her father had always called Polly a witch and forbidden his children to have anything to do with her. Getting to know and love Polly over the years had made Rachel forget her father's warning and the stories that used to travel round the village about Polly's 'gift' as it had been called.

She took one last look at the star then turned over. If Polly had powers, they were good ones, she thought. A witch? Or a pious hypocrite? She knew which one she would choose every time, was her last thought, before she slipped into the most peaceful sleep she had had in months.

*   *   *

Rachel stood back and studied the display of nightwear and underwear for the fashion show. It sold well. But she wasn't sure how profitable exclusive lingerie was going to be. As if echoing her thoughts, a voice spoke in her ear.

'I still think you're mad showing those,' Sarah said.

Rachel shook her head and grimaced. She remained silent, unwilling to admit she might have got something wrong.

'What happens if you get a big order? Who's going to make them?' Sarah stressed pointedly.

'I'm not in the market for big orders.' Her clothes were exclusive. She never made the same thing twice. That was why her customers always came back.

'You don't go around showing your knickers,' Sarah stated baldly. 'Surely you could make a few pairs of those the same!'

Rachel smiled at her sister's dry humour. Then turned away from the lingerie rail, dismissing the subject. They were here now, down on the programme. It was too late to change her mind.

'Is that everything?' she asked, walking over to inspect a large box of shoes and giving Sarah a smile. She had been a great help with the show. Giving in over the shop and school *had* turned her into a different person.

'All except the models,' Sarah said.

Rachel's smile vanished. She spun round to the dressing tables. 'Aren't they all here?' she asked worriedly, looking quickly down the row of scantily clad girls fixing hair and make-up with the help of the beautician. There were five. There should have been six! Her heart sank. 'Who is it?'

'Rosie,' Sarah replied, looking resigned.

Rachel immediately turned her attention to the programme, looking to see who could fill Rosie's place. There was no-one; not without changing everything around. Which could prove disastrous at short notice. The models only had a few minutes to change. The announcer only had the written details in correct running order. The woman had no idea of the models' names. Mess the outfits around, cut some out, and the whole thing could turn into a farce.

She had the image of a svelte model slinking down the catwalk in black silk underwear, accompanied by the announcer's voice describing the perfect business suit. She shuddered and groaned. It was too awful to imagine. She looked at Sarah. 'Go and get me a cup of tea, coffee, anything. I've got to think of something.'

She was sitting on an upturned crate, still trying to think of something, when Sarah came back. Her arms were held wide, a plastic cup in each hand. She was walking carefully, so as not to spill any. Her mini skirt showed the grace of her long legs. Her head, even with the danger of the spilling coffee, was held high and proud. She navigated the clutter of boxes and chairs without once dropping her gaze.

Sarah was tall, elegant – about Rosie's size! The idea came to Rachel in an instant and she did not give herself time to change her mind.

'Still no Rosie?' Sarah asked.

'It doesn't matter. I've found another model.' She whipped the coffee cups from Sarah's hands. 'You haven't got time for this. Get yourself dolled up.'

'What!' Sarah gasped, looking stunned.

'Get your face made-up. You are now a model, little sister.' The last was said with amusement, as she looked up into Sarah's face several inches above her own. 'Don't argue.' She quickly lifted a hand to stop the protest she saw forming on Sarah's lips. 'There's no other way. Besides, I'm confident you can do it. You're a natural.'

Sarah did not look so sure. Nevertheless she went obediently to the empty dressing table.

'Perfect!' Rachel beamed with pleasure. Sarah looked every inch the confident lady, as she pirouetted in a dusky pink mini-dress and matching duster coat. Her hair was fixed in a high top knot, making her look much older. 'Classic,' Rachel breathed under her breath. Sarah was stunning and she felt a moment of doubt. She had tried to keep her sister a little girl. Now, because it suited her, she was pushing her the other way.

'How's that?' Sarah struck a haughty pose.

Rachel laughed, and her doubts were forgotten. 'I said you were a natural.'

The show was at an end, the models all out on the catwalk together for the grand finale, before David appeared behind the scenes.

'Mary Quant! Who's she?' he joked, brandishing a bottle of champagne in one hand, glasses in the other. Had she not known for herself, the smile on his face would have told Rachel how successful the evening had been.

'Don't exaggerate,' she scoffed good naturedly. 'Where's Judith?' she asked, as she tossed the no-longer-needed programme aside. It was strange to see him alone, not pushing the wheelchair that had become Judith's only means of getting about outside the house.

His smile vanished. 'She didn't feel up to it.' His entire frame seemed to diminish right before her eyes. Then he took hold of himself and the smile was back. 'She said I had to take her a glass of champagne home.'

'You'd better get it opened then,' she said, forcing herself to sound flippant. His manner gave her the feeling Judith was worse than he was admitting. She felt suddenly guilty. With all the extra work for the show she had not seen much of Judith in the last weeks. Been too busy! she thought regretfully.

'Where's mine?' Sarah enquired, eyeing the champagne with great interest, as she came through the curtains with all the other models.

'You're too young.' Rachel tried to look stern, but failed. The picture her sister made contradicted the comment. She was wearing a red chiffon cocktail dress. Its slender lines clung to her lithe body and the low neckline, edged with sparkling rhinestones, made the most of her assets. She looked anything but childlike.

'You look beautiful,' David said, echoing Rachel's sentiments. 'I got a shock when I saw you walk out. What happened?'

'It's a long story,' Rachel said, once again asking herself what she had done. She had allowed Sarah to be a model and show herself off as the desirable creature she was. In one evening she had turned her back on all the insecurities, all the worries for Sarah's safety. Just because it suited her own needs. She did not feel very proud of herself.

'Come on, David,' Sarah urged, taking the glasses from his hand. 'Open up. Take no notice of big sis. She thinks I'm still seven.' She laughed affectionately at Rachel. 'If I can't celebrate tonight, when can I?' She looked down at the red dress. 'Can I keep this?'

'No you can't!' Rachel quickly replied, but she was laughing as she spoke. 'But we can all celebrate,' she declared. Sarah had been marvellous tonight; stepping into Rosie's shoes without making any mistakes. And they had all worked hard towards the show. They deserved a celebration now it was all over.

The popping of David's champagne cork was the first of many. Rachel made fifteen sales from members of the audience who came backstage to grab something they had immediately fallen in love with. She was also, much to Sarah's amusement, approached by a buyer from a large chain of shops who was interested in the lingerie.

'I told you so!' Sarah delighted in saying. 'You can't make exclusive knickers.'

'I can do exactly as I want to do.' Rachel took on a stubborn stance.

'Sarah might have a point there,' David said, looking interested. 'There's no law that says you have to make every garment yourself.'

'What are you suggesting?' Her stubbornness changed to irritation. It was not like David to interfere. She had done very well following her own ideas. Her instincts had proved spot-on every time. She did not welcome interference; not even from David or Sarah. 'You'll have me opening a sweatshop next,' she said mulishly.

'It's worth considering,' David continued.

Rachel looked shocked. 'Don't be ridiculous. People buy from me because they know my garments are unique. If you want to wear the same as every other person on the street there are plenty of chains around.'

'I don't mean for the dresses,' David explained. 'I mean the lingerie. Underwear and nightwear, surely, is not so important.'

'I already told her you don't go around flashing your knickers at everybody,' Sarah informed him, obviously pleased she had found an ally.

Rachel grimaced. She wished Sarah would not keep saying knickers so often. She wondered if her sister had drunk too much champagne. Then remembered she had been saying the word before touching a drop.

'It's something to think about, Rachel.' David had on his serious business voice.

She stared at him for a long moment. 'Perhaps,' she finally said, realizing he was expecting a reply; but having no intention of wasting a moment's time on it.

Feeling a sense of loss now that it was all over, Rachel made a final check to make sure nothing had been forgotten. Her first fashion show, she thought. Perhaps her only one. She would never have thought of holding a show if the local Red Cross had not made the suggestion. She was pleased it had been a success and had boosted their funds for them.

'Come on,' she said, urging both David and Sarah to the door.

'Can I be a model again?' Sarah asked, as they walked across the car park.

'We'll see.' Rachel was not prepared to commit herself. She looked up at the stars and moon and wondered once again if she had done the right thing in letting Sarah model for her. It was too late to worry now, she told herself, and turned to David. 'Thank you for coming.' She knew it must have cost him something to come alone and leave Judith at home. She found it rather worrying that Judith had not come to the show. She had always shown such interest in the shop and it had proved to be the lifeline that David had hoped it would be.

'Nothing would have made me miss it,' David said with feeling.

Rachel smiled as she climbed into the passenger seat of his car, happily unaware of how those words were going to haunt her for years to come. He would have made a wonderful father, she thought, and wondered if that was why they got on so well together: she looking for the father she never had, he the daughter.

'Straight home? Or do you want to come and share another bottle of champagne with Judith?' David asked.

'Oh, the champagne,' Sarah insisted, before Rachel could open her mouth.

David laughed. 'Champagne it is then,' he said, and turned the car out onto the road and headed home.

The full moon lit their way, its brightness almost as clear as daylight. No-one in the car spoke, but they all radiated a silent contentment, a shared glow of success.

Rachel looked out of the window at a bright star on the horizon. A magic star, she thought, feeling it was the same star that had peeped through her curtains the other night. It was a lucky star, she decided. Like Polly's rainbow.

It was not until the car turned down Mulberry Bush Lane, that she realized how wrong she had been. In an instant her euphoria vanished and she felt as if icy water had been plunged down her spine. Fear widened her eyes, as she turned to David and saw the same stark disbelief on his own face. Suddenly all she could hear were his parting words of the show: 'Nothing would have made me miss it!' She wanted to clamp her hands over her ears, but she knew it would have done no good. The words were engraved on her brain and nothing would erase them.

Her eyes flew back to the road, praying she was wrong. It was a dream. She had fallen to sleep she tried to tell herself. But she was wide awake and nothing had changed. It had not been some sick trick of the bright moonlight, whose shadows seemed suddenly to grow and stretch and reach out like grasping fingers. There, by the side of the wall bordering the river, its shining chrome picked out in ghostly relief, was Judith's wheelchair – empty!

Judith was nowhere to be seen.

Chapter Fifteen

No! No! No! Rachel wasn't sure if she was speaking or if the word was only screaming round inside her head. Tension filled the car: from herself, from the still and silent Sarah in the back seat, from the man by her side, whose knuckles looked bloodless as he clung fiercely to the steering wheel and stamped hard on the accelerator, making the car travel the last few yards at breakneck speed.

The brakes squealed as the car skidded awkwardly to a halt and David had the door open and was out almost before it had stopped.

Rachel was close behind him, and reached his side as he leaped halfway up the wall, and screamed, 'Judith!' his eyes frantically trying to take in every inch of the silver grey water at the same moment.

'It's probably a mistake,' she said, trying to convince herself. It had to be a mistake! She spun round to the house, panic growing with every second. The curtains were open, the downstairs' lights all on, giving a clear view into the rooms. There was no movement, no signs of life. The house emitted an aura of emptiness and she felt her heart sink even lower than it already was. Nevertheless, she said, 'She's probably inside. Go and look.' And she took hold of his arm and tried to pull him down from the wall. 'Go and look!' she repeated, panic filling her voice when he refused to move. She began to fear he might suddenly plunge into the water himself.

He turned then, looking at her with a bleakness that chilled her bones.

'Go and look!' she pleaded. 'You don't know for sure!'

As if suddenly seeing some sense in what she was saying, he jumped from the wall and raced across the road. Sarah dithered by the car for a moment, looking from Rachel to

David. Then, seeming to come to a decision, ran after him as he reached the door and once more screamed, 'Judith!'

Rachel stayed by the wall. She felt guilty for sending him into the house and raising his hopes. The evidence was too clear for any doubts. But she had been so afraid he would go into the river to try and find Judith.

'Oh David!' she whispered, again recalling his words as they had got into his car: 'Nothing would have made me miss it!' Nothing! She reached for the top of the wall, found a good foothold and pulled herself up.

Though it was summer and the river was low, that part from the bridge to the weir was always deep and dangerous. She shuddered. If Judith was in there, there was no hope. And she didn't think there was much hope that she wasn't in there.

She searched the gently rolling silver-black surface and pleaded for a miracle. Her hands began to tremble and she clutched the cold stone wall more tightly, but the tremor only moved further up her arms and she had to lean her body heavily against the wall to stop herself falling off. She could not believe how quickly things had changed. She had felt so happy at the fashion show, when she had had no right to feel happy. It all seemed so obscene now. To think they had been drinking champagne, while Judith . . .

That way of thinking was doing no good now, she told herself, and leaned forward to see beneath the wall. An old oil can and several bits of unrecognizable rubbish bobbed on the surface fifteen to twenty feet below her, but nothing else. She looked across to the weir. The water running over the top was reduced to a trickle and several tree branches and what looked like an old tea chest were trapped against the edge.

She had to be here! she thought, anxiously scanning the area from the bridge to the weir. There wasn't enough water to take her over the top. It was then that she saw it, and even though it was what she was looking for and she had known she would find it, her heart missed a beat. 'Oh Judith!' she moaned, as she stared at the far side of the weir, her eyes unable to move from their grisly find. An entire tree with sturdy trunk and crooked branches reaching up into the night and stretching over the surface, was lodged at a right angle to the weir. Inside the branches, as if imprisoned in a cage, was a small light-coloured bundle.

Tears misted Rachel's eyes and she clung desperately to the wall, as the shaking in her arms increased violently. She could no longer see properly. But she knew she was right, knew exactly what her clouded vision was staring at. She even knew what Judith was wearing: a cream linen trouser suit which she had made for her. It had been the first new outfit she had wanted in over two years. She had wanted it for something special, she said.

A great sob grew inside her chest and she almost fell off the wall. Special! she thought, realizing with horror that Judith must have been planning this for a long time.

'She's not there,' David announced unnecessarily, his voice seeming to tear from his throat as he bounded back across the road with Sarah still close behind him.

Rachel pulled herself together and stepped down from the wall. He was going to need her, she told herself, and turned slowly to face him. 'I know,' she said simply, not knowing what other way to say it.

'Where?' he demanded, taking her roughly by the arm and almost shaking the answer from her.

She could not speak as her throat clogged with the tension that seemed to flow right through his hand and into her. Slowly she lifted her arm and pointed to the tree on the weir. Then they both stood like statues, gazing at the ghostly moonlit bundle swaying gently within its prison of gnarled branches.

It was Sarah who broke the grim spell that held them. 'Shouldn't we be doing something?' she asked, her voice clogged with tears.

David did not move, did not speak.

Rachel looked at him for a long moment. Shock was rendering him dumb, she realized. 'Go and phone the police,' she suddenly ordered her sister, knowing David was incapable and she had to take control. 'Then stay in the house,' she added more gently, wanting Sarah to be spared as much as possible. She also wanted David to come away and go into the house. Judith was firmly trapped by the branches and she wasn't going anywhere. There was no need for him to stand staring and tearing himself apart. But when she took his arm and tried to pull him round, he shook his head, refusing to take his eyes from the pathetic bundle which was all that was left of his wife.

Rachel wished a cloud would come and cover the moon, cutting off its bright light and hiding the weir in darkness. But there wasn't a cloud in the sky and the moon remained like a huge spotlight, laughing at their distress.

'It's too late,' she said, keeping hold on his arm. 'It's too late. You can't do anything.' She felt dreadful saying these things to him, but fear made her speak out. She still felt he might suddenly take it upon himself to try and get Judith out. And if he did he would be killing himself, as well. The river was such a long way beneath the wall she would never be able to get him out again before help arrived.

'The police will be here soon,' she said, assuring herself as much as David, and tightening her grip on his arm.

It was less than ten minutes before the first panda car came down the lane. But it felt more like ten hours to Rachel, as she clung to him feeling the tension in him grow steadily. And when the uniformed sergeant stepped out of the blue and white car, she felt she might collapse with relief.

It was a large funeral. Rachel found it ironic that all the so-called friends who had shunned Judith in her final months, saw fit to crawl out of the woodwork now, when it was too late.

David was like a ghost. His skin had a frighteningly grey pallor and dark rings circled his eyes. She didn't think he had eaten or slept over the past four days. His misery cloaked him and it terrified her. She remembered so clearly the day he had talked of Judith wanting to die rather than become an invalid. And his parting comment at the fashion show wouldn't be helping to ease the burden of his guilt. Every time she looked at him she knew he was condemning himself for leaving Judith alone.

As he stood at the graveside with bowed head and slumping shoulders, she wanted to scream at him to cry. He wouldn't. He seemed to be beyond even that most natural of releases. She had the awful feeling he hadn't cried since the night of Judith's death. It wasn't a good sign. He was holding it all tightly inside him, where it could do the most damage.

She sighed and glanced sideways at Sarah. Tears were streaming down her face and in the baggy grey skirt and black cardigan she looked like the fifteen year old she was. The skirt was borrowed from herself and the cardigan from Polly. The only thing Sarah owned in black was the dress she had appeared in at Christmas two years ago, and Rachel had been quick to point out she was not wearing that!

Sarah snuffled loudly and she handed her a clean paper handkerchief and gave her a little smile. Unfortunately, when she had sent Sarah into the house alone so she wouldn't have to stand and look at Judith's body, Sarah had found the note Judith had left. It had upset her greatly and the funeral was bringing it all back.

It hadn't been a long note. 'My Darling David, Forgive me. Remember me as I was, before. I will always love you, your dearest Judith'.

It had been as he read it that David broke down. Handing the note to Rachel he had dropped on to the settee, cradled his head in his hands and sobbed. And without thinking what she was doing, she had gone to him and wrapped her arms around him and they had cried together. It never occurred to her that she was committing an intimacy she had forbidden herself. At that moment David had needed comfort and it had been the most natural reaction to his need.

Rachel's vision blurred as she looked at the enormous bouquet of red roses from David. Fifteen dozen in all, one dozen for every year of their marriage. He had loved her so much, she thought, and felt so very sad for him. Then suddenly felt sad for herself: there would be no-one to put roses on her grave!

'Come on.' She nudged Sarah's arm and turned slowly away. David's brother, Malcolm, was looking after him and she had no wish to linger there. In a way she felt as guilty as he did. If it hadn't been for the fashion show he would never have left Judith alone. She hadn't been alone for several months. He had always stayed with her in the evenings and, since she had stopped coming to the shop, he had employed a nurse to be with her through the day when he was at work. The fashion show had been what Judith had been waiting for, she realized sadly. She sighed heavily and thought, if only!

'Are you all right?' Sarah asked, looking concerned.

Rachel gave a thin smile and nodded her head. 'Yes. Are you?'

Sarah nodded. She had stopped crying but her eyes looked red and swollen. 'I wish today was over.'

'So do I,' Rachel agreed with feeling. 'So do I.'

It was almost three hours later before the first people left the funeral party. And that was what it had been for most of them, Rachel thought with disgust. A party! She looked around the room in despair. Dirty plates, cups, saucers, glasses and overflowing ashtrays littered David's lounge. She hoped the hangers-on would not be staying much longer and made a pointed gesture of looking at her watch. It was two minutes to five. She wished the old mill clock had still been there. No-one could have missed its loud chimes telling you clearly what hour it was.

She looked around for David, but could not see him anywhere. Sarah was sitting by the window, looking out as if reliving that night all over again. Rachel sighed. She wondered how many times David had done the same thing. Every night and every morning, and many times in between. The beautiful view from his window, prized by all the residents of Mulberry Bush Lane, had turned into a nightmare for him. She hoped he wouldn't stay there and let the memory haunt him, and, becoming worried where he might be, went to find him.

After searching the dining room and kitchen she went into the garden. But he was nowhere to be seen. She was on the point of panic, as she walked down the paved path running between the two large lawns, when she saw him through the window of his study. He was ensconced in the small room with Polly.

Rachel smiled. If anyone could get him talking, Polly could. She had been concerned about her old friend attending the funeral. She had not been out of the house for so long she had worried what the strain might do to her. But Polly had insisted she could get herself to a car at the gate and back again and lean on Rachel to get herself into church for the service. She had stayed in the car at the cemetery, Rachel feeling the long walk to the grave too much for her. She also considered that part of the ceremony too upsetting for Polly.

She stood for a time, watching them. David's head was no longer bent. He was looking straight into Polly's eyes and was obviously speaking in words of more than one syllable. Rachel turned away and began to walk down the path once more. She had been so anxious about David she had not realized Polly was also missing.

'Where's David?' Sarah called, looking worried as she ran up the path. 'No-one can find him.'

'It's all right. He's with Polly.'

'Oh good.'

It was a simple statement, but one that made Rachel stare at her sister. She understood far more than she gave her credit for, she realized. The silly young girl had well and truly gone. She smiled tightly. One more week and Sarah would be a working girl, an adult.

'What's the matter?' Sarah peered uncertainly at her odd expression.

'I hope your life is a happy one,' she said, surprising herself as much as Sarah.

Sarah smiled fondly. 'Course it is,' she said, and wrapped her arm around her shoulders. 'Come on back inside. Before we're both crying again.'

Rachel smiled and nodded in agreement. Her sister really was growing up, and she was warmed by the knowledge.

'Will you be all right?' Rachel looked anxiously into David's pale face. She wasn't happy about leaving him alone there.

He had seemed a bit more alive since receiving Polly's wise counsel, but there was still the bleakness in his eyes that chilled her.

'I'll be all right,' he replied, not very convincingly.

For a moment she wished all the funeral party, which she had been eager to get rid of, would come back and prolong the moment for a few more hours. But they would still have had to go at some time, she told herself, and David would have to be left alone. He wasn't a baby. But right then he looked as if he needed someone to take his hand and tell him what to do.

Polly patted his arm. 'Remember what I was saying. And if you want to talk some more . . . You know where I am.' She took hold of his brother's arm on one side and Sarah's on the other and let them help her out of the house to the car.

Rachel stood looking at him, not knowing what to say. She had to go but it was the last thing she wanted to do. She glanced round and saw the river through the window. It was too close for comfort while he was wrapped in the depths of his misery. If he should decide to follow Judith . . .

'You could come and stay with us for a few days. If you wanted to,' she suddenly said. She gave a nervous little shrug. 'We could turn the sitting room back into a bedroom.'

He shook his head and a weak smile stretched his pale lips. 'No. I will be all right.'

She shrugged again. 'Well, remember where Polly is.' He needed someone to talk to and she knew Polly would always know the right thing to say, and would find no embarrassment in saying it. Not like all the other mourners, herself included, who had passed on brief condolences, then seemed stuck for words. 'And if you change your mind, you know where we are.'

He nodded his head and she reluctantly turned away and followed the others.

David's brother was taking them home and, as she climbed into his car, her heart sank as the sound of the river filled her ears and she could not stop herself looking up. The wall seemed so near, the road suddenly so narrow. She closed the

217

door with more force than was necessary and sighed heavily.

'All right?' Polly questioned, peering round from the front passenger seat with a frown, as the car moved away.

'No!' Rachel sounded hopeless. 'He can't stay there.' Not with that view out of his front window. He'd never be able to look at the weir again without seeing Judith's body floating there.

'Don't worry,' Malcolm Morrell said. 'If I can't persuade him to come and stay with us for a few days, I'll stay here with him.'

'Thank you,' Rachel replied, as she stared bleakly at the back of David's brother's head. But she had meant he can't live there, ever. A few days wasn't any good. She fell silent and the car remained that way for the rest of the way home.

David went to stay with his brother initially for two weeks, which stretched into one month, then two, then three. At the end of the third month he came to see Rachel.

'I'm selling the house,' he announced, the moment he stepped through the door.

Rachel was pleased with the decision to sell up and make a fresh start. But when he said he never wanted to go inside the house on Mulberry Bush Lane again, she wasn't so sure he had come to terms with Judith's death enough to make that decision.

'Will you arrange everything for me?' he asked, and the desolation in his eyes made it difficult for her to refuse.

'But what about all your things?' She looked worried. He was not doing the right thing. Selling the house had been what she wanted him to do. But not this way. He was so changed, a pale shadow of the man he had been.

'Is there anything for sale over this side of the river?' he asked, ignoring her question. 'I'd like to stay in the village. But not over there!'

'Look. Sit down.' She swept the sewing clutter from the table and pulled the two chairs around so they could sit down. Placing her elbows on the table she clasped her hands and stared at them anxiously. 'I think you should sell,' she finally began. 'I wouldn't like to think of you there alone. But . . .'

'I never want to look out of that window again!' he put in, taking her aback with his viciousness. 'Will you do it? Arrange the sale, see to the furniture . . . everything?'

She gave a sigh.

'Please! Rachel. There's no-one else I can ask.'

No, she thought. There was no-one else who would be daft enough to do it for him when he should be doing it himself. She wanted to refuse. But then she thought about the shop and how, if it hadn't been for him, she might still not have one. 'All right,' she reluctantly agreed, feeling she owed him this much.

Within a month she had Mulberry Bush Lane sold and all his furniture moved into the big house which had come up for sale at the top of the hill, above her own cottage.

On the day he arrived to take up residence, she was waiting for him.

'We can move things round if you don't like the way I've arranged it,' she said, as he looked bleakly round his new sitting room. She hoped he still had enough enthusiasm left to want to make his own decisions on the layout of the house. She had not known if she should be trying to make it look similar to the old one, or arrange it completely different. She had settled for half and half, arranging the furniture differently but putting all Judith's treasured porcelain in the same little groups as she had had them.

'Perhaps I should have had all new furniture,' he replied flatly.

It was not the response Rachel wanted to hear. 'No you should not!' she quickly replied. She had given in over the bedroom and refurnished that one room for him. But he needed the rest, the memories, to make him come to terms with his loss. Judith could not be wiped away by having a big bonfire and the sooner he realized that the better he would be. When he did, the bits and pieces that had belonged to them both would mean everything to him. They would remind him of the happy times and help him forget his guilt.

'This is beautiful.' She picked up a Royal Doulton crinoline lady. It had been one of Judith's favourites. If she could just get him to talk about it, she thought, and held the figure up for him to see.

'Take it! You can have it!' He swung his arm through the air, as if dismissing Rachel as well as the ornament.

'I will not!' She rounded on him fiercely. 'These are all Judith. She loved them and she loved *you*, and she would want *you* to keep them!'

'Judith!' he cried, like an animal in distress. Then grabbed the figure out of her hand with such violence that she reeled backwards in shock. 'It's a piece of pot! Cold! Empty!' He brought his hand high above his head and sent the figure crashing into the wall.

Rachel looked on in horror, jumping visibly when the china cracked against the wall and shattered into tiny fragments.

For a moment there was silence. David stared numbly at the broken mess. Rachel could only watch anxiously, seeing both a broken ornament and a man who looked to be just as broken up inside. Then, slowly and painfully, the realization of what he had done moved across his grey features. He suddenly bounded across the room, fell to his knees and tried frantically to pick up all the pieces.

'Judith!' he groaned. 'Judith! Judith! Judith!' It was all he could say, her name over and over again, each time more painfully, as tears began to run swiftly down his cheeks.

In an instant Rachel was by his side. She sank to her knees and wrapped her arms around his shaking shoulders and held him as she had held him on the night of Judith's death. She felt her own tears welling up, but forced them back. This was David's time of release. From the way he had been acting, she had the feeling he had wrapped his grief in anger and refused to let it go for all the time he had been at his brother's house.

Now, maybe, he could begin to rebuild his life again, she thought, as she rocked him in her arms and felt the wetness of his tears on her blouse, and hoped she was right. Oh how she hoped she was right!

Chapter Sixteen

For the next two months David became a recluse. Every evening he came home from work, closed himself up in the house at the top of the hill, and didn't come out again until it was time to go to work the following morning.

Rachel tried persuasion, force, even trickery, but nothing could break him out of his depression.

Finally she gave up. 'It's useless,' she moaned to Polly one evening, after having a blazing row with him. 'He won't listen. He's happy being miserable. So he can do it on his own.'

'He'll come round, lass. In his own time.'

Rachel wasn't convinced. The new house had not been the new start she had hoped for. She felt sure he spent most of his time there staring out of the window, looking across the river to Mulberry Bush Lane. She'd caught him doing it often enough. 'He should never have had that house.'

'Maybe he shouldn't.' Polly gave a sigh and struggled out of her chair.

'What are you doing?' Rachel looked concerned and jumped up to help her. Polly's legs were getting increasingly more stiff and painful and it hurt just watching her move.

'I've got a pan of broth on the boil,' Polly said, and brushed Rachel away. 'I'm having a bowl. Do you want one?'

'Well, sit down. I can get it for you.'

'I'm still capable of getting my own broth,' Polly asserted stubbornly, and using the table and chairs for support, got herself across the room. 'Do you want one?' she repeated pointedly.

Rachel grimaced and accepted defeat. 'Aye, I'll have one,' she replied, teasingly mocking Polly's voice. 'But I'm capable of getting my own broth, too.'

Polly chuckled. 'We'd better go together then.' She pulled

221

a face and made Rachel laugh, and for the moment David was forgotten.

They were sitting at the table, eating the thick chicken broth, before Polly turned the conversation back to him. 'He's a man. You can't treat him like a child,' she said, as if she had been thinking about the matter but had not intended to speak.

'I can if he acts like one.' Rachel put her spoon in the bowl and looked hard at her old friend. 'Are you trying to say it's my fault?'

'No, lass. But stop trying to put the world to rights all by yourself. Leave him be for a bit. See what happens.'

'Oh, I'm going to do that!' She'd never meant anything so much in her life. She'd had enough of his sulks and his bad tempers. From now on he could come to terms with his grief on his own. 'I'm not going up there again,' she stated firmly. 'If he wants anything he'll have to come to me.'

The decision did not make her happy. She had been doing all his shopping for him since the day he had moved in. She worried that he was now going to starve himself. But she was determined she wasn't going to give in. He had been so nasty to her tonight, all because she had tried to make him talk about Judith. For his own sake he had to be shaken out of it.

But when a whole month went by and she hadn't seen anything of him, she began to get frightened.

'It's no good. I'll have to go up there,' she told Polly.

Polly looked at her oddly.

'What's wrong?' she asked, suddenly made anxious by the expression on her old friend's face.

'Haven't you heard?'

'What?' she demanded, feeling her heart lurch.

'He's bought the old chapel and is setting up in business.'

'*What*!' Rachel sat to attention in Polly's big armchair, her fingers tightening on the old worn arms. She felt surprised, shocked, and let down. After all she had done for him! She couldn't believe he had finally come to his senses and gone out and done it without her knowing.

'He's bought the old chapel,' Polly repeated. 'Well, him and somebody else. So Madge Jennison was telling me.'

'Who? Who else?' He didn't need her permission. And she was pleased if it meant he was getting over Judith. But it also meant he had recovered and was getting out and about again – and he hadn't had the decency to call on her!

'Don't know. Madge couldn't remember the name. Can't be anybody from round here or she would have done.'

Rachel fell silent, nursing her wounded ego.

'Didn't you know anything about it?'

'No.' Rachel shook her head. 'Oh well,' she said, forcing her expression to brighten. 'That's one problem I no longer have. He's obviously got himself back up and running.'

'Aye, lass.' Polly's wrinkled old eyes narrowed knowingly and she rubbed her knees, which Rachel had grown to realize could mean two things: either they were playing her up, or she was thinking deeply. 'Madge was telling me she's going to be a granny again,' Polly said, changing the subject. Rachel gave a little smile: she had been thinking deeply, she realized, and was grateful to be given something else to talk about.

Almost a week had passed before David finally showed up. Rachel had been to the shop for the afternoon to give Sarah the time off to visit the dentist and hairdresser. It was an unusual occurrence now. Since Sarah had begun working in The Boutique she had proved so able to look after things herself that Rachel only went in on Saturdays. She got on better working at home, rather than at the sewing machine in the shop's small back room, where she got constantly interrupted. The arrangement suited Sarah as well. She had thrived on the responsibility and all Rachel's misgivings had been unfounded. In the few months she had been there she had grown up and out of all her silly moods.

Rachel was spreading butter on to a slice of bread to make herself a ham sandwich when the knock came at the door.

'How are you?' she asked, not knowing what else to say, as she stood looking at him on the doorstep. Since first hearing of his business venture from Polly, she had told herself many times it was nothing to do with her. But she still felt he could have told her himself, rather than let her hear it secondhand.

'Fine,' he replied and stuck his hands in his pockets

223

and gave her a little consolation by looking ill at ease.

'You'd better come in then.' She walked into the front room and left him to follow.

'Are you busy?' He glanced round the clutter of material and thread and needles.

'I was just making myself a sandwich. Do you want one?' she asked, feeling she would be better if she had something to occupy her while they were talking, and was relieved when he said yes.

'What have you been doing with yourself?' she asked matter of factly, as she prepared a second ham sandwich. The stilted conversation was driving her mad and his obvious unease was not helping her. She glanced round at him. He had sat down at the table but still looked uncomfortable.

'I'm going into business. Hadn't you heard?' He gave an embarrassed laugh. 'I thought the entire village knew by now.'

'Polly mentioned something.' She showed little interest as she put the sandwich in front of him and sat down with her own.

'I've bought the old chapel. I'm going into partnership with a colleague. Engineering. Small components to begin with. But hopefully it will lead to bigger things.'

As he spoke, his nervousness seemed to evaporate and he brightened visibly. He still looked pale and thin. But it was good to see some of the life back in his eyes and a thin smile came to Rachel's lips.

'Will you be leaving Rolls-Royce?'

'No.' He shook his head as he bit into the sandwich. 'Not to begin with,' he added, when his mouth was sufficiently empty. 'We'll set a manager on and five or six chaps and see how it goes.'

'So you'll just be putting the money up?' She wasn't sure she liked the sound of it.

'I'll be making the designs and keeping an eye on the technical side. Jim, Jim Featherstone, that's my partner, will be looking after the accounts. But we'll both stay at Royces until it gets going properly.'

Rachel was disturbed by the speed of it all. One minute

224

he'd been fit to kill himself, the next ready to make the far-reaching decisions needed to begin a new business.

'Was it something you'd always wanted to do?' She'd never heard him talk of setting up for himself, but that didn't mean he hadn't wanted to.

'I hadn't thought about it, before . . .' Rachel frowned, as he found it impossible to speak of Judith's death. He smiled, but it was forced and unnatural. 'But things have changed,' he continued, still skirting round the words. Then added too quickly, 'I need something, Rachel.'

She nodded in agreement. He definitely needed something. But she wasn't sure this was it.

'Jim has been thinking about it for a long time,' he said, as if the fact that Jim had been wanting to do it made it all right. Rachel sighed. Then wanted to sigh again, when he added, 'But lack of cash prevented him from getting started.'

'How much . . . ?' she began, then stopped herself from asking outright how much money he was putting in. But she had a very nervous feeling about it all. 'What are you doing – going half and half?' she asked, feeling that was less rude.

'I'm buying the old chapel. Jim is providing the machinery. It will work out about even.'

Rachel wondered why they hadn't bought everything together. But David seemed happy with the arrangement and it really was nothing to do with her. 'Want another sandwich?' she asked, noticing he had demolished the other as if he hadn't eaten for a week.

Two days later Rachel came face to face with Jim Featherstone. She had gone up the hill in the evening, carrying a large bag of groceries. David hadn't asked her to do his shopping again, but the way he had eaten the sandwiches the other night had confirmed her theory that he wasn't feeding himself properly. If he wasn't, it was his own fault, she told herself. But then she thought of Judith and felt she owed it to her to make sure he was all right.

It wasn't until she was almost at the gate that she noticed a second car was parked behind David's large black Rover. He had company, she realized, and was about to turn around and leave it till another time, when David saw her and beckoned her through the window.

Jim Featherstone was younger than she had expected; thirty to thirty-two, she guessed. He had jet black hair and a swarthy complexion, and sharp bead-like eyes that ogled her the moment she walked through the door.

She took an immediate dislike to him and wondered what David was thinking of, getting himself attached to such a person.

'I brought you some groceries,' she quickly said, looking straight at David and keeping her eyes well away from Jim Featherstone. But she could feel him looking at her, almost as if his eyes were actually touching her, and she turned and went straight into the kitchen to put the food away, wanting to get the job done and get out of the house.

As she had expected, the pantry shelves were empty and the refrigerator was not much better. Its top shelf held half a pound of butter and a pint of milk that both looked fresh. The second shelf had two cracked eggs of indeterminate date, and in the bottom was a piece of cheese that looked as if it was going into the manufacture of penicillin. She looked around the kitchen, in the main clean and tidy because he had a cleaner come in three times a week. But on the breakfast bar was an open packet of biscuits, a loaf of bread and a pot of jam with the top left off. And on the side was the remains of a bottle of whisky and a selection of ginger ale bottles, some full, some empty and some in between.

Is this how he has been living? she asked silently, and looked to the ceiling with a sigh of despair. She began to unpack the bag of groceries and condemned the cleaning woman for not doing something about the food. She could have done a bit of shopping for him, she thought. Then remembered she had been the one to stop doing it for him, and felt guilty. He's big enough to do his own shopping, she told herself, but still felt as if she had let him down.

'There was no need.' David came into the kitchen and looked embarrassed.

Rachel picked the mouldy cheese from the refrigerator and

held it dubiously for a moment. 'No need!' she repeated, looking sceptical, then dropped it in the waste bin with disgust.

'I was going to do it . . . tomorrow,' he said lamely.

Or the next day, or the next! She looked at him pointedly. 'Well it's done now. I'll bring some every week. It will save you the trouble!'

'I really can do it myself.'

'Hey. If you don't want her doing your shopping, she can come to me.' Jim Featherstone came up behind David and leered at Rachel. 'I could find something for her to do.'

David flashed him a warning glare.

Rachel's lips fastened tightly together and her eyes flashed twice as hard as David's. 'I'll see you another time,' she said pointedly, glancing at David, before walking out. He can put his own food away, she thought rebelliously, knowing if she had stayed a moment longer, she would have told Jim Featherstone exactly what she thought of him.

He reminded her so much of Micky Caradine. He had the same cocky self-assurance that he was something good. She hadn't gone far before she was shaking. But not from fear for herself, for David. Jim Featherstone was typical of his type – on the make. He had played on David's low state to get what he wanted. She was sure of it. It was so blatantly obvious she couldn't understand how David couldn't see it for himself.

'You must be mad!' Rachel had brooded over Jim Featherstone for twenty-four hours and the moment David stepped through the door, she set about him. 'What are you thinking of? How can you let yourself trust *him*?'

'Who?' He looked surprised at her unexpected reaction. 'Jim?' he questioned uncertainly.

'Of course Jim!' She threw her sewing down and ignored the startled look Sarah was giving her. 'If I met him on a dark night, I'd run.'

David infuriated her further by laughing. 'Come on. He's harmless. He just thinks he has a way with the women.'

'Oh!' she groaned loudly and looked to the ceiling in despair. He thought she was upset by Jim Featherstone's lecherous attitude to herself. 'I don't mean the way he looked at me,' she snapped. 'I can handle that.' After all, she'd had plenty of practice. 'But his whole manner was untrustworthy.'

'You only saw him for a couple of minutes!' He looked and sounded amazed.

'It was enough. And you need your head examining if you get tied up with his sort.'

'I know what I'm doing.' His face hardened. 'And I think I know him a bit better than you do.'

Rachel sighed. Outwardly David didn't look the same man who had been Judith's husband. Now she knew he wasn't the same inside, either. 'Can't you give it a bit of time?' she asked, softening her voice, realizing he was still very much the awkward character she had tried to cajole out of the house. 'Perhaps it's a bit too soon to be making any big decisions,' she suggested, and wished he was still the recluse behind closed doors. If this was what he did when he was let loose, he needed locking up.

'No, I don't think it's a bit too soon. I need something to take my mind off . . . things.'

'Judith,' she put in sharply. 'Her name was Judith! Why don't you try saying it?'

'I'm well aware of my wife's name,' he grated. 'It's because of that I need to be busy.'

'I know that.' She looked guilty for speaking to him in that way. 'But I don't know that this is the right thing. If you'd just give it a bit more time, think it through . . .'

'I don't need to think it through,' he blazed, and there was more life in his eyes than she had seen for a long time, but it was the wrong type of life. 'I'm capable of making my own decisions.' He turned angrily for the door. Then stopped, pulled his wallet from his pocket, took out two five-pound notes and tossed them on to the table. 'For the food,' he said, glared at her for a moment, then turned and walked out, closing the door noisily behind him.

'You need some change,' she replied flatly, knowing he couldn't hear and, even if he could, wouldn't have stopped long enough to be given it.

Chapter Seventeen

'I think the waist needs taking in a bit more.' Rachel sat back on her heels and studied the dress she was fitting on Carol Land.

Carol turned to Sarah and grimaced. 'What do you think?'

'Yes, I agree.' Sarah cast a critical eye over her friend. 'You've lost some more weight. You're not still on that silly diet?'

Carol blushed slightly. 'It's fashionable to be thin.'

'You were never fat to begin with.'

'Yes I was. I look dumpy next to you.'

'Then don't stand next to me.'

The two girls continued to banter and Rachel folded her arms and smiled. It was always the same when Sarah's friends were having anything made. They all wanted to look like Sarah and thought that one of her dresses might do the trick.

She began to study Carol's waistline again. But a shadow passing the window made her look up and she realized, with some surprise, that it was David.

She didn't see much of him these days and she wondered what had brought him. He hadn't come to the cottage in over three months and the weekly grocery delivery trips had been their only communication. She had kept on doing his shopping even though he had continued to protest that he was capable himself. But he never did anything about showing her he could do it for himself. So, until she was happy he had learned how to walk into a shop and find more than jam and biscuits, she would continue to make the weekly visit, knowing Judith would be thanking her for it.

His new business seemed to be going well and she had to admit he was beginning to look better despite being tied up with work every evening. She never stayed long to disturb him. But he always took the time to show her the designs he was working on. Some she could recognize as large nuts and bolts, others she couldn't even imagine what they could be used for, but she always tried to sound interested. She even began to think she had misjudged Jim Featherstone and wondered if she had let her own past colour her opinions. He had reminded her so much of Micky that she began to feel she had not been seeing the real man, but a shadowy figure conjured up by her own insecurities.

'Go and take him into the kitchen. Tell him I won't be long,' she said to Sarah. Then quickly turned her attention to nipping Carol's waistline in by another inch. She was pleased he had come. Their relationship had been rather tenuous these past months and it had saddened her to recall what good friends they had been before Judith's death.

'That will do it,' she said. 'Get it off and I'll have it ready by Friday.' She picked up the tin of pins from the floor and stood up. 'And don't go losing any more weight.'

Carol grinned as she slipped the dress down her body and handed it to Rachel. 'I only want to look like Sarah.'

'Then you'll have to be put on the rack and stretched a good few inches,' she pointed out. 'Not that I don't know how you feel,' she added, and looked down at her own short form with a grimace.

Carol grinned again, and slipped into her skin tight hipster jeans and bright red skinny rib polo jumper.

'But you're pretty. I look like our beagle.'

'Get off with you!' Rachel laughed. She had never looked in the mirror and seen anything pretty. And, though Carol had a plain face, she had a lovely smile that seemed to fill any room she was in.

'David's in no rush,' Sarah announced, as she came back. 'Are you ready then?' she asked Carol.

As the two girls went out of the door, David came into the front room.

'Is something wrong?' Rachel stopped folding Carol's dress and dropped it on to the table. She looked hard into his face. He had deep lines of worry running across his forehead and dark rings under his eyes. He looked terrible. 'Are you working too hard?' she asked, leaping to the first conclusion when he remained silent.

He shook his head and the bleakness that had been his constant companion after Judith's death returned to his eyes.

'Whatever's the matter?' She felt herself go cold with apprehension.

'I need to talk to someone.'

She went colder still, recalling he had said the same thing once before: when he told her of Judith wanting to kill herself rather than become dependent on other people.

'Sit down.' She pulled the chairs round the table and pushed him into one before sitting down in the other. 'Now, what is it?' she asked, peering round into his eyes, which seemed to be glued to the table top.

'The business,' he replied flatly.

'What? Is it losing money?' she prompted, when he fell silent again.

He shook his head and gave a harsh laugh. 'No! We're making a fortune.'

'Then what? What is it?' Her anxiety made her lose patience and her voice was sharp, as she had to repeat, 'What is it?' before getting any reply.

'Jim,' he stated bluntly. He put his arms on the table and dropped his head into his hands.

'What has he done?' she asked flatly.

He looked up then, stared into her eyes for a long moment. 'He's been taking material and equipment from Rolls-Royce,' he finally said.

'What . . . borrowing?' she asked stupidly, knowing, yet not wanting to believe the truth.

'Stealing!' he grated.

'Oh, no!' She sat back in the chair, stunned.

'Well go on. Say I told you so!'

She shook her head. It had never crossed her mind to say such a thing. 'How do you know?' she asked.

He looked round the room with a heavy sigh, then fixed his gaze once more to the table top. 'I was so pleased we were making a go of it, I never stopped to think how we were making such a good profit after so short a time. Jim's always been in charge of all the supplies and I left him to it – thinking he was doing a good job,' he added dryly. 'I've been a fool, Rachel.' He gave a groan. 'What a fool!'

'Are you really sure of your facts?' she asked.

'Without a doubt,' he replied flatly, and sat back to stare at her with wooden eyes. 'With a place the size of Royces you always get a bit of pilfering. But recently it has increased. Even knowing that, I never suspected . . .' His voice trailed away in disbelief of his own stupidity.

'So how did you find out?' she asked, fixing him with concerned eyes.

'Last week I was in one of the workshops when it was discovered a drill had gone missing. The foreman was spitting blood. It was the second one to vanish in the space of a week. That evening it suddenly struck me that we had just *acquired* two of the same.'

'What did you do? Speak to Jim?'

He shook his head. 'I didn't know what to do. So I went down to the chapel and had a look at our drills. They were supposed to be new, but were obviously secondhand. I took the serial numbers and checked up.' He leaned heavily on the table once more and dropped his head into his hands. 'They were the ones from Royces.' He gave a sigh. 'I made a few enquiries about exactly what else had been going missing. The majority of it was what we use.'

He fell silent and for a while Rachel did the same. She stared at the crumpled heap of Carol's dress, but didn't really see it. All she could think was that David had been a fool not to listen to her. She would not say that to him. It had been his situation that had made him act out of character. She suddenly looked at his bent head.

'But you knew nothing about it?' she asked, unable to keep the uncertainty from her voice. If he could act out of character in one way, he could do so in another.

'Of course I didn't,' he said, and the hurt in his eyes was

too painful to be false. 'For God's sake, Rachel, you've got to believe me.'

'I do,' she replied, as gently as was possible in her present state.

'I don't know what to do.' He met her gaze with a hopelessness that cut through her and she had the feeling, had Jim Featherstone been there with them, she would have strangled him with her bare hands.

'So Jim isn't aware that you've found him out?'

He shook his head.

'Right!' she said purposefully, realizing someone had to take control and it wasn't going to be David. 'The first thing you have to do is tell Royces.'

'*What*! You must be mad!' He seemed more alive in that moment than all the time he had been there put together.

'Do you want it hanging over your head for the rest of your life?' she asked firmly. 'Or do you want it sorted out and have a clear conscience?'

'Yes . . . but . . . I'll lose my job!'

She looked at him steadily, refusing to bow down. 'You have two choices,' she pointed out. 'You can tell Jim to get lost, close the chapel and hope no-one ever finds out. Or you can make a clean breast of it and have a peaceful life.'

'And then do what?' His voice was incredulous. 'Who would take me on with that hanging over my head?'

For a moment she felt like telling him he should have thought of that before getting caught up with someone as shifty as Jim Featherstone. Instead, she said, 'Does anyone at Royces know about the business?'

'I haven't told anyone. But Jim's been going round bragging.'

He would! She gave a sigh. 'So if you closed up and the stealing stopped, there isn't much hope that somebody wouldn't put two and two together – sooner or later?'

He shook his head yet again, fetched his cigarettes from his jacket pocket and lit up.

Rachel reached over to the mantel and handed him her

father's old ashtray. 'So there's only one way to go,' she pointed out, in a tone that brooked no refusal.

'I might as well follow Judith,' he said, taking a noisy draw on his cigarette.

'No you won't!' Rachel leapt from the chair in a blaze of anger. 'Judith had good cause. You don't! Not unless you want everybody to think you're a coward!'

He gave a dry snort. 'Better a dead coward than a live idiot,' he said, refusing to look at her.

'Just you listen to me, David Morrell.' She grabbed his shoulder and yanked him around to face her. She glared fiercely into his startled eyes, the terror of realizing he was capable of throwing himself in the river and ending his life, spurring her on. 'How dare you belittle yourself in such a way? What would Judith think? She would never have taken her own life if the illness had not been slowly strangling it from her! You're healthy, you have a strong body. Use it! And stop feeling sorry for yourself!'

The glisten of tears in his eyes made her release his shoulder. But she would not apologize. He needed to see the truth and knocking it into him was the only way. With a sigh of despair she sat down again. 'You've got to get this cleared up.' She could see now her first suggestion of closing up and hoping for the best would not work. It would always prey on his mind and he would end up in the river. 'You've got to go to Royces and tell them everything. How much do you think the stolen goods will amount to?'

'I don't know.' He gave a defeated shrug. He had managed to force back his tears, but the way he sucked on his cigarette showed how tense he was.

'Has everything you have used been stolen?'

'Not everything. We have some invoices. I presume they're legitimate.'

She thought for several moments. 'The first thing you do is tell Royces everything. And that happens tomorrow morning,' she said, hoping he was too anxious at that moment to think of turning awkward.

'Right,' he replied meekly.

'You don't tell Jim beforehand. Explain that to Royces and tell them you'll help with whatever they decide to do. And you also offer to pay for everything he's taken.'

He looked stunned. 'It might be thousands!'

'You have the chapel to sell.' She paused uncertainly. 'That is still in your name, isn't it?'

He nodded and she heaved a sigh of relief.

'And you have the house,' she continued. 'If the worst comes to the worst you'll have to sell that.' He didn't need the great rambling place, anyway, she thought. He could manage in a little cottage like the rest of them. 'Whether you lose your job or not is up to Royces.' She gazed at him steadily. 'But you've got to do it, David. For your own peace of mind you've got to do it.' She leaned on the table, hoping to see some evidence that he agreed with her. He looked bleak, but she had the feeling it was a bleakness of resignation. 'If you bend over backwards to help them, they might look on it favourably and be lenient with you.' She hoped they would. She knew he would never have got involved in anything like this if it hadn't been for losing Judith. But she wasn't so sure Rolls-Royce would take the same view.

He nodded tiredly.

'Have you eaten?' she asked, knowing he wouldn't have and wanting to do something to take his mind away from the subject before he began backing down.

'A hearty meal for the condemned man,' he said dryly.

But she went into the kitchen and ignored him.

Fortunately, Rolls-Royce did take a lenient view on David's position. All the stolen equipment was returned and he managed to pay for the materials that had been used without having to sell either the old chapel or his house. It put an end to any chances of promotion, but he was too relieved at being kept in his job to think too much about that.

Jim Featherstone was tried, convicted, and given a three-year prison sentence. The association with David had not been his only business venture. It was discovered he had another, similar works, and another partner who had been led astray

235

the way David had. He had been supplying both concerns from Rolls-Royce stock and had also been fiddling both of his partners by falsifying the books: a fact that had helped Rolls-Royce accept David's total innocence and not make any charges against him.

David began to spend the evenings at the cottage with Rachel, needing her company to see him through the dark days of the trial. When the trial was over, Rachel suggested they keep up the arrangement. She was worried that if he began spending the evenings alone he might do something silly again. She didn't want to leave him open to any more Jim Featherstones.

'Don't you ever get fed up?' he asked one evening, as she struggled and chuntered over a piece of lace work on a pair of French knickers.

She gave a sigh. 'Yes,' she stated bluntly, startling herself by the admission. The fiddly lingerie had begun to get on her nerves of late, but she would never have let it be known before.

'Did you ever look into a prospect of setting up a factory for the lingerie?'

She gave him an amused grimace. 'I should have thought you'd be the last person to suggest that.' It was almost a year now since he had closed the engineering works. But the matter was still painful to him and she tried at every possible occasion to turn it into a joke.

'It would be very profitable,' he continued, his face deadly serious. 'You've got to admit you could sell more, if only you could make more.'

'Yes,' she replied guardedly. She also had to admit it had not been a suggestion she had taken seriously. Her thoughts had been turned more to stopping the time-consuming underwear altogether and concentrating on her dresses and suits. 'I wouldn't know where to begin,' she said, turning back to the sewing machine and dismissing the subject.

'Why not begin at the old chapel?'

'What?' She could not stop herself laughing. But when she saw his expression become even more serious, she brought herself up short. She stared at him for a long moment. 'Is that why you've never sold it?' she finally asked. Then suddenly returned to the sewing. 'Forget it. I couldn't afford it.'

'You don't need to afford it. It's doing nothing. You might as well use it.'

She forgot the sewing altogether and turned her chair around to face him. 'Are you trying to suggest we become partners?' she questioned seriously.

'Yes,' he replied confidently.

For another long moment she stared at him. 'Are you a good risk?' she asked teasingly, playing for time, her mind trying desperately to come up with the right answer.

'We did it once before,' he pointed out.

She nodded her head. But that had been different. He hadn't been directly involved, just a crutch to lean on if she had needed him, which she hadn't. And the shop was now fully paid for.

'And I don't think there's much chance of you cooking the books.' He gave a self-mocking grimace.

'No there isn't,' she agreed with feeling. She stood up and walked across the room. It could be just what he needed, she realized. And, if he was tied up with her, he wouldn't go getting tied up with someone else. But what about the shop? She scratched her head. Then gave a sigh. 'It wouldn't work. I couldn't run a factory and the shop.'

'Sarah can run the shop. You know she can. She does it already.'

She looked at him steadily. He had obviously been planning this for some time. He had all the answers nicely worked out. 'I don't know. I'll think about it,' she said, suddenly having the feeling she was having her arm twisted.

'What's to think about?' he insisted. 'It would be ideal.'

She bit her lip. The old chapel would be very convenient, placed as it was just a stone's throw from the bottom of the hill. It was almost on the doorstep . . . if she wanted a factory. She looked at the French knickers stuck in the sewing machine, the white silk crumpled beneath the needle, the time-consuming lace work that drove her mad. Why was she

237

resisting? It *was* what she wanted. It was the perfect solution, for both David and herself.

She suddenly laughed. 'Tell me I'm not dreaming,' she said, and he also laughed, and reached forward and pinched her gently on the arm.

Chapter Eighteen

Rachel's time was taken up with designing and making patterns and samples for use in the factory, as well as organizing the supply of all the machinery and other paraphernalia needed to turn the old chapel into a productive workroom. The old building had not been a house of worship for thirty years. The first twenty it had stood empty and decaying. For the majority of the last ten it had been a knitwear factory, followed by David's brief engineering works.

Rachel grimaced when she first set foot inside the place. She looked around the oily workshop and wondered if it had been such a good idea, after all. 'I hope it will clean up.' She ran her finger along a greasy bench and held the blackened tip up for David's inspection.

'Don't worry. All this will be thrown out. You won't recognize the place when the decorators have finished.'

Rachel looked uncertain. It was a far bigger job than she had bargained for. David had insisted he would take responsibility for organizing the complete refurbishment, but she was worried it was going to prove too much for him. She didn't want him doing anything that would wear him out and affect his job at Royces. His position there was still too tenuous to go upsetting them.

She didn't voice her doubts. She had done so several times previously and he had just laughed them off. And she had to admit the new interest had returned the enthusiasm for life she had thought he had lost for ever.

Pulling a handkerchief from her pocket she wiped the dirt from her finger and looked round at the tall arched windows, then up to the high rafters above her head. 'It still looks like a house of God,' she said flatly, and looked to the front, where the altar table would have stood. In its position was now the small office, large enough for one desk and a filing cabinet. 'I'll be sitting on the altar,' she said dryly.

David laughed. 'Then you'll have extra support,' he joked. 'Come and look at this. Do you think it needs a new door?'

She walked over to him and studied the large cupboard door he was scrutinizing thoroughly. 'What's wrong with it?'

'It's not very strong. The hinges are almost rotten.'

'Will we need it?' Her voice was flat. Just tiredness, she told herself. She had been working flat out to make all the preparations and keep supplies flowing into The Boutique. But the shop's stock was beginning to dwindle.

'You'll need some storage space,' David said, his concentration still on the cupboard. 'If it needs doing we should do it all now.'

'I suppose so,' she replied, without much enthusiasm.

'What's wrong?' He turned to her, looking concerned.

'Sarah thinks *her* shop is being neglected.' She gave a twisted smile. Now she was opening the factory, Sarah had come to think of The Boutique as her own.

David's frown increased. 'I told you to leave *all* this to me! I'm quite capable of ordering the machines, if you tell me which you want.'

'I know.' She sighed. It had not been her intention to push more work on to him. She wanted to lessen his load, not increase it. 'I'll manage. Most things are already ordered now. I'll have time for sewing while the decorators are in. Now what are we going to do with this door?' She forced her enthusiasm to return and picked up a note pad and pencil to list all the repairs and renovations David thought necessary.

When they had finished she went home alone, leaving David to go and see the joiner and make the arrangements for the first of the alterations. As she stepped through the door, she found Sarah waiting in the kitchen.

'You'll have to let me buy some stock in!' Sarah began, before she had got the door closed behind her.

'No!' Rachel was adamant. She threw her bag down on the chair in frustration. She didn't need this! 'Our customers want

240

something different. There isn't another shop in the county that provides what we do.'

'We'll be providing nothing soon!' Sarah set herself angrily against the kitchen table. 'I sold another four today. The place is half empty!'

'David is getting the work sorted out now. It won't be many more weeks before we're in production. Then you can fill the empty half with underwear.' She pulled her coat off and dropped it with her bag. She felt so lifeless. It had never happened before. And to happen now – just when she needed all her strength.

'*Great!*' Sarah threw her hands in the air. 'This is the swinging sixties. England has become the fashion centre of the world. And what do I have to sell? A window full of knickers!'

'Well they'll be posh ones!' Rachel retaliated, and walked out of the kitchen before she fell out with her sister. She didn't know what had got into her lately. More often than not Sarah was irritable and snappy. She pulled her sewing chair out, stopped and looked bleakly at the sewing machine. Not again, she thought, and had the intense desire to knock the machine off the table and send it crashing to the floor. If it was broken she wouldn't be able to use it, she told herself. Then looked up at the ceiling and gave a heavy sigh. It wasn't Sarah who was snappy and irritable, it was herself.

She sighed again and, realizing she needed her head sorting out, was out of the cottage before having time to go back into the kitchen to pick up her coat.

'Whatever are you doing? You'll catch your death!' Polly peered accusingly over the top of her reading glasses, as Rachel rushed through the door, arms wrapped around herself to fight off the cold evening air.

'I didn't think it was that cold,' she said, her teeth chattering.

'Or you didn't stop to think what you were about!' Polly put in knowingly. 'What's wrong now?'

'Am I so obvious?' She flopped into one of the large armchairs and held her hands to the warmth of the roaring coal fire. She smiled to herself, as Polly put the newspaper lying on her knee on to the table, then followed it with the blanket that had been tucked tightly round her knees. She was still too proud to be thought of as old.

'Aye, to me you are,' Polly replied, when she felt she looked suitable to entertain company. Then sat quietly and listened, while Rachel poured out her problems.

'Maybe you should listen to Sarah,' she said, when Rachel finally fell silent.

'What? Sell mass-produced? The same as you can buy anywhere. Never!' She folded her arms and looked obstinate.

'That wasn't what I was meaning. So you can get down off your high horse.' Polly gave her a look that instantly humbled her.

'You're all set up to get this fancy underwear made for you,' she continued. 'Why can't you get your frocks made as well? They'd still be yours. There's nothing that says you've got to kill yourself to make a few bob.'

Rachel stared silently into the fire. David had said exactly the same thing, on more than one occasion. What was wrong with her? She wanted the factory, for herself, as much as for David. But it was proving to be far more work than she had anticipated. She was not going to be able to keep up with her sewing, as well as running the workshop. What was it Polly had once said about a good boss being one who knew how to delegate? Was that her problem, why she was feeling fed up with it all? Because she didn't like the idea that someone else could do her work as well as she could.

She gave a sigh and turned to Polly. 'What you're saying is that I should get everything made in the factory, is that it?'

'They'd still be yours,' Polly repeated pointedly. 'Just the same as all the fancy frilly things will be yours.'

Rachel nodded in slow agreement. 'I'll think about it,' she said, not ready to bend to total acceptance of the suggestion.

'You do that, lass,' Polly replied. 'And you can start thinking while you put the kettle on.'

Two days before Sarah's seventeenth birthday, Coprell began business. The name had been made up from the beginning of

Cooper and the end of Morrell. They had eight staff: six machinists, one cutter-out, and Flo, who was cleaner, tea-masher, and general dogsbody.

Rachel did not plan on it staying that way for long. The conversation with Polly had been taken to heart and she had finally seen sense. There was no reason she had to make all her creations with her own hands. If she was there to watch over and make sure everything was done to her instructions then, as Polly had said, they were still hers.

When she put the prospect of an immediate expansion of the factory to David, he had been extremely happy.

'It's what I've been trying to tell you all along,' he said, and blessed Polly for good sense and the ability to get through to Rachel where no other could.

Rachel laughed. 'I seem to think you have the same ability, also,' she pointed out, and reminded him there would be no factory at all, if it hadn't been for him.

Too narrow-minded, that was what she had been. She had to smile when she thought of what she had been trying to achieve, single handed, and from one sewing machine. Well no more, she told herself. The Boutique would always remain as their shop, but she was going to supply to other shops, all over the country. One approach to a large chain had already received a promising reply. They had heard of her reputation and were more than interested in selling her products.

At twelve o'clock the girls knocked off for dinner and Rachel sank gratefully into her office chair. The first day! It was bound to be difficult, she told herself. Her head was spinning. Questions had been fired at her from all directions, nonstop since nine o'clock, as her new staff began learning their new jobs. Fortunately, four of them were experienced machinists and had known how to handle the industrial sewing machines and been able to assist the two raw novices, which had helped greatly.

They seemed a fine bunch, she thought, happy with her choice. She had paid more attention to personality rather than skill when she had had the daunting task of interviewing all the applicants. She smiled as she looked through the office window at the clutter already surrounding the workroom. She was pleased she had staggered the starting dates. The four extra machinists, taken on to deal with the fashion wear, were not due to begin until next week. Hopefully, by then, this lot would be working under their own steam, she thought, and began to open the packet of sandwiches Sarah had excitedly made for her that morning.

After she had eaten her lunch, she started cutting out. The girl she had employed for the job was inexperienced and slow. It wasn't a bad thing, she told herself. No experience meant she wasn't bringing along any bad habits picked up in another factory. It also gave her a viable excuse to get her hands on the material without looking as if she was interfering.

The afternoon flew by. At five o'clock the noisy hum of the machines came to a halt and for a moment the silence was stunning.

'Good night,' Rachel called, as the girls filed out, their happy chatter taking over where the sewing machines had left off.

'I'm off then,' Flo called, as she returned the brush and dustpan to the cupboard and began to put on her coat. 'There's nothing else you want doing?'

'No thanks, Flo. I'll see you tomorrow.' Rachel smiled, as she watched Flo scuttle out of the door in the same hectic manner she had used all day. Where did she get her energy from? she wondered, as she went around the empty room, checking all the machines had been covered up and un-plugged.

Everything had been left as she had instructed. She turned to the long bench running the length of one wall. The finished garments were beginning to pile up already. She peered into the tea chest where all the mistakes had been thrown. There weren't as many as she had imagined there would be after the first day. By the end of the week they would be working well, she thought, and went to collect her own coat and handbag, feeling happily content.

It was going to work she told herself, as she took a last look around the newly decorated room; all nice clean walls and new furniture. She shook her head. It was difficult to imagine it was the same greasy workshop she had first seen. David had worked wonders. Even the little office had been completely pulled down and re-erected with spotless white walls and crack-free glass.

As she switched off the lights and locked up, she felt better than she had in weeks.

She had not been at home for more than ten minutes, when David burst through the door.

'How did it go?'

'Better than expected,' she replied, with a certain amount of restraint. She did not want to raise his expectations too high. 'But I don't think we'll be millionaires, just yet,' she added jokingly.

His smile turned to a grin. The happiness on her face told him that the day had gone far better than her words explained.

'Anyway, what are you doing here at this time?' she asked. He was one hour earlier than his usual time and the dinner was not even thought about. 'I've not got the potatoes peeled yet.'

'Don't bother. We're going out,' he said, taking her by surprise. 'Celebrating,' he explained. 'You deserve it. It's all booked. You can't say no.'

'What about Sarah?' she asked stupidly. At that moment she couldn't remember if Sarah was coming home for a meal or not. But she did know she felt very nervous about the idea of going out with him.

'She already knows,' he said, leaving her feeling her line of defence had been swept from under her feet. 'She can't come. She's got a date.' He pulled a chair out and sat himself down at the kitchen table. 'Go and get yourself ready.'

She stared silently at him. She could see he wasn't going to budge until she walked through the door with him, yet still she could not move. Why? she asked herself. What was wrong with the idea of going out to dinner with a man? With David? she quickly amended. *It was David!* she told herself firmly. The man she spent every evening with. She was being ridiculous.

The last did it. 'Give me ten minutes,' she said.

'There's no rush.' He reached out to stop her before she got to the door. 'Do you still have the dress Judith and I gave you that Christmas?'

'Yes,' she replied guardedly.

'Put it on. I've never seen you wearing it. Judith never saw you in it.'

The dress had been tried on over and over again. Many times she had decided to wear it – tomorrow, the next day. It all seemed rather silly now. And the remark about Judith never seeing it had gone deep. 'All right,' she agreed.

'Thank you,' he said, his smile touched with something she did not understand.

It was only when he moved his hand to let her go, that she realized he had been holding fast to her arm for several moments without her being aware of it. She put her hand over the place and hurried through the door, quickening her steps as she went up the stairs and felt her heart strangely racing beneath her rib cage.

It was not until she slipped into a pair of chocolate brown court shoes that she stopped and studied her reflection, and realized what she had done. She had fixed her hair into a French plait that hung down between her shoulder blades. The soft cream jersey skimmed her figure to perfection, enhancing her curves in a very feminine way. It made her look more woman than she would have thought possible.

She gave a little shiver, apprehension taking over. Some of her business suits made her look like a woman, she assured herself. But not in the same way the dress did. It's only David, she told herself. Then took a deep steadying breath, grabbed a chocolate brown clutch bag that matched the shoes, and hurried down the stairs before she could change her mind.

'Ready?' David asked, taking only the briefest of glances at the dress before picking up the car keys from the table and heading for the door. 'Your chariot awaits,' he joked.

His smile was back, but there had been a tightness in his voice. It was the dress, she thought, as she walked out and left him to lock the door for her. It had been a mistake. It reminded him too much of Judith, she told herself as she climbed into his car and wished she could run back and change into something else.

'That was excellent!' Rachel leaned back in the comfortable chair in the restaurant's coffee lounge. Her earlier anxieties had vanished and she felt as relaxed and happy as David now looked, and that she would not need to eat for a week after the meal they had just consumed. Something suddenly occurred to her and she laughed.

'What is it?' David asked, smiling at her.

'I'm twenty-four. Run my own business. Have enough ambition inside my head for ten men. And this is the first time I've been out . . .' She had been about to say out with a man. 'Out for a meal at a proper restaurant,' she quickly completed, and felt heat creeping into her cheeks and wished she had never opened her mouth.

'I know,' he replied, with a quiet certainty. 'You've never bothered much with boyfriends, have you?'

'No,' she replied, a little too quickly. 'I've always been too busy,' she added more calmly. 'My dreams have always revolved around work.'

He frowned, making himself look much older. 'It worries me,' he said. 'You'll wake up one day and find you've achieved all the success you've been chasing. But will it make you happy? Or will you wonder what you've missed?'

The sadness in him reached out and touched her. She gave a thin smile. He was thinking of Judith, she thought. But their marriage had been made in heaven. They were not all like that. 'Does that have something to do with you suggesting the factory?' she asked. 'Do you think I should make time for other things, as well as work?'

He took a swig of coffee. 'Not exactly. You know I've always thought you should expand into a proper business. But,' he looked a little sheepish, 'I suppose I did twist your arm a bit.' He grinned at her. 'You need a bit of force at times. I only hope you don't go upsetting the staff by trying to take their work off them and do it better yourself.'

It was Rachel's turn to look sheepish then. She was thinking about the dinner break: cutting out because the new girl was slow. 'I'll try not to,' she said, considering it best to keep that bit of information to herself.

It was when the waiter came to refill their coffee cups, that Rachel realized if she was to drink another drop, she needed to find a lavatory first.

The ladies room was at the end of the corridor past the dining room. As she passed the door, she glanced at the sea of bent heads of the other diners. But it was not until she was on her way back that she realized she had known one of those bent heads.

He was leaning against the wall, obviously waiting for her. His silly grin beamed mockingly at her and her heart gave a leap. Micky Caradine! She couldn't believe it! He had to turn up and spoil one of her best days ever. Would she ever be rid of him?

'Fancy seeing you here.' He pushed himself lazily off the wall to stand in her way.

'Fancy seeing *you* here!' Her voice was heavy on sarcasm. 'Or are you being entertained?' she added pointedly, making it clear she thought the expensive restaurant above him.

His mouth twisted in a parody of a smile. She stopped right in front of him and stared into his hated face with a blank expression. His hair still hung long and lank in his neck and he was wearing an Italian-style suit that looked cheap and tacky. It could have been made for him, she thought acidly, and felt good in her dress.

'We're having a party. I've just got engaged,' he announced arrogantly.

'Congratulations,' she said. 'I hope you deserve each other.' The girl must be an idiot, she thought. He was here with his new fiancée, yet he was still on the prowl for anyone he could chat up. All she had to do was cock her little finger and he would have been outside with her in seconds. She almost wanted to laugh, but it reminded her too much of what he had turned her into, and her voice was bitter, as she said, 'Well, now you've told me your news, can I go?'

He gave one of his infuriating half-grin, half-leers and let his gaze run insolently down her body. She held herself stiffly, not allowing any of the emotion raging inside to show on her face. She suddenly wished they were outside, and she could lash out at him and make him move, the way she had done the night on the hill. 'If you're not interested in getting back to your dinner guests, then I am!' she said, and attempted to push him aside.

He stood firm and sneered at her. 'I see you're going for the older man now,' he said nastily, jerking his head in the direction of the coffee lounge and David.

Rachel felt her blood immediately come up to the boil.

'It's a crying shame, if you ask me,' he continued, as she began to silently seethe. 'Old hands on that lovely body.' His eyes rested deliberately on the swell of her breasts.

'Well nobody asked you,' she returned icily. That it was David he was insulting was of more importance than any insolent gesture he made towards herself. 'And I think it's about time you shut that dirty mouth of yours.' A couple came out of the dining room and looked at them oddly. But she was too wrapped up in her defence of David to let it worry her, and she continued, 'Or I might just find I have a few things to tell your fiancée. I'm sure she would find your past history very illuminating!'

Micky's colour heightened and Rachel smiled bitterly. She had hit the right spot, she realized, and it pleased her.

'Got high and mighty all of a sudden, haven't we?' he spat nastily. 'Think we're something better, now we've got our own factory.'

'I was always better than you,' she replied, with quiet confidence. Then her eyes flashed with the contempt she felt for him. 'You are nothing, worthless, an apology of a man who is not fit to lick the shoes of a man like David Morrell. Now . . .' She banged her little clutch bag hard against his chest and wished it was a suitcase. '. . . move aside and let me pass. And I think it would be better *for both* of us if you never speak to me again! Do I make myself clear?' She glared

249

into his face to convey the intention of her unspoken threat. Then she walked away.

A sneering laugh followed her down the corridor. 'You wait,' he called. 'There'll come a day when you want me, a *young* man, one with fire in his veins.'

Never! she thought, and carried on walking.

David was lighting a cigar when she got back to the table. She forced herself to smile. Her anger had stopped her fully realizing what Micky had been saying. Now her anger was on the wane, the full implications becoming clearer. Everyone knew David owned the old chapel. And they knew he had become her partner; in the small village it would have been impossible to keep it quiet, even if they had tried. But did they think she and David were . . . ? No, she quickly told herself. Only the likes of Micky Caradine, with evil minds.

'Is something wrong?' David asked, eyeing her oddly, as he put his lighter back in his pocket.

'No.' She shook her head. 'This has been a wonderful evening,' she said, smiling into his eyes and realizing it was the truth. At first she had resented Micky being there. Now she was pleased. He had boosted her ego. She had matched up to him with a feeling of superiority. Maybe she had been right all along. The factory had lifted her higher, making her feel she was at last in a position to look down on him.

'Do you want another coffee? Or something stronger?' David asked.

'Another coffee please,' she quickly replied. She hadn't quite finished with Micky Caradine yet. Sooner or later he would come through to the coffee lounge and, she suspected, would not expect to find she was still there. He would now be imagining she was making a rapid departure, getting out of his way. Well he was wrong. She was staying right where she was, with the hope that she might see him cringe.

Rachel got her wish. When Micky came in, ahead of a party of ten, he took one look at her and his eyes nearly jumped out of his head.

She smiled secretly. 'Shall we be going?' she said, and

swallowed the last drop of coffee she had been holding on to long after David had finished his.

Then she walked out, walking right past Micky as if he didn't exist.

'I haven't seen him for a while,' David said dryly, showing he held no respect for the man.

Rachel glanced up at him uncertainly. Did he know? she wondered. Then told herself it was impossible.

As they drove home the only noise in the car was the purr of the engine. David concentrated on driving and Rachel stared into the headlight's beam, watching moths performing fantastic last dances, before being hurled against the car's body. She remained silent. Now she had succeeded in making Micky nervous it all seemed rather silly and childish, and she found his words preying on her mind. She began to wonder again if everyone in the village thought she was having an affair with David. Then she thought of David's caustic comment as they had left the restaurant, and she began to worry that he might know everything about her. And, if he did, other people might also know.

What did it matter? she thought angrily. It was history now. It didn't concern anyone else.

'It has been a lovely evening,' she suddenly said, echoing her sentiments of earlier, and wanting to turn her mind in a more pleasant direction. 'I've really enjoyed it.'

'Good!' he replied with feeling, and glanced a smile at her before turning his attention back to driving. 'We'll have to do it more often.'

'Yes,' she replied without thinking. But even after thinking it still seemed a good idea. Her sentiments had been sincere, she had enjoyed being with him. She felt rather silly now for her earlier insecurities. She had not felt uncomfortable in the cream dress, after all. In fact, she had forgotten she was wearing it, and there was certainly nothing cheap or tacky about it. Perhaps it's time you grew up, she told herself, wondering if the dress had also helped her with Micky. She didn't think it had: she always felt herself better than he was, even in her baggy clothes of home. That was a feeling born

251

out of the anger she felt just thinking about him. But the dress had showed her to be the woman she now was and not the silly child who had been so easily taken in. She smiled to herself. There wasn't any need to make herself grow up, she had the feeling it was happening of its own accord. It wasn't a frightening feeling, she rather liked it.

When the car pulled up at the end of the yard, David was out of the driver's seat before Rachel could speak. 'I'll make sure you get in safe,' he said, ignoring her protests that she was quite capable of putting the key in the lock herself.

Always the gentleman, she thought, smiling in amusement, as he took the key from his pocket, where it had been since she left him to lock the cottage for her, and wouldn't let her have it.

'Do you want another coffee?' she asked, as they walked into the kitchen. She felt it only polite to offer but, if he was like herself, he was awash with the stuff.

He shook his head. 'Thank you for wearing the dress,' he said, his eyes moving gently down the length of cream jersey. Then he looked into her eyes. 'You look beautiful in it. I was very proud to be with you.'

'Thank you.' It was all she could say. There had been nothing of the insolence of Micky Caradine in his gaze, nothing in the least insulting, but she felt colour creeping into her cheeks. She wanted to return the compliment and say she had also been proud to be with him, but the words stuck in her throat. 'Thank you,' she repeated, feeling foolish, and suddenly insecure.

'We will have to do it more often,' he repeated the words he had said in the car, and looked into her eyes as if expecting to see some reaction there.

'Opening factories or having dinner?' she joked, trying to cover her unease, as she realized, for the first time, he had lovely turquoise green eyes, almost the same colour as her own.

He laughed. 'Both, if you like,' he said, and his laughter faded, his face becoming serious, intent. 'Rachel . . .' he began, then words seemed to fail him.

For a moment she was unable to understand the sudden change in him, but only for a moment. The next he had pulled her into his arms and was kissing her on the lips.

At first she was too stunned to react. The shock was too sudden, too unexpected. She stared numbly into his eyes, so close they seemed to be drawing her into him, sucking her into his body as his lips sucked her lips.

Then suddenly it wasn't David, it was Micky before her. The memories came rushing back. 'No!' she mumbled from beneath his mouth and tore her lips free. 'Please no, David! No!' She pushed her hands into his chest in just the same way she had done to Micky all those years ago, and felt an overwhelming relief when he put up no resistance and moved away.

'No! No!' she begged, the plea in her voice sharp and edged with the pain of her memories. 'I can't. Don't make me!' She backed away, putting the length of the small kitchen between them and wishing she had taken him into the front room, which was bigger and would have given her more space.

'Can't?' David questioned gently, his eyes narrowing in concern.

He was not angry, not hurt, as she had expected, and his reaction confused her further. She dropped her head into her hands and groaned with a pain that was too deep to be physical, too intense to be washed away.

'It's me, Rachel,' he continued, standing very still and watching her carefully. 'I would never make . . .' He suddenly stopped, paused for a long moment, then said, '*I* won't do anything to hurt you. Don't be afraid of me.'

'I'm not afraid,' she insisted, but when she lifted her head her eyes were those of a frightened animal. 'I'm not afraid of *you*, David. It's just . . . just . . .' She could not tell him. In a way she wished she could and that she could have it all out in the open, and perhaps get rid of some of the tension that made her fear to walk round corners, made her shun the neighbours and everyone she did not know too well. For fear they asked some probing question she would not be able to answer truthfully. But David respected her for what he thought she was. How could she shatter his illusions by allowing him to know she was no better than one of her father's harlots.

'Don't . . . don't let's spoil a beautiful friendship,' she said, forcing her voice to lightness as she pulled herself together, realizing her reaction had already made David think she had something to hide. 'We can't risk anything upsetting the partnership,' she added, and recalled her own thoughts in the car about growing up, and wanted to cry.

For a long moment David continued to watch her. He seemed to be assessing her, she realized, and felt embarrassment growing. She wanted to speak, get him on to another subject and get the friendship back to its normal level, but her tongue was tied up with embarrassment and guilt.

'I've grown to love you, Rachel,' he finally said. He made no move towards her, but his sincerity reached across the room and she felt a terrible shame for the way she had treated him. She suddenly wanted to go to him, wrap her arms around him and comfort him for the wrong she had done. But she did not move and her confusion increased. If that was what she wanted, then why didn't she do it? she asked herself. Her mind was spinning too fast to come up with the answer. All she knew was that she was wanting, yet fearing that same want.

'I'd like to think you had some affection for me,' he continued, with the same sincerity. But she could only remain as she was, still and silent, and being torn apart.

'Talk to me, Rachel!' A plea entered his voice. 'Tell me what you're afraid of! Let me help you. I can help you.'

She shook her head in despair. If only it was that easy. If she thought confession could cleanse her of her sins, she would be shouting it from the rooftops.

'I've never wanted a close relationship,' she said, her voice edged with bitterness, as she realized what Micky had taken from her. David was there, right in front of her, offering everything that she knew was missing from her life. But she could not cross that barrier because she knew she would never be able to offer in return everything he wanted from her. 'It would get in the way of my work,' she insisted, too fiercely.

254

'Marriage and careers don't go together. Not for a woman. I'd put work first. No man would like that.'

'I know you, Rachel,' he began, the gentleness of his voice holding no demand, and his stillness offering no threat. 'I know how much your career means to you. I would never get in the way of that. I'm not some arrogant young stud who thinks his every whim should be catered to.' She had the sudden fear he was referring to Micky again, and her eyes pivoted anxiously to his. He smiled fondly, almost knowingly, and her fear increased.

'Coprell belongs to both of us,' he pointed out. 'It means as much to me as it does to you. I wouldn't expect you to push it into second place.'

'Please, David!' She held up her hands to stop him. She couldn't listen to any more. 'I do have my reasons for my decision,' she said, half hoping he might bring Micky to light himself. He didn't and she thought it was only because he was waiting for her to do so. But she might be wrong. If he didn't know, she didn't want him to know. She put her hands to her head, feeling her brain was going to burst. She was being ridiculous, she told herself. 'But I won't discuss them,' she said, feeling he deserved at least half the truth. 'Not with you, not with anybody. It's my decision and I know it's right for me.' She lifted her head with the return of the calm determination that had evaded her for the last minutes, and looked him straight in the eyes.

For a long moment he only stared at her, watching the new resolve grow slowly on her face. 'All right,' he finally and reluctantly agreed. 'But one day I'll get you to open up. Everyone needs someone . . . And you are no different to anyone else!' he added pointedly. Then he pulled the car keys from his jacket pocket. 'I'll see you tomorrow,' he said, and turned for the door.

'Yes,' was all she could reply, as he walked out. But as the door closed behind him, a great weight of guilt settled on her shoulders, and she was filled with the fear that she would never see him again. And her heart wanted to run after him, but her head wouldn't let her.

Chapter Nineteen

The new machinists were taken on, the factory began running smoothly and the orders came flowing in. Rachel soon found that managing the place was a full-time occupation. She never got the chance to touch a sewing machine or pick up a needle and thread. And she found she liked it.

David still came round each evening. They would discuss the daily progress of Coprell, any new designs she was considering, any amusing incidents that had happened that day. They never spoke of the evening they had gone out to dinner.

Rachel thought about it constantly. The following day she had lived in fear of him not turning up at the cottage in the usual way after work. She had spoilt everything, she told herself. Her stupid fear had made her lose David and she would also lose Coprell. She couldn't see him wanting to stay in partnership with her after the way she had treated him. Strangely, it was losing David that caused her the most concern.

The relief she experienced when he walked through the door as if nothing had happened was plain for him to see. But he made no comment and they had both acted as if the evening before had never happened.

As time went by, Rachel tried to rationalize her feelings towards him. She liked him, of that she was sure. In fact, when she was honest with herself, she found she had strange and unexplainable feelings towards him. He was the nicest, kindest man she had ever known.

But he was a man! And when she allowed that reality into her mind, she was overtaken with the grotesqueness of the act of sex with Micky. There had been no tenderness there. None of the nice feelings she had read about in women's magazines.

On her part there had been nothing but pain and revulsion. She neither knew nor cared what Micky had felt. Yet they had made a baby! The course of procreation had been completed. It wasn't right, she thought. She could not understand how it could be right to produce an innocent child out of such brutality. The more she thought about it, the more it troubled her, and it strengthened her opinion that there was something obscene about sex.

When Rachel made her regular visit to Polly before going to the factory, she found her old friend sitting in the chair by the window, watching the steady flow of people going down the hill to work. The teapot was on the table and a cup sat in front of her. But there was also a plate containing a half-eaten slice of toast.

It wasn't like Polly to leave food. Rachel looked from the plate to the old wrinkled face with a frown. Polly had been looking increasingly more tired of late and she looked as weary now as she had done when she had left her the night before. 'Did you sleep?' she asked, unable to keep the anxiety from her voice.

'A bit, lass.' Her voice held the same weariness as her eyes and something tightened in Rachel's chest. 'My knees were playing up so I got up early.'

Rachel imagined 'early' had been the middle of the night. 'Shall I get Doctor Mellor to come and give you something for them?'

Polly shook her head. 'I'm past his help. It's you I want to talk to.'

'Oh!' Rachel looked and sounded surprised. She wondered what it was that could not have been said last night or have waited until this evening. David! she thought. He was always with her when she made her nightly visits to her old friend. She tightened her lips, suddenly knowing what to expect. She wasn't disappointed.

'David might be old enough to be your dad, but that might not be a bad thing – in your case!' Polly stated baldly.

'We're just friends, Polly,' she said, suddenly on the

257

defensive. 'Don't try to make it into something it isn't. You'll only be disappointed. Anyway, why bring it up now?'

'Because I might not have another chance,' she said, speaking the words so matter of factly that it took a moment for the real meaning to sink into Rachel's brain.

'Don't say that!' she suddenly insisted, wishing Polly did not have to be so disturbingly straightforward.

'Facts have to be faced, lass. I've had a good run for my money and, to tell you the truth, I'm ready.'

A large lump rose in Rachel's throat. Don't cry, she ordered herself, having the overwhelming feeling she wanted to drop her head into Polly's lap and cry as she had done when she was younger: when she had been a child with a woman's problems.

'Get yourself rid of Micky Caradine,' Polly said, the weariness gone and the old determination back in her voice. 'You've got a chance of something more with David. You needn't try to deny it,' she quickly put in, putting an end to the protest she saw forming on Rachel's lips. 'It's plain to see in the way he looks at you. If you don't know it already, you soon will.'

Rachel dropped her head and toyed nervously with her fingers. 'He tried to kiss me,' she finally said, in a very small voice and unable to look Polly in the eyes.

'And I can guess what happened!' Polly replied sagely.

Rachel nodded.

'What happened after that?'

Rachel shrugged. 'Nothing. He wasn't angry.' She thought that maybe if he had been angry things might have been different. She would have felt guilty and it would have softened her resolve. But that would not have been the right reasons, she told herself. She looked at Polly then. 'It's never been mentioned again. He acts as if it never happened.'

'And how do you feel about that?'

She gave another shrug. 'Sad. I suppose. If I'm truthful. I like David. I never think about him being older. It's just . . . well . . . I thought about Micky and . . .' Her voice trailed away and she stared out of the window with a bleakness filling her eyes.

'Why don't you bring the subject up?' Polly suggested, narrowing her eyes into shrewd little slits. It seemed an eternity since Rachel had seen that once familiar expression and she smiled. 'Talk to him,' Polly continued. 'Tell him how you feel.'

'And the rest,' Polly agreed, and folded her arms beneath her sagging bosom and hoisted it higher up her chest, the way she had done when her chest had been of more ample proportions. Rachel bit her lip, the memories bringing the stab of tears to her eyes. 'I don't think it will come as any surprise to him,' she added with quiet certainty.

Rachel gave a nod. She did not think it would come as any surprise to him, either. But that did not make the words any easier to speak. 'Oh Polly!' she gasped, rushing forward and wrapping her arms around the old shoulders. The once robust frame had diminished greatly, the bones now felt sharp and frail, a shadow of what they used to be. The lump in her throat made further speech impossible and she could not speak of how much Polly's friendship meant to her.

'Don't go crying over me, lass,' Polly said, reading her mind as astutely as she had always been able to do. 'I've had my life. Yours is still waiting for you. Most things happen for a reason. You'll see that when you get older and can look back. Look back and laugh. And you will laugh, lass. One day. You'll have the last and the longest laugh.'

'I've laughed with you, Polly.' Panic filled her voice and she pressed her face against Polly's cool cheek and held on to her with a desperation born of fear. Ninety per cent of the laughter in her life had come from Polly and she was suddenly filled with the fear she was losing it.

'Aye, we've laughed together.' Polly fondly patted her hand. 'And I thank you for it.' A smile came to her wrinkled face and the old eyes sparkled. 'We've had some tears, but we've had more laughs.'

Rachel's smile was small and tight. Her heart went out to her old friend. In that moment she would have given up the factory, all her ambitions, everything, just to have Polly well again. All she wanted to see was the short dumpy figure waddling down the hill, her bosom seeming to counterbalance the rest of her body, her eyes twinkling with the wisdom that had guided her through her darker moments.

'I'll go and open up and come back and sit with you,' she said. 'They can manage without me for a morning.' She was suddenly of the opinion Polly knew the end was near. She had given up. There was a calmness about her, a quiet resignation. Dread trickled through Rachel's veins like icy water and she did not want to leave her old friend alone.

'No, lass.' Polly's eyes seemed to say she knew what she was thinking. Her next words confirmed she did. 'I've had a good life. Remember that, lass. David's a good man. Remember your rainbow. He'll show you the way.'

Rachel's throat constricted but she forbade herself to cry. 'Yes, Polly,' was all she could say. She gave her a big hug and kissed her on the cheek. Then, even though it was the last thing she wanted to do, respected her wishes to be left alone, and walked out.

The morning dragged by in a wakeful nightmare. Rachel did not know what she was doing, or if she was doing it right. She glanced constantly at the clock on the factory wall. It seemed to be going backwards.

At ten minutes to twelve she could stand it no longer. Without a word of explanation to the surprised staff, she grabbed her handbag and ran out of the old chapel. She raced along the lane and up the hill, her feet flying with a speed she had not found necessary since the day she fled from Micky Caradine.

Her heart was pounding as she reached Polly's door and let herself in.

Polly was still sitting in the chair.

For a moment Rachel thought her old friend was sleeping!

Chapter Twenty

She knew it was too late, but Rachel still raced round to the next-door neighbour to get them to fetch the doctor. Then she returned to Polly, sank to her knees by her side and took hold of her hand. The wrinkled old flesh felt so cold against her own warmth, and emotion finally trembled through her and broke through the numbing stupor that had grasped her from the first moment of realization.

She felt a great weight closing round her heart and lifting to her throat and she wanted to scream, but no noise came from her. The grandfather clock in the corner ticked on: tick, tick, tick. It seemed to be mocking the still and silent form in the chair and if she could have thrown something at it without letting go of Polly's hand, she would have done, smashing the glass, the long ornate brass fingers, anything to stop the constant beat that echoed the emptiness of the once cosy little room.

She clung more tightly to Polly and dropped her head into her lap. But the old hands did not stroke her hair as they used to do, and she wanted to cry, but was too numb.

Dr Mellor found her that way. He spoke, but she did not hear, and her hands were clasped so tightly to Polly's that he had to use force to prise them away. Then he pushed her across the room until she was backed up against the table and could move no further.

She seemed to be locked in some dreadful dream. And she clutched the table top to stop herself falling over, as the doctor made a cursory check for any signs of a pulse. He shook his head. 'She's been gone two or three hours,' he pronounced matter of factly.

As soon as I left, she thought, and knew she would never forgive herself for leaving her alone. Dear, kind,

Polly, who would have done anything for her.

Even when Polly was taken away by two burly ambulance men, Rachel still could not move. She pressed herself against the table, her hands still gripping tightly to the wood, the lace edging of the table cloth crumpling beneath her fingers.

'Can you send for Sarah?'

Dr Mellor's voice brought her back to life. She looked at him vaguely. Then shook her head. 'I'll be all right,' she said. She wanted to be alone. For a moment she stared silently into his face, trying to find any hint of emotion in his cold exterior. There was none.

'Well you'll have to leave here,' he informed her shortly.

Rachel looked at him for another moment. Then, suddenly realizing what she was doing to the table cloth, turned around and tried to straighten it out. Polly's best cloth, she thought anxiously. She had been so proud of the Nottingham lace. It had always been kept spotless, perfect. She brushed furiously at the creases, trying to flatten the crumpled edge down again.

'Come on.' Dr Mellor took her arm. 'That doesn't matter,' he said, impatience entering his voice.

It does, she thought. What did he know? Polly always called him an old fool. She was right!

Dr Mellor was having no more. He tugged at her arm until she relented and allowed him to lead her out of the cottage. Then he locked the door and handed her the key. 'You had better keep that!' he said, waggling the key irritably in front of her.

Rachel took the key and walked away from him. It was time he retired, she thought. He was too old, too uncaring for his profession.

When she reached home she dropped into a chair at the kitchen table. For a moment she stared blankly at the wall. Then she slumped forward, her head fell on to her arms and she began to cry, feeling a grief greater than any she had ever experienced before; greater than for Judith; greater than for her mother!

She was still in the same position when David arrived that evening.

'What's wrong?' he immediately asked. He lifted her by the shoulders, making her look at him. His gaze fixed anxiously on the tear-stained cheeks and the red puffy eyes, and his frown deepened. 'What is it?' His concern added impatience to his voice.

'Polly . . .' she said, her voice little more than a whisper. It was a moment before she could continue, 'She died this morning.'

A groan rumbled from David's throat. He lifted her to her feet and pulled her to him and held her tightly in his arms.

Rachel's arms went round his waist. She clung to him, needing him in a way she had never imagined she would need anyone – only Polly. But Polly was gone and there was a great void inside her.

'Why didn't you send for me?' he asked, lifting her chin and looking deep into her eyes with concerned rebuke.

Rachel shook her head. 'There was nothing you could do.' There was nothing anyone could have done – only herself! She could have stayed with Polly. Instead she had gone off to the factory, as if that had been more important. She had always thought she had understood how David must have felt, knowing he had chosen to go to the fashion show and leave Judith alone. She hadn't. She had not understood half of it. But she did now!

The funeral was a quiet affair. Most of Polly's friends had already died before her and there were only six people to stand with Rachel, Sarah and David around the graveside.

The loneliness of the event added to Rachel's desolation. There should have been crowds, she thought. All the good things Polly had done.

Don't go crying over me, lass. I've had a good life. Rachel heard the words as clearly as if Polly had been standing right there by her side. She looked up, startled. David was looking down at her, concern shadowing his kind sea-green eyes.

He's a good man, Polly's voice said.

Yes, Polly. A very good man, she replied silently, and sank gratefully into the arm he held out to her. Polly's wisdom and

263

knowledge had seen her through many a crisis, and it would see her through many more, she thought. Polly wasn't lost. She would never be lost. Her words of wisdom would stay with her for ever.

'How many more?' Rachel looked bleakly at the debris in the front room. The table was littered with dirty cups and saucers. Half-eaten sandwiches lay on discarded plates. It looked as if there had been ninety mourners, not just nine.

'They've all gone!' Sarah stated, and gave her an odd look.

'I don't mean them,' Rachel replied irritably. She rubbed her hand across her head, where the first signs of a headache were beginning to be felt. 'I mean funerals. Life seems to be a constant procession of death.'

'Don't be morbid.' Sarah grimaced with disgust.

'It happens to everyone . . . sooner or later,' David put in soothingly.

'Well, I've had my fair share for a good while.'

She began to collect the dirty crockery. For a good *long* while, she thought. Ten years, that was all it was! Her father, mother, Judith – now Polly! She was sure other people managed to spread their deaths out a bit better.

'Oh damn!' She knocked a cup over, a brown tea stain spreading over the cream linen cloth. It wasn't her habit to swear, but at that moment she didn't much care if she would be consigned to hell for it. 'Damn! Damn! Damn!' she repeated with feeling, telling herself hell could not be any worse than life.

'Here! Let me do that.' Sarah elbowed her aside. 'Sit down and have a rest,' she ordered, taking over and leaving Rachel to stare first at her sister, then at David, feeling totally hopeless.

'Come and sit down,' he said, and with a sigh she went to him and sat down on the sofa by his side.

At least we didn't have to lug the furniture about, she told herself, and let her gaze wander slowly around the front room and tried to imagine it as the untidy sewing room. It reminded her of the time they had struggled to get it all back downstairs for Christmas Day. The first Christmas she had spent with David. Judith had been there as well. And Polly. It had been the year she made Polly the hat to go with her coat. She could see her now, parading proudly in front of the mirror, the hat perched on her head. It was difficult to believe she would never see her again.

'Will you go to work tomorrow?' David asked.

She nodded slowly. 'Yes,' she replied simply. She had not been to the factory since the morning of Polly's death. She had wanted to close herself off, not have to meet or talk to anyone. She needed the solitude to work out her grief, she had told David, when he showed concern for her behaviour.

It was strange, she thought, how she had not given any interest to the factory. It could have stopped working and she would not have minded. But now it was over. Polly had been laid to rest and she had to get on with her life; Polly would have been the first to tell her so.

David looked both relieved and pleased with the news. 'Right now it's what you need,' he said.

She looked at him in the dark-grey suit and black tie. Then at her own plain black suit. They looked so funereal, she thought, then asked herself what they were supposed to look like? They were dressed to fit the occasion. But it reminded her of the days of Jim Featherstone's trial. David looked as sombre now as he had done then; when he had needed her so much. She gave a little grimace. The tables had turned, she realized. It wasn't just the factory she needed. It took a moment to pluck up the courage, but she finally managed it. 'I also need you,' she said, her voice small and uncertain, her fears not completely banished by the new realization of what David really meant to her.

He smiled fondly. 'Good!' The word was little more than a breath, as he took her hand and cradled it in his own, his eyes never leaving her face.

He was watching for any reaction, she realized guiltily, and let her head fall against his shoulder to keep the uncertainty clouding her eyes concealed from him. Please don't rush me, she silently begged. She had come a long way, but there was still a lot further to go. And she had to do it on her own now. There was no Polly to run to and talk her insecurities through. She gave a resigned sigh. 'You'd have thought by now I would have learned to make my own decisions,' she said, the words tumbling out before thought. When she realized what she was saying, she looked up at him embarrassedly.

Fortunately he saw nothing odd in the statement and did not ask her to explain. 'When have you ever not made your own decisions?' he asked, smiling with amusement.

'You pushed me into the factory,' she pointed out. 'You said yourself I needed a bit of force at times.'

He shook his head, still smiling, and affectionately tightened his grip on her hand. 'I only hurried you up a bit. You'd have made the move yourself, eventually. It was only because I had the old chapel. I didn't keep it for that. I just . . .' He sighed, as his mind went back to unhappier days. 'At first I couldn't work up the enthusiasm to do anything, and selling the place seemed like an awful lot of trouble. I'd have been happy if it had rotted away.' He gave a self-mocking grimace and Rachel responded with a thin smile. She was thankful those days were over and he had come out of it all on the right side.

'It was only later that it occurred to me it would be ideal for you.'

'You never said that before.' She eyed him suspiciously.

He laughed. 'You're a very stubborn lady, Rachel Cooper. You don't like anyone telling you what to do when it comes down to your work. I felt I had a better chance of success if I played on your sympathies.' He looked a little sheepish. 'So I made you think you were doing it for me.'

She looked amazed. 'How did you know that?' The initial decision had been for his benefit, but she'd soon come round to thinking it was the best idea for herself as well.

He laughed again. 'Masculine intuition can be just as good as feminine,' he pointed out, bringing his eyes down to smile closely into her own. 'And it was nice to know you were willing to do it for me.' He leaned back again and looked suddenly serious. 'Call it male pride, call it what you will, but I had to know you thought about me the same way I thought about you.'

She began to smile, then changed it to a mocking glare and aimed a playful punch at his ribs. 'You should go on the stage, David Morrell!'

He warded her off and they both laughed for a moment. It was Rachel who fell silent first. Oh, Polly, I should not be laughing at your funeral, she thought guiltily. Then she remembered how much Polly had liked a good laugh, and she knew her old friend would have forgiven her and, wherever she was, she would be laughing with her.

'All the evenings we spent together,' David said, turning Rachel's mind back to him. He shook his head, as if in wonder. 'They were so nice. I could never have got over Judith without your help.'

The mention of Judith put a thin smile on her lips. 'I know,' she said. It was good to hear him talk of her.

'But you never showed anything other than friendship.' He sighed reflectively. 'You never gave any indication that you'd be willing to let the relationship go further. And, I suppose . . . I hoped if we got together over the factory, we might get together over other things.' He paused and gazed deep into her eyes. 'I was falling in love with you a long time ago.' He lifted her chin, bringing her face upwards. His eyes never left her own as his head slowly descended, watching for any reaction in the same way he had done when taking her hand.

She was ready, she told herself, and prepared to accept the touch of his lips. But even though the kiss was gentle and undemanding, she felt her body stiffen with anxiety, and her lips were trembling when he moved away.

'I won't rush you,' he said, making her wonder if she had spoken out her fears. 'We'll take it as slow as you want . . . All right?'

She could only nod in acceptance. The strength of his concern was so great that emotion clogged her throat and her voice was lost. Tell him, Polly's voice urged inside her head. It won't come as any surprise to him. The time was right, she told herself. Perfect, in fact. He had, himself, given her the opportunity without asking directly. 'David . . .' she began nervously.

'Right, I'm off out!' Sarah announced, as she breezed through the door.

Rachel looked round startled. She had forgotten her sister was in the kitchen doing the washing up. She edged away from David and tried to pull her hand free, embarrassed for Sarah to see them in close intimacy.

David held on tightly, refusing to let her go, and Sarah grinned as she glanced knowingly at their clasped hands, and Rachel felt her cheeks redden.

'Will you be late?' she asked, attempting to cover her embarrassment. But she immediately regretted speaking. Sarah was always late coming home. Making a point of asking made it seem as if she was checking to find out how long she would be alone with David, and only added to her unease.

'Who's the lucky fella tonight?' David put in, giving her hand a reassuring squeeze and increasing her discomfort by making it obvious he knew how she was feeling.

What must he be thinking of her? she wondered, too anxious at that moment to listen properly, and missing Sarah's reply.

'He's lasting a long time,' David teased. 'It must be serious.'

Sarah blossomed visibly. 'It is,' she chirped, and ran upstairs to get herself ready.

'I wish she *would* settle down with one!' Rachel glanced at David with concern. 'It worries me sometimes.'

'Sarah's got her head screwed on the right way,' he assured her, and put his arm around her again. 'Come here,' he said, pulling her back to him.

'I know,' she replied distractedly. She moved into the cradle of his arm, but her mind was fixed on her sister. She had planned to make Sarah more worldly wise, but there were times when she had the feeling she had let things go too far.

She did not speak of her worries and for a long time David looked silently down at her. 'Well . . . ?' he finally asked.

'Well what?' She looked puzzled, her mind still taken up by Sarah.

'You were going to say something,' he pointed out. 'Just before Sarah came in.'

'Oh . . .' She felt colour rushing to her cheeks. 'It couldn't have been important. I've forgotten.' She let her head fall against his shoulder, once more concealing the uncertainty in her eyes. It was obvious he did not believe her. But the moment had gone now. He was prepared to let her go at her own pace without knowing the full facts. So there was no point in dragging it all up when there was no need. It was best forgotten.

'I've got to come up with some ideas for the advertising campaign,' she said, changing the subject. 'Have you got any?'

'As a matter of fact, yes, I have.'

She smiled; half in pleasure that he was interested enough in the factory to have thought about it himself; half in relief that he was willing to let the previous matter drop. 'So tell me,' she said.

'I was thinking about the model needed for the shots,' he said. 'Why don't you use Sarah?' He looked as if he had found the answer to a prayer.

Rachel was not so sure. 'Sarah?' she repeated, showing her surprise. The idea of her sister's photograph spread across the pages of national magazines – wearing nothing but underwear – was not one that appealed to her. 'I don't think . . .'

'She's more than capable,' he put in. 'And she would jump at the chance. You could turn her into the Coprell girl. All the big names have their own model.'

'We're not a big name,' she pointed out, feeling her reservations increasing.

'Not yet. But I have faith in my partner's ability,' he teased.

She had to smile. 'Stop trying to flannel me. I'll think about it. She is *my* sister! You're not twisting my arm on this one!' she stressed meaningfully.

'OK,' he replied, as if conceding. Then immediately went on to explain further points in his favour. 'It would be far better to have Coprell's own face. One that became as

269

recognizable as the label. Rather than a succession of unfamiliar models.'

'I said I would think about it!' she insisted, unmoved by his persuasion.

'All right! All right!' He held his hand up in surrender. 'I won't mention it again.'

A knock at the door stopped her making any reply. She got up to answer it, hoping it was not someone rude enough to turn up on Polly's funeral day to get something made.

'Doctor Mellor!' She did not try to conceal her amazement at finding him standing on the doorstep. He was the last person she had expected to see. .

'I've got this for you.' He waggled a long white envelope in front of her nose and walked in without waiting to be invited.

'Oh?' It was all she could think of to say, as she stared blankly at the envelope.

'It's Polly Webster's will,' he announced bluntly, making no attempt to hand it over. 'She left it with me when she asked me to witness it.'

'Shouldn't it have been with a solicitor?' she asked shortly. It was the first she had heard of any will. She wanted to grab the envelope from him. If it had belonged to Polly he had no right having it. She would never forgive him for his unfeeling treatment of her old friend.

'I think *I'm* qualified enough to be able to look after it,' he snapped, and continued to flap the envelope around in the air.

Rachel stared at him coolly. She wasn't going to apologize. He's nothing but an old fool, she heard Polly say, and almost smiled.

'Can I have it then?' She made a pointed gesture of holding her hand out flat in front of him.

The doctor hesitated, looking put out. 'Don't you think I should read it to you?'

'That won't be necessary.' She bristled with indignation. If he thought she was going to listen to Polly's last wishes from his lips he could think again. 'I think *I'm* qualified enough to be able to read it!' she snapped, taking on his manner as well as his words, to let him know exactly where he stood.

'Uh!' he snorted loudly, followed by several minor huffs and grunts of disapproval. Then he turned deliberately to David. 'I think you had better have this,' he said, and handed the envelope to him.

David looked questioningly at Rachel. She shrugged her shoulders and gave a nod to tell him to take it. Anything to get rid of the silly old fool, she thought, and quickly showed him to the door. She did not say goodbye. Neither did he.

'If he was a horse they would have shot him years ago,' she said, as she returned to the front room and ran her hands nervously down her black skirt in anticipation of what the envelope contained.

'Shall I open it?' David asked, looking into her face with a concern that suddenly crushed her. He looked so bleak, and it reminded her of all he had gone through, all he had lost. And she clapped a hand over her eyes feeling a need to cry like she had cried on the day of Polly's death: for her old friend who she would never see again and whose last wishes were in that envelope; for herself because she had to look in that envelope and she really did not want to do it; but most of all for David, for what she was denying him: the ability to give herself in love to another person, which Micky had taken from her.

'Yes, you open it,' she spoke sharply, concealing her grief in anger, as she removed her hand and looked into his eyes with a bleakness that matched his own.

He smiled thinly and patted the sofa. 'Come and sit down,' he said, and she went to him, knowing she needed him but doubting she would ever be able to give him everything he needed in return.

There wasn't much. Just a short note stating that anything Rachel wanted was hers. The grandfather clock, and a gold locket Rachel had never seen, Polly had pointed out as being the only things of value. The rest, she suggested, would make a good bonfire.

A grandfather clock and a gold locket! Rachel stared

numbly at the sheet of writing paper she had taken from David's hand. It didn't amount to much after ninety years. Yet what Polly had possessed had been of far more value. In many ways Polly had been the richest person she had known. She smiled with the fondness of her memories. Would she ever know half the riches? she asked herself. Remember the gold at the bottom of the rainbow, the voice said inside her head.

'Are you all right?' David asked, and wrapped his arm around her and pulled her close.

'Yes.' She nodded and reached out to place Polly's meagre will down on the table. She looked up into his concerned eyes and wondered if he was the gold at the bottom of the rainbow. If he was, she was in danger of losing it – unless she tried harder!

Slowly she lifted her arms and curled them around his neck. A moment's surprise passed over his face. Then he wrapped both arms around her and pulled her right up close to him, and waited. With the same slow uncertainty she moved her head towards him, little by little, until her lips were a hair's breadth from his. She had a moment's hesitation and allowed panic to take over briefly. But David did not move. He understood she needed to do this for herself, she realized, and felt a kind of relief in the knowledge, as she stared uncertainly into the closeness of his eyes. They were kind eyes, she told herself. Gentle. They held no leering gleam, like Micky's did when they looked at her. Forget Micky, she ordered herself, and, crossing the final barrier, touched her lips to his, carefully and tentatively. It was a moment before he responded, allowing her the time to assess her feelings and to withdraw if she decided to.

She did not withdraw. Her lips remained still, her eyes staring into his. She felt a smile curve his mouth, before it slowly began to move against her own in a softly testing caress. He closed his eyes and she quickly did the same. She wondered if she was doing it right, but if she wasn't, he hadn't got a clue to what she should be doing. So she took David's lead and moved her mouth gently in time with his.

But the next moment Sarah's footsteps were running down the stairs, and in an instant she was moving away from him, putting space between them.

Once more David held on to her, allowing her to sit back but not to remove his arm, which stayed firmly round her shoulders.

Sarah hurtled through the stairfoot door like a tornado. 'Don't mind me. Got to rush. I'm already late.' She was out of the cottage before Rachel could blink.

David began to laugh, until she realized he was laughing at her and she looked hurt and he became serious. 'There's nothing wrong with Sarah knowing how we feel,' he said, lifting her chin and looking right into her eyes. 'There's nothing *wrong* in what we are doing,' he added pointedly.

'I know.' Her voice was small and she sighed. It all felt so odd and alien. She was trying to change the habits of nine years in a few minutes. 'You'll have to give me time.' She looked uncertain, hoping her sudden forwardness had not given him other ideas.

'I know that.' He pulled her head down to rest on his shoulder once more. 'I won't ever hurt you, Rachel. Don't ever fear that I will.'

They remained in the same position for the rest of the evening. They talked about the factory, Polly, Sarah, and even Judith. On several occasions, she prepared herself to tell him the truth, always finding a good excuse to back out at the last minute.

He did not try to kiss her again and she did not try to attempt to prove she could do it again. There had been nothing objectionable about the feel of his lips on her own. They had been soft and warm, not cold and wet like the memory she held of Micky's. But she had asked him to give her time and she was not going back on her request. When things got more intimate she was still not sure she would be able to see it through. If she rushed herself she knew she wouldn't. And that would have been even more unfair to him.

It was after eleven when David looked at the clock, and

said, 'If I don't go, Sarah will be back. Then what would she think?'

The teasing light in his eyes made Rachel laugh. 'Thank you for being understanding,' she said with feeling, and gave a little sigh, realizing she was not sure he knew what he was being understanding about.

'If something is worth having, it is worth waiting for.' He tilted her chin and kissed her gently on the lips.

Rachel was glad he did; the action hid the colour that leapt to her cheeks from the intimate suggestion of the remark.

'You're beginning to sound like Polly,' she teased, using humour to cover her embarrassment, as he stretched his tall frame out of the sofa.

'Maybe I am, maybe I'm not,' he quoted, in exactly the same manner Polly would have used. Rachel laughed as he took hold of her arms and lifted her to her feet. 'You loved Polly well enough,' he said, looking suddenly serious. 'If quoting her makes you love me half as much, then I'll go . . .'

'I do love you, David.' She spoke before thinking. She needed him. He was the kindest man she had ever known and she felt an affection for him she had never experienced before. If that wasn't love, then she didn't know what was.

'Do you mean that?' He looked uncertain and she felt a crushing guilt for all she had put him through.

She nodded her head. 'Yes.' Her voice was small, coming stronger, as she added, 'I think I must have loved you for a long time, as well. But it frightens me.'

'I know,' he replied gently.

'About the baby?' she asked, suddenly deciding the time was right and if she didn't do it now she never would. Then she had second thoughts. Polly had seemed so sure he would already know, but she felt her courage slipping and wished the words back. She dropped her gaze, unable to watch as the look of disgust and condemnation spread over his face.

But he placed a finger under her chin and forced her head up. 'Yes,' he said simply. And there was no censure in his lovely eyes, only compassion. A lump constricted her throat.

She had tried to fool herself that nobody knew and she was suddenly incredulous of her own stupidity. There wasn't much went by in a village the size of Millbridge.

'It was Micky Caradine,' she said, knowing if she did not complete the story now, she never would.

For a moment David looked taken aback.

'He attacked me,' she quickly added, wanting to make it plain she had not been a willing party.

'I guessed that,' he said gently. 'After your reaction when I suddenly leapt on you after we went to dinner.'

Rachel bit her lip, she didn't want to remember that evening.

'I'm sorry,' he said, and she shook her head.

'I'm sorry, too.'

He shook his head then. 'You have nothing to be sorry about. I charged in like a bull at a gate. I'd forgotten about the baby. Well, I never really knew for sure. It was only a brief rumour and it had gone from my mind.'

A nine-day wonder, as Polly would have said, she thought, and was thankful for the small mercy. It was obvious the neighbours had had their suspicions, but no-one could have worked out the whole truth, or the place would have been ablaze with it.

'Where is the baby now?' he asked.

'I had her adopted,' she replied, and tried to push the image of a little girl from her mind.

'Does Sarah know?' he suddenly asked, his eyes narrowing in an uncertain frown.

Rachel shook her head. 'I've never been able to tell her,' she said with regret. 'She was so young she didn't notice anything at the time.' She smiled grimly. It would have made it so much easier if Sarah had been more inquisitive. 'There might come a time,' she said, not really believing herself. Then she saw his chest rise and fall in a silent sigh and felt her heart dip in despair. 'Does it matter?' she asked, fearing the worst.

'No! Of course not,' he was quick to reassure her, and he pulled her into his arms and held her so tightly she felt her bones might break. 'Thank you for telling me,' he said.

She smiled, feeling safe and protected by his arms. I'm glad I listened to you, Polly, she thought, as she listened to the steady beat of his heart beneath her ear. There was nothing threatening, nothing to fear, and she wrapped her arms around his waist and offered her mouth to him.

The kiss was long, building up in pressure as he felt her body relax against him. The tip of his tongue snaked out to caress her lip. She jumped, her body immediately tense. Stop it, she ordered herself. Slowly her body responded to the command and she loosened up and relaxed against him once again. For the second time his tongue snaked out. This time she was prepared, and her lips parted and allowed the intrusion.

The sound of a car drawing up at the end of the yard made David finally look up. 'Is that Sarah?'

'I think so,' she replied, the regret in her eyes putting a smile on his face.

'Then I'll see you tomorrow.' He planted a small kiss on the end of her nose, then reluctantly released her and turned away.

She followed him to the door and watched him walk down the yard, and realized she felt better now he knew the truth. It was as if a barrier had been removed and they could now reach each other without any hindrance. As if the lie had got in their way. But she hadn't actually lied, she told herself, and tried to throw off the remnants of her chapel days; she just hadn't told the truth. There was a difference, she assured herself, and glanced at her watch as David met Sarah coming the other way. It was only just after half past eleven. Every other night she had to pull Sarah up for being out after midnight. She would choose tonight to listen to me, she thought dryly.

Then she almost died with embarrassment. Sarah glanced cheekily at her own watch and gave David a wide-eyed look of shock. 'Whatever have you been doing until this time?' she asked, mocking Rachel's own words of other nights.

'Mind your own business, young lady,' he tossed back good naturedly.

Rachel breathed again, thankful he had not taken exception

to Sarah's rudeness. She really did go beyond the limits, she thought, and hoped she would settle down with this boyfriend, and calm down a bit.

But it was only a few moments before she was taking her sincere hopes back. The car Sarah had got out of had gone up the hill to turn around. As it came down again, it stopped at the end of the yard. The young man driving stuck his arm through the open window and waved. Sarah turned and gave a vigorous response.

Rachel did not need to hear David call, 'Good night, Alan,' to have her worst fears thrust in her face. The street light at the end of the yard shone directly on the young man's face.

The warm glow David had left in her body trickled out through her feet. She had the feeling it had been replaced by icy water and clasped her hand over her stomach as nausea rose up inside her. She leaned back against the door frame and felt the sickness get worse and beads of perspiration form on her lip and forehead.

Sarah breezed past her without much concern and she turned slowly to her sister, feeling if she moved quickly she might faint. 'How . . . how long have you been going out with Alan Caradine?' she asked, begging to be told that she wasn't, that it was all a big mistake: he had just brought her home, picked her up at the bus stop and given her a lift. She could accept anything, except a firm relationship.

'A few months,' Sarah replied.

A few months! 'How many months?' she demanded, suddenly filled with anger. Her sister could not do this to her! 'I thought you were going out with someone called Philip?'

'Oh, he's ancient history.' Sarah gave a dismissive shrug and threw her handbag on the table. 'These shoes are crippling me.' She pulled first one shoe off, then the other and tossed them on the floor. 'What's wrong with you?' she asked.

'I think you could find better than Alan Caradine,' she insisted, and closed the door and turned the key and drew the bolt with such viciousness the hounds of hell might have been trying to follow her in.

'Don't be such a snob! There's nothing wrong with Alan.'

277

Sarah massaged her aching feet, giving them more attention than she was giving Rachel.

'I'm not a snob,' she retaliated hotly. 'The whole family is rough. You've got to admit that!'

'Alan is not the family!' Sarah got to her feet and glared at her. 'Alan is different. You don't know him. Don't condemn him before you've given him a chance.'

Rachel looked around the room in despair. She could not believe this was happening. Sarah had no right to be associating with *that* family. 'You're too good for him,' she insisted. 'You've got the looks to get anyone you please. Why go for someone like him? Why didn't you tell me you were going out with him?' she asked, suddenly wondering why it had been kept a secret.

'You never asked!' Sarah pointed out fiercely, and lifted her chin and glared down her nose. 'And anyone I please happens to be Alan. You'd better get used to the idea. We're getting engaged – whether you like it or not!' With a toss of her head, she swept her shoes from the floor, grabbed her handbag and stormed upstairs.

Rachel felt icy cold. She sank into a chair and folded her arms protectively round herself. Engaged! The thought filled her with horror. Her own sister marrying into Micky Caradine's family. Sarah would be his sister-in-law!

She dropped her head into her hands and sighed loudly. Then sat up straight and began to pull the pins from her hair. How could she expect Sarah to understand? She'd never told her the more illuminating facts about her own life and it seemed it was now too late. She stared blankly at the wall and wondered how she was going to cope with this. Maybe if she let it run its course, Sarah would eventually come to realize there were better fish in the sea, she told herself, but didn't feel very confident with the theory. They were talking about getting engaged. At least Sarah was. She didn't dare to hope it was just a fantasy of Sarah's and that he knew nothing about it.

She wished she had more friends herself and was able to introduce Sarah to some more fitting men. She wondered if

David knew any at Rolls-Royce. She sighed again, seeing herself attending a wedding as sister of the bride with Micky as brother of the groom, and she stood up wearily and shook her hair out, and made her way up the stairs wishing it had just been her own funeral she had attended and not Polly's.

At her bedroom door she paused and looked up the second flight of stairs to Sarah's firmly closed door. For several moments she tossed over the idea of going up and coming clean. But the way Sarah was banging around in her bedroom told her she was in no mood to listen. And she had already told David tonight, and once a night was enough confession for anybody, she decided, and finally went into her own room and closed the door with a sigh. Besides, in Sarah's case, she had the awful feeling it was too late – much too late!

Chapter Twenty-one

The following morning the cottage was cloaked in a tense silence. Sarah quickly threw down the slice of toast and cup of tea that Rachel had prepared for her. Then she grabbed her coat and handbag and walked out with only the briefest of acknowledgements to Rachel's simple goodbye.

Rachel felt as despairing as she had the night before. She gave the breakfast pots a quick wash, then left them on the drainer to dry themselves and grabbed her own coat and bag and hurried out of the cottage with the same haste as Sarah.

It seemed strange going to the factory without popping into Polly's on the way. Oh Polly! she thought sadly. Just when I really need you. She looked up at the mill chimney looming overhead as she hurried down the hill. She was surprised to find that scaffolding had been put up its length and two workmen were right up at the top. Life had been going on while she was locked away in mourning. Just one more thing she hadn't known about, she thought bitterly, her mind turning back to Sarah and Alan Caradine. And she felt her own life, at that moment, to be as precarious as the men perched on the chimney top and in touch with the clouds.

Stop feeling sorry for yourself, she ordered sharply, and bent her head as the first stirrings of rain touched her face. Summer was over, she thought, as she reached the bottom of the hill and turned on the lane. But it didn't concern her. She had seen sweet little of the good weather, always cooped up inside the factory or the cottage.

It made her wonder if a holiday would do her good. Sarah, as well, she thought, her mind beginning to revolve. If she took Sarah off, somewhere nice, perhaps abroad! The idea suddenly appealed to her. It might make Sarah realize there was a lot more to life than the close-knit community of the village and the Alan Caradines of the world.

She sighed. It would be nice. But it wasn't possible at the moment. Not with the factory so new. Perhaps next year, she told herself hopefully. Then she realized next year might be too late for Sarah. She sighed again. She would have to think of something else.

It was raining hard by the time she reached the factory and she ran up the steps and quickly unlocked the big wooden door. As she entered, she turned back to look at the clock above the door. She had been in such a hurry to get out of the cottage and away from her own company, she had not looked at the time and had forgotten to put on her watch.

She was only fifteen minutes early, and most of that was the time she would have spent with Polly! She looked around the large room, at the silent sewing machines, the multitude of clutter. She looked up at the high vaulted ceiling which would never lose its religious identity, and the emptiness seemed to crush her. Half of all this belonged to her. Yet did it make her happy?

At one time, yes. But just then she had the strangest feeling there must be more to life.

'Morning, luv.' Flo came bustling through the door and a smile came to Rachel's face.

'Morning, Flo,' she returned, thankful to be saved from herself. 'Has everything been all right?'

'Right as ninepence.' Flo dropped her shopping bag and umbrella, hung up her coat and bustled into the office. Then she began to relate everything that had been done, and what had not been done, until Rachel was finding it difficult to keep the smile from her face. In her absence, it appeared, Flo had taken over and she was obviously feeling very proud of herself. And rightly so, Rachel thought, looking at all the neat piles of paper lying on her desk. Flo had proved very competent.

At the end of the day Rachel was tired, but happy. The brief moroseness of the morning had vanished as she fell back into the busy routine as if she had never been away.

She was picking up her keys and handbag, ready to leave, when the telephone rang. It was the photographer who was dealing with the new advertising contract. He wanted to know dates, location, model's name, type of settings – he wanted to know everything!

Rachel grimaced into the telephone receiver. 'I'll sort it all out tomorrow,' she replied firmly. 'I'll call you in the morning.' She put the telephone down before the man had time to object. Her mind began to whirl. She had done nothing about it. She knew all the garments she wanted to use. But the model? And the settings?

When David arrived after work, she was sitting at the front room table, its surface obliterated by glossy photographs. 'Which one do you think?' Frustration filled her voice. She had gone through them all, over and over again, and none of the models had leaped out at her as being *the* one. She held two photographs up for his inspection: Kathy, dark and sultry; Norma, blonde and bubbly.

He studied them for a long time.

'How about a redhead?' She introduced a third photograph, hopefully.

He still appeared less than convinced.

'You must have some preference!' she insisted, impatient to have the problem dealt with.

David grinned. 'I prefer the blonde. But I don't think we have the same thing in mind.'

Rachel blushed. 'Be serious,' she snapped. Her voice was more harsh because she was angry with herself. She felt stupid for her silly reaction, just because he had made a suggestive joke. Thankfully Sarah chose that moment to come down-stairs.

'Are you seeing Alan?' She knew it was a stupid question. Who else would she be seeing! But her irritation at knowing the answer took the fire out of her cheeks.

'Yes,' Sarah replied shortly.

Rachel gave an inward sigh. Sarah's red mini-skirt showed an indecent amount of long leg encased in white knee-length boots. The white skinny rib sweater, moulded to her body like a second skin, defined the outline of breasts not completely concealed by the swathe of long golden hair. Make-up gave her blue eyes a large, innocent appearance. While at the same time pale pink lipstick gave her mouth a seductive pout.

'Going somewhere special?' David said, attempting to break the icy atmosphere.

Sarah turned to him, making it plain the smile she gave was for him alone. 'Alan's taking me to dinner – at the Palm Court!'

The Palm Court! *That* had been for her benefit, Rachel realized bitterly. Sarah had wanted her to know Alan had a bit of class.

'Have a nice time,' David said, with a sincerity that made Rachel want to scream.

'We will,' Sarah chirped. Then turned to Rachel. 'See you later,' she said, her voice uncertain, a touch of contrition entering her eyes.

'See you later.' she replied, reluctantly accepting the olive branch Sarah offered, even though she did not know what she was going to do with it.

As soon as Sarah had walked out, Rachel turned back to the photographs. 'Let's get this sorted out,' she said, her voice stiff with anger caused by fear.

'Leave those,' David insisted, grasping her arm and pulling her hand away from the glossy portrait she was about to pick up. 'Didn't you know?' he questioned.

She shook her head. Then gave a small smile of gratitude that she had him on her side.

'It is *Alan* Sarah is with,' he pointed out gently. 'Don't tar everybody with the same brush.'

'They're brothers!' she ground through her teeth, the bitterness she had nursed for almost twenty-four hours exploding inside her.

'And you and Sarah are sisters. But you are as much alike as ice and fire.'

And she knew which she was! she thought, his reassurances doing nothing to calm her. Ice! Cold! Unapproachable! Sarah was fire: warm, welcoming, needed.

She dropped her head forward and groaned, realizing she was jealous of her own sister. It had never occurred to her before. But it was true. Sarah's vivacity and easy-going nature, her ability to get on with everybody – that was how she wished she could be. It was a numbing realization.

'If you dig your heels in it will make Sarah more determined,' David continued.

'I know.' Her voice was flat and resigned. She picked a photograph up and threw it down again, and sighed.

'Let it run its course,' he said.

Hadn't she told herself the very same thing? It wasn't any easier to accept from David's lips. 'You're right,' she reluctantly accepted. 'Let's eat.' She scooped up the photographs and threw them on to the sofa. Then she hurried through to the kitchen, the subject dropped from conversation – if not from her mind.

While they were eating the meal, talk became easy and relaxed, covering this and that, uncomplicated and unimportant topics. Rachel began to relax, enjoying David's company as she always did.

The photographs lay strewn across the sofa where she had dropped them and one caught her eye. A girl with long blond hair, paler than Sarah's, but the same heavy fringe and long straight waterfall over her shoulders. She was wearing a pale blue mini-skirt with a white skinny rib sweater and white boots. If the skirt had been red she would have looked identical to the way Sarah had looked when she walked out of the door.

'We've had a lot of new orders while I've been away,' she said, as her mind began to turn over the uncertain possibility. David thought Sarah would be perfect for the job. Coprell's own model! No, she couldn't do it. It wouldn't look right having her own sister parading around in underwear. Only a few photographs would be in underwear, she reasoned. The rest would be fully clothed. They needed someone with nice long legs to carry off the short skirts that were now the height of fashion. Someone tall, slender, pretty . . .

'Are you listening to me?'

His voice made her wake up to find he was peering at her

suspiciously. She looked apologetic. 'I was just thinking about Flo,' she said, not wanting him to know she might be susceptible to persuasion. If the decision was to be made, it would be her own. 'Flo's been running the place while I was away. Now she's back to running errands and making tea.' She looked regretful. It didn't seem fair.

David laughed. 'You could always give her some more to do.'

'Then we would need another general dogsbody, and I don't want to put the wages bill up, not just yet. Or take on another member of staff just for the sake of it.' Or pay a model's fee when it wasn't necessary, a small voice said at the back of her head.

She turned her gaze to the photographs. The girl in the blue mini-skirt had a lovely figure. But her face, though pretty, was in no way striking . . . Not like Sarah's. Sarah would jump at the chance, she told herself, remembering how thrilled she had been to take part in the fashion show. How easily she had done it, as well. But would it be right?

Then her mind turned another corner. She realized it might open up a new career for Sarah and was suddenly more than interested. She had never wanted Sarah to work in The Boutique, always thinking she could do better for herself. Maybe . . . She looked up, meeting David's curious appraisal. If Sarah thought she had a worthwhile career, one that might be hindered by permanent ties – like a steady boyfriend – she might think twice about Alan Caradine!

'Do you really think Sarah would be right for it?'

David did not have to ask what 'it' was. 'You know I do. She would be perfect. Are you having second thoughts?'

For several seconds she bit her lip and stared at him. She couldn't tell him her real reasons; they showed her to be too manipulative. It was for Sarah's good, she told herself. Forget what Micky had done, Sarah could do better for herself than Alan Caradine.

'It would be nice to have our own girl,' she finally stated, as if speaking more to herself than to David. 'None of these inspire me.' She waved her hand over the array of photographs. 'I'll see what she thinks in the morning.' She returned to the meal in front of her. It was the perfect solution, she thought.

'Sarah will bite your hand off,' he replied confidently, and Rachel hoped she would be forgiven her scheming.

Sarah did bite Rachel's hand off. Two days later the photographic session took place. One week after that Rachel had the job of sorting out which shots to use and which to reject.

'How about that?' She held the photograph up for David's inspection. She had got the folder full of shots out immediately after they had finished their evening meal.

David sighed. 'How about forgetting work and going out for a drink?' He took the photograph from her hand, reached over and picked up the rest, piled them together, stuck them back in the folder and shoved it across the table.

Rachel looked surprised, more with the request than his actions. Apart from the one night they had gone to dinner, he had never suggested they go out before. She wondered if it was because he was going away for five days. A Saudi Arabian airliner had crashed and he was one of the investigation team. A lot of people had been killed. Perhaps it was playing on his mind!

'What's wrong?' David prompted her silence with impatience. 'Am I not allowed to take you out and show you off?'

'I thought you were happy just coming here,' she replied, rather lamely, feeling guilty that she often let it slip her mind that he had another job that did not concern the factory or The Boutique.

'I am,' he agreed. 'But sometimes all you can think about is work. How am I supposed to get close to you? How can we make any progress when all you talk about is your blessed factory!'

'*Our*! factory!' she pointed out fiercely.

'*Ours! Yours!* What does it matter? It's always there inside your head. Right where you want it to be. Where it stops you

286

having to think of other things. More important things! I'm going away for almost a full week. Can't I leave you with more inside your head than your blessed work?'

That it was her dreams he was crushing angered her. That he had hit the nail right on the head inflamed the guilt in her and doubled her anger. '*What is more important?*' she demanded hotly, and leapt from the sofa and paced across the room and away from him. When she reached the wall she turned and glared at him.

'*Us!*' he declared with equal fire. 'Or doesn't that mean anything to you?' His eyes lanced her with something she had never seen before and, taking her cue, she also stood up, then paced the floor with taut steps.

He reminded her of a tiger in a cage, she thought, fixing him coolly, her gaze moving with him; to the fireplace, to the dresser, back to the fireplace. Stop it, she wanted to scream but not from fear. There was no fear inside her, only anger; directed not at David, but at Micky Caradine and all the Caradines, for what they had, and were still, putting her through. Only because she was letting them, she suddenly thought. Polly had known, she had told her it was time she got herself rid of him. But, as usual, she'd thought she knew better.

'I know you've been hurt,' he said, suddenly stopping and facing her squarely. 'And I'm trying to go at your pace. But you always keep work between us. It's like a bloody great wall I've got to get over before I can reach you. Rachel, please . . . !' He held his hands out before him.

An act of resignation, or one of appeal. She did not know and could only stare at him silently. What he was saying was the truth. She liked to know his opinions on things that concerned the factory, because it belonged to him, as well as herself. But there was never any need to bring the work home the way she did – to fill their evenings! She dropped her gaze, suddenly unable to look him in the eyes.

He sighed loudly. 'When Polly died I thought it was all going to change,' he said. 'For a few days there was something more important to you. The night of her funeral I thought you'd made the first step. You let me get closer to you than I'd ever been.' The emotion in his voice cut through her like a knife and she looked up with a great sadness in her eyes.

He fell silent and for several moments only watched her. He was waiting for her to say something, she realized, but she couldn't find the right words, and all that came out was a pathetic, 'Sorry.'

He sighed again. 'Don't you understand what I'm talking about? Since then you've filled the evening with plans, projects and bloody models.' He swept his hand angrily over the folder of photographs. 'As if you're frightened if you don't keep me talking I'll leap on you.' With another sigh he fell silent and looked defeated.

'I . . .' she began, then gave up. To say sorry again was pointless. He had every right to be angry. She had known exactly what she was doing. She had wanted to stop herself, yet fear had made it impossible. But fear of what? She wasn't afraid of David. She wasn't even afraid of Micky any more. The emotion she now felt for him was a raging anger for all he had taken from her. And by feeling that way she was letting him take more from her. Her virginity was gone and irreparable; her self-respect she had been fighting for every day since; but there was no fighting to be done for David, yet she was allowing Micky's memory to rob her of both David and the rest of her life.

She took a deep breath and looked him in the face, the new realization softening her eyes. She did not speak, there was no need, he sensed the change in her and his own expression lightened noticeably. She smiled crookedly and took a step forward. Before she had taken another, his arms were opened wide to her and she stepped into them knowing it had to be her decision. There would be no force on his part, she had to go to him, willingly, of her own free will. And it was with complete free will that she wrapped her arms around his neck and offered her lips readily, as his mouth came down to kiss her.

He pulled her so close she could feel the entire length of

him, but there was no fear, only a feeling of safety and the protection she craved from him. Then she closed her mind to everything except the warm sensations running through her body.

It was David who finally pulled away. She looked up into his face and felt joy, as she saw the happiness spilling from the eyes that had previously looked so hurt.

'What do you want me to do?' she asked, feeling sure the time had come to break down the final barrier and give herself to him completely.

He sighed, and for a moment looked torn in two with indecision. 'Go and get your coat and let's be normal,' he suddenly said, and Rachel looked taken aback.

'But . . . ?' she began, but he placed a finger across her lips to stop her words.

'There's no hurry,' he said. 'When it happens it won't be because I've bullied you into it.'

Rachel's smile was thin and uncertain. Even though she found she was experiencing a certain relief, she also found there was a sinking feeling in the bottom of her stomach. Disappointment? she wondered. No, she told herself, and quickly went to get her jacket and handbag.

'Well it was *your* idea!' Rachel laughed, as she linked her arm through David's and they walked back up the hill to the cottage.

'I know! I know!' He laughed with her.

'Did you see Flo's face when we walked in hand in hand?' Her laughter increased and a cat, which had been sniffing around the gutter, looked up in surprise, its eyes catching the street light and looking like amber jewels. 'It's all right, puss,' she said, and bent to scratch its head as they passed by. Then she looked up at David and her laughter returned. 'At least they didn't talk about work.' At his suggestion they had gone to the Beehive; only to find Flo and all the factory girls were there, having a night out.

'No,' he agreed. 'And neither did you . . . And it was very nice!' he added pointedly.

'Point taken,' she said. She had learned more than one lesson tonight. She guessed he had chosen the village local on purpose. To make their relationship public and to make her face up to, and accept, a real relationship with him. Normal, as he had said earlier, and not something that had to be hidden behind closed doors.

She sighed inwardly for all the silly things she had done. For so long she had been living with secrets that it had become the normal way of things for her. Well, no more, she thought with determination. He'll show you the way, she heard Polly telling her.

Yes, she replied silently. He was showing her the way: gently and without force.

'It raised more than just Flo's eyebrows,' he said, and looked suddenly serious. 'Does it bother you?'

She shook her head and held tighter to his arm. 'I'm glad we went,' she said, and he looked into her eyes with a smile that spoke for him.

They walked in silence for a while. An owl suddenly swooped low across the road and came to rest in the branches of a heavily laden apple tree. Rachel wondered if it was Polly's owl. She hoped it was the one that had sat in her old friend's tree and kept her company, as she had called it. The owl hooted and she felt it was telling her it was, and she felt it was a good omen, a message from Polly. And, when they reached the cottage door, she was filled with a warm contentment and a quiet certainty that what she was going to do was right.

But when he unlocked the door, David handed her the key without coming inside. He gave her a brief peck on the cheek and left her standing there.

She had expected more, and she felt a strange emptiness rolling over her as she watched him walk to his car and then drive to the top of the hill. She remained standing there while the car's headlights faded and watched the electric light above his front door illuminate his tall, narrow frame as he went inside. She was going to miss him while he was away, she thought, and turned into the cottage. As she closed the door behind her, she realized she had actually wanted him to make love to her, not because she felt guilty that she was denying him something he wanted, but because she really wanted it – for herself!

It was halfway through the morning of David's fourth day away. Rachel was struggling to make the cash-book balance, when the telephone rang.

'I'm back! We're going out tonight,' his voice said in her ear, before she had time to speak.

'Oh!' she replied thoughtfully. She had not expected him until late the following day and the joy of surprise added to her smile, but she didn't let it show in her voice. 'Perhaps I have other plans,' she teased. 'I'll just check my diary.'

There was a chuckle at the other end of the line. 'You'll have to put him off. Get dressed up. I'll pick you up at seven. And don't bring any damned photographs with you.'

She grimaced at the ledger on the desk. 'How about the cash-book?'

'Just yourself,' he growled, and put the telephone down before she could reply.

She replaced the receiver and looked thoughtful. Get dressed up! Did he mean she should wear the cream dress? Wasn't it time she learned to dress herself? a voice at the back of her head enquired. She thought for several moments. The voice came to the front of her head.

Why not? she asked herself, and did not wait for a reply. 'Flo!' she called pushing the cash-book aside, her business-like tone gaining Flo's immediate attention.

'What is it?' she asked peering through the office window.

'Has the red suit for The Boutique been pressed?' She had admired the suit earlier, a part of her wanting to try it on. The skirt was plain red and straight cut, the hemline ending just above the knee. The long length jacket had a softly fitting waist and wide lapels. A broad band of navy blue ran round the edging and there was a matching navy-blue blouse to complete the outfit. It was totally different from anything she had ever worn before.

'It's all done and hanging on the rack,' Flo reported, putting her head round the office door a minute later.

Good, she thought. 'Bring it here, will you. I want to try it on. And will . . .' She stopped herself. The rest she would do for herself.

The suit fitted perfectly and she replaced the plastic cover and hung it on the office door. Then she waited until dinner time, when the workshop emptied for one hour.

She felt almost sinful, furtively going through the lacy bras and briefs while everyone was away. She supposed it was sinful – planning in advance. But nothing was going to stop her. She had waited so long and she wanted everything right and to be perfect.

She chose three matching sets of underwear: one white, one pale oyster, one cream silk with coffee-coloured lace. She set them out on the desk and tried to decide which. Then suddenly wondered at her own thoughts. Perfect! She gave a huff. Would *she* ever be perfect? Would a bit of silk and lace really make her feel any different? She hoped so. She needed David, of that she was sure, needed him to be close to and to be a companion. She had missed him so much these last four days. But the final part still made her nervous. She wished he had made love to her the night before he went away, when she had felt that she wanted him to. She hoped she would be able to reclaim that feeling when the time came.

Suddenly, from nowhere, the memory of Micky and a lonely field invaded her mind. She placed a hand across her mouth to still the bile rising inside her stomach. No! she insisted, throwing her hand away. She would not let him do this to her any more. What was it Sarah had said about Philip? 'Oh, he's ancient history!' Well Micky was ancient history: in the past; gone!

She looked back to the bras and briefs lying on her desk. She still couldn't decide which would be most appropriate. She pondered a moment, then swept all three sets up, marched out to the large roller dispenser of brown paper in the workroom and tore a piece off. Tonight she would put paid once and for all to Micky Caradine's ghost, she thought, and wrapped the underwear into a neat parcel, tied it with string and put it down by the side of her handbag. Then she returned to the errant cash-book, determined to think only of work for the rest of the afternoon.

Chapter Twenty-two

'To the most beautiful woman in the room!' David lifted his glass, his eyes lingering on Rachel's face with an intimacy that caused her to blush faintly.

'Stop it!' She flashed him a glance of reproval from beneath lowered lids. 'Or you'll have me the same colour as my suit.'

A smile tugged at David's lips. 'Keep looking at me that way and I'll have you any colour you like.'

Rachel smiled. It had been a bold statement for him to make. He would never have spoken with such teasing intimacy before, not to the Rachel he had left behind at the beginning of the week. He could sense the change in her, she realized, and it pleased her to know the change that had been slowly taking place over the past days was not only in her head. She thought of the woman – the very different woman – who had looked back at her from the mirror earlier that evening, and her smile broadened.

The red suit could have been made for her, Sarah had exclaimed, bubbling with such excitement that Rachel had finally seen the light, even though she felt the skirt could have been several inches shorter!

She had stared long and hard at her reflection. But, no matter how hard she tried, could find nothing in her appearance to make her change her mind. The red suit looked as smart as any of her dull-coloured ensembles hanging in the wardrobe.

It was strange, she thought, as she sipped slowly at her wine, how putting on different clothes had made her feel so different; the woman she had been trying to tell herself she was going to be – for David! Even the underwear, she thought, feeling a touch of embarrassment at the way her mind was suddenly working. After much deliberation she had decided on the pale oyster. The coffee and cream had looked more sexy than she wanted to appear. The white had seemed too virginal. She did not want to give him the impression she was under any illusions of being something she was not.

Sarah had even been allowed to add a touch of lipstick to her face. She had not been so sure of the bright colour; but Sarah had insisted it had to be red to match the suit, so the lipstick had stayed where it was, and the expression in David's eyes when he first saw her removed any doubts.

'Was it hot in Saudi?' In only four days his skin had taken on a fresh glow and his blond hair seemed a shade lighter. He really is a very attractive man, she thought happily.

'Like an oven. How those chaps work permanently out there, I'll never know.' He put his glass down and leaned forward, rested his chin on his hands and looked suddenly serious. 'I have something for you. Do you want it here?' His eyes glanced sideways, taking in the restaurant's other clientele. 'Or shall I keep it until we're alone.'

She looked uncertain. Then recalled the other evening, when he had forced her into realizing there was nothing to be ashamed of in their relationship. She smiled fondly. There was no shame in what she felt for him. 'Now please,' she said confidently, knowing she had said the right thing when his eyes responded with warm gratitude and he began to fumble in the pocket of his jacket.

Looking into her eyes, he reached silently for her hand and slipped a ring on her third finger. 'Will you marry me?' he asked.

The noisy diners continued to talk, the clatter of cutlery rang through the air, waiters bustled around with precariously balanced trays on their hands. She saw or heard none of it. The room became silent. All she could hear were his words. All she could see was his face, his gaze held in quiet expectancy, waiting – waiting for her reply.

She looked down at her hand. Three large diamonds winked silver, blue and yellow fire from her finger. Tears misted her eyes. Her hand, her finger, the ring, all blurred. But the sparkle of the stones remained, reaching out to her through the tears that clouded her eyes, just as David had reached out to her, his love and compassion breaking through the mist that had clouded her life.

'Yes,' she replied, her voice a shaky whisper. She blinked back her emotion. 'Yes,' she repeated, loudly and clearly. The past was gone. The bad, Micky Caradine, was washed away. The good, Judith and Polly, would always be there in memory to share their future: the future that was for herself and David.

'Thank you.' He gave her hand an affectionate squeeze. His other hand went out to catch a passing waiter. 'A bottle of Moët and Chandon and the largest cigar you have.'

The waiter took the order with a knowing smile and David grimaced as the man left the table. 'He thinks I'm trying to impress my secretary.' He became serious. 'I am twenty-two years older than you,' he pointed out. 'Do you want to reconsider?'

'No!' There was no doubt in her voice. Her head shook in slow wonder. Even now he was giving her the chance to back out. 'I love you, David. What does age have to do with that?'

'When you are forty, I shall be sixty-two,' he persisted.

'Stop it!' she ordered, laughing at his concern, as the waiter returned with the champagne, popped the cork and filled two glasses. Then he unwrapped David's cigar, handed it to him, produced a box of matches and lit it for him.

David took a long draw on the cigar. Rachel lifted her glass, then paused and looked down at the beautiful ring. 'I'd already made my decision,' she pointed out. She had known since his phone call that morning that tonight she would cross the final barrier and become his in every way. The ring, the proposal, made no difference. She wanted to make that clear to him.

He glanced quickly at the ring and jumped to the conclusion she had feared. 'That does not mean . . . !'

'Hush!' She lifted her finger, placing it across his lips to stop the words. 'I missed you,' she said, feeling her love for him swell inside her.

'I missed you,' he repeated, and a smile grew gently on his face.

'To the most beautiful man in the room!' She lifted her glass and touched it to her lips.

As the car turned the corner and began the steep climb up the hill, Rachel turned to David. 'Take me home with you,' she said.

He glanced round at her. 'Are you sure?' he asked, and turned his attention back to driving.

'Yes,' she replied simply. She had never been more sure of anything in her life. She wanted it to be at his house. There were no memories there. No dark corners filled with ghosts from the past that could lift their heads and fill her with doubt, just when she didn't want to be filled with doubts. It held no shadows. It didn't even hold much of David. Since moving in he had done little there except eat and sleep.

Now they could change all that, she thought. Together they would fill the house, turning it into their home. She smiled into the darkness, warmed by her thoughts.

As they passed the end of the yard, she turned her head to see if the lights were on in the cottage and Sarah had come home early. The cottage was in darkness. Even if it hadn't been, she doubted she would have stopped David.

When she walked through the door into the hallway, then into the sitting room, she felt no doubts. She looked around at the furniture, at all the ornaments, and felt a strange detachment from Judith's memory. All she could see was the future – and David.

She turned to him, her smile slightly crooked. He stood very still and looked somewhat uncertain. She wondered if, at the age of forty-seven, it was possible to be assailed by schoolboy nerves. Knowing very little about the subject, she cast the thought aside and dropped her handbag on to the chair.

'You'll have to . . .' Her voice failed. Teach me, sounded rather absurd under the circumstances. She had been the one to make all the plans, forcing the issue.

He smiled gently and, as if knowing what she had been about to say, held out his hand. 'Don't worry,' he said, his voice as gentle as his smile. 'Everything will be all right.'

She slipped her hand into his, but her eyes were suddenly filled with the uncertainty that had evaded her the rest of the evening.

He did not speak. He led her slowly from the room and up the stairs.

It wasn't the first time she had seen his bedroom. She had chosen the furniture and the colour scheme because at the time he had not been interested. It was the only room he had had refurnished, wanting to get rid of the bed he had shared with Judith. At the time she had thought he was wrong. Now she was grateful it wasn't Judith's bed he was taking her to.

She looked around at the dark-green bedspread and the striped curtains, put there by her own hands. Yet suddenly it all looked new, different, as if she was entering somewhere she should not be.

'All right?' he questioned, taking both her hands in his and looking deep into her eyes, as if he might find the answer there.

'Yes.' She nodded her head jerkily. The fears were coming back. No, she ordered herself firmly. They would only return if she allowed them to.

'Hold me,' she said, moving against him and pressing her cheek to his chest. Everything usually seemed so right when he was holding her.

He wrapped his arms around her and stood very still. The room was silent and the only sound she could hear was the thumping of his heart beneath her ear. She smiled. It was such a comforting sound.

'I'm sorry,' she whispered.

'Do you want to go home?' he asked.

'No,' she replied without hesitation. She had not come this far to back out now. If she did, she feared she would never get this far again. Her mind could now handle Micky's memory. Now it was time for her body to be rid of it; washed clean by David's hands, by David's touch.

His arms tightened around her. He lifted her face and kissed her gently. There was no hesitancy in her response and he smiled. He kissed her again. Then he moved away and took off his jacket. All his movements were slow, controlled and carefully thought out. They made her feel easy, as if there was no pressure being placed on her.

She removed her own jacket, then stood nervously holding it, until he took it from her hand and draped it over the back of the green Lloyd Loom chair she had given him as a house-warming present.

Then he came to stand right in front of her and took hold of her arms. She stared silently into his eyes. 'You can stop me whenever you want,' he assured her, a moment before his arms encircled her and his lips touched hers.

Rachel opened her eyes to bright autumn sunshine spilling through the gap in the curtains and dappling the wall. She had the feeling she had woken from a dream where she had been floating on a cloud. She thought she might have seen Polly. But the dream began to fade and all she could recall was the pleasant floating.

She looked at the clock. It was six-thirty. She should be going, she told herself, and looked fondly at David's sleeping face: silent and relaxed. It was the most beautiful face in the world and it would always be so, she thought, enjoying the moment of secret intimacy.

She smiled, remembering the night. She had not stopped him. She had finally conquered her fears – with his help. His gentle persuasion had undemandingly broken through the final vestiges of her dread, proving to her, once and for all, that love really did make the difference. There had been nothing in what they had done last night that had even the remotest connection to the act with Micky. There had been no using, only giving. David had given of himself and had invoked a response from her that she had never dreamed she possessed.

She brushed the blond hair that had fallen over his forehead to the side and he opened his eyes and smiled at her.

'I'd better get going,' she said, responding to his smile with all the love she felt for him. 'Stay there. There's no need for you to get up so early.'

For a moment he only looked into her face. Then, coming to life, sat bolt upright. 'Oh Lord!' He rubbed his fingers through his hair and undid all the good work she had done. It fell in spikes over his forehead once more and Rachel smiled. 'I didn't intend to keep you here all night,' he said, and stared at the clock as if he wanted it to tell him it had gone wrong.

'Sarah won't be up yet. I've got plenty of time,' she assured him, and sat up, drew her knees up and wrapped her arms around them, and smiled at his concern.

'Oh well,' he said, and grinned at her. 'I'll have to make an honest woman of you now – and pretty quickly!'

She laughed. 'Sarah won't know!' she said, and wrapped his dressing gown around herself before getting out of bed.

'No,' he agreed. 'But do you think you're going to get from here to there without some eagle-eyed neighbour spotting you?'

'Probably not,' she replied simply. Strangely, it did not concern her. 'It'll be a nine-day wonder. Then they'll start talking about somebody else,' she tossed flippantly over her shoulder, and vanished into the bathroom.

'Yes, Polly,' he called teasingly.

She smiled with fond memories of her dear old friend. 'You were right, Polly,' she whispered, as she studied her reflection in the bathroom mirror. She had half-expected to see someone else standing there. But she looked exactly the same as she did every other morning and it disappointed her. She was sure Sarah, in the same situation, would have risen from bed looking serene and desirable. Not have bleary eyes and hair sticking up all over the place like a gorse bush. She was grimacing at herself when David came through the door, unselfconscious about his nakedness.

'What's wrong?' he asked.

'I don't think this robe was exactly made for me,' she said, pulling the towelling folds more tightly round herself and keeping her gaze fixed firmly on her own reflection and away from his body. She still had a lot to learn, she realized anxiously.

'You look beautiful,' he assured her, and wrapped his arms around her from behind and pulled her up against him. 'As beautiful as you were last night,' he said, and kissed her neck.

She managed a little smile, and thanked heavens the robe was made of thick towelling and provided more of a barrier between their bodies than a thinner fabric would. It was silly, she told herself, after last night. It was daylight now. That was the difference. It had been more private in the dark.

'Let me go,' she insisted, playfully slapping his hands away. 'Or we'll both be late for work.'

'What a good idea,' he purred suggestively in her ear, and she felt her cheeks growing hot. She really did have a lot to learn! She gave him a mocking scowl through the mirror and slapped at his hands once more, and finally he let her go.

He was at the door, before he stopped and turned back to her. 'Do you want a big wedding?'

She laughed then. 'Who would I invite?'

'In that case I'll get a special licence. We'll do it as soon as possible.'

Despite Rachel's protests, David drove her down the hill to the end of the yard.

'I'll see you later,' she said, and leapt out of the car and hurried down the yard with a speed that made him smile. She suddenly felt like a criminal and turned the key in the lock as if she was breaking into a safe.

She gave the door a shove. Nothing happened. She shoved again. The bolt! Only then did it occur to her that when Sarah got in at night she pulled the bolt. 'Damn!' she muttered, and was too anxious to even think she was swearing, as she turned around to see David's car was already halfway home.

Oh well, she thought. Then gave a sigh, resigned herself to her fate, and rapped loudly on the door. It took several attempts before Sarah's bleary head poked through the tiny garret window.

'What's up?' she enquired fuzzily.

'Let me in!' Rachel insisted urgently.

301

'What are you doing out there?' Sarah's bleariness turned to amazement.

'Just let me in!' Rachel repeated, having no intention of going into details on the doorstep.

It seemed to take an eternity for Sarah to get down the stairs. Rachel stood trying to look calm and composed, while her insides danced the tango.

'Where've you been?' Sarah grimaced and scratched her head, as Rachel rushed past her into the house.

'I've been at David's.' Honesty was the best policy, she had decided. To try and cover up would make it seem as if she was ashamed of what she had done.

'Oh.' Sarah yawned and scratched her head again. 'Well, you might have told me,' she grumbled, and went back upstairs.

For once, Rachel was grateful for her sister's easy going attitude and, although she was bursting to tell her about her engagement, she kept silent and let her go.

She had changed out of the scarlet suit of the previous evening into her sombre business clothes and had been downstairs for sometime before Sarah reappeared.

'I'll make some fresh toast,' she said, looking at the breakfast she had prepared for her, which had now gone cold and rubbery.

'Don't bother. I don't want anything.' Sarah's voice was short and she flopped into a chair and rubbed her forehead as if she had a headache.

For a moment Rachel stared at her. She looked pale and tired, and her usual energy seemed to have vanished. 'Are you all right?' she finally asked, concern entering her voice. 'Did you have a late night?'

'Not particularly,' she replied, her voice still short.

'I've got some good news.' Rachel was far too pleased with herself to take much notice of her sister. 'David and I are getting married.' She stuck her hand out, displaying the diamond ring.

'*Married!*' Sarah's amazement quickly turned to disgust. 'Don't you think he's a bit old?'

'No, I do not!' She stiffened against the unexpected attack, leaping to David's defence. 'I love him. Age has nothing to do with it. He's been very good to me. No-one has been kinder!'

'I know he's helped with the business,' Sarah said, helping herself to a cup of tea. 'But for God's sake, Rachel, you don't have to marry the man!'

For a moment she could not reply. The crude insinuation of her sister's comment sent a shiver of disgust through her. She obviously thought it would have been perfectly acceptable to go to bed with him as a kind of payment. To use herself and let David use her. Only a short while earlier she had wished she could be more like her. Now the thought repelled her. That she had brought Sarah up and so the fault must lie with herself, fuelled her anger.

'David has done me the honour of asking me to be his wife!' The frosty clarity of her voice lifted Sarah's disbelieving gaze from the cup of tea she was drinking. 'I was proud to accept!' she continued heatedly. 'The business has got nothing to do with it. And I'll thank you to remember that and keep your cheap comments to yourself.' It was Alan Caradine's fault, she told herself. That's where the blame lay. If Sarah had not got tangled up with him she would never have been capable of such dirty thoughts. She sighed angrily. She hoped someone spotted Sarah's photograph in the promotional ads and made her an offer she could not refuse – and quickly!

Sarah put her cup down very deliberately. Then she stood up and turned squarely to Rachel. 'I still think he's too old. You could find someone your own age easily enough – if you allowed yourself to have any social life!' She turned away, then stopped and gave a cutting bark of laughter. 'It had to be someone who was connected to your precious work, didn't it?' Her eyes pivoted to Rachel's face and there was a hardness in her gaze that she had never seen before, and it chilled her.

'That's enough, Sarah.' She returned the cool glare. She had done everything for her, everything she possibly could. Sheltered her from their mother's condition, worked her fingers to the bone to keep her clothed and fed. She had never wanted for anything. Suddenly she had the feeling it might have been better if Sarah had not been given everything on a plate. If she had had to struggle for something she might now know the meaning of giving, the meaning of caring for someone above yourself.

Sarah was heartless and cold, she thought, and in that moment all the love she had ever felt for her turned inside itself. But, as Sarah tossed her head and walked out of the kitchen, it was herself Rachel hated: for what she had allowed her sister to become.

Half an hour passed. Rachel had drunk several cups of tea and had just gone to the sink to wash the cup and saucer with the idea of going to the factory and leaving her sister to herself, when Sarah came back into the kitchen.

Rachel glanced round at her, then returned to the cup and saucer in the water. The anger had gone, she realized. But it had been replaced by something she could not immediately recognize, and it disturbed her. She dropped the saucer back into the water and turned to face her, suddenly concerned, but careful not to make it too apparent. What Sarah had said had made her relationship with David look cheap, and she was not ready to forgive her. Not yet.

'Can we talk?' Sarah asked, and there was a desolation in her eyes as she looked at Rachel.

It confused her further and she frowned as she wiped her hands on the towel. 'Do you want another cup of tea?' she asked.

Sarah nodded and Rachel set two fresh cups and saucers on the table and filled them up, using the time to think, but unable to come to any startling conclusions. Then she sat down, having the feeling it was the best position to hear what Sarah had to say.

'What is it?' she asked.

'You weren't the only one to get engaged last night.' Sarah stuck her hand out.

Rachel's astonished gaze fell on the tiny single diamond on her finger. In the next moment her right hand was covering her left, hiding the three large stones on her own finger. She bit her lip. She was angry that Sarah had got herself tied to Alan Caradine, but still her heart went out to her. All her ill-humour was due to envy, she thought. Sarah must have been so proud of her new ring. Until *she* had unthinkingly stuck David's under her nose.

'I . . .' she began, then paused to try and choose her words carefully. She wanted to be pleased for her. But all she could see was herself becoming sister-in-law to a Caradine.

'I know you don't think much of Alan,' Sarah began, as if reading her mind. She stuck her chin out defiantly. 'But *I* love him. And he loves me. Nothing else matters.'

Rachel's eyes opened wider. Was this the same person who, only a short while ago, had been asserting that David was too old for her?

'I know what you're thinking. And I'm sorry for what I said. I . . .' She hesitated and looked uncertain and, to Rachel's comfort, a little ashamed. 'It was such a shock. I never thought . . . Well, I suppose I had thought about you and David in that way. But I thought if you hadn't married each other by now, you never would.'

Rachel's incredulous gaze swung to the wall, then back to her sister. 'Just for the record, last night was the first time we . . .' She felt her cheeks heating up. 'The first time,' she repeated uncomfortably.

'What?' Sarah gasped, obviously disbelieving.

Rachel dropped her head into her hands in despair. 'It isn't any of your business, Sarah,' she pointed out firmly. Then looked her straight in the eyes. 'I thought it was *you* who wanted to talk?'

It was Sarah's turn to drop her head into her hands and it was several moments before she spoke. 'We *were* going to get engaged, anyway. That has nothing to do with it. But . . .' She hesitated again, and looked up with a deep sigh of resignation.

Rachel went cold as she looked into the desperation filling her sister's eyes. It wasn't new. She had seen it before. Something very heavy and solid sank in the bottom of her stomach and she knew what Sarah was going to say next.

'I'm pregnant.' Her voice was little more than a whisper. Yet the words rang inside Rachel's head like the death knell of a great bell.

She leapt from the chair and paced across the small kitchen, wishing it was larger and she could get further away. She wanted to slap Sarah, take hold of her and shake her. How could she have done it? she asked herself. Then suddenly she checked herself. The memory of herself and David in bed filled her mind and she realized she could no longer stand in judgement.

'How . . . How do you know?' It was a stupid thing to ask, she realized, and quickly changed the question to, 'How long have you known?' She had been so happy, she thought angrily. Now everything was falling round her ears. Sarah had tied herself to Alan Caradine as securely as if she had chained and padlocked herself to him.

'A couple of months.' Sarah's neck seemed to diminish and her head sank into her slumped shoulders.

Rachel went back to the table, sat down and dropped her head into her hands once more. This time there was no way out. She had allowed Sarah to be Coprell's model in the hope it would lead to greater things! She almost wanted to laugh. But she knew if she gave way to any emotion she would end up crying. First Micky and herself; now Alan and Sarah. If nothing else she could say one thing for the Caradines – they never gave up trying! It was ironic. Not only would her sister be related to Micky's family. She would have to watch her baby growing up, knowing its parentage was shared by the Coopers and the Caradines – and knowing that somewhere there was another child, a little girl, of very similar parentage.

'I'm sorry,' Sarah whispered.

Rachel looked up. 'Do you feel well enough to go to the shop?' She needed time to think, to get the bombshell into some kind of perspective – if there was a perspective!

Sarah nodded. 'I've not been sick or anything. I feel tired, but that's through lack of sleep with worrying.'

Rachel's heart went out to her sister. In the few minutes they had been talking, she seemed to have shrunk. All the confidence and self-assurance had slipped away. She looked like the old Sarah: the young girl in need of care and protection.

'Don't worry. We'll sort something out,' she said, laying a comforting hand on her arm. 'Let's both go to work and save the talking till tonight. Neither of us is in any fit state at the moment and we'll have more time tonight. You will be in tonight?' she quickly asked, suddenly wondering if she had any intention of letting her new condition change her busy social life.

'We were going to come and tell you tonight,' she replied. 'Alan said he should be with me when I told you.'

At least he was willing to take responsibility. She wasn't sure if she was pleased or not: it might have helped her if he had vanished off the face of the earth. She sighed. She supposed she should be grateful for the small mercy; for Sarah's sake. But she wasn't looking forward to meeting him. 'Maybe it would be better if it was just the two of us . . . to begin with,' she quickly added, seeing a look of objection forming on Sarah's face. 'Let us get things clear ourselves first,' she suggested. She needed time to get used to the idea, before she had to confront a Caradine.

Sarah nodded her head in meek acceptance. 'I'll let him know not to come before nine o'clock.'

It wasn't exactly what Rachel had planned. She had been looking for at least one day's respite, if not more, before having the pleasure. But she agreed, for Sarah's sake, and resigned herself to having to face a member of the family she had treated like dirt for the past nine years.

Sarah got up silently and fetched her coat and handbag and made herself ready for work. Just before she went out of the door, she threw her arms round Rachel's neck and pressed her cheek to hers. 'I'm sorry, sis,' she said.

Rachel attempted a smile of encouragement, but she knew it came out tight and unconvincing. 'Stop worrying. We've got over far worse. We'll work everything out – tonight!'

Sarah's shoulders were still slumped and there was no bounce in her step as she went out of the door.

Rachel shook her head. She had thought she was doing right, giving Sarah all the freedom her parents had denied her. She could remember all too clearly feeling like a caged animal. She'd wanted so much more for Sarah. Now she was in a cage of another sort, but just as restricting.

As she walked down the hill to the factory, she wished Polly was still there. Polly would have immediately known what to do, she told herself.

'Here you are, Rachel!'

She looked up, startled. She had almost walked into George Rowbottom as he made his daily postal round.

'Looks like one's from your Joseph.' George handed her three letters, the top one an airmail. His red face beamed with the smile that seemed to be a permanent fixture. 'Is he getting on all right?' he enquired.

'Yes thanks, George,' she replied, not knowing if it was true or not. His letters had become fewer and fewer since his marriage. The last one had been over six months ago.

She went on her way, the letters clutched in her hand. If she was to blame for Sarah's condition, then so was Joseph, she told herself. He should have been the head of the family. Instead he had washed his hands of them, leaving them to get by on their own. She was glad she had been in a position to stop him sending them money several years ago; she felt sure now he had only done it to ease his conscience.

It had been a long time since she had thought about her brother. But as she turned the corner and walked along the lane, each footstep jarred the hurtful memory of his desertion. His letters had become monotonous essays on his life in Germany. He never asked how they were getting on. He just took it for granted they were fine, she told herself angrily, and turned the key in the great wooden door with more force than was necessary.

She dropped the letters on her desk, took off her coat and reached for the telephone.

David was not in his office and she had to stand tapping her fingers while he was paged. It was several minutes before he finally spoke down the line. 'Hello, darling,' he said, his voice breathy, as if he had been running.

The sound of his voice finally cracked her. She dropped on to the chair, thankfully right behind her or she would have landed on the floor. She held her breath, forcing the threat of tears away, and could not speak.

'What's wrong?' he asked, becoming anxious.

She took a deep breath. 'Sarah's going to have a baby!' she gasped, not knowing a better way to put it.

It was then David's turn to be silent.

'What did I do wrong?' she asked woodenly, knowing she was searching for impossible answers.

'You! It's not your fault!' he was quick to insist.

She smiled tightly. She had found someone who was on her side. It felt so good. Tears pressed at her eyelids and again she ordered them back. She was at the factory, she reminded herself, and work was no place to be caught crying.

By the time she replaced the receiver, Flo and all the girls had arrived. Sewing machines whirred and voices rose above the mechanical clatter and the old chapel was in production.

She looked around the room and smiled. She might be pretty useless at the personal side of life, but she more than compensated for it on the career side. It was a comforting thought.

The talk with David had also been comforting. He had provided answers to all the problems she felt were insurmountable and he had come up with a good solution. But she wouldn't think about that – until she'd had time to talk to Sarah.

She had to find out Sarah's real feelings before she began putting suggestions forward, she thought, and picked up Joseph's letter and slit it open. It took her all of thirty seconds to read the quickly scribbled note, she couldn't call it a letter, the two pages filled with impersonal information.

It was no good looking to him for help, she told herself, and screwed the letter and envelope into a ball and dropped it in the bin.

There were times when the day dragged, each minute

seeming like an hour. Those were the times Rachel was thinking of Sarah and wishing she had been more able to cope with the situation that morning. She felt guilty for sending her off to work the way she had. It would not have mattered if they had both been late for once, she told herself, realizing Sarah must be going through hell, anticipating what was to come that evening.

At other times the day seemed to be flying by. Those were the times she contemplated the necessary meeting with Alan Caradine. Since the day of Micky's attack she had shunned the entire family, now she had to welcome them with open arms. The thought chilled her.

Then there were the other times, the worst times: when the day, the room, even the sky seemed to be closing in on her. Trapping her in a dark cave filled with pictures of a little girl and the sound of a childish laughter that was strange and unknown to her.

She tried to push the images away by telling herself she had done the right thing. She would have made a terrible mother. It wasn't the first time she had thought the same thing, but now Sarah's situation proved it to be a fact. Wherever she was, whoever she was with, her daughter was far better off than if she had kept her, she insisted, and ignored the tiny voice that told her she had no way of knowing that.

'Did you send the order to J.C.?' Flo asked, one minute before closing time.

'Oh heavens!' She began to scrabble through the paperwork on her desk. 'No I didn't. I forgot!' She tossed things aside willy-nilly. She had been so tied up in her problems she had forgotten the large fabric order she had intended phoning through first thing that morning.

'Well we need some more of that pale blue double jersey. Shade D146. The last lot they sent has got a fault running right through it.' Flo took the pile of papers from out of Rachel's hand and pulled the order out of the middle. 'Here it is!' She held the sheet up and looked triumphant.

'What would I do without you, Flo?' She forced herself to sound cheerful, joking her unusual neglect away at the same time as clearing up the mess she had made on her desk. 'I'll sort everything out tomorrow,' she said, making one large pile and pushing it across her desk.

'What about the order?' Flo enquired.

'That will wait until tomorrow, as well.'

Flo looked askance at her strange attitude. Under normal circumstances she would not have left the factory until everything was done.

But these were not normal circumstances, she told herself, and, having no wish to pursue the subject with Flo, left her standing there and set about making the final check to see everything had been switched off properly.

Then she put on her coat, ushered Flo out of the door, and hurried home.

Chapter Twenty-three

'Are you really sure you want to marry him?' Rachel's gaze levelled on Sarah's tear-stained face. They had been talking since they arrived home, and seemed to be getting nowhere.

'Yes!' Sarah's chin rose in defiance.

The insistence in her voice confused Rachel. She feared she might be trying to convince herself. Or perhaps that was what *she* hoped.

'I love Alan!' Sarah repeated, as she had stated at regular intervals throughout the evening. 'We'd planned to get married . . . before this.' Her head dropped. She toyed nervously with her fingers.

'There are other ways,' Rachel explained gently. 'You don't *have* to get married. You wouldn't . . .'

Sarah did not let her finish. 'I won't give my baby away!' she insisted hotly, the defiance back in her expression.

Rachel's heart curled painfully. She would never have asked her to do that. She was only too aware of the pain that would follow such a decision. Unfortunately Sarah was ignorant of that, and now was not the time to put her wise.

'I was going to say,' she began, turning her back on Sarah to hide the shadow of pain on her face, 'you would not be the first to bring up a baby alone.'

'I don't need to bring it up alone. Alan wants the baby . . . And he wants me. Can't you understand that?' Sarah's voice was filled with the anger that had caused them to go round and round in circles since beginning to try to talk to each other.

They were getting nowhere, Rachel realized disappointedly. And she was to blame. Sarah was obviously of the opinion Alan was right for her. You have to accept it, she told herself, feeling as if a dark cloud was sinking round her shoulders.

Her sister was going to be a Caradine. If she did not back down and take a grip on her repugnance of the idea, she would alienate her and lose her completely.

'You're so young.' She turned back to Sarah with a great sadness in her eyes, and her voice cracked when she said, 'You could have done so much!'

'Well I can't do it now, whether Alan marries me or not,' she replied bluntly.

For a long moment Rachel stared silently at her. It was such a waste, she thought. She was so pretty, beautiful in fact. She could have had anybody she chose! 'All right,' she finally and reluctantly agreed. 'Have you made any plans? Where will you live?'

'We've got to sort all that out.' All the defiance and anger left Sarah. Her head bowed once more. 'I had thought you might let us live here with you. But you're marrying David now.' Her shoulders lifted in resignation and she looked defeated.

Rachel stared at her blankly. One part of her wanted to go to her and hold her and rock her as she had done when she was young. The other part wanted to slap her and knock some sense into her silly head, because there wasn't much sense there. She could see now how her sister's mind had been working. Sarah's morning anger had not been because she was marrying David. She would have been angry whoever she had said she was going to marry. For no other reason than that it upset her plans. She had had it all nicely worked out. Rachel would let them move into the cottage with her. Rachel would help. Rachel wouldn't mind. Rachel had always been there to sort things out. Because Rachel had always been soft!

Before her anger got the better of her, she turned away again. She fiddled with the tea tray ready laid for Alan's arrival. Discussing things over a cup of tea had seemed more civilized, she had reasoned earlier. Now she had the feeling she would gain more satisfaction from throwing the entire tray at the wall. For several unchivalrous moments she was of the opinion this was all Micky Caradine's doing. He had put his brother up to it! It was a sick joke and Alan was not going to turn up

313

at nine o'clock. He'd have gone to ground by now, the way his brother had done nine years ago. The way all rats did!

Fortunately David chose that moment to arrive and saved her from herself, before she expressed her opinions to Sarah.

'Hello, sweetheart.' He kissed her on the cheek.

'Hello,' she responded simply, looking into his eyes and giving a grimace of resignation.

'I'll go and tidy my face up.' Sarah pushed herself out of the chair as if her body was so heavy she was already about to give birth.

Rachel remained silent, sadness spilling from the eyes that watched her sister go.

'Don't worry, love,' David said, in his reassuring manner. 'We'll sort things out.' He was speaking to Sarah's back and received no reply. She walked silently through the front room and up the stairs.

Rachel took hold of his hand. 'I'm glad you're here,' she said, the relief in her face echoing the words. She had told him to arrive at quarter to nine, wanting him to be there when Alan arrived. She shook her head. 'Oh, I'm so angry!'

'I know.' He nodded in agreement. 'But anger isn't going to get us anywhere,' he pointed out, levelling his gaze into her eyes. 'Did you tell her my suggestion?'

'No.' Her voice was bleak, turning bitter as she went on, 'She had it all planned that they'd move in here – *with me!*' She gazed at him hopelessly. 'She's spoiled. And I'm the one that's spoiled her!'

David shook his head, his expression conveying that he was having none of that. 'Stop thinking this has got anything to do with you,' he insisted, kindly but firmly. 'You've done your best for Sarah. She'd be the first to agree. It happens. They don't need anyone's recriminations. All they need is a bit of help. And we can give it to them!'

He was right, she reluctantly agreed. Sarah did need help and, no matter how angry she was, she could never have turned her back on her. She couldn't disregard all the years they had, only had each other, but it wouldn't stop her saying her piece.

'Come on through.' She tugged at David's arm, leading

314

him to the front room. 'We can't interview my prospective *brother-in-law* in the kitchen,' she said dryly.

'Talk to,' he corrected, with an admonishing glance.

Rachel had never imagined she would live to see the day she felt compassion for a Caradine. But she had to admit that was the emotion she was feeling right then.

Alan turned up on the dot of nine o'clock. She had the feeling he must have been standing by the lamp-post at the end of the yard, like a greyhound in a trap, waiting for the off.

Sarah had returned downstairs and was waiting for him, and he went straight to her, taking her hand in his. As if seeking reassurance as much as giving it, Rachel thought, and went to fetch the tea tray, grateful she had not given in to her earlier fury and slung it at the wall.

When she returned, Sarah and Alan were sitting on the sofa and clinging almost desperately to each other: squashed together from shoulders to knees like two nervous orphans.

Rachel's heart went out to the pair of them. For a moment she paused, the tray suspended in mid-air. When she finally placed the tray on the table, the rattling cups and saucers showed the unsteadiness of her hands. She wanted to speak, yet remained silent, her voice locked away in the tangle of her emotions, feeling both compassion and anger for the pair on the sofa.

'We're sorry for causing trouble,' Alan said, looking from Rachel to David, then back to Rachel, his voice filled with a regret that seemed genuine enough. 'We had planned to get married – next year.' He gave an embarrassed little smile. 'We'll just have to hurry it up a bit.'

Rachel remained silent, unable to take her eyes off Alan – Micky's brother! She had to admit he was nothing like Micky in looks, except for the mid-brown wavy hair that all the Caradines were endowed with. His manner was totally different. Which was a definite good point. There was none of big brother's cockiness; no arrogance.

Perhaps it was just the situation, she thought, reminding herself that he was a Caradine after all.

At Rachel's continued silence, David took the initiative and began speaking. She woke up with a start to realize she had missed some of the conversation, as he said, 'That isn't much to live on. Have you thought about where you will live?'

Her eyes pivoted to her sister, expecting to hear once again that she had spoiled all her plans by deciding to get married herself. Sarah remained silent and she was thrown into confusion.

'You'll have to think,' she suddenly put in. 'And pretty quickly!' Her voice was short and clipped. Sarah was being too quiet, she thought, and wondered what game she was playing at now.

'We will think, Rachel.' Alan's voice remained calm and he looked at her levelly. 'We know it won't be easy. But we'll get by. We'll have each other. And that will make it all worthwhile.' He turned to Sarah and gave her a fond smile, receiving the same in response.

'Have you fixed a wedding date?' Rachel enquired coolly. She should be angry, she told herself. She wanted to be angry. Yet there was something so loving, so genuine in Alan's manner and his actions, that she felt her determination to speak her mind crumbling.

Sarah was also a revelation in his presence. The look in her eyes was one of almost adoration; something Rachel had never encountered before; something she didn't understand. It confused her further.

'We haven't fixed anything yet. We wanted to speak to you first.' Alan looked glum. 'We haven't got a lot of money saved up. So it will have to be a small do.'

'I . . .' Rachel began, then hesitated. It was for Sarah, she told herself. She had to do it. She looked to David for help. He gave an almost imperceptible nod of the head, his eyes telling her he knew what she was about to say, and to carry on, she was doing the right thing. 'I'll pay for the wedding,' she suddenly continued. 'So there's no need to worry about that. And,' she continued, before either of the two amazed faces on the sofa had time to speak, 'David thinks you might be able to keep this on.' She waved her arm around the room.

The cottage rent-book had been transferred to her name after her mother's death. Recently the Strutt Estate, which had owned most of the cottages in the village, had begun to sell off the properties when they became vacant. But David felt, under the circumstances of it being Sarah's home as well as Rachel's, that Sarah would be able to keep it on when she left.

'You'd have to go and talk to the Estate Office,' David said. 'I'd be willing to come with you. If you wanted me to.'

Rachel looked at Alan, expecting an arrogant refusal.

'I'd be grateful if you would,' he replied meekly, and she felt about two inches high for her unchivalrous thoughts.

'Thank you, Rachel.' It was almost a whisper from Sarah.

Rachel's gaze moved to her sister, and in that moment she knew Sarah had grown up at last. The flighty young thing had turned into a young woman with responsibilities. Yet, strangely, she was more like the Sarah she remembered with such fondness, the child she had loved so much.

A lump closed her throat. 'Look at me.' She spoke rapidly, covering her emotion. 'I've made this tea and I'm letting it go cold.' She quickly set about pouring four cups and handing them round. If this evening had been anything to go on, she had to take back everything she had said and thought about Alan Caradine. His care for Sarah seemed too genuine to be put on just for the occason, she realized, and sat down feeling happy that he felt enough for Sarah to stand by her, yet at the same time very sorry for herself.

She still had the displeasure of being linked with Micky to come to terms with. That was her own problem, she realized bleakly. One she would have to deal with as it arose. Sarah and Alan were now a *fait accompli*. Whether she wanted it or not, she was going to have a Caradine for a brother-in-law. She also realized that, now things had gone so far, Sarah must never be allowed to discover the truth about herself and Micky. If she did, it would spoil her future. The secret she had kept locked away over the years must now remain locked away – for ever!

*   *   *

317

On a Saturday morning four weeks later, Rachel married David. It was a very simple registry office ceremony. Sarah and Alan were witnesses and then the four lunched at a nearby restaurant. Rachel wore a pale blue suit. On the wide lapel she pinned a white rose to complement the frilly neck of the white silk blouse. For the first time in her life she went to the hairdressers and her long blonde hair was a profusion of curly loops piled on top of her head and hanging down her neck. In her hand she carried another single white rose.

Stunning, was the description David used, when he arrived at the cottage to take the four to the registry office in his car.

Rachel had wanted to delay the wedding. Wait until after Sarah and Alan were married, she suggested, feeling her sister's wedding was more urgent and more important. It was only when David pointed out that if Sarah and Alan were to move into the cottage, she would need to be out first, which made her see she had to go along with his plans for a quick ceremony.

Exactly three weeks to the day of Rachel's wedding, Sarah walked down the chapel aisle. She had chosen the chapel of their childhood, though Rachel had the feeling Alan's mother might have had something to do with it. Mrs Caradine was rather like their father had been, feeling it was one of the deadly sins to miss a Sunday service.

In the oyster satin and guipure lace dress, Sarah looked like a princess. Rachel had tears in her eyes as the bridal procession walked slowly down the aisle. She hoped with all her heart that the affection Sarah and Alan now felt for each other would last for the rest of their lives. Not once in the past four weeks had she found any reason to doubt his sincerity. She had constantly tried to find similarities to his elder brother, but had not been able to. And, at times, had found herself almost liking him.

Rachel had returned to the sewing machine to make Sarah's dress herself. She also made the dresses for the two brides-maids, the two youngest members of the Caradine brood.

Looking at the two little girls, one aged seven, the other nine, Rachel told herself there could have been three, and she felt the old sadness rising up. She slipped her hand in David's, seeking comfort, and tried to turn her mind to another topic by studying the two magenta-pink bridesmaid dresses to see if she had made any slips. She couldn't find any, but it didn't stop her looking. The dresses had been made in such a rush. She turned her gaze to Sarah's dress, just as Alan was slipping the ring on her finger. She smiled secretly, as she looked at the row of tiny pearl buttons down the back, which held the tightly fitting bodice together. She'd sewn the last button on at ten-thirty the previous evening. She recalled Sarah's anxious pacing as her fingers had worked feverishly to put the finishing touches to the dress. She hadn't dared to complete it too soon, for fear Sarah suddenly blossomed and could no longer get into the narrow-waisted design.

She had tried to talk her out of such a fitting design. Now she was pleased Sarah had been adamant in refusing to be put off. Her tall form was still as slender as ever and her waist looked tiny above the fullness of the lace skirt. She looked wonderfully graceful and poised.

She should have been a model, Rachel thought with regret. Then told herself sharply to stop such thoughts. It was too late now, and thinking about it would only cause grief.

Rachel had hired the hut for the reception. Anything Margaret Land can do, we can do better, she had laughingly told Sarah, when they were in the midst of all the rushed and hectic planning. And, with all Sarah and Alan's friends, they needed a large room.

It was not until the lunch was over and the cake cut and speeches made, that Rachel had the chance to approach Micky. Since arriving at chapel she had been constantly aware of him: where he was, what he was doing. But she had not allowed herself to look at him directly, or get close enough to speak.

She had thought carefully about what she was going to do during the evenings she had sat diligently over the sewing machine, the bridal gown growing before her eyes. To say nothing would be too risky, she had decided. Micky was more than likely to let something slip in his arrogant assumption that Sarah already knew. Of course Alan might already know. She felt Micky was more than capable of bragging to his younger brother. But she didn't think that was so. She was certain Alan was not aware of anything, assuming that, if he had been, he would have said something to Sarah. And she knew her sister would not have kept it to herself if she had found out. The more she thought about it, the more she was convinced her secret was safe. And she had every intention of keeping it that way.

David was involved in a deep conversation with Alan's father when Rachel took the chance to slip away. Micky was leaning against the bar, loudly extolling the virtues of the new sports car he had purchased that very week. He was wearing yet another cheap imitation of an Italian suit, in a shiny copper-coloured fabric with a black velvet band on the lapels. He had grown his hair even longer and it hung around his shoulders in curls any girl would have been proud of; but at least it looked clean now and nothing like the rat's tails that used to hang in his neck.

For a moment Rachel stood behind him, feeling very superior in her matching dress and jacket of sea-green silk shantung, the colour exactly matched to her eyes. She did not have to summon up courage. It was there already: just the sight of him made her hackles rise and put an unmistakable stiffness in her voice.

'I'd like a word with you,' she finally said. It would have been easier to tap him on the shoulder to get his attention, but she drew the line at actually touching him.

Micky turned, his initial surprise turned to a knowing leer. 'Any time, Rachel. You only have to say the word.' She stared blankly into his face, ignoring the insulting suggestion of his words. 'Over here!' She jerked her head in the direction of the wall, where the only empty space in the hall seemed to be.

He flashed his drinking partners a cocky grin, placed his pint of beer down on the bar and followed her. 'What is it, love?' he enquired suggestively.

'Don't you call me love!' Her lips curled with distaste as

his beery breath wafted in her face. 'I just want you to know that if you do anything – *anything* – to upset this marriage, I'll finish you.'

He gave a dry laugh. 'Strong words from the big lady!'

'Strong!' She gave a sarcastic huff. 'You haven't heard anything yet. Neither has your girlfriend.' She flashed her eyes to the table where his girlfriend was knocking back vodka and limes with as much gusto as he had been drinking his beer. Then she let her gaze move deliberately to Mrs Caradine. 'Or your mother!' she added pointedly.

At mention of the doyenne of the Caradine household his beer-reddened face became brighter. 'You wouldn't dare,' he scoffed, but was obviously ill at ease.

Rachel smiled. 'Oh yes I would! If you don't care enough about your brother to upset his marriage by not keeping your big mouth shut, I warn you, I'll make such a stink that your precious mother will never be able to hold her head up in the village again.' She paused, her smile broadening and twisting at the same time. 'And you know what chapel's like for a bit of scandal. They'd close the doors to her.' She had never thought to see the day when she would find the chapel, the cause of her torment, useful to her. Micky's mother was typical of all that she despised about the place. A regular Sunday saint and a six-day sinner, as Polly would have said.

'It would kill her.' He had visibly blanched and she wondered why she had never thought of it before.

'Yes,' she replied simply. No other words were needed. He understood her far quicker and far better than she had expected. 'Now go back to your drinking partners and enjoy the rest of the reception,' she insisted. 'But don't forget one word of what I've said!' She turned and walked away before he had the chance to respond. Though, from the look on his face, she didn't think he had had much to say.

David was still in conversation with Mr Caradine when she returned to the table. He glanced round. 'All right?' he asked, making it obvious he had seen everything.

'Fine,' she said, grasping his hand beneath the table and giving it a reassuring squeeze. She did feel fine. She felt a sense of release. As if for nine years Micky had held a knife to her throat and now, in a matter of minutes, she had twisted the position. Suddenly she was the one holding all the dice and, if need be, she would throw them. After all, what harm could it do her now? A bit of scandal would do nothing to harm the business. And David already knew everything, so it wouldn't harm their relationship.

It had taken Sarah's marriage to open her eyes, and it was the same marriage which had given her the power over Micky. Life was a strange business, she thought.

There's a reason for everything, lass, Polly's voice said. You'll find out, have no fear.

Yes, Polly, she replied, her smile deepening, as she toyed with her wine glass and stared into the empty bottom, and thought of her dear old friend.

Mr Caradine obviously took her action for a hint. 'Let me get that filled up,' he said, taking the glass from out of her hands and vanishing in the direction of the bar.

'Was he causing trouble?' David asked.

'No,' she shook her head. She was confident there would be no more trouble from him. 'I was just thinking that this is the end of the Misses Cooper,' she said, changing the subject. 'I only hope Alan will be as good to Sarah as you are to me.'

'Of course he will,' he was quick to assure her. 'Just look at the two of them. Nobody could be happier.'

Rachel looked across to where Sarah and Alan were dancing. Sarah's arms were around Alan's neck, Alan's wrapped around Sarah's waist, gazing into each other's eyes as if they were the only people in the room. Sarah's face was aglow with the radiance that always seemed to shine from her when Alan was around. She turned back to David. She loved him, she was sure of that. But it was a quiet love, based on friendship and caring. She had never known the euphoria that Sarah was at present experiencing. It frightened Rachel, not for herself, but for Sarah. She worried that it was not the lasting type, that when they fell into the humdrum routine of daily life with a baby, the bubble would burst. They're young, she told herself. David was older, more mature, and she had been forced to grow up before her time. Love was different for the young, she thought, hoping it was true.

'Mr Morrell,' she suddenly said, shaking off her doubts, 'I do believe it was in this very room that you taught me to dance.' She grabbed his arm and pulled him from the chair. 'Come on,' she insisted. 'We can't let that tuition go to waste.'

David was still laughing as he took her in his arms. 'It's been a lovely day for Sarah,' he said. His smile faded. 'I wish you could have had one the same.'

'I didn't want one,' she assured, and clung tighter to him. 'I only wanted you!'

'You got me.' His face flooded with a warmth that reached out and touched her. 'Don't ever stop wanting me.' He pulled her closer and wrapped his arms more tightly around her, as if he feared she might run away.

'I won't,' she whispered, and settled her cheek against his chest. She smiled. Even with the noisy background music, she could hear his heartbeat in her ear.

How she loved that sound. It warmed her right through. It is a new era, the end of the Coopers, she thought happily. Suddenly she frowned, recalling a time long ago, when she had had the very same thought. The day the mill clock had been stopped. The day her mother took her own life. She thought back to that day with sadness. Then she let her mind travel over the years. They'd had their sorrows, more than enough at times, but the years had been good. She had achieved most things she had set out to achieve. There couldn't be many people who could say that.

Yes, it was a new era, she assured herself, smiling again. One of happiness and certainty. And new hope, in the form of Sarah and Alan's baby. The first of a new generation . . . She suddenly checked herself. The second, she corrected, and clung more tightly to David, as her mind filled with a picture of an unknown child. One that looked the way Sarah had looked at the age of nine, and dressed in a magenta-pink bridesmaid dress.

Chapter Twenty-four

1971

Despite her doubts as she watched Sarah grow and blossom, when Christopher Andrew Caradine was born Rachel found it easy to love her new nephew. He was a beautiful baby, taking after his father in looks, although the mandatory mass of Caradine curls were of traditional Cooper blond.

At first Rachel found herself studying the tiny face, looking for any sign of the baby's uncle. The only occasions she thought there might be a faint likeness was when Christopher screwed up his face in the agony of wind, and she was reminded of Micky at school: screwing up his face in petulance when he was being told off for one of his many misdemeanours. But those times were few. Christopher was a very placid, easy-going baby, always ready to give a smile, or content to amuse himself if left in the pram.

'You don't know you're born. He's so good.' Rachel glanced a look of rebuke at her sister, as Sarah scolded Christopher for spilling orange juice down the new blue dungarees Rachel had just given him.

'That stuff stains. It might not come out.'

'Then we'll buy him another pair,' she replied, without much concern.

'You spoil him,' Sarah retaliated. 'He must be the best-dressed baby for miles.'

Rachel took Christopher out of her sister's arms. 'Go and get his dinner and stop nagging,' she said, and held him up in her hands and brought his face down close to her own. 'We can spoil you if we want, can't we? You haven't any objections, have you Christopher?' The baby gurgled happily. 'See . . .' She turned to Sarah. '. . . he approves.'

Sarah shook her head hopelessly. But she had to smile. 'All

right! All right!' Realizing she was outnumbered she went into the kitchen.

Rachel sat down and cradled Christopher on her lap. He caught sight of the gold chain bracelet around her wrist and his tiny fingers began to play with it. She looked fondly on the mop of white-blond curls and he looked up and gave her a toothless grin.

She smiled and gave him a little hug. He was a beautiful child. She could not have wished for better. If the baby had been a girl, and had looked like Sarah, she was not sure she could have coped with it. As it was, he made her think more and more often of her own daughter.

She had hoped that she and David would have had a child of their own by now. They had been married for eighteen months. She thought if she had a baby to look after and care for, it might help her to forget by filling the void that she felt deep inside herself. But it had not happened. There was time, she told herself, brushing her lips across the silky hair on the top of Christopher's head, and receiving another toothless grin and a happy gurgle.

'Put him down and drink this in peace,' Sarah said, as she came back through the door with his dinner in one hand and two mugs of coffee in the other.

Rachel lifted him up and placed him in his highchair and his attention immediately moved to the string of coloured ducks fixed to the tray. For a moment she watched him. 'You're very lucky!' She looked meaningfully at her sister, a shadow in her eyes. So far all her reservations about Sarah's marriage had proved unfounded. Alan seemed to be the perfect husband and Sarah was as happy today as she had been on her wedding day.

'I know.' Sarah smiled fondly as she pulled a chair close to Christopher and began feeding him.

Rachel picked up her coffee from the table and fell silent.

'Would you like a baby?' Sarah suddenly asked.

'Me?' she replied too quickly. It wasn't something she had ever talked about with Sarah. 'What would I do with the factory?' she edged, looking for excuses.

'Employ someone to run it for you,' Sarah replied, obviously amazed that she could not see that for herself.

Rachel shrugged. 'David's too old to want the bother now.'

For a long moment there was silence. Sarah stared pointedly at her and she felt her embarrassment increasing. She had the feeling Sarah could see right through her. But to admit that it just had not happened seemed unchivalrous to David. Sarah might not know that she already had a child, but she knew, and so did David. Although it had never been spoken of, she had seen the look in his eyes: the feeling that he was letting her down. She took a long swallow of hot coffee and felt it burning her tongue. The last eighteen months had been the happiest of her life. David had done so much for her, yet she did not know how to explain that to him. She tried to pretend the lack of a baby of their own didn't really matter to her. It will happen, all in its own good time, she would say to him. She could never have told him how much it was hurting her and make it seem as if she was pointing the finger of blame at him.

'Maybe, one day.' She shrugged her shoulders again and changed the subject. 'Did you find a babysitter for Wednesday?' she asked. Wednesday was David's birthday. Sarah and Alan were going out to dinner with them to celebrate the occasion.

'Yes,' Sarah replied. Then became pensive. 'I don't know what to wear. I can't decide if the black and silver I had at Christmas is too . . .' She shrugged and grimaced, causing Rachel to smile. 'Well, it is a bit revealing.'

Rachel laughed. Her sister had become a respectable wife and mother after all. It was very heart-warming to see.

'Have I told you lately that I love you?' David pulled Rachel into his arms and held her tightly.

'Not since this morning.' She looked into his eyes and the smile slowly slipped from her face. 'You look tired,' she said, studying him with concern. She had worried earlier about him and had even suggested they forget the birthday dinner.

David grinned and the tiredness seemed to vanish. 'I'm too old to keep up with you young ones,' he joked.

'You'll never be too old,' she confirmed with feeling. Forty-nine! What was that? In Polly's terms he was only just over halfway there.

'Thank you for this evening.' He became serious again and the tiredness returned. 'I really enjoyed myself.'

'Good!' She looked steadily into his eyes. She had to admit the evening had gone exceptionally well, and he had seemed to enjoy every minute of it. But he did look worn out. She couldn't understand it. 'Do you really feel all right?'

He smiled at the concern on her face. 'Work is a bit tense at the moment. It's nothing for you to worry about.'

'Have you got problems with an engine?' Engine trouble was the usual cause of any concern for him, as a Rolls-Royce engineer.

'No.' David shook his head and laughed the subject away, by adding, 'We could do with you for chairman. If R.R. was expanding as quickly as Coprell, you wouldn't be able to see Derby for jet engines.'

Rachel laughed. Coprell was thriving. She had taken on their twentieth member of staff only that week. 'Stop flattering me, Mr Morrell. Or I'll think you're trying to get round me!'

'Now there's a good idea.' He gave a mocking leer and pulled her hard against him. Then kissed her long and deeply.

'I love you, Mr Morrell,' she said, when she finally came up for air. And she knew, in that moment, she would rather have David and no children, than a house full of babies and any other man. I found the rainbow, Polly, she said silently. And the gold.

She received no reply. Are you asleep, Polly? she asked, as he began to lead her to the stairs.

When they reached the bedroom David kissed her again, with a gentleness that grew in intensity as she pressed herself to him. His fingers slowly began to unfasten the buttons of her jacket. When his hands brushed the jacket aside the silk whispered over her shoulders and drifted down her arms like a caress. His hands followed the path of the fabric and she

327

smiled, unable to contemplate that any other hands could ever make her feel so warm and wanted.

I definitely found the rainbow, she thought, as he led her to their bed. A moment later she forgot all about Polly.

Rachel woke at first light. Something was troubling her, yet she didn't know what it was. She looked at David, sleeping peacefully by her side, and smiled, recalling the night. In all their time together there had never been any occasion when his lovemaking had become forceful and demanding. His treatment of her was never anything but tender. She sometimes worried she was not adventurous enough for him, but supposed that if he wanted her to be more adventurous, he would lead the way.

Feeling too awake to go back to sleep, she got herself out of bed and crept downstairs, careful not to wake him. Then she began to prepare breakfast.

'Good morning!' She breezed into the bedroom at the usual time for getting up, carrying a large tray laden with bacon and eggs and a pot of tea.

'Good grief!' David peered in bleary disbelief. 'Breakfast in bed! What day is it? Is there a special occasion?'

'February the fourth. The day after your birthday,' Rachel chirped, happily unaware of what the day was going to bring.

David pushed himself up and propped the pillow behind his back. Rachel sat facing him, legs curled beneath her, the tray balanced between them.

'I don't need a special occasion to spoil you.' She grinned mischievously over the top of a forkful of bacon. Then she leaned forward and pushed it into his mouth.

'I haven't reached my dotage yet,' he joked, forcing the fork from her hand, as he got his teeth round the overlarge piece of bacon. 'Or are you trying to choke me and get your hands on the insurance money?' He gave her a playful tap on the leg and almost tipped the tray over.

Rachel laughed and grabbed the tray to steady it, the uncomfortable unease on waking now forgotten.

They had finished eating, before David fell quiet and

serious. 'Thank you for making my life worth living again,' he suddenly said.

'Thank you for making my life worth living,' she said, echoing the sentiments, the sincerity. She did not think there was another man alive who could have turned her into a woman the way he had, through patience and understanding, unlocking the emotions that had been frozen to stillness inside her. Emotions she had kept locked away because she had feared if that part of her came to the surface it would be hurt again.

As if treating a bird with a broken wing, David had taken her in his hands and taught her to fly. She owed him much, much more than he owed her, she told herself, and lifted the tray and put it away on the floor.

'Never stop loving me,' she said, a pleading in her voice that made her sound like a frightened child once more.

'Never!' he assured her, and pulled her to him and turned her into a woman again.

When Rachel arrived at the factory, she pulled the folder of new designs out of the filing cabinet and sat down to study them. She had to decide which would go into production for the autumn/winter collection.

After a while she had two piles of designs sitting in front of her. One contained items for the general market. She never allowed herself to refer to the mass market, even though that was what she had now entered. She never churned out great numbers of any one garment, although economics had dictated she had to give way and allow some duplications. It didn't entirely please her, but she was enough of a businesswoman to know they could not have succeeded making a continual line of one-offs.

The other pile was the exclusive items, the evening and day wear for that extra special occasion. On that section she was adamant. No two garments were ever made identical. It was a principle she would never change. Her exclusive gowns were expensive, but that did not put the customers off and the market was always there.

As she worked, Rachel began to hum, the happiness of the morning still with her.

'Someone sounds happy,' Bob Smith said, as he came up to her desk, grinning from ear to ear as he heard her cheerful tune.

She looked up and stopped humming. 'You don't have the monopoly on happiness, Bob.' Bob whistled constantly while he worked. 'Puppet on a String' was his usual masterpiece, until someone complained about the monotony. Then he would go into a rousing rendition of Tchaikovsky's 1812.

'The van's all packed,' he said.

Rachel pulled a sheet of paper from beneath a box of paper clips. 'Come back via Derby and pick these up.' She put the order into Bob's outstretched hand and leaned back in the chair. 'How are you getting on? Are you happy with the job?' He was one of the latest editions to the staff. The accountant who did the yearly audit had pointed out to her that it would be cost effective if she took on her own van driver, rather than pay outside despatchers to make the deliveries.

'Champion!' Bob replied with feeling. Then suddenly became serious. 'You haven't got any complaints?'

'No,' she quickly assured him. 'But if you have any problems come straight to me with them.'

'I will. Shall I be off now?'

'Yes.' She smiled as he walked away. Before he reached the door the first strains of 'Puppet on a String' could be heard.

Still smiling to herself, she returned to the designs. The smile changed to a thoughtful grimace. She wasn't entirely happy with the selection and reaching for her pad and pencil she began to create some new ones. As she worked her mind turned to David. The smile returned to her lips and her happiness spurred her creative talents. By lunch time there were several new creations lying on her desk.

When Rachel finally looked up, the girls had gone off for their break. Flo was still there, busily scuttling round with a huge roll of lemon-yellow seersucker in her arms.

Rachel shook her head in despair. 'I've told you not to carry those yourself,' she called. The rolls were too heavy for the biggest of the girls to handle single handed. But Flo always managed. Talking to Flo was, at times, like talking to a brick wall, she told herself, and got up and went out of the office to have a serious word with her.

But Rachel did not have time to open her mouth.

The door flew open and Bob rushed in, no cheerful tune on his lips. 'Royce's have gone bust!' he gasped.

'What!' It was all Rachel could say. She heard Flo's roll of fabric hit the floor with a bump, but didn't turn to see if Flo was all right. Her gaze was too busy trying to catch the headlines of the midday edition of the *Derby Evening Telegraph*, which Bob was flapping around madly in the air.

'They're in liquidation,' Bob continued, his voice stunned and disbelieving.

'Hold it still!' Rachel demanded, and grabbed the newspaper from his hand so she could get a chance to see it for herself.

'It can't be true!' She held the newspaper out and stared at it numbly. The headline leaped out at her:

ROLLS-ROYCE CALL FOR RECEIVER
SHARE DEALINGS HALTED

Still Rachel could not believe it. It wasn't possible. Rolls-Royce? Companies that size didn't go broke!

'Never!' Flo breathed in equal disbelief, as she peered over Rachel's shoulder to get a look at the stunning news.

'They can't close Rolls-Royce!' Rachel looked at Bob for confirmation of her theory.

His expression did not look very reassuring. He shrugged his shoulders. 'If the receivers are in . . . it's bad. There'll be a lot out of work.'

David! she suddenly thought anxiously. She must talk to him. She thrust the paper back at Bob and flew to her desk, grabbed the telephone and feverishly dialled the number. It seemed like some sick joke. The newspaper's headline glared in her mind. It was not a joke, she told herself, yet still could not accept the truth.

331

She stopped dialling and waited, listening. Nothing happened. She looked numbly at the two stunned faces who had followed her into the office and were standing before her, as unable to take in what was happening as she was.

It was several seconds before she told herself she had dialled incorrectly and put the receiver down and started again. She could feel her hands shaking, but forced herself to dial slowly, so there was no mistake this time.

Still nothing. The line remained ominously dead. Slowly Rachel put the receiver back in the cradle. Then she looked at Bob and Flo. 'The phones are off,' she said, her voice echoing with disbelief. It was true. The impossible had happened. Rolls-Royce, one of the largest employers of Derby's industry, had stopped trading.

'Let's have a cup of tea,' Flo said, scuttling over to the kettle.

Rachel's gaze frozenly followed her. Just like Polly, she thought. A brew up was the cure for all.

Rachel flopped on to her office chair and dropped her head into her hands. She wished she could contact David in some way, to know he was all right. She thought of how tired he had been looking the last few days, now she understood why. She tried to telephone one more time, knowing, before she heard the continued silence, that it was useless.

'It's a bombshell all right,' Bob said, dragging a chair up to her desk and sitting himself down.

'What's Derby like?' she asked, forcing herself into conversation to try and get rid of the overwhelming need she was feeling to speak to David. She knew it was impossible until he came home.

'There's crowds everywhere. Nobody can talk about anything else.' Bob went into graphic detail of Derby's town centre, leaving Rachel with the feeling everyone must be walking around as if they were in a drugged stupor, believing the end of the world had finally come.

The news travelled fast and every time a new face returned from dinner, the story was retold. Then it was the topic of conversation for the entire afternoon.

Two of the machinists had husbands working for Rolls-Royce and were very worried over the fear of redundancies: wondering how they were going to manage without their husbands' wages coming in; worrying how their husbands would find another job. If the whole of Royce's was out of work then there wouldn't be enough employment to go round.

Rachel kept very quiet. She did not share the same problems, she told herself, watching the minutes ticking away and praying David would not be late home. Coprell was thriving enough to keep both of them in more than comfort and there was no reason he needed to keep his job; there hadn't been for some time now. But the business was hers. David had always thought of it that way and preferred to keep his job for himself.

Rachel returned the designs to the folder and stuck them back in the filing cabinet. She was no longer in the mood. She couldn't think of anything but David. He didn't need his job, but she wasn't sure he could be happy without it. If he came to Coprell she felt he would feel he was working for her and not his own person.

Nevertheless, she made a mental list of all the jobs he could take over, if the worst came to the worst. The cash-book and all the accounting was at the top of the list.

By the end of the afternoon she had it all worked out and had a list of jobs as long as her arm. If she could persuade David to take over the administration, it would leave her free to concentrate on designing, ordering and selling. The place would run a whole lot smoother. It was perfect, she thought. If only David would agree!

As she locked the old chapel door and closed up for the night, she was feeling very pleasantly enthusiastic about the future. She just hoped David would not be late home. She did not want him worrying any longer than was necessary.

It was eight forty-five before she found out that all her planning had been for nothing.

David never arrived home. On the way he had a heart attack. The car went off the road, crossed the pavement, through a hedge, over someone's lawn and crashed into the garden wall.

It was a massive attack, the doctor said. He would have been dead before the car hit the wall.

Chapter Twenty-five

'For God's sake, Rachel! Get yourself out of it!' Sarah tossed the tea towel across the kitchen. She had just washed the plate on which she had brought a meal up for her. The dinner had only been half-eaten, but that was an improvement to previous months. 'What's the matter with you?'

Rachel looked incredulous. 'My husband is dead!' she returned, her voice sharp and bitter.

Sarah softened. 'I know that. We all know that. But you have to go on living – painful though it is. Why don't you go to the factory tomorrow? I'm sure it will help you. It's what you need. Work will take your mind off things.'

'Nothing will take my mind off it!' she returned fiercely.

Sarah sighed. She could see she was getting nowhere. 'It won't if you lock yourself up here day in and day out,' she snapped, losing patience with her. It was four months since David's death and, apart from his funeral, Rachel had not set foot outside the door. 'You've got to make the effort – for David's sake, if not for your own.'

'I don't know what you mean.' Her tired eyes looked puzzled. 'How can anything be for David's sake – now?'

'The factory was his as well as yours,' Sarah pointed out. 'Don't you think you owe it to him to keep it going?'

'It is still going,' she returned lamely. But she saw Sarah's point. She hadn't really cared if Coprell continued in production or not. Left to her, it would have closed. It was only Sarah, stepping in and taking the helm, that had kept it going. Maybe she had been wrong, she thought. Maybe David would want her to carry on. She sighed. It all seemed so pointless now.

'Well, it won't be going any longer. Unless you get off your backside,' Sarah stated bluntly. 'I've had enough! How do you think I'm coping with Christopher?' She stared unrelentingly into the pale face of her sister. Fixed her gaze to the eyes that looked as if they hadn't seen sleep in the last four months.

Rachel turned away, unable to take the condemnation of her sister's glare. Christopher was all right, she tried to tell herself. Alan's mother had been having him during the day, so Sarah could be free to stay at the factory.

'It isn't fair to him,' Sarah persisted, making Rachel wonder if she had spoken her last thoughts out loud. 'Besides, I want to bring my own child up!' She used emphasis to make her point. She had only taken responsibility for Coprell, thinking Rachel, with her history of working herself to death, would only be away for a few days. She had thought the problem would be the other way round: trying to stop her working. She looked at the back of her sister's bent head and shook her head. Her present reaction was so out of character and she was worried sick about her. She had tried gentle persuasion to get her to share her grief. But she was a closed book and wouldn't let anyone in.

Sarah hated being angry with her. But Alan had pointed out that it might be to Rachel's benefit to shock her out of it. So she summoned up her will power, and said, 'I'm not going there any more. I've got Christopher and Alan to think about. They come first with me. If you don't want to run the place yourself, you'll have to sell it!'

Rachel turned to the kitchen window and gazed out across the grassy mound that led up the top. It wasn't fair, she thought. After everything else, David being taken from her. She turned back to her sister. 'Just another week,' she said, a pleading in her eyes that tore Sarah in two.

'No,' she replied firmly, keeping hold of all her courage and forcing herself not to relent in the face of Rachel's devastation. It had gone on too long and something had to be done about it. 'I'm so tired in the evenings I've got no patience with either Alan or Christopher. It's spoiling our lives. It's your factory, not mine. It's your decision.'

Rachel dropped her head. Oh David, she thought. But

it was Polly who replied. Life goes on, lass. Life goes on!

'But the rainbow has been and gone – and taken the gold with it!' she replied, very angrily and very loudly.

'What?'

Rachel lifted her head to find Sarah looking askance at her. Then what should she expect? Speaking out like that! She shook her head. 'Nothing,' she said dismissively. Then stared at her sister for a moment. 'I'll sell the factory,' she finally said.

It wasn't what Sarah wanted to hear. She knew if Rachel didn't get herself back working she would never get over David's death. 'Well, you'll have to go in and wind it all up,' she said, hoping if she could get her back through the doors she would change her mind. 'I'm not doing one more day there. And you owe it to the staff to give them proper notice.'

Rachel felt trapped and it showed in her eyes. But Sarah had come too far to back down now. For four months she had seen only the numb devastation of her loss in her sister's eyes. Today had been the first hint of anything else, of signs of any other life still left in her.

Rachel sighed and turned back to the window. She didn't want to go to the factory. It would remind her too much. If it hadn't been for David she would never have had it. He had been so pleased to give it to her and she had always thought of the old chapel as being him. But she wasn't being fair to Sarah, she realized. Or Christopher, she told herself, and suddenly had the horror of seeing her nephew, brought up by Mrs Caradine senior, turning into another Micky. The thought provided the final spur. She took a deep breath and turned to Sarah. 'Will you do just one more day? With me?' she added, seeing the objection forming on her sister's lips. 'I can't go back on my own,' she said, and tears misted her eyes.

Sarah smiled. 'Of course I will!' she said, and went to her and wrapped her arms around her and they cried together; but her tears were those of joy.

The following morning Sarah went up to the top of the hill to come back down again. She felt it was necessary to make sure Rachel kept her word. But her fears had been for nothing. When she arrived at the house, Rachel was just on her way out, dressed in a very sombre black dress that looked totally out of place in the June sunshine. Sarah hoped it didn't herald a return to the drab clothes she had always worn before David. She'd never been able to understand why she'd always dressed like a nun. But she realized now was not the time to make any comment on her attire.

All the girls were very kind to Rachel when she reached the factory and Flo fussed round her like a mother hen. They were pleased to see her back, she realized, and did not miss the sense of relief that had also run through them. They had obviously been wondering what she was going to do. If she was going to close down. If they were going to lose their jobs.

She felt guilty that she had raised their hopes when she was going to squash them again. 'I think I should tell them straight away,' she said to Sarah, after closing the office door so no-one else could hear.

'If you must,' Sarah replied, showing little concern, even though she was greatly disturbed by the speed Rachel was trying to go at. She sorted calmly through the new orders and arranged them into stacks for the appropriate machinists. 'But don't you think it would be a shame?' she added casually.

Rachel frowned at her.

'I mean . . .' Sarah left the orders and turned to look through the office window at the busy work room, and spread her arms wide. 'This is what David left you. I don't want you to do something you'll later regret. What would you do if you suddenly began to think you'd given part of him away?'

Rachel's frown deepened and she moved up behind her sister and looked over her shoulder.

'I'm not saying you shouldn't sell, if that's what you want to do,' Sarah persisted. 'But I think you should give yourself more time to think about it.'

Rachel wasn't listening. Suddenly she was not seeing the old chapel building with the noisy sewing machines and the chattering girls. Or the roll upon roll of fabric and the piles of cotton spools of every shade and colour imaginable. She was seeing her baby: the child she and David should have had but never did. This was it! It had been *theirs*! Their creation.

The feeling that she had been left with nothing except cold bricks and mortar in the shape of his large rambling house and the dour old chapel began to diminish. Coprell was the child David had given her. And this time she would not give her child away. She would nurture it with tender loving care and watch it grow and expand – for David, and for all he had meant to her.

She suddenly turned to Sarah. 'Thank you,' she said with feeling.

'For what?' Sarah's smile was small and uncertain. She couldn't believe her hopes were coming true so quickly and so easily.

'For making me see the light,' Rachel replied, and Sarah's smile grew boldly on her face.

From that day Coprell went from strength to strength. Rachel gave it her all, working from dawn to dusk and well into the night on many occasions. She knew exactly what she was doing and she wasn't going to stop until she had realized her dream and could see it with her own eyes. Their baby, hers and David's, was going to grow into an adult. One that was as tall and proud as its father. The only part that made her a little sad was that she would have to move from the old chapel. But she felt David would understand; when she had built him his fitting memorial.

Chapter Twenty-six

1979

The rain stopped and a watery sun pushed its way through the grey November sky. Rachel turned the car radio on and began to hum to the music. As the car went round the final bend, the sun won its battle and the factory came into sight and the white walls and gleaming paintwork were circled by a halo of light.

Rachel stopped humming and fell silent. It looked so beautiful and she wished David could have been here to see it. On an impulse she stopped the car and sat staring at the realization of her dream. Eight years it had taken, of hard work and, at times, sheer bloody-mindedness. She had travelled all over the country, begging and even stealing contracts from right under her competitors' noses.

'I did it, David,' she said, her voice filled with the determination that had driven her through the years. Pride glowed from her face and her fingers went to Polly's gold locket hanging round her neck. 'I reclaimed the rainbow, Polly.' She laughed, recalling the other time, so long ago, when she had spoken out loud to Polly, and made Sarah think she was going mad.

She sighed, and was thankful she had been able to see the light before she had given away David's legacy. Then she started the car and drove on. The factory was almost complete and she had to meet the surveyor to make the final checks that everything was all right, before she took possession.

As she stepped out of the car, she paused and looked up at the two large workshops: Coprell and Morrell! The names blazed out at her from the newly erected sign boards. Coprell was for the popular fashion lines. The cheaper, mass produced. She grimaced, remembering how she had been so against entering that side of the market. But it was what the younger generation wanted: modern clothes which changed with each new year of altering fashion. Cheap and cheerful, was the motto of the Coprell range.

Morrell was the alter ego: the exclusive designs closest to her heart. It covered the luxurious lingerie and the evening and day wear that would not have looked out of place on the catwalks of Paris. Designs for the more mature, wealthy woman, who knew exactly what she wanted. Very much like herself, she thought, and turned her gaze to the third, small, building. The brick-built office block with large picture windows and a massive arched doorway, which, though mostly glass, had been designed that way to imitate the large oak doors of the old chapel.

As she admired the doors, Geoff Lavender, the surveyor, came out to meet her.

'No more problems?' she enquired pointedly. They were already one month behind schedule. Nothing major had gone wrong, but a string of minor complaints had needed to be rectified. And at one point the builder's men had been reduced to half by a tummy bug that had run virulently around the site.

Geoff shook his head. 'The floor coverings are all down and the carpet in your office looks wonderful.'

Rachel breezed through the office block doorway before he had time to open it for her. She made no comment about the carpet. She would reserve judgement until she had seen it for herself. She had learned by trial and error that when Geoff said something was wonderful, it was because it was not exactly what she had ordered and he was trying to persuade her it was better than her choice.

She stopped and studied the reception area very thoroughly. The long curved desk was now in the right place. The vertical blinds were the correct colour of pale grey and the turquoise and gold carpet, with the names Coprell and Morrell woven into it, really did look wonderful. She nodded her head with a certain reservation, not prepared to make any wild statements until she had seen the rest.

341

There was one large general office and four small offices: a larger one for herself and smaller ones for her production manager, personnel manager and accountant. The general office looked fine with two-tone grey carpet tiles on the floor. The three smaller offices were also looking good. Then she walked into her own office.

Wonderful, she thought, as she glanced briefly at the carpet and immediately saw the reason for Geoff's statement. She turned her attention to the windows and made no comment. She studied the blinds. Then the cupboards and the paintwork which she had already seen before. Then she turned to him. 'Everything seems to be right.' She paused and watched the relief pass over his face. '*Except* the carpet!' she added pointedly.

His face fell and he looked down at the cause of his problems. 'I thought it was rather nice.'

Rachel remained unmoved. She had learned some hard lessons since first signing on the dotted line to get all this in progress. Not least that if you were a woman in a man's world, you needed to be twice as crafty as they were. She looked at the carpet and pursed her lips. What he was saying was true. It was nice. But she'd be damned if she'd let him know that. She kept her eyes fixed on the carpet. It was the right colour and the design was almost identical to what she had chosen. The only difference was there was more gold in it. She had picked turquoise and gold as the colours for Morrell's logo: they were the colours of David's eyes and hair, and the colour scheme ran right through reception and into her own office. She frowned and looked thoughtful. It *was* better than her own choice. But Geoff was never going to know that.

She looked him straight in the eyes. 'How much?' she asked.

'Oh,' he gave a little shrug. 'They'll let you have it for the same price as the other.'

'I was meaning how much are they going to knock off for a wrong delivery?' she pointed out firmly.

Geoff shrugged again and looked uneasy. 'It's almost the same.'

'But it's not the same!' she quickly put in. 'I want twenty-five per cent knocked off the original price.'

'I don't think you can ask them to do that.'

'Not me!' She folded her arms and levelled her eyes at him. '*You!* You will tell them I either get twenty-five per cent off, or they come and take it up and put the right one down.'

'It might take ages. You could be without a carpet when you open.'

Rachel never blinked. 'Do they want paying for the rest?'

'Well, yes . . .'

'They don't get one penny until all the contract is complete. Tell them to read the small print very carefully.' She had been very thorough when setting up the deal and it had been such a large order the suppliers had not quibbled about her additions to the clauses.

He seemed about to object. But her eyes hardened and he had second thoughts. 'I'll see what I can do.'

'You do that. Remember I'm the one who's also paying your bill!'

Sarah giggled that evening, when Rachel related the carpet saga to her. 'You do push your luck at times,' she said, as she ironed Christopher's football kit.

'I do not!' Rachel looked affronted. 'If I'm to successfully run a place that size, I'll have to show them who's boss. So I might as well start now.'

Sarah nodded as she folded the blue and white shirt and laid it on a chair. You started a long time ago, she thought, keeping it to herself. She had dragged Rachel back to work after David's death, but there were times she wished she hadn't. Her sister had changed, slowly at first, but over the last eighteen months, since she began to see her dream becoming reality, the changes had speeded up. There was now a hard edge to her that the old Rachel would never have been capable of. It was, at times, as if she was blaming the rest of the world for David's death. The old chapel wasn't the same any longer. It was bursting at the seams with sewing machines and, Rachel said, production had increased four times over since David's day. But it wasn't the happy little work room it used to be. All Rachel was interested in was getting the orders out and getting more in. She hoped she would relax a bit more once the new factory was running and she had a full management team to run it for her. But she couldn't really see her ever giving the reins over completely. In fact, she saw her upsetting the staff and causing trouble by her interfering.

'Flo's coming with us,' Rachel said, and looked pleased. She had worried that having to take a bus journey to and from work might put Flo off. 'I think she thought I was trying to get rid of her when I asked her.'

'You didn't upset her?' Sarah looked concerned.

'Of course not. I told her I didn't want her to go, but I would understand if she didn't want to come.'

Sarah breathed a sigh of relief.

'Am I so totally unfeeling?' Rachel asked, seeing the reaction.

Sarah looked at her levelly. 'Yes,' she finally said. 'Sometimes.'

'Thank you!' Rachel did not get time to say more.

Christopher came bounding through the door. 'Hello!' he called, grinning from ear to ear when he saw Rachel there.

'Where's Dad?' Sarah asked.

'He's gone to see Gran. He said I was too dirty. I'd got to come straight home and wash.' He held his muddy hands out and looked down at his equally muddy knees. Then he gave a little shrug as if to say he didn't know what all the fuss was about.

'Where've you been, tiger?' Rachel asked, smiling with the fondness that came so easily to her face when she looked at her nephew.

'Dad's been to look at Mr Slater's car. We came back over the fields and through the woods.'

'You've not ripped your trousers again?' Rachel looked exaggeratedly serious. The wood in question was only small, but perched on the side of a steep grassy bank that was perfect for sliding down.

'No.' He grinned and turned round to show a muddy bottom, but trousers still intact.

'Thank goodness for that,' Sarah put in. 'Now go and get straight in the bath before you spread mud all over the place.' She affected a scowl, but was smiling before he had gone through the door.

Rachel laughed. 'You wouldn't change him,' she said.

Sarah shook her head. 'No, I wouldn't. But I wish he realized the value of money a bit more and wasn't of the opinion clothes grow on trees.'

Rachel looked steadily at her sister for a time. She knew they were struggling at the moment. Alan was trying to get a bit put by to buy his own car-repair business. She'd offered to help him. But Alan was fiercely proud and wanted to do it on his own. She respected him for that. In fact, she respected Alan for many things. Over the years he had never once given her cause for complaint. He was nothing like his elder brother and he and Sarah had always known the contentment that had passed Rachel by.

'You know there's always a job at the factory . . . If you want one?' she said. She didn't think it would be accepted. But there was no harm trying.

Sarah shook her head again. 'The money would be nice. But there are some things money can't buy. And I'd rather be a proper wife and mother.'

Rachel smiled and fell silent. Her flighty sister had changed so much. She shook her head and her smile broadened.

'What's wrong?' Sarah stopped ironing and eyed her suspiciously.

'Nothing's wrong. I was just remembering one Christmas Day, when a rather wayward thirteen year old came tottering down the stairs on high heels and with make-up plastered all over her face.'

Sarah laughed. 'I thought I looked so good. And I thought you were so stuffy for objecting.'

They both laughed at the memory. 'I was stuffy,' Rachel agreed. Then she fell silent as the memory of that day brought David and Polly back to her.

Sarah also fell silent, knowing the thoughts in her sister's head. She smiled sadly. It was good to see the old Rachel still existed. But she came into evidence less and less often of late. She gave an inward sigh and wished Rachel could find someone else to love. She felt sure that would be the cure. But in the eight years since David's death she had never looked at another man: she was too obsessed with the factory to have the time!

Chapter Twenty-seven

On the last day of the year Rachel stood in the old chapel for the final time. The sewing machines had all gone. Not one roll of fabric could be seen. She ran her hand down the yellowing office wall and recalled how white it had been when David first had it all fixed up for her. She looked at the high arched ceiling. It still looked like a house of God. It made her sad. The building's original identity would never be lost. But now, apart from the odd bits of cotton and little scraps of material cluttering the floor, the work room was anonymous. It had all gone, she thought sadly. And, as she looked around the bleak room, she could see David, busy with his tape measure, working out where everything was going to go and instructing the decorators how to do this, how to do that. Tears misted her eyes and she gave a deep sigh.

'Forgive me, David,' she whispered. It had taken a great deal of heart-searching before she had finally been able to agree to selling *their* chapel. But she couldn't think what to do with it and it would only have stood empty and decaying. And she needed the money for the new place. But she felt that she was giving part of him away.

She took one last look before hurrying through the great oak doors for the last time. Then she jumped into the car and took the keys to the agent, and, despite her sadness, forced herself to look forward to the new decade of the eighties with hope.

Rachel had been at her desk for ten minutes, when Flo came bustling in with the pile of mail. The factory had been in production for one month and everything was going surprisingly well.

'Thanks, Flo.' Rachel took the pile of letters from her hand

and placed them by the side of the four letters she had picked up off the mat at home that morning.

'Keith's going to be late,' Flo announced importantly. 'He phoned to say I had to tell you. He's calling in at Leatherbarrow's to see Roy Gibson.'

'Right.' Rachel nodded, then smiled as Flo scuttled out of the office. Now she was looking after the office block and the creature comforts of the office staff, she felt herself to be much more important. And Rachel was convinced the scuttling had increased in speed to match the position.

Still smiling, Rachel picked up the pile of mail and thumbed through the envelopes: orders, bills, an income tax form. She put the pile down and picked up the four personal ones brought with her. Again there were two bills, a reminder that she had missed a dental appointment, and a long white envelope with 'Private and Confidential' printed boldly across the top.

She frowned, picked up the paper knife and slit the envelope open. Inside was a single sheet of paper.

Her breath stopped as she began to read and her eyes travelled rapidly down the lines to the signature. Pauline Chapman! The name meant nothing. She read the entire contents again, more carefully, hoping she had got it wrong, knowing she had not. A feeling of sickness rose warm inside her, then vanished, leaving behind a cold dread.

It had happened. She looked at the calendar and did a quick mental sum. Last June her daughter had celebrated her eighteenth birthday. How could she have forgotten? She kicked herself for her neglect, yet knew, even had she been waiting for it, the letter would have been no less stunning. She had lived in fear of the day since a new law had made it possible for adopted children, when they reached the age of eighteen, to find their natural parents.

Last June, she thought incredulously. She had been so tied up with the new factory she had let the very significant date slip by unnoticed.

She shook her head, a feeling of despair coming over her. She had tried to tell herself her daughter would not want to find her. Who would want to look for someone who cared so little about you that they had given you away? It seemed a reasonable enough assumption, more than reasonable – to Rachel!

She looked once more at the letter and read it over again, word for word. Nothing had changed. Pauline Chapman was a social worker. Miss Chapman explained that her daughter had requested to be given the name of her natural mother. She then went on to explain the details of the Children's Act 1975. Children adopted after the twelfth of November of that year would be given their parents' identity on request. If adopted before that date the natural parents had, first, to give their permission. Because before that date the parents would have been given an assurance the child would never be able to find out who they were.

Pauline Chapman then went on to ask Rachel to get in touch to arrange a meeting so they could discuss this matter.

Rachel stared woodenly at the sprawling signature. Pauline Chapman! Who was this woman? she asked herself angrily. Some do-gooder who thought she could meddle with her life! Well she would not reply. She was coldly adamant. She would not give her permission. They couldn't make her if she didn't want to. This Miss Chapman stated the law very clearly and it was not against the law for her not to reply.

She folded the sheet of paper and pushed it back in the envelope. Then she crushed it in her hand. She was about to drop it into the waste bin, when she suddenly stopped. She was never sure what had made her stop. She had had no conscious thought to prevent the action. But, instead of throwing the envelope away, she placed it down on the desk and began to carefully brush the creases from it. Then she slipped it into the top drawer of her desk.

Forget it, she ordered herself, as she closed the drawer up again. Then she set about the daily routine of running the factory.

Unfortunately, she found it beyond her control to forget either the letter or the unknown Pauline Chapman. She felt suddenly very open and vulnerable; as if the whole world had become privy to her guilty secret. As she sorted through the works' orders in progress, ready for the weekly production meeting later that morning, she found her mind filling with the image of a tiny baby. She took herself off to the two large workshops, as she always did before the meetings, to check everything was running to plan. But she found the images increasing and she was seeing a little girl toddling across a lawn with her hand clasped in a woman's. But she didn't know where the lawn was and the woman was only a shadowy image.

By the time she was seated at her desk with the four faces of her management team sitting on the other side looking back at her, she was ready for war; anything to take her mind off the letter.

Keith Broadhurst was her production manager and he had been with her for just over a year at the old chapel. Ted Richardson was Keith's deputy in the Morrell work room and he had also been at the old chapel. The two new faces were Colin Wilson who did Ted's job for Coprell and Kate Prince, who was the accountant and company secretary. Kate had been the final choice after Rachel had reduced the candidates to two. The other had been a man and their experience and qualifications had been much the same and it had been Kate's sex which had finally swung it in her favour. Rachel had felt it would be nice to even up the score a bit and not be totally surrounded by men.

It was Kate who began. She gave her usual summary of the financial progress and what was expected in the coming week. 'The lingerie figures are down because the Rhapsody and Georgette bras are not reaching full production,' she said, to finalize her statements. 'We have quite a number of orders waiting but they're not getting processed.' She turned pointedly to Ted and peered at him over her large blue-framed glasses.

Ted, who could be a cussed devil at the best of times, was immediately on the defensive. 'Everything else is going to schedule,' he countered belligerently. 'Why pick on just those? I've got a machine down. What do you expect? They stitch them by hand!'

350

'Why is the machine still down?' Rachel enquired, taking over where Kate left off. Her hackles had immediately risen but she kept her cool. She had learned over the years that getting heated served no purpose. Cool determination always won, and her voice was like ice, as she said, 'It's been out of action for four days. Haven't you done anything about it?'

'I've phoned them every day. But they're busy. They're getting someone to us as quickly as they can.'

Rachel turned deliberately to Keith. 'Get it sorted out today. Tell them Swainson's can have a replacement here tomorrow morning and if they can't do the same by five o'clock this afternoon, *theirs* will be standing out in the car park waiting for them to collect.'

Ted sank lower into his chair and took on a more belligerent appearance. Keith scribbled a note on his pad and thought Rachel had definitely got out of bed the wrong side this morning. She was always firm and no-one got the better of her when she was determined. But her present manner was almost manic, and she hadn't stopped the frantic waggling of the pen in her hand since he had walked through the door and got his ears chewed off for taking longer than she felt was necessary at Leatherbarrow's. 'Have you made the final decisions on the next season's designs?' he asked, hoping he could successfully change the subject and draw her away from Ted, before he started ranting and raving and the meeting turned into a complete waste of time.

'Yes.' Rachel handed a folder to each one of them and the meeting returned to a more normal state.

Rachel fired back answers to the barrage of questions that was the usual culmination of the weekly event. But, for once, she wasn't entirely sure she was giving the correct replies. She felt almost fuzzy headed, as she tried to concentrate on work, yet found the letter constantly nudging into her thoughts. And she heaved a sigh of relief when the meeting ended and Kate, Ted and Colin filed out of the door.

Keith hung back, as he always did, to move the row of chairs from in front of her desk and put them back in their correct positions around the wall.

'There are times I could willingly strangle Ted,' Rachel said, leaning back in her chair and finally tossing the pen, which had remained jiggling in her hand for the entire meeting, on to the desk.

'I know,' Keith agreed with feeling, and perched himself on the corner of her desk and pulled a packet of cigarettes from his pocket. 'But he's marvellous with the girls.'

Rachel nodded. 'Because they know he'll come out fighting for them.'

Keith laughed and stuck the unlit cigarette in his mouth and fished in his pocket for his lighter. Rachel watched him intently. The way he lit his cigarettes reminded her so much of David. He wasn't like David in any other way. He wasn't so tall and he was broader than David's lean frame, and his hair was dark brown and wavy.

'How do you think Colin is getting on?' he asked.

'He seems to be doing all right. The work is coming through. Why? Is there a problem?' She looked questioning.

'No.' He shook his head and took a long draw on the cigarette and reminded her once more of David. 'I just wondered if you'd got any?'

'No.' She leaned forward and dropped her head into her hands and rubbed tiredly at her temples.

'So, what's troubling you?' Keith levelled her a knowing stare, as she glanced up at him with a scowl.

She smiled and leaned back once more. 'Nothing,' she said. 'I didn't sleep well.' She made a mental note to remember Keith was too astute for comfort and turned the conversation to Ted's broken machine. 'Go and get it sorted out straightaway, will you?' she said, wanting to get him out of her office. She wanted to be alone to think.

Keith pushed himself from the desk. 'And tell them you're dumping it in the car park?' He lifted his eyebrows at her in mocking amusement.

Rachel grinned. 'Well, perhaps not in quite so many words. But I want it sorting out today!' she added firmly. 'Tell them we'll be wanting a dozen more by the end of the year and if they don't get their act together now, they won't stand a chance.'

Keith grinned. 'Aye, aye, cap'n.' He gave a swift salute and went out.

Rachel had to smile. She'd made a good choice in Keith. He'd come ready qualified and was conscientious and ambitious, and he had liked the idea of helping to get the new factory off the ground. Most of the other candidates had stuck their noses up when they had seen the size of the old chapel. But Keith had seen the potential and had listened to her plans for expansion with a keenness in his eyes that had told her more about him than any amount of talking could have done. And he was younger than most of the others had been: thirty-six, just a year older than herself.

They made a good pair, she thought, and collected up the designs which had been left strewn across her desk. As she was putting the designs back into the folder, the letter leapt into her mind again. She slammed the folder shut and pushed it across the desk. She really couldn't imagine why the girl wanted to find her. She grabbed her pen back and began to jiggle it nervously once more. Novelty value, she tried to tell herself. It was nothing more. The girl just wanted to see what she looked like, what she did, what she was like. Once she had done that she wouldn't want to know her any more.

No, she thought determinedly. She wasn't going to open up a hornets' nest for herself, for someone who probably only wanted to take one look, then vanish again.

But, as she pulled the production schedule across her desk and tried to concentrate on it, she found unwanted questions bombarding her mind. What was her name? Did she still look like Sarah? Were her parents good to her?

The last one made her pause. She felt if the answer had been yes she wouldn't want to be looking for her. The thought disturbed her and she couldn't concentrate on the production figures. The guilt which had weighed heavily on her over the years suddenly increased. *Her daughter was not happy!*

She tried to tell herself she was jumping to conclusions. She tried to picture Sarah at eighteen; tried to imagine a carefree teenager. It didn't work. At eighteen Sarah had been married with a baby on the way.

Was her own daughter pregnant? Was she already a mother? She suddenly sat back. She could be a grandmother and not know it! It was a frightening thought.

The more she tried to convince herself she was being unrealistic, the worst the images became. Finally, she knew she could not ignore the letter any longer. She had let her daughter down once before. Now was a chance to make good some of the wrong she had done her. Before she could change her mind, she pulled the letter from the drawer and reached for the telephone.

Chapter Twenty-eight

'Miss Chapman!' Rachel breezed across the small dark office with an air of businesslike confidence. She held out her hand, giving the one offered across the cluttered desk a firm handshake.

The tiny, dark-haired woman smiled warmly and offered Rachel a chair, and they both sat down, one on either side of the enormous old desk that looked far too large for the diminutive Pauline Chapman.

Rachel sat very straight and erect. Her face remained blank and she gave away none of the emotion she was feeling inside. Since making the phone call to arrange the meeting she had changed her mind several times each day. And, even though she was now there, she still was not entirely convinced she was doing the right thing.

'Now,' she began, having every intention of keeping the upper hand in the conversation. She was not going to allow herself to be browbeaten into something she did not want. 'Let me make it quite clear that my coming here does not mean I am willing to comply with my daughter's request.'

'Of course not,' Pauline Chapman agreed, positioning her hands before her as if she was in prayer, her voice holding a gentleness which Rachel felt was of the deceiving quality.

It made her bristle with indignation and there was a hard edge to her voice as she continued, 'I want to know all the facts before I make any decision.'

Pauline Chapman's reverent hands swept wide. 'But you must understand I am limited in what I can divulge, if you are not going to meet your daughter. If you are unsure of making any contact it would be detrimental to yourself to know too much about her. In these cases it is far better to be left in the dark.'

Then why have I come here? Rachel wondered, her irritation increasing at the woman's sanctimonious attitude.

'*You* asked to see me, so we could discuss *this matter*!' She used emphasis to make her point. 'If there is nothing to discuss, then we are both wasting our time. I did not come here to discuss *my* emotions. I want to know those of the girl. Why does she want to see me? Has something happened to make her feel the need? Is *she* happy?'

Pauline Chapman paused and looked thoughtful.

Rachel stared at her blankly, waiting. If she could not have the answers she was seeking there was no point in continuing. She thought of the factory, of the one hundred and one jobs waiting for her attention. She wished she had never given in to the urge to come.

The silence continued. Rachel reached down and picked up her handbag – a sure sign she was ready to leave.

'All right,' Pauline Chapman reluctantly agreed.

Rachel kept the handbag on her knee, refusing to make the gesture of compliance by putting it back on the floor. 'This is a special case,' Pauline continued. 'Which presents special problems.' She paused and looked suitably serious and Rachel's interest suddenly picked up. 'Unfortunately, when your daughter was only four years old, her adoptive mother was killed in an accident.'

Rachel's eyes widened. She immediately let the handbag drop to the floor. Then she straightened purposefully, listening intently.

'The father has never married again. So,' Pauline Chapman's hands made another sweeping gesture, then returned to praying, 'from that age she has been cared for only by him.'

Rachel looked away, turning to the drab fawn wall. Who chose that colour, she wondered, as she forced the harsh, dry bark of ironic laughter not to leave her mouth. She had given her daughter away so that she could have two parents, be given twice the love she, alone, could have given her. To have the comfort of a real home with a father *and* a mother!

'Under the circumstances, it is understandable that she wants to find the mother who is still alive.' Pauline Chapman's voice broke into Rachel's mind and she returned her despairing gaze to her, as she said, 'But, you must understand the situation is full of exceptional problems.'

Rachel nodded her head. Then lifted her hand to her forehead and rubbed, as if the action would rub away this new, disconcerting bit of information. She did not speak. She could not. She needed time to think. This changed everything. Her determination to walk in, ask the questions she wanted to, and walk out again, began to crumble rapidly. Her heart was crying out for her motherless child. But she had to be rational, she told herself. There was still the father to consider. And she was not sure it was what she really needed. She had made a successful life for herself since David's death. The factory, work, business . . . It was what she was good at. Her parental control of Sarah had never been a raging success because she had always put work first. Fortunately, Sarah's mistakes had not blighted her life and she and Alan's happiness seemed to grow with each passing year, but it could have been very different.

She rubbed her head again. If she agreed to her daughter's request, what would happen? Would the girl be disappointed? If she was expecting some warm maternal type she was in for a shock!

'What is the father like?' She looked up into Pauline Chapman's assessing gaze and felt naked, torn apart by the all seeing eyes.

'He is very nice, very understanding. He has looked after her very well.'

'Does he know she wants to see me?' She hoped he didn't, clutching at a straw that would give her the reason to stand up and walk away.

'Yes,' Pauline Chapman replied simply.

'And?' Rachel questioned, feeling her heart sinking to somewhere in the region of her knees.

Pauline Chapman gave a little shrug. 'At first, naturally, he was not very happy with the decision.'

No, he wouldn't be, Rachel thought dryly. Why couldn't he have married again, given the child a mother? she asked herself, her mind placing all the blame on the man's shoulders.

'But he has come to understand his daughter's reasons,' Pauline Chapman continued.

My daughter! Rachel thought mutinously – and Micky Caradine's! The last thought just popped into her head. She didn't want it, tried to push it away. It stuck. All in the same moment she was walking up the top with Micky, could see his silly grin, was in the field, could feel the nausea rise as he invaded her body.

No, she thought rebelliously. She pushed herself upright in the chair once more. She had allowed her guard to slip. Stiffening her back, she took command of her body, along with conversation. It was the cool businesswoman who said, 'There is little point in our continuing, Miss Chapman. I really don't have any wish to drag up the past. I don't feel it would accomplish anything for the girl.' She made a deliberate point of not referring to my daughter, for her own benefit, as much as Pauline Chapman's. 'She seems to have a good father. I don't think I could do anything for her that he has not already done. She'll forget about it. I'm sure it is merely a whim.' If the army of do-gooders had not passed the silly law there would have been no need to go through this, she thought belligerently. Did they know what harm they caused? Turning people's lives upside down with their meddling. Her anger formed in an unrelenting glare at Pauline Chapman's frozen face.

'A whim!' The frozen face displayed the displeasure of her comment. 'The father and daughter have been talking about this for several years.' Her voice was hard with accusation. 'I can assure you, Mrs Morrell, this has not been a decision taken lightly. The father is an intelligent man. He has brought his daughter up the same. This is no silly teenage *whim*! It is the carefully considered decision of a very capable young woman. But . . .' She gave an all encompassing shrug. '. . . if you feel you cannot cope with the situation . . .' Her voice trailed away, the rest left unsaid.

Rachel looked away from the condemning gaze, her anger

doubling that this pious woman thought she was not capable of facing her own daughter; that it was true, increased her rage. She turned back to face her opponent, her eyes pivoting coolly to the challenging ones across the desk. 'I am a businesswoman,' she said, her voice bitter with the recriminations that were aimed mostly at herself. 'My life is too wrapped up in the working of my company. I do not have the time for a child. I think it could be disastrous for *her*. Hurting her far more than concealing the truth from her.'

'As you wish, Mrs Morrell.' Pauline Chapman's tone was dismissive. She picked up the case papers lying in front of her, made a very deliberate gesture of straightening them up, placed them back inside the folder, then closed the folder with a negligent action of one finger.

Rachel's expression remained blank and unmoved. But inside she gave a bitter smile. She knew exactly what the woman was doing. She had used the same psychology herself, many times: making it obvious to whoever was sitting on the wrong side of the desk that she was of the opinion they were wasting her time, of little consequence, a nuisance to be got rid of with all speed.

Rachel picked up her handbag once more. She stood up and stretched her five feet three inches to their full limits and looked Pauline Chapman straight in the eyes.

'Goodbye, Miss Chapman!' She held out her hand politely, gave another confidently firm handshake, and turned for the door.

Rachel had assumed the conversation was at an end and was taken completely by surprise when, halfway to the door, Pauline Chapman asked, 'Does your husband know about your daughter?'

She turned slowly around, her surprise doubled by the fact that the Social Services had not pried enough. The dark little woman sat gazing at her and she felt her whole body stiffen with indignation. 'I am a widow,' she spat. Then she turned back to the door, but had second thoughts. 'And yes!' she said, slanting her eyes coolly at the woman. 'He did know – *everything*!' she added pointedly, bridling at the insinuated slur that she had kept secrets from David; that they had not been close enough to share everything.

'Was it his baby?'

Rachel's mouth dropped open. She knew it had, but was powerless to stop it. What did this woman think she was?

'It does happen,' Pauline Chapman pointed out, her manner softening once more. 'Especially with someone like yourself. A committed career woman who would find a baby too much of a drain on her time.'

Angry heat rose rapidly to Rachel's cheeks. 'If you must know,' she began with fierce acidity. 'I was attacked. I was sixteen years old and had a sick mother to care for. I was only married for eighteen months before my husband died. We thought we had time to wait,' she added bitterly. She would not tell this woman the truth. It was none of her business. She did not know what caused the sudden restriction in her throat: the sorrow of not having David's baby, or the lie to cover the hurt. But whatever the initial cause, she was overtaken by an emotion that clogged her throat and prevented her from telling the prying little woman to keep her nose out of her affairs.

Pauline Chapman sensed the change that suddenly came over her. 'Sit down,' she instructed gently. 'I think we should start again, from the beginning. Don't you?'

For a moment Rachel wanted to turn and run. Turn her back on Pauline Chapman and all the bad memories and all the guilt she had kept locked deep inside her for the long years. It would be so easy, she told herself. All she had to do was walk out of the door. But, she realized sadly, that would only close Pauline Chapman away. The rest would go with her, following her to the day she died.

Slowly she returned to the chair and sat down. If she did not face it now, she never would. It might not bring her peace, but at least she would have a clearing of the conscience. She would know that, at least once, she had done the right thing by her daughter.

It was one and a half hours later before Rachel finally left Miss Chapman's office.

She told the woman everything, except Micky Caradine's full name. Pauline Chapman accepted her refusal of that without question, and they referred to him only as Micky.

Rachel became surprised to find the social worker growing on her. She seemed to understand all her feelings, all her anxieties and fears.

It was strange, she thought, as she finally walked to the door, how the woman had been able to draw her out of herself. She had never opened herself up in that way before, not to a stranger, only to David and Polly, the two dearest friends she had ever possessed.

'Goodbye, Rachel.' Pauline Chapman took the door in one hand and held the other towards her.

'Goodbye,' she said, taking the offered hand and realizing the handshake she was receiving was as firm as her own. She smiled, realizing she had met her match.

'Now go away and have a good think about everything we've talked about,' Pauline Chapman said. 'Don't leap to any decision. Make sure it is what *you* really want to do. If you have any questions give me a call.'

Rachel nodded. 'Thanks,' she said meaningfully. She had decided she definitely liked Pauline Chapman. They were two of a kind, could play the game whichever way, soft or hard. She smiled. 'And if you ever think of changing your job, give *me* a call. We'd make a good team.'

Pauline laughed. 'Until the day we crossed swords and neither of us would give in.'

For one whole week Rachel did think. She found it difficult to think about anything else. Fortunately, the factory ran smoothly, with only the usual minor hiccups, but nothing major. For that Rachel was grateful. She felt that her mind, usually able to cope with several problems at once, would have let her down.

Every day she made up her mind to telephone Pauline Chapman. Say yes. Set the wheels in motion for the meeting she was both wanting, yet dreading. Every day she picked up the phone. Every day she put it down again.

'Ted's just phoned across,' Flo announced, as she bustled importantly into Rachel's office.

Rachel actually jumped, as Flo's sudden presence jerked her away from her pensive gazing out of the window.

'He wants you to go across and take a look at that new black taffeta. He thinks there's something wrong with it.'

She looked blankly at Flo. 'What does he think is wrong with it? Why couldn't he have phoned me?' she enquired irritably. If Ted had called her direct he could have explained on the phone, saving her the job of having to go trailing to the workshop.

'He's been trying for ages. Said you were always engaged.'

'I've not . . .' Rachel followed Flo's gaze to the blue internal telephone. The receiver was lying on the desk, where she had put it first thing that morning. She grimaced. She had intended to have a peaceful half hour to herself, before being bombarded with questions. She looked at her watch. She had forgotten all about the telephone and the half hour had turned into two.

'All right, Flo. Leave it with me,' she snapped, irritation increased by the addition of guilt. She began to dial Ted's number, then stopped, looked pointedly at Flo, who was standing staring at her. 'Was there something else?' she enquired stiffly.

'Is there something up?' Flo looked concerned.

'No,' she replied sharply. 'Why should there be?'

'You're not your usual self,' Flo persisted. 'You've worried me these past few days. Snapped at everybody you have.'

Rachel gave a sigh of resignation. Then attempted a smile, but it was thin and light. 'I'm sorry,' she said. 'I've got things on my mind. It's nothing to do with the factory. So you've got no need to worry about it.'

Flo didn't look convinced. 'I'll worry if I want to,' she insisted. Then walked out, continuing to grumble, as if speaking to herself but loud enough for Rachel to hear. 'Life's too short to go getting yourself into a tizz,' was her parting comment.

Yes, Polly, Rachel thought, leaning her chin thoughtfully

against the telephone receiver held in her hand, the comparison putting a sad smile on her face. She fingered Polly's locket hanging round her neck and wished her old friend was here now. She wished David was also there. They would both have known what to do.

She suddenly put the telephone receiver down. The black taffeta would have to wait, she thought, and got up from the chair and returned to the window.

There had been a heavy frost that morning. Now the sun was shining and the sky was blue and dotted with fluffy white clouds. Everywhere glistened wetly in the brightness. The two workshops stood like soldiers on guard, proud and erect. Her dream, her legacy to David's memory, she thought, and smiled. She had not failed him. She looked at the Morrell sign board: sea green with gold lettering, like the carpet, to match his colouring. She had done it. And all alone!

Yes, she thought, slowly realizing the fact. No-one had helped her. There had been no-one to run to, to check she was making the right decision, planning the right moves. Yet all the decisions and moves had been exactly right. She had done it all by herself, once she had faced the irrefutable fact of David's death. The proof was staring her in the face. And this was the same. If she could face the problem squarely . . . She had to face it squarely, she told herself, and suddenly knew exactly what she had to do.

Five minutes later the black taffeta problem had been handed over to Keith. An astonished Flo had been given orders to inform everyone Rachel was not available until tomorrow. And Rachel was in her car, driving home with the sure conviction that by the end of the day she would have come to a decision and would know what she was going to do about her daughter.

The wind was biting as she walked over the brow of the hill. On reaching home she had taken only the briefest time to change into a pair of jeans and wrap herself in a sheepskin coat and boots. Then she had set off up the top. Facing David's death all those years ago had given her the strength to build her empire and shown her how to succeed in her professional life. That was the easy part. The other part, the personal side, had always been difficult for her. David had taught her how to love through patience and understanding. Now she had to understand herself and the reasons why she had closed herself off, erected the brick wall which kept other human beings at a safe distance. She had to face the past, her past, the part that hurt the most.

The dirt track cut a line between the grassy banks: one side glistening with sparkling jewels of moisture where the sun had softened the frost, the other side shaded and still white and hoary. Rachel walked on, her steps driven by purpose. Her nose turned red and her eyes began to water in the chill air. A lonely robin bobbed along the top of the wall on her right, obviously pleased to have some company. She had found a friend, she thought, also glad of the company.

At last she reached the place. She stopped, looked at the wall for only a moment, then climbed carefully up the slippery bank.

She had walked up the top many times since that day. But she had never stopped there, never approached the wall to look down the fields, to where . . .

She reached the wall and grasped the copestones, held her breath in nervous anticipation, but refused to turn back now, and pulled herself up so she could see over the top.

The robin stopped a few yards away and stood, its head on one side, watching her. The valley was flooded with the bright winter sunlight, the fields edged with white where the frost clung beneath the walls. It all looked so peaceful, so unreal, a bit like a Christmas card. There did not seem to be anything belonging to the horrific memories she held of the place. She looked all around: at the farm, the wood, part of the river down at the bottom, everywhere, before slowly allowing her gaze to settle on the corner of one field.

For a moment there was nothing, only the increasing feeling that she had got the position wrong. It was too peaceful, too docile to be a partner in any crime.

Then it came. So sharply that she flinched and gasped in shock, as the nightmare was lived again in stunning 3D images so real she felt she could have reached out and touched them, raised her hand and stopped Micky.

But she could not stop them. She was powerless, until the end, when the pictures stopped of their own volition. She had been just as powerless as she had been on that day. She had seen it all now, relived with shocking clarity.

Her arms trembled as she clung to the wall. But a peace, a serenity was settling over her. So many times she had relived the repulsion of the attack: the touch of his hands, his body tearing out some very special part of her. So many times she had gone through it all, again and again. But always as a partner to the crime. She had always felt to blame, that in some way she had been responsible. Suddenly she knew the truth. Had seen it with the eyes of an innocent observer.

She suddenly threw back her head and glared up at the white clouds scudding across the blueness of the sky. 'I hope you are rotting in hell, Daniel Cooper!' she shouted, the intensity of her feelings vibrating the cloud of her breath and sending the robin fleeing to a safer distance.

It was all clear now. Just as she had been powerless to stop the images of her mind, she had been powerless to stop Micky on that long ago day. The horror of what had happened had, in a way, been engulfed by the shame of turning into one of her father's well-used names: harlot, common hussy, brazen trollop, whore!

The names had spun round inside her head, like magnets dragging her down to some unspeakable degradation which had clung to her through all the years. Not even David's love had fully washed away the guilt she had wrapped herself in.

Well, now she knew the truth. The blame, the guilt, the shame, all lay on Micky's shoulders. And on her father's, for his pious hypocrisy. She recalled her mother's words of warning on the subject of men and sex. The ravings of a mad woman, she had thought at the time. Now she changed her mind. Her father had been a hypocrite over everything else, she could not see any reason to assume he had changed his attitude behind closed doors.

She shuddered on the imaginings of what her mother might

have had to put up with. Then she turned away and jumped down the bank and back on to the track. There was no reason to stay any longer.

The robin, having overcome its fear, bobbed along the wall once more, as she retraced her steps. She was in no way to blame for what had happened, she told herself, and neither was her daughter. It was not the child's fault that she had Micky Caradine for a father. The girl was as much an innocent victim as she herself. And, no matter who her father was, she was still half of her. More than half, she told herself, recalling the tiny spitting image of Sarah. The baby was all Cooper. A female Cooper, she quickly inserted, having no wish to label her daughter with any of her father's characteristics.

The robin stopped, held its head on one side, and peered at her. She smiled. 'It's all right,' she said. 'Everything is all right now. I'm going home to make a very important phone call.'

The robin seemed unimpressed and began to hop along the wall once more. Rachel laughed, and suddenly had the feeling Polly was right there with her.

Do you approve, Polly? she asked silently, and was convinced she heard Polly chuckle.

The first thing she did when she got home was to put some crumbs out for the robin, who had followed her all the way back. The second was to telephone Pauline Chapman.

Chapter Twenty-nine

The restaurant was crowded with the usual midday flock of business men and women. Rachel sat down at the table and looked around to check there was no-one there she knew. The faces were all those of strangers and she breathed a silent sigh of relief. Neutral ground, she had thought, when choosing the venue for the first meeting. It would be best for both parties. Now, watching all the faces, listening to all the noise, she was having second thoughts. The privacy of home might have been better. Her own home. Not her daughter's, where the father's presence would have been in evidence even if he himself was not.

Pauline Chapman had offered to be there. It had been the girl's decision that they should be alone. Rachel was pleased with that decision. She felt they would be better left to themselves with no third party to interfere. It also pleased her that her daughter was confident enough to come alone. She knew very well that at the same age she would have needed someone to hold her hand.

Rosemary! The name of the imagined face she had watched growing up in her mind. She wondered how the reality would compare to the fantasy. She toyed with her fork. Would she be disappointed? It was a question which had never occurred to her before. Any disappointment, she had thought, would be the other way around. It would be herself who did not measure up to anyone's ideal of the homely mother.

She glanced down at the apple-green suit she was wearing. The straight figure-hugging skirt and the broad-belted jacket in no way resembled the dull, sexless two-pieces she had worn in earlier days. But the suit was smart and businesslike, chosen specifically to portray her as she really was – a career woman, the leader of her own empire. She had wanted no false frills to give any wrong impression. If Rosemary Ellicot was looking for a kitchen sink mother, one who could produce mouth-watering chocolate cake at the drop of a hat and the remedy for every known childish ailment, then she was looking in the wrong direction.

She is eighteen, you idiot, Rachel was reminding herself, just as the restaurant door swung open.

The breath caught in her throat and she knew immediately who was walking in. Her hair was a shade darker than Sarah's and cut in a short bob that framed her face. She was not as tall as Sarah and her face was no longer the spitting image. But there was no denying the ancestral connections. She was pretty, as beautiful as Sarah and, as the waiter showed her over to the table, she walked with the same bouncy confidence as Sarah had at that age; an enthusiasm for life which Rachel had never known.

'I'm Rosemary.' The girl stuck out her hand and Rachel was pleasantly surprised to find her grip was as firm and confident as the infectious smile on her face. She was wearing a plain chocolate-brown dress with a bright orange jacket of the quality that could have come from Morrell's own workshop, and expensive looking chocolate-brown knee-high boots.

Rachel smiled her approval. 'Sit down,' she invited, and wondered what to say next. How to begin the conversation. Should she talk about the weather and inconsequentials, or row right in?

The decision was taken from her. 'I'm so pleased you agreed to meet me,' Rosemary said. 'I don't want you to think I'll go making demands on you. I have a wonderful dad, couldn't have been better.'

Could have been worse, Rachel thought, images of Micky flying past her eyes. Strangely there was no bitterness with the thought.

'I've been very happy with Dad, even though we lost Mum.'

Rachel smiled. She liked the way the girl said 'we', as if they were inseparable, a pair. It told her more about the girl's relationship with her father than any detailed monologue

368

could. It also hurt a little. 'Why did you want to see me?' she asked.

'I want to know where I came from. Can you understand that?'

'Yes, I can understand,' she replied, a quiet pride growing inside her that this confident, self-assured young lady was her daughter. The father had done a good job she grudgingly allowed.

The waiter arrived and they quickly looked at the menus, smiling together as they realized they had both forgotten they were supposed to be there to eat. They quickly ordered and the waiter went away.

'Tell me about yourself,' Rachel said, feeling the need to know everything: how every year had been spent, what she had done, what she liked, what she disliked, how she felt about anything and everything. She knew she was asking the impossible. It would take years to catch up on a lifetime. She suddenly wondered if Rosemary had any intentions of seeing her again. She had said she would make no demands. Perhaps this one meeting was all she wanted. The thought alarmed her. 'Where did you go to school? Are you working?' She spoke quickly, her voice suddenly urgent, a demand there that she had not intended. Her voice softened. She smiled. 'There seems so much to know in so short a time.'

Rosemary smiled a little embarrassedly. 'Yes,' she replied simply. Then dropped her gaze and stared thoughtfully at the Canaletto scene of Venice imprinted on the table mat. When she looked up her smile had gone. 'I think we should see how we both feel after this. Miss Chapman explained that you are a professional woman, that you might not have time for any . . .' She looked around, searching for the right word. 'Complications,' she added, with a wry smile.

Rachel leaned forward and rested her chin on her hands. 'I think we should forget Miss Chapman. We're both intelligent enough to make our own decisions.'

Rosemary smiled at the compliment. 'What exactly do you do?' she asked.

'I suppose you could say I was in the rag trade.' Rachel

gave a little laugh, making a deliberate attempt to lighten the previous tension. 'I design and manufacture clothing. Dresses, suits, evening wear, lingerie. Have you heard of Coprell and Morrell?'

Rosemary's eyes widened. 'You're *that* Morrell!'

Rachel laughed. She was by no means the first woman to succeed in the fashion industry. But the reaction was always the same. She often felt like asking if they had heard of Coco Chanel or Mary Quant. If she had been a man no-one would have batted an eyelid. She was never offended, the attitude always added to her pride in her accomplishments and successes.

'Yes, I'm that Morrell.' She lifted her eyes expressively. 'And I'm also the Coprell.' She explained how the name had been invented, and she told Rosemary about David.

'David was not your father.' Recalling Pauline Chapman's assumption that he might be, she wanted to put the matter straight. She knew it would lead to a question she would rather not hear, but it had to be faced. And the sooner it was out of the way the better.

She was not disappointed. Rosemary looked her straight in the eyes. 'Who was my father?' she asked, her voice suddenly very serious.

Rachel commended herself on not blanching, not allowing any emotion to show. 'We were very young. I was just sixteen, he wasn't much older. Not long after I found I was pregnant he was killed. Motorcycle accident,' she said, keeping words to a minimum, thanking heaven for all the experience earned in the weekly production meetings. Experience that had given her the ability to remain calm in all situations. She knew only too well if you lost your cool, you lost the upper hand. She hated lying, beginning what could be a good relationship with an untruth. But, after considering all the aspects of the situation, she had felt a lie was the best course. The girl deserved better than to be told she had been conceived in an act of violence, without love.

'Had you known him long?' Rosemary persisted.

The waiter arrived with the meals and Rachel waited until

he had gone, using the time to carefully prepare her reply.

'Not very long. He was from Manchester. He moved down to the local mill as part of his training.' Manchester fitted in well with the local mill. The head office was situated there.

'What was his name?'

'Michael Holden,' she returned without any hesitation. Half truth, half lie. It comforted her a little to know the story was not a complete fabrication.

'Was he nice?'

Rachel did not miss the anxiety which had crept into Rosemary's voice. She dully performed a fond, reminiscent smile. 'Yes,' she said softly. You should have gone on the stage, she thought dryly. Then, considering the line of questioning had gone too far, turned the tables. 'So, tell me about yourself while we eat. Or the food will be cold.'

Rosemary began to relate the story of her life between mouthfuls of lasagne verde. Exotic food – another similarity to Sarah, Rachel thought with approval, as she picked at her chicken salad.

Rosemary certainly had a good life. Far better than Rachel could have given her, at the beginning. Rosemary's father was a doctor, an orthopaedic consultant. It was obvious he doted on the girl, and the way Rosemary's face lit up when she spoke of him showed how clearly she returned his love. She was also following in his footsteps and had begun university in September, although she wasn't sure she wanted to go into the same line of medicine.

Rachel began to feel a niggling jealousy towards the man. You gave her away, she reminded herself. Yet she could not help feeling Rosemary would have made the perfect successor for the factory, the successor she was sadly without. In her mind she had considered Christopher to be her heir. But Christopher was more like Alan than Sarah. From the moment he could sit up he had loved tinkering with things, taking bits to pieces so he could put them back together again. It was obvious that he was another car mechanic in the making, just like his father. Rachel had kept hoping that Sarah and Alan would have another child, but Christopher was nine now, and still the only one.

'Have you always wanted to go into medicine?' she asked.

'Oh yes,' Rosemary replied with enthusiasm. 'My dolls always had bandages and splints on them.'

Rachel smiled, though she felt sad inside. If only she had realized what she had been giving away. It was too late for regret, she told herself. Besides, Christopher would appreciate the money. He could buy himself his own garage and perhaps . . . She looked thoughtfully at Rosemary for a moment. No, perhaps not, she told herself, and turned to gaze out of the window. Rosemary had given no indication that she wanted to see her again. Leaving her a legacy might be looked on as guilt money.

Rachel watched a man slowly manoeuvre a long Jaguar car out of the crowded car park. At the exit he paused, allowing a woman with a pram to pass by. Her mind's eye filled with the image of a tiny baby. She looked quickly to Rosemary, that tiny baby, now a young woman. So many years gone by, lost!

'Do you want another coffee?' she quickly asked, peering into Rosemary's empty cup, having the sudden need to reach the inevitability of the end. And get it over with before the pain got any worse.

Rosemary shook her head. 'No thanks. I'm meeting Dad. We have some Christmas shopping to do.'

A nice little arrangement on father's part, Rachel thought bitterly. A set appointment to make sure his daughter did not stay too long. 'Well, I'll pay the bill and let you go.' She spoke pleasantly enough, though the bitterness was curling painfully around her heart. The writing was on the wall, she told herself, and caught the attention of the waiter.

'How did you get here? Can I drop you anywhere?' Rachel asked as she opened her purse and placed the money on the plate. And she found she was having a change of heart and wanted to put the moment of separation off a few minutes longer.

'No thanks. I have my own car.' Rosemary stood up first,

not waiting for Rachel, but concluding the meeting for herself.

Rachel's heart dipped. It seemed her daughter was only too eager to be away. She followed the young woman through the twist of tables to the door, her mind whirling over a procession of unanswered questions.

It was too late, she told herself, as they stepped out into the cool December air. Rosemary wanted nothing more. Now she had seen her mother with her own eyes and had asked the questions she wanted about her father she was content.

She was not sure if Rosemary was happy with her discoveries. She had been pleasant enough, but she had not shown a great deal of emotion. She gave a wry smile. Perhaps her daughter was a lot like herself, able to cover her feelings.

'At least it isn't raining,' Rosemary said, looking up at the grey sky as Rachel stopped by her car.

'No,' she replied simply, feeling despair expanding within her. The end, it seemed, was to be lost in useless trivialities. When there was so much more she wanted to say . . .

Rosemary cast a look of approval on her red BMW car. 'That's nice,' she said.

'Yes,' Rachel replied, and wanted to scream. A thousand words were stuck in her head, yet none would reach her lips.

'Look!' They both spoke together.

'You first,' Rachel quickly insisted, before Rosemary had the chance.

Rosemary looked embarrassed. A tight smile pulled at her lips. 'I know I said I wouldn't make any demands – and I won't!' she quickly inserted. 'But I would like to see you again.' She looked apologetic, and Rachel smiled as the pressure left her heart, lifting it high.

'I'd love to see you again,' she said, pleasure flooding her face as relief washed over Rosemary's. 'I thought . . .' She moved forwards, taking Rosemary's hand in both her own; the first time she had touched her daughter, really touched her, not just the polite handshake of meeting. 'I know the fault is all mine,' she said unsteadily. 'I've had years to regret what I did. I know you belong to your father now. But there is no reason we can't be friends.'

Rosemary smiled emotionally. For a moment she looked very young and vulnerable: the confident young woman turned back into the child. So like Sarah, Rachel thought, and wanted to wrap her arms round her, the way she had done for Sarah. She held back. It was too soon, she realized. She had the confirmation she had been wanting. Her daughter wanted to see her again. It was enough for now, for both of them. If things did not work out they would both get hurt – herself possibly the more so. Rosemary had her father to run to. She had no-one!

Rosemary visited Rachel five times in as many days; in the evenings after she had left the factory, and always in the privacy of Rachel's home. It was the first time in years that she had finished work on time and she raised quite a few eyebrows when she left her desk along with the rest of the staff.

Each night they talked until the lateness of the hour prompted Rosemary's departure. They learned about each other and how each had felt a part of them missing: Rachel from the day she had left Rosemary at the hospital, while in Rosemary it had grown slowly, as she had grown.

Rachel never mentioned Rosemary's adoptive father. She tried not to think about him too much, or of all the hurt and anxiety she must be causing him. And, fortunately, Rosemary never brought the fictitious Michael Holden into conversation again. Rachel was grateful for that. The lies still weighed heavy and she had no wish to enlarge on them.

Rachel began to feel more content, and more a whole person again, than she had since David's death. She found herself looking forward to the evenings. She knew it could not last. When Christmas was over, Rosemary would return to university and there would be no chance of seeing each other until the Easter break.

She also began to get more worried about what Dr Ellicot, Rosemary's father, was thinking. She was somewhat surprised he had not already made his objections clear and, as the evenings wore on, began to have a vivid picture of him anxiously pacing the floor in Rosemary's absence.

He certainly could not feel happy about the situation, she realized, and found herself feeling pity for the man. She had known Rosemary for one week, yet she knew what it would mean to lose her again. He had known Rosemary all her life. He must be going through hell, she told herself, and unable to keep the subject silent any longer, asked. 'What does your father think of you spending all this time with me?'

Rosemary's face darkened. 'I think he's worried.'

Rachel thought that must be the understatement of the year.

'He tries not to show it.' Rosemary gave a thin little smile that conveyed all the fondness she felt for the man. 'He knows we have a lot to catch up on. He understands why I want to come here.'

Rachel stared pensively into the flickering flames of the large log fire. She wasn't sure she would be able to understand. He had done everything for Rosemary, given her everything. All she had done was abandon her. The man must hate her, she thought sadly.

'Perhaps it would be better if we gave it a rest for a few days.' She looked concerned and hoped Rosemary would see the reasonableness of the suggestion. 'Your father must miss you. He must have been looking forward to having you home for the holiday.'

'Yes.' Rosemary dropped her gaze and stared at her feet. 'I was thinking the same myself. It's just . . .' She looked up, a crooked smile on her lips. 'I want to see you both. It's very difficult,' she added, her voice sounding plaintive and child-like.

Rachel was once more reminded of Sarah. She smiled fondly. 'You'll have to work out a timetable,' she joked.

Rosemary laughed. 'And you could bet your bottom dollar Dad would be called out to an emergency when it was his turn.'

The following morning Rachel was in the general office, when the telephone rang.

'It's for you,' Keith announced, and handed her the receiver, at the same time taking the stock record card they had been looking at from out of her hands.

'Hello, Rachel Morrell speaking,' she said, her mind still lingering on the record card which Keith was now frowning at – it seemed to have a large discrepancy.

'This is Edward Ellicot, Mrs Morrell,' a daunting male voice announced. 'I would like to have a word with you.'

'Edward?' she began uncertainly. The next moment she was standing to attention. '*Doctor* Ellicot?' she questioned, just to make sure she had got her facts right, feeling her heart hit her throat.

'*Mr*! Mrs Morrell,' he pointed out, and she remembered that for some reason consultants never used the title.

For a moment she could not reply. A dozen reasons for his call flashed through her mind, none very pleasing. Gathering herself together, she responded with clear confidence. 'Would you hold on for a few moments. I am not in my own office.'

'Certainly,' came the reply.

She thrust the receiver back at Keith, whose frowning interest was now directed at her, and marched across the large general office to her own door. 'Transfer that call,' she instructed the telephonist as she passed by, then quickened her steps as she became aware that she was creating interest throughout the office staff.

With her office door closed securely behind her, she lifted the telephone receiver and listened for the click to indicate the switchboard had completed the connection and was no longer listening. Then she gathered her courage, and said, '*Mr*! Ellicot. How can I help you?' As if she didn't know!

'You have been seeing rather a lot of *my* daughter recently.' The deep voice laid particular emphasis on the ownership. Rachel felt angry colour creeping into her cheeks.

'Yes, Mr Ellicot,' she replied coolly, biting her tongue from pointing out that Rosemary also belonged to her, more so in fact, they were the same flesh and blood.

'I think it is time we had a talk about the situation and

found out exactly what it is we are both expecting to come from it.'

Both! Rachel almost laughed. He wanted to know what *she* was expecting to come of it. Be honest, she thought irritably. 'What *exactly* do you mean?' she questioned, her voice stiff, filled with the disapproval she was feeling for the man.

'I do not think the telephone is the correct place to do it,' he said, his voice attaining equal stiffness to hers. 'I think we should have a meeting to discuss things thoroughly.'

'Oh!' It was out before Rachel could stop herself. But meet him! The thought filled her with dread.

'Unfortunately, I am conducting a surgery this evening. It is impossible for me to leave the house. Which means I must ask you to come here, to me.'

Must ask! An order! A command! 'What about Rosemary?' she asked, trying to find any excuse she could think of to refuse. 'I don't think it would be advisable to meet with Rosemary present.' They were not going to get on, she told herself. She could feel it, every time he spoke needles of tension raced down her spine. 'We should wait until Christmas is over, when Rosemary is back at university.'

'Rosemary will be out this evening,' the faceless voice replied, its tone slightly mocking. As if he was laughing at her attempts to wriggle out; as if he knew he had all the answers up his sleeve.

He did have all the answers, Rachel realized bleakly, as he continued, 'I have given Rosemary two theatre tickets. She is going out with a friend.'

Perfect, she thought. He had it all sewn up, planned to the last degree. Or had he? She suddenly paused, wondering when he got the tickets. He hadn't known Rosemary was not visiting her that evening, not until late last night. She smiled grimly. He had got the tickets purposely to stop Rosemary's evening visit to her.

The thought angered her. If he wanted to play dirty . . . Well, fine by her, she told herself, wondering just why she had been frightened of meeting the redoubtable *Mr* Ellicot. He could not take Rosemary away from her, not unless

Rosemary herself decided to let him. And Rosemary, she was sure, was her own woman and would make her own decisions.

'What time do you want me there?' she enquired, putting on her best business voice, the one she reserved for awkward customers, polite but determined.

'I have a space between seven and eight,' he said. 'If I overrun, my receptionist will show you in.'

'Then I shall see you at seven, Mr Ellicot.' Rachel put the phone down; no goodbye, no false gratitude, nothing to give him any impression other than that she was ready and willing to do battle with him. With all claws bared, she thought.

It was only after she sank down into the chair, that she realized she was trembling.

Chapter Thirty

The large, dark-grey stone building was very imposing. It had a very grand black door with highly polished brass bell and pull and knocker, and an equally shiny name plate by the side. Two brass coach lamps emitted a warm glow on either side. Rachel smiled grimly. The only warm glow she was going to feel tonight, she thought, and gave the bell one long tug.

She glanced at her watch: ten past seven. She was purposely ten minutes late, assuming it would give him plenty of time to be rid of his last patient. She wanted to spare herself the anxiety of having to sit and wait for him.

She was wrong. The door was opened by a silver-haired lady wearing a dark suit that reminded her of herself in days gone by. She had a pair of gold-rimmed spectacles hanging from a chain around her neck and a fountain pen poised in her hand, as if she was about to stab whoever had dared to try and get through the door. She looked the epitome of efficiency and Rachel gave an inward grimace. The lady added up to everything she imagined Edward Ellicot to be.

'This is not a general practice,' she said haughtily. 'And if it is Mr Ellicot you are wanting to see, you will need to make an appointment.' she looked very disapproving.

Rachel smiled to herself. She could not imagine many malingerers getting past this one. 'Rachel Morrell,' she said, just as haughtily. 'I am expected,' she pointed out, when the name seemed to make no impression.

'Oh . . . Yes!' The receptionist stepped back and glanced pointedly at her watch. 'Mr Ellicot did say you might be coming.'

Might! Rachel thought. So the arrogant voice of the telephone had not been so sure of her compliance. The thought pleased her, as she stepped through the door into an oak-panelled waiting room with a large reception desk at the far end. 'Do I wait here?' She glanced round at the oak, high-backed benches that reminded her of the pews in chapel. They looked extremely uncomfortable. She wondered if he had them on purpose: to drum up custom for himself. She couldn't imagine anyone sitting on them for long without getting backache.

'This way,' the receptionist instructed, and led the way to one of three doors at the far end. 'Mr Ellicot won't be long. You can wait in here,' she said, holding the door open and eyeing Rachel interestedly as she passed by.

It was a small sitting room and, as Rachel entered, she decided the oak pews had not been put there to make more business, but to decrease it by giving his patients the fright of their lives and making them run away and forget their pains. She gave an inward grimace. The man was proving to be everything she had contemplated, and more.

She sat down on one of the three high-backed leather chairs and wished she had not come. She looked around the very masculine room and felt her doubts increase. Apart from the three chairs there was a low coffee table in the centre, with an empty fruit bowl in the middle. Two walls were covered with ceiling-high bookshelves, crammed full of books of assorted sizes and subjects. A brass carriage clock sat on the mantel above a roaring fire and, in the corner, a small Christmas tree was the only acceptance of the season.

'Would you like a cup of tea or coffee while you're waiting?' the receptionist offered, as she hovered in the doorway.

Rachel declined, she hoped she was not going to be waiting that long, and the receptionist closed the door and left her alone.

So this was Edward Ellicot! She smiled grimly. The deep austere voice of the telephone fitted perfectly the dark sobriety of the room. She could see she was going to need all her mental factors working to precision this evening, she realized.

The carriage clock softly ticked the minutes away. Rachel

looked at the time, at the books, at the time, at the Christmas tree, back to the time. Frustration turned to anger and she began to boil. He was doing it on purpose, she told herself. Keeping her waiting until her nerves were at snapping point.

Realizing Edward Ellicot was winning the battle before he even entered the room, she forced herself to calm down.

She heard a door open. 'Good night, Mrs Critchlow,' the receptionist's voice said. The unknown Mrs Critchlow responded and Rachel heard the black outside door open and close.

The last patient leaving, she thought, and felt her heart begin to hammer as the moment of encounter came closer.

Again the sound of a door opening. 'I won't be needing you again, Jessie.' It was a deep voice, the one of the telephone call. Rachel felt sure the hairs on the back of her neck stood up.

Jessie gave several verbal messages, then said good night, and Rachel heard the outside door open and close once more.

There was a long silence. She strained her ears, listening for the slightest sound to indicate he was on his way. There was nothing. She began to have the feeling that he must have gone out as well, that she was alone in the large stone house.

The next moment the door handle was grasped and her heart hit her throat. The door swung open and the tall dark form of Edward Ellicot stepped into the room.

'Mrs Morrell!' The deep voice rose slightly towards the end, as if in surprise. His back stiffened, lifting his head higher as he peered at her with intense eyes.

Uncertainty, disbelief, shock. Rachel was not sure which, or if all three had taken him by surprise. Her brain would not work. All she could do was stare into those dark eyes that seemed to be as confused as her own.

It lasted only a matter of seconds. Then Edward Ellicot regained his poise. For Rachel it was more difficult. She was still reeling with nervous anxiety as he crossed the room and took up position in the chair opposite to her.

'Now, Mrs Morrell.' He smiled, and Rachel found her gaze dropping to her feet.

Stop it! she ordered crossly, and forced her eyes back up, feeling an embarrassed warmth as they met once more the dark ones across the room.

'I asked you to come here so we could discuss Rosemary,' he continued, seemingly quite unperturbed now.

'Yes,' Rachel agreed, forcing her voice to a confidence she was far from feeling. 'I think it would be best if we both got our feelings into the open.' She paused, waiting for the argument to begin, wanting the argument to begin, so she could get rid of the feelings that had entered her body as Edward Ellicot had entered the room. She had never before met anyone who had affected her so badly. She could not understand it. It's just the situation, she told herself. It wasn't every day you came face to face with your daughter's father. The thought sounded ridiculous. But she knew what she meant.

'How do you feel about Rosemary seeing me?' she continued, when he remained silent. She succeeded in keeping her eyes fixed firmly on his face, knowing she had to see his reactions, as well as listen to his words, to know the truth; even though she would rather have looked anywhere but at him.

Edward Ellicot paused thoughtfully for a time. Rachel waited. He seemed to be assessing her and she felt her discomfort grow. 'I was not very happy with the decision,' he finally began. 'But Rosemary seemed to have the need to see you and find out what you were like. I respected that wish.' He smiled grimly, and gave Rachel a brief respite from his penetrating gaze by turning his attention to the far wall. It was not for long. His eyes soon pivoted back to her and she felt the same shock as before, and she thanked heavens for the roaring fire, hoping he would see that as the reason for her heightened colour.

'I can understand that,' she said, suddenly wanting him to know they were on the same side, that she was not a threat to him. They need not be enemies . . . if they were sensible, she found herself thinking.

'Can you?' Disbelief echoed through his voice. He gave a

self-mocking grimace. 'I thought it best to let Rosemary find you. Then, if it seemed a close relationship was developing . . .' He gave a resigned huff. 'I had intended to offer you money . . . To buy you off.' His smile was as bitter and self-mocking as the grimace had been.

Rachel's back and shoulders stiffened in offence. She sat very erect, glaring at him coolly, words failing her.

'I realize that is not a commodity you are in need of,' he finished dryly.

Rachel's eyes suddenly blazed. 'You think you have enough money to pay a mother for her daughter!' Her voice was icy with condemnation. She saw a flicker in the dark eyes and was pleased she had touched a nerve.

'I would not have thought it would have taken that much,' he responded, returning her condemnation in both his voice and in the gaze that hardened on her own. 'After all, the mother originally gave her daughter away for nothing!'

Rachel felt the colour drain from her face. 'You don't have any right to sit in judgement of me without knowing the facts, the reasons. There are reasons for everything, Mr Ellicot,' she bit out hatefully: one of Polly's sayings slipping from her tongue. She turned away, looked at the mocking merriment of the dancing flames. I wish you'd tell me the reason for this, she asked Polly.

Edward Ellicot gave Polly no time to reply. 'Reasons!' he barked. 'You mean some cock-and-bull story about her father dying!'

Rachel's eyes pivoted to his, wide, anxious and fearful. 'Didn't Rosemary believe me?' she asked, without thinking.

'Oh, Rosemary believes it,' he sneered. 'For now, at least. I can't comment on what she'll believe when she's older and can see what a neat little story it made. How nicely it fitted in with your plans.'

'What plans?' she demanded, jumping up from the chair and pacing to the fireplace, rage making it impossible to sit still a moment longer.

'Concocting a little story that conveniently disposes of her

383

real father, means you only have one more left to get rid of
– me!'

'Don't be stupid!' she retaliated, wondering at the man's
sanity.

'Then why did you lie?' Edward Ellicot stood up, rounding
on her.

As she looked up into the blazing eyes towering at least
twelve inches above her, she wished she had never left the
chair, never given him the chance to see how his extra height
could dominate her without the necessity to speak.

'I did not lie,' she insisted, and turned away, knowing she
did not sound sincere, knowing she had no ability to lie
convincingly. It was a throw back to her childhood. Lying
was a sin. She had always believed so. She had hated herself
for lying to Rosemary, but there had been a good reason for
that.

'You did lie!' His voice blazed close to her ear. She could
feel the hot angry gasps of his breath on her neck, and almost
flinched, as he continued, 'You've as good as admitted it
already.'

Rachel kicked herself for allowing her defences to slip.

'It didn't surprise me,' he grated. 'It was just the sort of
lovey-dovey story I imagined you would spin.'

Lovey-dovey! She was shocked and amazed. She might
have added a bit of reminiscent fondness, for Rosemary's
benefit, but there had been nothing lovey-dovey about it.

Edward Ellicot gave her no to time to disagree. 'You gave
her away because you didn't want her,' he said cruelly. 'It's
too late now to concoct some fantasy, some *reason*, as you
put it, for abandoning her. And if you won't face the facts
and tell her the truth, *then I will*!' The firelight glittered in his
eyes, like sparks of animosity that pierced her as she rounded
on him.

'Oh, you will, will you?' She stretched to her full five feet
three inches, her eyes flashing with a fierce gleam of purpose
that usually made people take a step backwards. Edward
Ellicot did not move. 'What will you tell her?' she hissed.
'That her mother was nothing but a little tart, a whore, a slut?'

All her father's names came flooding from her lips so easily. The names she had silently called herself after Micky's attack. Well they were not true, never had been. She knew that for a fact now. And no-one was ever going to use them again to her: not her long dead father, not herself, and certainly not Edward Ellicot!

'We're getting to the truth now, are we?' A vicious gleam of victory entered his eyes and she wanted to slap him, lift her hand and bring it across his pompous face. She never knew how she managed to stop herself.

Pushing past him she retrieved her handbag. Then she rounded on him once more, held her head high in the air, and said, 'All right, you want to tell Rosemary the truth. You tell her. Tell her she was conceived in the middle of a field in an act of violence so repulsive I still wake up at night wanting to be sick. Tell her she was made out of lust, hate, brutality, without any love whatsoever. Tell her that. See how that makes her feel!'

Before he could reply she was out of the room, past the reception desk and the austere benches, and out in the street, the large black door closing very noisily behind her.

Rachel arrived at work two hours early. She had not slept a wink and considered work the best place for her to be. It was, she had felt, the only place she could keep her mind occupied and away from the happenings of the previous evening.

She had blown it, she realized. Edward Ellicot would never allow Rosemary to see her again – not after what she had foolishly admitted. But he had made her so angry. She had lost all control. She felt ashamed of herself and humiliated that she had divulged the truth to him – a total stranger. It wasn't something you went round telling everybody!

She thumbed through the expenses sheets, initialling each one without really looking what she was doing. This had got to stop, she told herself firmly, and went back over the pages she had just supposedly done. Nothing came between her and her work, she reminded herself, and heard a little voice add, not usually.

She tossed the expenses sheets aside and dropped her head into her hands and gave a loud groan, just as Flo came through the door with the early morning mail.

'What's wrong with you?'

'Nothing, Flo.' She leaned back in the chair and tried to look relaxed as she took the pile of envelopes from her hand.

'You look as if Armageddon's just around the corner.'

Rachel gave a small laugh. Perhaps it is, Flo, she thought. Perhaps it is! Armageddon could not be worse than she was expecting.

'We haven't got problems, have we?' Flo looked concerned. 'Everything's running all right. Or so they tell me.'

'Everything is running fine,' she confirmed. Then, just to make sure no production-interfering scare began to take shape, added, 'It's personal. Nothing to do with the factory.'

'Oh!' Flo mouthed, slowly and thoughtfully. Then looked about to expand on her thoughts.

'Fetch me the lingerie production sheets from Ted,' Rachel put in first, having no wish to know what was in her mind.

Flo hesitated, still looked as if she had something to say.

'Now, Flo!' she insisted, returning her attention to the expenses sheets. 'I need them urgently!'

'All right! All right!' Flo bustled off indignantly.

Rachel smiled, knowing she had saved herself from one of her lectures.

Before Flo closed the door behind her, Rachel's mind had already leaped back to the previous evening: to Edward Ellicot; to the angry words she never should have spoken. She had given him the perfect tool to use against her, she realized worriedly.

She could not see him being stupid enough to tell Rosemary, she tried to tell herself. He loved his daughter and would not want to tell her something that would hurt her, possibly damage her. It seemed a reasonable assumption to believe the man was too intelligent to do something so damaging. Yet still she could not forget the look in his eyes, the anger possessing him, fuelled by the fear that she was taking something very precious away from him. It made her fear he would not act rationally. Neither of them had been rational last night. What the consequences could be increased her worry. If Rosemary had arrived home before he had calmed down, he might have spilled it all out, in the desperate hope of keeping his daughter to himself.

She stared at an expenses sheet; the figures blurred as Edward Ellicot's ominous features expanded in her mind. Suddenly she knew she had to phone him, make it clear she would have nothing more to do with Rosemary. It would tear her in two, but she had to do it; to stop Rosemary learning the awful truth. She picked up the phone. She put it down again.

What was the matter with her? she asked herself irritably. He would not tell Rosemary. Only an idiot would do such a dreadful thing. And Edward Ellicot was no idiot.

'Ted's up in arms,' Flo announced, bustling through the door and thumping the requested production sheets down on the desk in a manner which displayed her annoyance.

Rachel looked at her, grateful to have something to take her mind off her troubles. 'What's the matter with him?'

'Winterton's have sent their order back. They reckon as it's not the right material.'

'I'll sort it out.' Rachel was on the telephone to Ted before Flo had gone through the door. Her only thought was to take the problem out of his hands before he caused trouble. Geoff Mead, at Winterton's, had been very good to her and had put a lot of business her way when they had still been at the old chapel and her name wasn't so well known. The last thing she wanted was for Ted's irritability to cause friction.

After speaking to Ted, she phoned Geoff Mead to get his side of the story. Then she went to inspect the suspect garments for herself. Ted was at his most irascible and she had to be the height of solicitude to calm him down and get things straightened out.

It was not until she was crossing the yard to go back to the office, that she smiled, realizing she had not given Edward Ellicot one thought since Flo had come bursting into her office.

Determined to keep it that way, she hurried through reception to her office door.

'There's been a delivery for you,' Linda called from the switchboard.

Rachel was in too much of a rush to notice the speculative glances she was receiving. She hurried through her office door and came up short.

On the desk lay a huge bouquet of flowers. For a moment she could only stare at them. She had just reached them and picked them up when Flo came bustling through the door, supposedly to deliver a cup of tea.

Rachel glanced at her watch. 'It isn't tea time,' she pointed out, knowing exactly why Flo had appeared. She wanted to know who the flowers were from. So did Rachel. She pulled the small envelope from the cellophane wrap and lay the bouquet back on the desk.

'Aren't they beautiful. Have you got a secret admirer?' Flo poked noisily around the array of assorted blooms. 'What's that?'

Rachel paused with the envelope open and looked at the orange-and-black-spotted flower she was pointing to. 'Tiger Lily . . . I think,' she replied uncertainly, and pulled the greeting card from the envelope. Her gaze fell on the three words. Her heart stopped and a tiny sound of dismay came from her throat. 'Sorry! Edward Ellicot.'

'Well?' Flo looked on expectantly.

'Well what?' she replied irritably, and shoved the card quickly back in the envelope before Flo's eagle-eyes picked up the name.

'Who are they from?' she persisted, obviously feeling no shame in her prying.

'Just a friend,' Rachel said dismissively. She dropped the card in the drawer and closed it tightly. Then she shoved the flowers across the desk to Flo. 'Find something to put them in. They can go in reception.' She did not want them in her office, where she could see them all the time, where they would be a constant reminder of the sender. She sat down and returned once more to the expenses sheets. Just when she'd got him under control, she thought despairingly.

Flo made her surprise at the instruction clear. 'If I'd got a fella who'd send me flowers like this, I'd want them on my own desk.'

'I did not say they were from a man,' she pointed out stiffly.

Flo chuckled with amusement. 'I knew you'd got yourself somebody at last. Leaving work on time and personal phone calls.'

Rachel looked up in disbelief.

'Doctor is he?' Flo continued.

'How did . . . ?' Rachel began, then stopped herself very quickly, realizing what she had been about to say would have done more to confirm Flo's theory than disprove it. But . . . ? Oh no! She suddenly remembered the phone call, her own loud and clear repeating of the name *Doctor* Ellicot! In the general office, where they were all listening!

'I knew you'd had a spat with somebody as well. It was plain to see. I could tell.' Flo sounded exceedingly pleased with herself. She grinned knowingly as she added, 'A peace offering these are.' She picked the flowers up and waved them in the air. 'It's as plain as the nose on your face.'

'Haven't you got anything to do?' Rachel levelled her a dismissing glare.

'Yes.' Flo chuckled again, then added mischievously, 'I've got to put these in water.' Then she went out, the bouquet in her arms, still chuckling.

Rachel threw her pen across the desk. Sorry, she thought angrily. Was that all he had to say? All he could . . .

No! No! No! She grabbed the pen back. He was not going to interfere with her work, she told herself. Beginning with the expenses sheets she threw herself into the job with a fanaticism that made every pair of eyebrows in the general office lift in surprise.

Despite telling herself not to look, as she walked through reception at the end of the day her gaze was drawn to the large vase of flowers standing at the end of the long curved desk. She paused and let her gaze linger on the beautiful blooms. The sweet fragrance filled her nostrils and she lifted her hand and touched the softness of a petal. If only they had been from someone else, she thought.

'I knew you liked them, really!'

Rachel spun around to come face to face with Flo. She was all muffled up against the weather in an overlarge duffel coat and wearing a red woolly hat with a long tassel perched precariously on the top. As always, she was armed with the statutory shopping bag and brolly.

Rachel had to smile at her. 'I was just thinking how wonderful it would be if someone could produce a fabric as soft as that.' She turned back and ran her finger once more over the petal.

Flo did not look convinced. 'There's nothing wrong with having a fella,' she stated bluntly, and turned to go. 'I wish I'd got one to send me flowers like that,' she added with feeling as she walked out and left Rachel standing, shaking her head in despair.

Flo had completely got the wrong impression. Putting two and two together and making five. She gave a sigh. She imagined there was more than just Flo doing the same thing. Well they could think what they liked. Fella! she thought, and had to smile. Under no circumstances could she have labelled Edward Ellicot 'a fella'.

'Hi!' Keith came out of his office door and she turned to him with the smile still on her face. 'Have you got an admirer?' he asked, and looked very serious.

Rachel's smile vanished. 'Oh, don't you start!' She flashed him a weary scowl. 'I did a favour for a friend. They're just a gesture of appreciation.' She nearly choked on the word 'friend'. But she wasn't going to get into any involved explanations.

'Oh!' Keith's face suddenly brightened, as they walked out of the door together and passed the night watchman on his way in.

'Evening, Frank,' they both said together.

They were almost at their cars, before Keith said, 'I was going to try that new Chinese place. Fancy joining me for a chop suey?'

Rachel thought for a moment. It would have been nice not having to cook for herself. But, on the other hand, did she want food? She wasn't sure she would be able to force anything down her throat. The flowers and the brief note might have eased her anxiety that Edward Ellicot wouldn't be stupid enough to tell Rosemary what she had told him. But? Sorry! Edward Ellicot! Did he really expect her to accept that? The nerve of the man made her boil. She really wouldn't be able to eat, she realized.

'No thanks, Keith. I'm going to put my feet up and get an early night.' A peaceful evening alone, to catch up on the sleep she had missed the previous night, was all she craved. 'Perhaps another time,' she added. She didn't make a habit of socializing with her staff. But she felt Keith was the exception. He was almost her equal and they had often had lunch-time meetings at one or other of the many restaurants he frequented regularly. An evening meal would be no different and they always had plenty to talk about. But she wasn't in the mood. 'Sorry,' she said, as she watched him climb into his car and felt a stab of guilt. Like herself, he lived alone, and she had the feeling he had wanted a bit of company and she was depriving him of it. But she couldn't force herself to change her mind, and she got into the car and drove out of the car park before him.

Chapter Thirty-one

The best laid plans, Rachel thought. She tossed the pile of designs in her hand to the floor, where she had six already spread out. The evening was turning out to be anything but restful. With nothing but her own company she found her mind spiralling from Rosemary to Edward Ellicot. She sighed and looked at the jumbled designs. She had to make a choice for a new range of advertisements. But she could not concentrate. She was missing Rosemary. They hadn't been seeing each other for long but she had got so used to seeing her in the evenings that the house felt empty without her. She stared at the designs: dresses, suits, jackets and coats all lay mixed together; she hadn't even got them into separate piles. She sighed again. She had thought she was over the feeling of loneliness that had filled her for the months after David's death.

She shuffled the designs around like playing cards and tried to concentrate, and kicked herself for slowing Rosemary's visits down because of *him*! She thought of the bouquet she had received and of the brief note: Sorry! Edward Ellicot! What was she supposed to make of that? she wondered. Did he really expect her to forgive and forget after one little note and a heap of flowers she had found embarrassing?

'Oh!' she groaned loudly and swept her hands across her head in frustration. Several wisps of hair had escaped from her ponytail and she tugged the bobble free, scraped her hair back up and stuffed it into the bobble again. The peaceful evening she had longed for was not going to be hers, she told herself, and left the designs scattered on the floor and leapt up and grabbed her coat. Then she jumped into the car and drove down the hill to Sarah's.

'I didn't expect to see you!' Sarah's smile was infectious but there was a touch of rebuke in her voice.

'Sorry,' she apologized. She hadn't seen Sarah for over a week with her evenings being taken up by Rosemary. 'My own company was driving me mad.'

Sarah laughed. 'You'd better come in then,' she said, and stood back to let her through. 'But I can't promise much better here. My two men are driving me mad.'

Rachel walked into the front room and immediately saw the reason. Alan was perched on top of a step ladder, garlands in his hands and round his neck. Christopher was sitting on the floor with the contents of a large box of Christmas decorations being rapidly strewn around the room.

'Hi, Rachel.' Alan twisted around unsteadily and flashed a grin at her. 'I'm glad you've come. I could do with a hand up here.'

'You're doing a grand job, Alan. I wouldn't want to spoil your efforts,' she countered with dry humour.

'Auntie Rachel!' Christopher leapt up from the floor. 'Dad's nearly fallen off twice.' His childish excitement at the prospect made her laugh.

'Sit yourself down. If you can find a chair.' Sarah looked bleakly at the mess of her usually perfect room. 'Do you want a cuppa?'

'Yes please!' Alan was quick to reply.

'I wasn't asking you,' Sarah scolded affectionately.

A knowing smile passed between husband and wife and Rachel felt something tighten in her chest.

'Rachel wants one, as well.' Alan looked to her for support. 'You'd love a cuppa, wouldn't you?'

She laughed. 'I might be able to force one down,' she said, and Sarah went off to the kitchen mumbling about her impossible husband and how long it was going to take him to get the mess cleared up if he was going to keep stopping for refreshments.

Rachel removed a box of fairy lights from a chair and sat down. She looked around the little room that had once been her own home. It looked nothing like it now. The old sofa and chairs had been exchanged for a bright and cheerful flower-patterned cottage suite. A blue carpet had taken the place of the old worn out brown thing and the muddy coloured walls had been exchanged for the lightest grey that made the little room look twice its size. Her past had been spring-cleaned and wiped away. She gave a little smile and wished it was that easy. She looked down at the clutter of the happy family Christmas and thought of all the festive seasons she had spent alone. She came to Sarah and Alan for one day, Christmas Day or Boxing Day, depending on which day the Caradines were having their family party. Even if they had not had Alan's family to go to, she would not have forced herself on them. She always made a conscious effort not to lean too heavily on her sister and her husband. They had their own lives to lead, she told herself, and kept herself to herself many times when she would have preferred their company.

'I'm getting a Scalextric,' Christopher announced proudly.

'You don't know what you're getting,' Alan put in firmly.

Christopher grinned at Rachel, glanced furtively round to make sure his father's attention had returned to the garland he was pinning to the wall, then nodded mischievously. 'I am,' he whispered confidentially. 'It's in the back of the closet. I saw it.'

Rachel nodded in solemn acceptance of the secret shared; then had to force herself not to smile when, over the top of his son's head, Alan's eyes lifted in resigned despair.

Christopher returned to sorting through the shiny balls on the floor and Rachel watched him, feeling her love for him warm her inside. She loved her nephew as if he was her own son. A Caradine, she thought. She would never have thought it was possible.

She was still pondering over the complexities of life when Sarah returned. 'What's wrong with you then?' she asked, as she stuck a mug of coffee in her hand and plonked Alan's on the table for him. She cleared the tinsel and crepe paper from the chair next to Rachel and sat down. 'What is it?' She looked concerned.

'Nothing really,' she replied. She took a sip of coffee and

studied the garland Alan was in the process of fixing to the ceiling. She could feel Sarah's eyes watching her and she knew she was not fooled. Just as she would not be fooled if the boot was on the other foot. They knew each other too well. 'It's Christmas,' she said, knowing she had to come up with some excuse. 'It makes me remember.'

'What?' Sarah's concern increased. 'David?'

'David, Polly, Judith, Mum,' she said. Rosemary, she thought, and stared pensively into her cup.

'Who's Polly?' Christopher enquired.

Rachel smiled fondly. 'A very nice lady who was a very good friend to me.'

'Is she dead?' he asked with childish bluntness.

'Yes,' Sarah replied quickly, and cast a glance of rebuke at her son to tell him to be quiet.

'Pass me those balloons,' Alan instructed Christopher, turning the boy's attention from the conversation.

Sarah gave her husband a fond appreciative smile and Alan responded with the same warmth.

A silent message immediately understood, Rachel thought, and felt the all too familiar tightening in her chest for something she had missed. Her mind span back over the years and she recalled the first couple she had seen use that silent language of love: David and Judith. She tried to remember David looking at her with the same intensity. His smile had always been fond and caring. But, try as she might, she could not recall him ever giving her that *special* look. She did not doubt he had loved her, in a way. But she had never been foolish enough to believe he had not loved Judith more.

'What time do you want me here on Christmas Day?' she asked, forcing her mind to other things.

'I imagine we'll be woken up around five.' Sarah's eyes pivoted pointedly to Christopher, now lurking around the bottom of the ladder with a look of intent in his eyes. 'So any time after that.'

'I think we'll make it closer to eleven.' Sshe forced a smile to her face, though in her heart she felt a pain for all the things she had missed. She had no memories of being woken in the early hours of Christmas morning to be shown a new teddy, a new doll, a new anything. And now she never would. Her thoughts turned to Rosemary and all she had given away.

You're getting maudlin, she told herself. The company of her sister's happy family was only increasing her gloom. She quickly finished her coffee and stood up.

'I'll get out of your way and let you get the decorations finished,' she said, buttoning up her coat.

'You're not in the way,' Sarah protested. 'And you're not stopping them.' She jerked her head towards the step ladder, now with Alan still perched on the top and Christopher close on his heels. Then she collected the empty cups and swept into the kitchen.

Rachel gave an inward grimace. She could read her sister's actions and was well aware she was supposed to follow, so they could be alone. After a quick goodbye to Alan and Christopher, she dutifully obliged.

'What's the matter with you?' Sarah immediately asked, pulling no punches, as she went on, 'You look terrible. I haven't seen you for days. What have you been doing?'

'The factory is busy.' She knew it was a lame excuse. Part of her wanted to tell Sarah the whole story. But, she thought. A very big but!

'Why don't you have a holiday?' Sarah's voice snapped with the irritation she was feeling for her. She would work herself into the grave one day. 'The blessed factory won't close down just because you have a few days off!'

Rachel smiled thinly. 'I know,' she replied simply, and lodged her bottom on the table and folded her arms. It was not the first time they had pursued this argument. Sarah had taken over from Polly and David, and was now the one who continually told her she was working too hard. But Polly and David had known the truth. Sarah didn't understand. Sarah had Alan and Christopher. She had nothing – except the factory. It was her reason to be alive; her way of forgetting what had been taken from her and what she had given away. She thought of Rosemary. Then she found her mind turning to the bouquet of flowers and recalled how she had wished they had been from someone else, someone she cared for. It seemed an odd thought to have had. She had never considered any other man since David died. He had been too special to her. He was irreplaceable she told herself. No-one could ever be as patient and understanding with her.

Sarah filled the washing-up bowl and began to wash the mugs, and continued to remonstrate with her. 'I thought once you got the new place going you would have more time to yourself.'

Time to do what? she wondered bleakly, as she remained silently watching her sister.

'You've got an army of managers now. They should . . .' Sarah fell silent. She dropped the last mug back into the water and stared out of the window. 'You've got a visitor,' she finally said.

'Where?' Rachel went to peer over Sarah's shoulder. Beneath the street light at the top of the hill was a long dark car. 'I can't see anyone.' She peered into the darkness surrounding her garden wall.

'Wait a minute,' Sarah said. 'They haven't got out yet.' As she spoke, the driver's door swung open and a tall dark form emerged. 'It's a man,' she stated unnecessarily.

'I thought it was a lady wrestler,' Rachel put in dryly, feeling she had to say something as she felt her throat go dry with apprehension. She watched carefully as the tall form walked along the front of the house. She was not sure, but perhaps she did not want to believe. Her heart seemed to have stopped beating and she knew her breath had stopped. He reached the garden gate, paused, then entered. She was still not sure. When he reached the front door and lifted his arm to the bell, the single light above the door silhouetted his large frame to perfection. As he waited he turned first one way and looked around, then the other. Then she was sure.

'I'd better go and see who it is.' Her voice was hasty, as she rushed to the door, wanting to leave before Sarah started asking questions. Why the devil was he here? she wondered anxiously. Sending flowers to work. 'I'll see you,' she tossed at her open-mouthed sister, with the door already in her hand.

Then she closed it quickly behind her before Sarah could get the words out. Now turning up on her doorstep, she thought angrily, where anyone could see him. And had, she reminded herself, knowing full well Sarah would be glued to the window until she had got home and got him inside. And long after that, she thought. Sarah wouldn't give up looking until she had watched his car leave.

She flopped into her car and slammed the door in frustration. Edward Ellicot was the last person she needed to see. She thrust the key fiercely into the ignition and wished she could turn the car and drive off down the hill and away from him. But she knew if she vanished it would mean more questions from Sarah. She had no idea how she was going to explain him away now, adding to her complications would only make the explanations more difficult.

When she pulled her car up in front of his, he was at the gate, had given up, was leaving. If she had stayed at Sarah's another two minutes she would have missed him, she thought, and climbed out of the car, aware she had to accept the inevitable.

'Hello,' he said simply.

'Mr Ellicot!' She sounded surprised. 'I did not expect to see you again so soon!' She swept past him, having no intention of making their argument public.

He followed her back to the house and stood silently while she unlocked the door. Then, with the same silence, accepted her stiff instruction to enter and sit down.

Rachel took off her coat and hung it in the closet beneath the stairs. For a moment she stared at herself in the large wooden-framed hall mirror, psyching herself up for what was to come. Then she took a deep breath and went through to him in the sitting room.

'Is Rosemary out again tonight?' she enquired pointedly. Had he provided more theatre tickets to keep her occupied?

'No,' he replied quietly, taking the wind from her sails.

She stared at him blankly. Why was he here? she wanted to ask, yet she remained silent, trying to find some clue in the dark eyes.

'Rosemary knows where I am.'

She felt the blood drain from her face. 'You haven't told her?' she gasped, suddenly seeing him as the messenger of doom, sent by Rosemary to tell her she never wanted to see her again.

'Of course I have not told her!' He looked angry at the suggestion. 'Rosemary is not aware we met last night.'

She reached for a chair and sat down, the support of the chair diminishing the trembling she only now realized had been in her legs. 'Then why . . . ?'

'To begin all over again,' he said. His voice had returned to normal. At least, she assumed it was normal. She could imagine it was the quietly confident tone he would use with his patients. She certainly hoped he didn't rant and rave at them, the way he had done last night. 'I think it would be best if we both forgot last night ever happened,' he suggested.

Forget! Did he think it was so easy for her to forget? He would be asking her next to forget she had ever had a baby, ever been raped!

'I think you can safely say last night has been pushed to the back of my mind.' As she spoke a small voice called her a liar. It didn't matter, she told herself. What she felt inside was of no concern to Edward Ellicot. She just wanted to make a sufficient peace with him so he would leave. She felt uneasy with him in the house and she didn't like to see him sitting in that chair, which had been David's. 'I'm glad you understand the need to keep what I told you to yourself – for Rosemary's sake,' she added. She was sure he would do anything for his daughter. She was not so convinced she would be granted a quarter of the same concern.

'Do you really want to go on seeing Rosemary?' He leaned forward in the chair and clasped his hands and frowned.

The question surprised Rachel. 'Yes,' she replied confidently, looking him straight in the eyes and finding his sudden concern difficult to explain.

'After what you told me I would understand if you did not,' he continued. She shuffled nervously in the chair. He was definitely using his patients' voice on her now, and he was also looking at her as if she was one. She felt those dark eyes were seeing right inside her, to all the bits and pieces that were throbbing erratically in his presence. 'I thought, maybe, you were bending to Rosemary's pressure.' He made a sweeping gesture with his hands, then returned to clasping them. Rachel found her eyes following the movement. He had beautiful hands. Surgeon's hands, she thought. Delicate without losing any of their masculinity.

'No,' she suddenly replied, wondering at the way her mind was working. He might have nice hands but that was the only part of him that was beautiful. To confirm her theory, she looked into the dark assessing eyes and felt a shiver trickle down her spine. 'I did not choose to have a baby,' she quickly continued. 'But, no matter how she was conceived, she was still mine. I have always regretted giving her away.'

She watched the muscles at his jaw clench and realized she had been clutching at straws, hoping that he was about to see reason. He had been hoping she would not want to continue seeing the child thrust on her by violence. She felt her backbone stiffen in preparation for the coming onslaught and sat more erect in the chair.

She wasn't disappointed. 'You have no rights to her!' he pointed out coolly.

'I realize that,' she replied quickly and forcefully, realizing if she showed any hesitation she would be lost. 'But it was Rosemary's choice. *She* wanted to find me. Not the other way round!'

His gaze hardened, swept across the room, then pivoted icily to her own. '*You* have done nothing for her!' His voice was filled with a hate that almost made her flinch and she grasped tightly to the arms of the chair, fearing if she did not he would see the tremor of anger in her arms. 'Where were you when she was crying in the night? When she was ill and needed nursing? When she needed a hand to hold to give her the confidence for the first day at school? Were you there?'

Rachel's head dropped forward. She knew how much she had missed without him thrusting it in her face.

'No!' he continued, his voice blasting round the room like

400

a gale. 'You were never there. But *I* was! I did everything for her – *everything*! After my wife died.'

The pain around her heart was too severe and it was a moment before she could speak. She finally looked up to meet the rage bubbling violently in the dark eyes.

'I don't want to take her from you,' she said with simple honesty. 'I know you are her father and I'll always accept that you come first. But if Rosemary wishes to see me – occasionally,' she quickly added, seeing the dark eyes narrow purposefully. She sighed. 'I really don't see what all the fuss is about.' Impatience put an edge to her voice and she shook her head in despair. 'I don't see why we can't come to some amicable arrangement.'

'You don't!' He gave a bark of dry laughter. 'She is *my* daughter. Eighteen years of love and care stand for far more than a few regrets.'

Rachel heaved a sigh and gritted her teeth. She really couldn't see why he had bothered to turn up this way, if they were only going to continue where they had left off the night before. 'I know she is your daughter. I'm not trying to change that,' she countered acidly. 'But surely we are both intelligent enough to handle this in a more reasonable manner – for Rosemary's sake. Do you think putting up a barbed-wire fence between us is going to help her? She searched me out because she felt a need to find me. I don't know why . . . I can't explain the reasons she should want anything to do with me – after what I did to her.' Her voice trailed away in sadness and she fell silent, the old guilt, recriminations and regret overwhelming her.

He watched her steadily and she forced herself to return the unblinking gaze. The anger seemed to leave his eyes to be replaced by something she could not name. It wasn't exactly sadness that matched her own, and she couldn't believe it was pity. Unless it was for himself.

She sighed once more, in despair and frustration. 'Don't you think we should both respect the need in Rosemary? And at least try to understand a little. We don't have to accept each other into our hearts. But to act like two warring factions will only cause her grief.' And herself, she thought. She was only too ready to agree to a truce and accept a limited access to Rosemary. So long as she never had to see him again!

He looked very serious and totally immovable. For a long moment they continued to stare at each other in a silence that began to tug at Rachel's nerves. She had the feeling she was banging her head against a brick wall. Nothing was going to make him see reason, she realized, and, unable to stand the close scrutiny any longer, turned her attention to looking round the room. She was seeking comfort in all the familiar objects. But she didn't find any. It suddenly occurred to her that all the so-called familiar objects had really belonged to David – and Judith. She hadn't done anything to turn the house into her own. Everything had been theirs. Only the bedroom had really belonged to herself and David. It didn't seem much. But then she had never really had much of David. Eighteen months was only a speck in a lifetime.

She leaned her elbow on the chair arm and dropped her chin into her hand. What was wrong with her? she asked, wondering at the way she had allowed her mind to go, when there was a much more pressing problem at hand. She stared bleakly at the pressing problem.

'I thought you said you had come to make a fresh start?' she said. 'That we should forget last night ever happened,' she added, realizing they had, in truth, started all over again, exactly where they had left off. But not in the way he had been meaning.

For several more moments they only stared at each other. She began to think he had lost his voice.

'I won't lose Rosemary,' he finally said, firmly, but with none of the previous rage. 'But I suppose you are right,' he grudgingly allowed, and Rachel couldn't help the thin smile that came to her lips. 'We should make the effort – for Rosemary's sake!'

He made it sound as if she was asking him to sleep on a bed of nails, she thought dryly. But the meagre truce was enough for her and she remained silent. And he said no more. He dropped his gaze to stare pensively at the carpet. She wondered what he meant by 'make the effort'. She hoped he didn't expect them all to have cosy chats and tea every Sunday. She looked at his bent head, his serious expression, and felt it best not to pursue the matter just then. She stared at the black hair slanting over his forehead and at the intense eyes, which she felt could have the power to stop a tank in its tracks. His long straight nose was arrogant and perfect for him, she thought. Then she had a second thought. She tried to tell herself it was silly, but the more she looked at him the clearer the image became: give him a beard and a pair of horns and he would have looked like the devil.

Which also fitted him perfectly, she thought. But nevertheless she found the idea disturbing. 'Well,' she said, suddenly jumping from the chair. 'If you've said all you came to say, I really am rather busy.'

She looked pointedly at the designs strewn across the floor by the window and was grateful she had left them there before going to Sarah's. 'I have to make a choice for some new advertisements,' she said, looking half-apologetic, but feeling none of it.

He stood up without any objection and she felt a rush of relief and hoped it didn't show too clearly on her face.

'What will you tell Rosemary about this evening?' she asked, suddenly anxious that he might try to turn the tables in his favour.

He gave a shrug. 'I suppose I'll have to tell her we are bosom pals.'

Rachel grimaced. 'I don't think there is any need to go that far!' Doctor he might be, she thought, but a psychologist he was not.

He suddenly smiled and, for a moment, she had the feeling another person had stepped into the room. The angry eyes glittered with an amusement she would not have thought possible and the previously tight lips made a warm curve that quite took her aback. 'Perhaps not,' he agreed. 'But you can be assured of one thing. No matter how much we fight, I would never tell Rosemary she was the product of rape.' He fell serious again and Rachel was doubly relieved: she felt

403

her secret was safe with him, for Rosemary's sake, not her own; and she felt she could handle the dour man far better than the stranger who had made a brief appearance.

He was at the door, before he said, 'Did you get the flowers?'

'Yes. Thank you,' she replied stiffly. If he was expecting overwhelming gratitude, he was in for a disappointment.

'I meant what I said. I am sorry. I never thought . . .'

'Yes, well, it doesn't matter. Good night, Mr Ellieot.' She had closed the door and was leaning back on it heaving a great sigh of relief, before he had got off the step.

Chapter Thirty-two

Rachel stood by the makeshift bar in the factory canteen and smiled to herself. The Christmas party was in full swing and the entire work force had turned out for this first event at the new factory. They had always had a drink and a mince pie at the old chapel, but there hadn't been the room to have a full knees-up, which this evening was fast turning into.

'Can I tempt you on to the floor?' Keith asked, coming up by her side and looking her over with appreciation.

She had never seen him look at her in that way before and she felt a faint blush come to her cheeks. 'Only if you promise to keep it sedate,' she said, and nodded pointedly to the dance floor where Ted and Flo were giving an outrageous display of the jitterbug.

Keith laughed. 'I didn't know Ted had it in him.'

'I didn't know Flo did, either,' she replied. Then gave a groan and hid her face in Keith's shoulder. Flo, at the age of fifty-eight, had gone sliding through Ted's legs and ended up sitting on the floor in tears of laughter with a great amount of pink satin, long-legged bloomers on show. 'I think I'd better go and tell the DJ to play something slow.'

'No!' Keith was quick to disagree. 'They're enjoying themselves. Come and do the same.' Before she could object, he had taken her hand and was dragging her to the dance floor.

'Sedate!' she warned seriously, as she turned to him and began to bob around to the music.

He grinned at her. 'How could I be anything else, with a lady like you?'

'Stop flattering! You're not getting a rise,' she joked, to cover the warmth she felt coming once more to her cheeks. She was not used to male compliments but she didn't find anything offensive in Keith's manner. In fact, she rather liked it. It wasn't until the record changed and Keith wrapped his arms right around her for a slow ballad that she realized he was only the second man she had ever danced with. David had been the only one – until then. It was strange. She had never thought she would be able to get close to another man. Yet she found she was liking dancing with Keith as much as she had liked his earlier compliment.

The realization put a smile on her face and Keith responded. His brown eyes crinkled up, and with his brown curls he looked suddenly very boyish, and her smile broadened.

'You're looking very beautiful tonight,' he said, and made her blush again by holding her away and looking her up and down with the same appreciation he had used earlier. 'That dress could have been made for you,' he said, as he pulled her close again and rested his mouth close to her ear.

'Idiot!' she said, and laughed. 'You know it was.' The sapphire blue crêpe, shot through with silver, had been made up for the occasion in Morrell's workshop. She didn't usually have things specially made for herself. If she needed anything she would go and choose something out of the stockroom. But as soon as she had seen the material, she had fallen in love with it. And she had known immediately how she wanted it making up: in a classical Grecian style with a draped top over one shoulder and a full, flowing skirt. It was a very daring design for her. She had cast off the dull sexless ensembles a long time ago, since the evening she had worn the red suit for David. Apart from the few months following his death, when she had felt it only right to show her respect for him by wearing black, she had never gone back to dowdy colours and shapeless garments. But, although her clothes always looked elegant and smart, she had never had anything that was so obviously feminine. And she felt good in it. It was a revelation, she thought. She looked like a woman and she was dancing with a man who was not David. And she liked it. Forcing herself to come face to face with her past had done more than return her daughter to her, she realized happily.

She had finally shaken off the last remnants of Micky's black legacy, and that felt good, too.

Happiness shone from her eyes as the music stopped and Keith pulled away from her. For a moment he seemed to have lost his voice and could only look back at her with what, she imagined, was a kind of wonder. Finally he said, 'Can you stand any more, or are you ready for a drink?'

She never got time to reply. Ted was suddenly elbowing Keith away. He grabbed her by the arms and dragged her further on to the crowded dance floor. She had time for only a beseeching glance at Keith, then Ted's arms were round her and the music had started up again, thankfully keeping up the slow tempo.

'I'm not in Flo's class,' she said, a warning in her voice. But she was smiling as she spoke. Ted was a revelation tonight. She could never have imagined that Morrell's irritable manager would be capable of letting his hair down and looking so happy. His appearance was also stunning. His silver hair, which usually stood up like a gorse bush around his head and gave you the impression he had just had an electric shock, was neatly slicked back. And he was wearing a light grey suit that went perfectly with the shade of his hair and made him look very executive.

He grinned at her. 'Not many people are in Flo's class,' he said. 'She's got a shelf full of cups and medals at home. From her younger days, of course.'

'Flo!' She couldn't imagine the bustling Flo being the belle of the ballroom. She laughed, thinking how strange, she had thought she knew Flo so well, and she hadn't known the half of it.

After dancing with Ted, Colin came and claimed her for the next two. Then Keith took over again and after one more dance, they retreated to the bar.

Kate was there, peering suspiciously at everyone because she refused to wear the thick-lensed glasses that were necessary for work.

'Rachel?' she asked, and frowned. 'I'm not used to seeing everybody dressed up. I can't recognize anyone. I was talking to Ted for five minutes before I realized it was him. I thought he was someone's husband.'

Rachel laughed. She could fully understand Kate being confused by Ted. 'Why on earth don't you get some contact lenses?'

'Can't wear them,' she said dismissively, and turned to Keith. 'And Keith?' she questioned, to make sure she had got him right.

'No. Attila the Hun,' he replied teasingly. 'I hope you're not driving!'

'No, I'm looking for someone to take me home. How you fixed?'

'Uh, uh.' He shook his head and lifted his pint of lager from the bar where he had left it. 'I came to enjoy myself. If I can't find a taxi I'm on shanks's pony.'

Kate gave a huff. 'You're no good,' she grumbled good naturedly, and went off into the crowd in search of a better offer.

Rachel shook her head and smiled at her retreating back. 'I thought she was sensible. Or I wouldn't have taken her on.' She looked around the noisy canteen with music blaring out and balloons and streamers everywhere. 'Then I thought most of them were sensible – before tonight!'

'They are sensible,' Keith assured her, and handed her glass of bitter lemon to her. 'But tonight is different. It's a once a year occasion to let your hair down and not be sensible.'

She nodded and took a drink. It was Christmas. Everybody enjoyed Christmas. She lowered her glass and stared thoughtfully at the packed dance floor, recalling another Christmas she had told herself the same thing. When she had gone to the Beehive to get crisps and bitter lemons for Polly. So long ago. So much happened. So much achieved. She lifted her glass again. Here's to you, Polly, she said silently and took a sip. It never occurred to her that it had also been the night she had come into contact with Micky again, for the first time after his attack.

'Something wrong?' Keith asked, looking suspiciously at her suddenly serious face.

She immediately smiled. 'No. I was just remembering Christmases past.'

He smiled tightly. 'How long were you married?'

She was taken by surprise and it was a moment before she could reply. 'Eighteen months,' she said, the smile slipping from her face.

He shook his head. 'Not long.'

'No, not long,' she replied. Then, before he could pursue the subject, she took his pint from out of his hand, placed it on the bar alongside her bitter lemon, and dragged him back on to the dance floor. It was not a night for moroseness, she told herself, suddenly seeing no reason why she shouldn't enjoy herself, if everybody else was.

It was two o'clock before the party finally came to an end. Rachel looked around the debris cluttering the canteen. Burst balloons, ripped streamers, empty glasses and beer mats everywhere. She was glad she hadn't got to clear it up, and heaved a grateful sigh as Keith held her coat up for her to slip into.

'I'm glad it only happens once a year,' she said with feeling. But as they walked to the door, switched off the lights and locked up, she realized she couldn't remember feeling this happy for a long time. Nine years, she thought. Well almost. Come February it would be the ninth anniversary of David's death. Surely that was long enough to be a dutiful widow? She checked herself, as she stepped out into the frosty night air, wondering where the last thought had come from. Is it you, Polly? she asked. Putting ideas in my head? She looked up at the clear star-filled sky. It seemed strange the way her mind had suddenly begun working. Since Edward Ellicot's blessed flowers, she thought, recalling once again how she had wished they were from someone else – someone who had meant something to her.

She gave a sigh and looked at Keith, buttoning his black leather overcoat and turning the collar up in preparation for his walk. 'Come on. I'll give you a lift,' she said. It would only take him a few minutes to walk, as he didn't live far away. But it would take even less time in the car, she reasoned.

And she didn't like the idea of him walking the streets at this time of night – morning, she corrected, as she set off walking across the car park and refused all his objections that it would take her out of her way. Besides, she had the feeling she might be better off with his company for a few more minutes. She had allowed her thoughts to turn to the depressive and she wanted to get out of it. If Keith's lively chatter couldn't do it, then nothing could, she thought.

But as she reached the car, she turned back and for several moments gazed on the factory's twin buildings, illuminated in the bright floodlights that were left on all night for security. And she found herself thinking her dream was complete. She had repaid David for all he had done for her. So what would she do now?

You'll keep it going, she told herself sternly. Then she got into the car, and thought, if this was what enjoying herself did for her, she had better return to being her usual work-obsessed self.

'This should be the other way round,' Keith said apologetically, as she drove out of the car park. 'I should be taking you home.'

Rachel glanced a teasing smile at him. 'I had one glass of wine with the meal. How much have you had?'

'I lost count,' he admitted. 'But I'll most probably have a head like a bucket to remind me in the morning.'

Rachel laughed as he mimicked pained regret. 'Well, you'll know you enjoyed getting it.' She fell silent, contemplating the new Keith she had seen tonight. She had always liked him. She admired his ability to get the work done and his never diminishing energy. It was because he was like herself, she had always thought. He had no family, no home ties. Work was his life and he put everything into it. But tonight she had seen another side of him: the man, not the machine. He pulled a packet of cigarettes from his pocket and lit up. She smiled. It was only one small action. But it was so like David: the way he held the cigarette, the way he positioned the lighter and brought his head down towards it, rather than lift the lighter to the cigarette. She found herself wondering if Keith was the reason for her strange thoughts. Had she grown closer to him then she realized? They worked so closely together that a kind of kinship had naturally evolved. If it hadn't they wouldn't have got on so well and been such a good team. But was there more?

She never reached an answer. They arrived at his gate and she stopped the car and turned to him. 'That'll be thirty bob, squire!'

'Thirty bob!' He wound the window down and disposed of his cigarette. Then he turned to her and leaned across the seat. 'Sorry, I went decimal with the rest of the country. You'll have to take it in kind.' Before she could reply, he had closed the gap between them and was kissing her.

She was surprised by the suddenness. But there was no shock and she accepted his lips without any objections. It was only when his hand began to run up and down her side and got dangerously close to her breast, that she pushed him gently away. She wasn't sure if he was acting with thought or if the amount of alcohol he had indulged in was speaking for him and he was doing something he would wake up to regret in the morning. And she wasn't totally sure it was what she wanted.

She smiled at him crookedly. 'You'd better be getting yourself off,' she said, nodding towards his front door.

'Should I be apologizing?' he asked uncertainly.

She laughed. 'Go on,' she urged. Whether he apologized or not had to be his own decision. When he was stone cold sober. 'I want to get some sleep tonight, even if you don't!' she added pointedly.

He looked sheepish. 'I'll see you tomorrow,' he said, and opened the door and climbed out.

'No you won't,' she called laughingly. 'It is Sunday,' she pointed out, as he bent down to look back into the car. 'And it's a good job, too!'

'So it is.' He grimaced and closed the door.

She watched him walk up the path and let himself in. He walked straight, she thought. And he hadn't looked or sounded drunk.

411

Before closing the door, he raised his hand and she returned the wave. Then she started the car and drove away, one half of her wishing she could have been sure he had known what he was doing, the other half telling her it was best to go steady.

It was Monday morning before she learned the truth. Keith's car was already in the car park when she arrived at work and she had only just reached her desk, when he followed her into the office.

'Morning,' she said quite normally. She had decided if he didn't bring the matter up, she wouldn't. It was best forgotten, she reasoned.

He didn't respond. He looked as sheepish as he had done the other night. 'Should I be apologizing?' he asked once more.

She dropped her briefcase by the side of the desk and looked at him with a smile. If he had to ask that then he had not been so drunk he couldn't remember. Which, she assumed, also meant he had known what he was doing. 'For what?' she asked, wanting to hear it from his own lips, so she knew for certain they were both talking about the same thing.

'It wasn't very gentlemanly of me.'

She frowned at him. 'Having to take you home?' She shrugged her shoulders. 'It was no trouble.' She picked up the pile of mail lying on her desk and began sorting through it.

'Damn it, Rachel!' he suddenly gasped in frustration. 'You know what I'm talking about. I jumped on you. Or did it leave so little an impression?' His face fell and she had to smile.

'I wasn't sure you'd remember,' she said. 'And if you did, whether you'd prefer to forget it.'

'Of course I remember. I wasn't plastered.' He looked affronted and her smile broadened.

'Well, it doesn't matter,' she assured. 'It's gone and forgotten.' As he had said himself, that night was a time for not being sensible. Everyone had been a little mad, and some of it had rubbed off on her. She had had all day yesterday to think about the strange effects of the party. She hadn't drunk much alcohol, but she had come to the conclusion she had been intoxicated by the success of the evening. Everyone had enjoyed themselves and she felt it had been a fitting tribute to all the hard work they had put in for her during the first year of the factory's production. But it had made her have strange thoughts and do strange things. She knew she liked Keith, and liking was enough for a business relationship. But, when she had sat back and thought things through properly, she became worried that if anything happened between them that didn't work out, it could make their working life intolerable. And she wasn't going to do anything to risk losing him, he was too valuable to the company.

'Forgotten?' He looked put out. 'I wasn't acting in a drunken stupor.' He scraped his fingers through his brown curls and sighed. 'I only did what I've been wanting to do for ages.'

Rachel dropped the mail back on to the desk and bit her lip. 'I didn't know that,' she said.

'Well you do now,' he replied frustratedly, and there was something in his eyes that reminded her how useless she was at being a woman. She should have realized, she thought, and kicked herself for being so dense when it came to anything other than work.

'I'm sorry,' she said. 'I didn't realize . . .' She shrugged her shoulders nervously, not knowing what to say. 'It's too risky. We can't do anything that might upset our business relationship.' She knew she was speaking her true feelings, but her voice sounded lame.

'Christ, Rachel!' His taut hands swept wide through the air and displayed his anger as clearly as his voice. 'Doesn't anything mean anything to you except the factory and work?'

She smiled grimly. He sounded like Sarah, she thought. No, she amended, he sounded more like David. Her mind was suddenly filled with the image of David and how he had been forced to turn to anger to force her to accept a proper relationship with him. But David had been different. She didn't know why, but he had. 'Perhaps we should leave it, Keith,' she insisted.

'No.' He shook his head and refused to bow down. 'What's wrong with trying it out to see how things work out?'

She stared at the pile of letters on her desk. David had been so gentle with her . . . Because he understood everything about her. She gave a little sigh. She had thought she had come to terms with Micky's memory. But she had to admit she was scared: frightened that, with someone who didn't have the same understanding as David, she might regain all her old fears and return to the feelings of disgust and repulsion that had haunted her for so long. She didn't want that, for herself, or for Keith. But she wasn't willing to tell him the truth. Too many people already knew. She trusted Pauline Chapman and Edward Ellicot not to let Rosemary ever know how she had been conceived. They were both involved in a way that gave them the understanding of what that knowledge would do to her. But she couldn't risk it ever becoming general knowledge and Rosemary hearing of it from some unthinking gossip.

'Have dinner with me?' Keith persisted. 'No strings. Let time work it out. There's no harm in that.'

'But . . .' she began, then fell silent. To say she didn't want to lose him, sounded rather silly under the circumstances.

'But nothing. We're both adult enough to be able to continue working together.'

She glanced at him uncertainly. Then turned her gaze back to the pile of unopened letters. She was being silly and insecure again, she told herself. She was still letting Micky spoil her life. 'All right,' she suddenly agreed, and turned to face him squarely. 'I'll have dinner with you.' She spoke with a confidence that belied the butterflies performing a fandango inside her stomach.

'Tonight?'

She nodded her head. 'Yes, tonight.' It all seemed to be happening faster than she would have liked. But Rosemary was not visiting that evening and she couldn't think of any real reason to say no.

The smile he gave her crinkled his eyes and gave him the little boy look she had first seen at the party. As he went out of the office, obviously satisfied with the result, she found herself smiling, although it was somewhat reserved and uncertain.

Rachel arrived home that evening still in a state of uncertainty. For the entire day she had blown hot and cold about the idea of going out with Keith. She had almost cancelled on several occasions and felt sure it was only that Keith had kept all their further meetings strictly on a business level that had stopped her broaching the subject.

She hadn't been in the house for many minutes when Sarah arrived. 'Could you have Christopher tonight?' she asked, as she walked into the sitting room to find Rachel standing in front of the fire reading the headlines of the evening newspaper.

For a moment she was struck dumb. Christopher often stayed with her. She liked having him and she liked being able to give Sarah and Alan a trouble-free night out.

'I know it's short notice,' Sarah continued, and looked at her oddly. It wasn't like her to refuse.

'I'm sorry. I can't.' She bit her lip. Then thought she might as well tell her. 'I've got a date,' she said casually and turned her attention back to the newspaper.

'A date!' Sarah's interest was immediately bubbling. She plonked herself down in a chair and grinned wildly, as Rachel cast a glance of resignation over the top of the paper. 'Come on then!' she urged. 'Who with? Where?'

She groaned loudly, tossed the newspaper aside and sat down opposite her sister, knowing she wasn't going to get rid of her until she had milked all the details.

'It's with Keith. And I don't know where.'

'Keith!'

Rachel scowled. 'If you say one word about it having to be someone connected to work, I'll . . . I'll thump you.' She kicked off her shoes and rubbed her feet, just for something to do.

Sarah looked sheepish. 'I've grown up since then.'

'Good!' she replied dryly.

'Why don't you know where you're going?' Sarah looked dubious, as if she wasn't being told the truth.

Rachel had to smile. 'We're going to dinner. That's all I know. I didn't ask the exact location.'

'Oh!' Sarah groaned and glanced to the ceiling in disbelief. 'You're impossible! How will you know what to wear?'

Rachel laughed then. 'I shall wear what I usually wear. I'm not like you, dear sister. I don't need to have a specific dress for every establishment in town.'

Sarah grinned. 'I'm so pleased.'

'What about Christopher?' she asked, wanting to save herself from one of her sister's psychology lectures. Then suddenly thought she had found a good excuse to back out. 'I can phone Keith and tell him I can't make it. We can go another night.'

'Don't be ridiculous,' Sarah scolded. 'That's no problem. Alan's mum will have him. So, when did you decide all this?'

Rachel gave up rubbing her feet. She sat back in the chair and sighed. 'This morning.' She looked at her watch. 'I really should be getting ready,' she said, even though she had plenty of time.

Sarah immediately stood up and smiled down at her. 'David wouldn't mind,' she suddenly said.

'I know,' she replied simply, and gazed into her sister's face for a long moment. There were times when she was amazed how understanding she could be. She did feel she was being unchivalrous to him. But that wasn't the only problem. Sarah didn't know that. Maybe it would have helped if she could have told her everything. But the truth would have hurt her. She sighed again.

'What's the matter with you?' Sarah demanded, and received a noncommittal shrug. 'Go out and enjoy yourself,' she insisted. 'You deserve it. You work hard enough. You need some relaxation, something to take your mind off the blessed factory.'

Rachel grimaced. Perhaps it was just that she had been alone for too long now, she thought. She was too set in her ways to welcome changes to her routine.

'You're not going to back out?' Sarah prompted her continuing silence. She looked worried and she bent her head to peer right into her eyes, as if she was chastising Christopher.

Rachel forced a smile. 'No. I shall go. But don't go expecting too much.' She knew Sarah too well. She could see the glisten of church bells and apple blossom was already in her eyes. 'We're friends. Nothing more.'

'But friends can turn into lovers,' Sarah pointed out knowingly.

'Not tonight they can't,' she replied very firmly. Then she stood up to show Sarah out, before the conversation reached depths that really would make her change her mind.

Chapter Thirty-three

Boxing Day was one of the days Rachel most hated. It was a holiday, a family day, a day for being with people. She had been invited to the Caradines along with Sarah and Alan. Every year Mrs Caradine passed an invitation through Sarah. Every year she politely refused, knowing Micky and wife and ever-increasing brood would be there.

She wished she had been seeing Keith. But his parents lived in Essex and he had gone to spend the holiday with them. She had only been out with him three times, but the occasions had been enjoyable. He was very easy to get along with and she found his company always diminished her uncertainties and made her relax. He had kissed her good night each time, but he had never got intense and she was grateful he seemed content to take things slowly.

After eating a slice of Christmas cake for lunch, she fetched a bottle of white wine from the fridge and sat down by the window in the sitting room. She poured herself a glass and held it cradled in her hand, but didn't take a drink. She gazed out down the hill. The place was deserted. All the doors of the grey-stone cottages were closed. Everything was quiet. Silent as the grave, she thought morbidly, and felt as if she was the only person left alive in the world.

She wondered why it had begun to happen again: the feeling of isolation, much like the time immediately following David's death. It was Rosemary, she told herself. Rosemary was not dead. But today she was at home with her father. She realized it was where Rosemary should be, but she couldn't get rid of the feeling that part of her was missing.

It was only the time of year, she insisted, trying to find reassurance that the feeling would pass, along with the festive season. She tried to think of something else. But found her thoughts drifting to Rosemary's father. She had not seen or heard from Edward Ellicot since the night of his visit. Rosemary had not said much about him. She had asked if he had upset her. He could be very pompous, at times, she had said. A point that Rachel already knew from experience. But she had denied any cause for upset and told Rosemary that they had got on well together, which, fortunately, seemed to tie in with what he had told her. Rosemary then seemed content to let the matter drop and he had never been brought into conversation again.

She looked bleakly at David's chair and tried to imagine him sitting there on the one Boxing Day they had shared as husband and wife. The image was hazy and then suddenly cleared. But it was not David she could see, it was Edward Ellicot's dark, unforgiving eyes that looked back at her.

He had had no right to sit in David's chair, she thought angrily. She turned quickly back to the window and took a large gulp of wine and screwed her nose up. Then wasn't sure it was the wine's fault, or if her previous imaginations had left the bitter taste on her tongue.

She lifted the bottle and studied the label. It was a brand she had not tried before and it hadn't been very expensive, but neither had it been that cheap! It was definitely her imagination, she thought, assuring herself there was nothing wrong with the wine, just as movement on the hill caught her eye.

She looked up. She wasn't the only person alive! The thought cheered her, but only for a moment. The next, the bottle in her hand landed on the table with a thud. Her eyes widened on the car coming up the hill. Oh my God! she thought, swearing in a manner that seemed to be the normal way of things when a certain person entered her mind.

'No!' she said out loud. She couldn't believe it. There was more than one black Jaguar around, she tried to tell herself. But as the car came to a halt by her house, she had her worst fears confirmed. She felt a certain relief when she saw Rosemary was in the passenger seat, but it was very small and insignificant, compared to the heart-sinking feeling she experienced when seeing the driver.

Why? she demanded. What had possessed him to make him come today? And why the devil had Rosemary brought him? She could think of a hundred questions but not one answer, as she went reluctantly to the door to let them in.

'Happy Christmas,' Rosemary chirped as Rachel swung the door open and stood looking dumb. Edward smiled uncertainly, but also remained silent.

It was a moment before she found her voice. Then she invited them in and followed them into the sitting room, still wondering why they were there. She was pleased to see Rosemary. But she couldn't say the same thing about her father. And she wasn't sure it was a good idea for them all to be together at the same time.

'I wasn't expecting you.' She tried to sound calm and casual, as she looked from Rosemary to Edward, then back to Rosemary, judging that to be the safest place to look.

'I remembered you said you weren't doing anything special today,' Rosemary began. 'So we came on the chance of catching you in. We thought it would be nice.'

We! She wondered if that was correct. Had *we* decided? Or had it been Rosemary's decision and he had been dragged along? She looked into the dark eyes across the room and hoped to find some clue. But all she found was an assessing gaze that seemed to see right inside her and she quickly turned away again. 'It's very nice to see you,' she said, looking directly at Rosemary. If he found her action offensive, tough, she thought. She really couldn't imagine why he would want to be here, unless it was to watch over everything she did with Rosemary. He didn't trust her, she told herself. She recalled the theatre tickets which must have been purchased with ulterior motives, and she wondered if this was another little plan he had concocted. Well, if he had come to goad her into another argument, in the hope of making Rosemary see her in another light, he was in for a disappointment. No matter what he did or said, she was determined to be nothing but sweetness and light. She glanced at him suspiciously.

'Were you going out?' he asked. 'We don't want to spoil your plans.'

'No,' she replied without thought. Then she kicked herself for not saying yes and getting him out of her home.

'Good!' Rosemary looked delighted. 'Then we made the right decision. We didn't like to think of you all alone today.'

Rachel forced a smile. It made her sound like a lame dog. 'I'm used to being alone. I enjoy my own company.' She glanced once more at the dark presence which seemed to be filling the room and hoped he couldn't see it for the lie it was: the way he had seen right through her on their first meeting. 'Please, sit down,' she invited, suddenly realizing they were all standing round like spare stools at a milking.

Rosemary accepted. Edward moved to the window and looked out. Rachel watched him, feeling safe with his eyes turned away from her. She wished he didn't have the uncanny knack of positioning himself in the same places David had done.

'You have a lovely view.' He glanced round at her.

'Yes', she replied simply, and wondered how long they intended to stay. She hoped it was not for the rest of the day. She didn't think her nerves were up to it. Every time he looked at her she had the feeling she was treading on broken glass: one wrong move and she would be speared.

'Was that the reason you decided to live at the top of such a steep hill?' he asked.

'My husband had this house . . . before we were married.' She did not tell him she had, herself, often wondered why David would have chosen the house with that particular view – the weir and the house he had shared with Judith and could never go back to.

Edward nodded with an understanding that made her think she must have spoken her thoughts out loud. 'Would you like a drink?' she asked, needing the relief of an occupation.

'We've brought our own.' Rosemary produced two bottles of wine from the large bag she had been carrying. Then she produced a gaily wrapped parcel. 'We've also brought you a present.'

There it was again. We! Was it just a figure of speech? For no other reason than that her father was there with her.

'Thank you,' she replied calmly, though calm was the last thing she was feeling. All she could think was if *we* had brought us a present, then one half of *we* was going to be disappointed, because she had nothing to give him back. 'I'll just get yours,' she said, keeping her eyes fixed firmly to Rosemary so she would not give the wrong impression. Then she made a quick exit from the room. She had not wanted Rosemary to have anything from her to open on Christmas morning along with her father's presents. She had felt that might hurt him. Now she wondered why she had given him a moment's consideration and wished she had got the present giving over and done with. She considered getting a bottle of wine from the fridge and wrapping it up. Oh to hell with it, she thought irritably. She didn't want to give him anything.

As she returned to the sitting room, Edward's eyes turned to her, and she felt heat rush to her cheeks, as if he was aware of all the unchivalrous thoughts that had been going through her head. He was still standing by the window and she wished he would sit down and make himself look smaller and less conspicuous. Turning quickly to Rosemary, she handed her the large, red-foil-wrapped parcel and took the smaller one in return. Then she sat down and began to remove the wrapping paper.

'It's beautiful,' she said sincerely, as she carefully lifted the silver jewellery casket from its box. The top was covered in the most intricate filigree and the sides were decorated in a bold pattern of roses and lily of the valley. And it was very expensive, she thought, her heart taking a dive as she recalled how much the silver cigarette box for Joseph's wedding present had cost. That had had nothing like the workmanship of this one.

'Thank you,' she said simply, looking first to Rosemary, then meeting Edward's intense gaze for the briefest of moments. It had obviously cost too much to have come from Rosemary alone and she felt very guilty for the bottle of wine still standing in her fridge.

Fortunately Rosemary's shrieks of joy gave her something else to think about.

'Look at this, Dad!' She held the chiffon cocktail dress in front of her. It was chocolate brown, the colour Rachel had noticed she often chose for herself. It had a dainty gold thread woven into the sleeveless bodice and the skirt was straight and tightly fitting: another point Rosemary always went for.

'It's lovely,' Edward agreed. 'One of yours, I presume?' He levelled his gaze at Rachel.

'Yes,' she replied, and turned her attention back to Rosemary, wondering just what he was looking for when his eyes x-rayed her.

Rosemary put the dress down and gave the tailored suit the same enthusiastic treatment.

'I hope you like the colour,' Rachel said uncertainly. Her preferences seemed to range from dark brown to old gold. The most startling thing she had seen her wearing was the orange jacket of their first meeting. She had deliberated long and hard over the scarlet suit. Remembering how red suited Sarah, she had finally overcome her doubt and taken the suit from Morrell's stockroom.

'It's great,' Rosemary confirmed, with an enthusiasm that lacked no sincerity. Rachel smiled her relief that she had not made a mistake.

'It makes a change from your usual dull colours,' Edward said, making it obvious Rachel had his approval. But she showed no reaction.

'Oh, Dad!' Rosemary gave a sigh of despair and looked to Rachel. 'He doesn't know the first thing about fashion,' she said, in a good-natured tease.

Rachel smiled and kept looking at Rosemary. But the smile soon slipped away, when she realized she was to be left alone with Edward.

Rosemary swept both outfits into her arms, and announced, 'I'm going to try them on and give you a fashion show.' Then she vanished up the stairs before Rachel could think of a good reason why she shouldn't.

The silence in the room seemed suddenly to turn electric.

Rachel got up from the chair and collected all the discarded wrapping paper. 'Christmas always makes twice as much rubbish,' she said, just for something to say. He didn't reply and she could feel his eyes moving around the room with her and she wished she had sat still. She folded all the used paper into a neat pile and put it on the dresser. Then she turned to him.

'Shall we . . . ?'

'Do you . . . ?'

They began together, stopped together.

'You first,' she prompted, wanting to know what he had been about to say before she opened her mouth again.

'Shall we have that drink now?' His eyes danced in a manner that she found strange and unexplainable. He was laughing at her, she thought, for her unease in his presence.

'Get the glasses,' he instructed. 'I'll open the bottle.' He moved easily across the room and picked up the corkscrew from the table, where she had left it alongside the opened bottle of wine she had sampled before they arrived.

He eyed the bottle. But she did not offer it to him. She remembered the taste and could see the Chablis he had brought had not come off the same supermarket shelf.

Instead of going into the kitchen, she took two Georgian crystal glasses from the display cabinet, feeling the moment called for it. She did not think the inimitable Edward Ellicot would look right drinking out of Woolworth's best. A tiny voice told her she was only trying to impress him and let him see his daughter was in good company when she was with her. But she held the glasses out for him to fill, and told herself she had no need to impress him. She didn't care what he thought of her.

Edward put the bottle down. Then he took one of the glasses and raised it in salute. 'To the future, Rachel,' he said, and fixed his eyes on hers in a manner that instantly alarmed her.

'To the future,' she repeated, finding the glass in her hand was shaking. What future? she asked herself. Her own? His? She didn't know. But she did know she didn't like the new look in his eyes any more than the usual expression of animosity. And she also knew he had spoken her name in a way she had never heard it spoken before. She took a quick sip of wine to steady her hands and she turned away from him. Confusion rolled around her brain like waves hitting a rocky shore: back and forth, back and forth, never finding an anchor or a place to rest. Yet she didn't know why.

She glanced up at him. The expression in his eyes was still there and it was so strange: deep and intense, as always, but there was a light, a glitter that she found disturbing. She walked over to the fireplace, suddenly feeling the need to put space between them. She gazed at the mantelshelf, wanting to speak and break the tense silence, but she couldn't find words in a throat suddenly dry with apprehension.

A log dropped in the fire and her taut nerves jumped, sending a visible shock through her body.

'Are you all right?' He was right behind her and he rested a hand on her shoulder.

She jumped again. 'Oh!' She gave a nervous laugh. 'I didn't know you'd followed me,' she said, turning around to face a gaze that was as warm and welcoming as the leaping flames behind her back. No, she thought. He had to be joking.

'Ta-ra!' Rosemary leapt through the door, arms open wide and setting a saucy pose.

Edward moved away and Rachel breathed again. She turned to watch Rosemary pirouette around the room in the chocolate chiffon.

'How do I look?' she asked.

'Exactly how you think you look,' Edward replied, with a knowing smile.

'The fit is perfect,' Rachel said, studying the dress with the eye of a connoisseur. She was very pleased with her choice. But the smile slipped from her face when she glanced at Edward. He was looking almost guilty, as if his daughter had caught them in something he had not wanted her to see. Yet it had been of his doing.

She rubbed at her temple, wondering what game he was playing. She felt sure he was up to something and was suddenly nervous.

Fortunately, Rosemary was too entranced by her new dress to notice anything odd about her father. She performed several more circuits of the room, made a final bow and went back upstairs to change into the suit.

'I think you made the right choice,' Edward said.

'Yes,' she replied, watching him uncertainly. 'I hope the suit fits as well,' she said, and felt her heartbeat increase as he moved closer to her.

'Rosemary is very like you,' he pointed out, stopping right in front of her and looking down into her eyes with an intensity that almost made her flinch.

'You should see my sister.' She spoke quickly and turned away, and kicked herself for not moving from the fireplace when she had the chance. She suddenly felt trapped by the warmth of the flames behind her and the heat of his gaze before her. 'You would think Sarah and Rosemary were sisters,' she added, and tried to convince herself she was being stupid. He was Rosemary's father, she reminded herself. He wouldn't do anything to her. He didn't like her. But his closeness was doing nothing to prove her reassurances held any merit.

'Then your sister must be very like you,' he persisted.

She glanced at him uncertainly. She had never considered herself to be like Sarah. It certainly wasn't in their characters. 'Rosemary has all the bubbling self-confidence and love of life that Sarah has,' she said, giving a twisted smile of self-mockery. Sarah would also have known exactly what to do in a situation like this, she told herself. Then, realizing the fire's heat was becoming too intense on her legs, had to make a move to get away from both it and him.

'I'm scorching,' she said. But he did not move and forced her to squeeze past him in a way that sent colour to her cheeks. Once free, she walked across the room. For God's sake, Rachel, she thought angrily. She was a woman, an adult, yet she still continued to blush like a schoolgirl.

She didn't stop until she was at the far side of the room and, she had thought, a distance away from him. But when she stopped, he spoke right in her ear. 'Don't you have a love of life, Rachel?' he asked, speaking her name in the way he had before, making it sound like a caress.

She edged away again. 'I was the one who had all the responsibility,' she said, forcing her voice to a confidence she was far from feeling. She continued walking as she spoke. 'I had to bring Sarah up from the age of seven and take responsibility for both of us.'

'Did your parents die?' he asked, and for a moment seemed full of genuine concern.

'Yes . . . they died,' she replied stiffly. She had not told Rosemary the full story of her life and she had no intention of telling him first. She had made a full circuit of the room and was back at the fireplace, before irritation got the better of her, and she turned to him. 'What are you doing?' she asked. He had followed her every step of the way, like a tiger stalking its prey.

He smiled and lifted one eyebrow quizzically. 'Don't you know?' he asked, and lifted his hand and ran it down her chin.

She swiped him away. 'I know that you're driving me mad,' she hissed. 'But I refuse to have an argument with you in front of Rosemary.' She was convinced now that was what he was trying to do. Her previous thoughts had been too ridiculous, she told herself. Edward Ellicot making romantic overtures to her. She almost wanted to laugh. But his next words proved just how wrong she had been and laughter was a million miles from what she was feeling.

He took hold of her shoulders and pulled her closer to him. 'What is wrong, Rachel?' he said, making more of a meal over her name than he had before. 'There's no need to be afraid of me.'

She stared into his eyes like a frightened rabbit, feeling totally trapped there. 'I'm not afraid of you,' she insisted. It was the truth. She wasn't afraid. She was terrified. She tried to pull away. 'Just let me go and we'll forget this ever happened.' She narrowed her eyes at him. 'We're good at that,' she reminded him pointedly. 'Forgetting things ever happened!'

He shook his head and pulled her back to him and, before

she had time to speak another word of objection, he had her trapped in his arms and her mouth was being crushed by his.

The shock was so severe that it was several moments before she could react. Then she was pushing at his chest with all her might. She tore her lips free. 'What the hell are you playing at?' she demanded fiercely, rage trembling through her like the after effects of an earthquake.

'I'm not playing at anything, Rachel. I'm deadly serious.'

She stared frozenly into the purpose filling his eyes and she had the awful feeling he was mad. She wanted to scream at him to stop speaking her name in that way. He had no right. God, she thought, as she forced his arms away and quickly put space between them. Did he think because she was the mother of his daughter he had the right to . . .

Suddenly remembering that Rosemary was upstairs, helped return her sanity. '*Your* daughter is within calling distance,' she said, laying emphasis on his ownership. She had wanted to say our but, after her previous thought, considered it wouldn't have been wise.

His smile told her he didn't believe she would do it. He moved towards her and her hands went up protectively. 'One more step and I'll scream my head off.'

He shook his head and continued to follow her as she backed away. She glanced nervously at the door. Then she realized that had been a foolish move: it showed her anxiety that Rosemary should not come back and see them, which also told him her threat of screaming had been worthless. She looked back into his face. 'Don't come any closer,' she demanded, and earned another cynical smile for her trouble. Then she came up against the dresser with a heart-sinking bump.

Before she could change course he had her trapped by his large body. He ran a finger down her cheek and she felt a shudder run down her spine. 'Stop it,' she said, but fear rendered her voice almost inaudible. He pulled her so close to him that she could feel the beat of his heart and, as his head descended on her, she could only stare numbly into the darkness of his eyes. When his lips touched hers again she felt another tremor run through her. She heard a whimper and prayed to God it was coming from herself and not from Rosemary standing in the doorway. When he finally pulled away the victorious light in his eyes made her shudder with a revulsion that was all aimed inward at herself. She hated herself for letting him do that to her, but all she could see was the huge chest and broad shoulders and she knew she hadn't had any choice.

'That was much more preferable to screaming,' he said, and gently brushed a wisp of hair from her face that had strayed from her bun.

'Let me go.' Humiliation put the fire back into her voice and she glared at him coolly. 'I don't know why you did that. But it wasn't for any genuine reasons. So let me go!'

He never had time to reply. Rosemary's footsteps were heard running down the stairs and the next moment she was at the door. She came up short and looked from one to the other.

Rachel looked at Edward, and suddenly she knew exactly what he had been playing at. He looked like a naughty boy caught with his fingers in the biscuit jar. He slowly released her from his arms and moved guiltily away. She reached behind her and gripped the dresser for support. Her fingers brushed against one of Judith's treasured ornaments and she felt she would have gained much satisfaction from throwing it at him. He had done it all on purpose, just to let Rosemary find them that way. He was still so insanely jealous of her that he wanted Rosemary to think she was a threat to her. And, from the look of horror on Rosemary's face, he had succeeded.

She pushed herself away from the dresser and looked at Rosemary's suit. 'That looks nice,' she said, realizing someone had to break the electric silence. The red suit did look good. It fitted as perfectly as the dress but, at that moment, Rachel couldn't really have cared if she was wearing a black plastic bin liner.

'It looks lovely,' Edward confirmed, and Rachel felt her heart sinking. Rosemary gave him a smile warm enough to

429

toast bread. All she had received was a blank stare. It told her clearly that he had won.

The afternoon went from bad to worse as far as Rachel was concerned. Rosemary decided to keep the red suit on, making it very obvious she did not trust them to be left alone together. She was polite to Rachel, but there was a coolness that had not been there before. And when she finally went upstairs to collect the brown chiffon dress and the clothes she had been wearing when she arrived, in order to take them home, Rachel was ready for him.

'You bastard!' She found no shame in the word. It fitted him perfectly. 'Are you so insecure that you couldn't have shared just a little of her?' She didn't wait for his reply. 'Well, I feel sorry for you,' she snarled bitterly. 'And I feel sorry for her as well! What will happen the day she finds a boyfriend? What little plan will you concoct to put a stop to that?' She held her balled fists tightly to her side, feeling if she had given them any freedom she would have set about him. 'And if you don't ease off then, believe me, you'll lose her completely.' She didn't know why she had said that. Because he deserved to find out the hard way. He was as obsessed with his daughter as she was with work. But at least her work was productive, not destructive.

She saw a tightening in his eyes and was pleased she had hit a nerve. But she never found out what his response would have been. Rosemary came down the stairs again faster than lightning.

She showed them silently to the door. She wasn't surprised when Rosemary turned to her, and said, 'I forgot to tell you something has come up tomorrow. I won't be able to make it. I'll . . . give you a call.'

You do that, she thought. She merely nodded her head and kept her eyes away from Edward as he walked out. As she closed the door and walked back into the room, to look bleakly on the empty glasses and the pile of secondhand wrapping paper on the dresser, she was shaking with rage.

Chapter Thirty-four

Ted came storming through the office door and Rachel lifted her head from the letter she was writing. 'The girls won't have this!' he blazed. His silver hair was standing up on end and the redness of his cheeks gave her the impression he was about to explode. He flapped the new work schedule furiously in front of her nose and glared at her.

She glared back at him. 'They'll have it – or else!'

'Or else what?' he demanded.

'Or else there are plenty of others looking for jobs!'

'You'll have a strike on your hands.'

'And they'll all be out of work!' She stood up, positioned her hands on the desk and leaned towards him in a threatening manner. She'd had enough of Ted and his militant girls.

He took a step back. 'You can't sack them if they're out on strike. You'll have the union on your back.'

'I can do what I damn well please. And if they walk out I'll close the place down. No-one can stop me doing that.'

'Then what would you do?'

'Live very comfortably on the proceeds. For the rest of my life!' She sat down again, the gaze she pinned to his face no less cool. 'So I suggest you go back and tell them exactly that. The choice is theirs.' She returned to the letter with an air of silent dismissal.

Ted shuffled uncomfortably for several seconds. Then he turned and walked out with his tail between his legs.

As the door closed behind him, she looked up and gave a heavy sigh and rubbed wearily at the tension in the back of her neck. She was tired of it all and her words had been no spur of the moment threat. She meant exactly what she had said. She could have closed the factory and walked away without a backwards glance. She was a rich woman. But what good did it do her? All she had was work, work, work. And for what? She had proved herself now and didn't need to go any further. She had no-one to take over when they finally wheeled her out. Which, if she didn't watch herself, would be happening very soon.

She felt she had been robbed of her last chance of contentment by the manic Edward Ellicot. It was Easter at the end of the week and she had not heard from Rosemary since Christmas. She had considered sticking her neck out and trying to make contact with her. But she realized it had to be left to Rosemary to make the first overtures. And, if she didn't want to make the first overtures, *she* had to accept it. She had even, at times of desperation, contemplated going to see Edward Ellicot himself to try to reason with him. She called those her times of insanity and was grateful they never lasted long enough for her to do anything about.

With a heavy heart she got up and walked to the window and gazed out on the twin buildings of the factory, once her pride and joy. She was still proud of them, she told herself. But she recalled more and more often the times David had chastised her for working too hard. It was ironic, she thought. The first little factory had been his idea of stopping her working like a slave. She knew he would have been proud of what she had done for him. But she also knew he would have been the first to put her straight on the errors of having nothing in her life but work.

She and Keith, she told herself. But that wasn't progressing as quickly as he wanted it to and she was well aware he was getting irritated with her. She didn't know why she couldn't feel more for him. She liked him. But that was all. Their nights out together never started any violins and his kisses had never caused any lightning. And when he tried to go any further she always stopped him. But she liked him. She shook her head and turned back to the desk, just as he came through the door.

'What have you been saying to Ted?' he asked, giving her a crookedly knowing smile. 'He's spitting blood.'

She grimaced and sat down in her chair. 'I told him a few home truths. If he doesn't like them – tough!'

432

Keith pulled out his cigarettes, perched himself in his usual position on the corner of her desk, and lit up. Rachel watched him. The significant little action still reminded her of David. She looked at his curly hair, always neat and tidy, at his kind eyes, always ready to give a smile of approval or encouragement. He was a very good-looking man, she thought. And he deserved better than she was giving him!

He took a long draw on the cigarette and exhaled noisily, and reminded her once more of David. 'So, are you going to tell me?' he asked.

'Hasn't Ted already?' She displayed her surprise. She had imagined it would be all over the factory by now.

He shook his head. 'All I caught was something about irritable women.' Ted's actual comment had been, 'frustrated bloody women who should be at home bringing babies up!' But he knew better than to let that be known.

Rachel smiled grimly. 'I told him if he didn't sort his bolshie lot out, I'd close down.'

Keith froze with the cigarette halfway to his mouth. 'You don't mean that?'

'Oh yes I do,' she replied with a steely determination, and he dropped his hand to his side, the cigarette forgotten. 'I've had enough of "we're not doing this, we're not doing that". They only do it because they know he'll come out screaming for them.' Ted was a good manager in many ways. But the girls had soon learned he was always ready to stick up for them and they played on it. 'Why can't he be like Colin?' Colin got the same capacity work out of the Coprell workshop without half the trouble.

'But you wouldn't really close down?'

She shook her head. 'I don't know.' She looked into his anxious face and felt a stab of guilt, realizing the concern in his eyes was genuine. 'How do you fancy spending the rest of your life on a desert island?' she joked, attempting to lighten both Keith's, and her own, moods. 'We'll sell up and buy one.'

'If I thought you meant that I'd already be on the way to buy the tickets.' He returned to the cigarette and watched her thoughtfully. 'Is it us that's causing you concern?' he finally asked.

She shook her head. 'No,' she said simply.

'Are you sure? It isn't exactly working, is it?' He levelled his eyes at her and she felt ashamed for the way she was treating him.

'It isn't you. It's me.' She leaned back in the chair and rubbed her neck once more. 'Just ignore me. I'll be fine in the morning.' She didn't really believe herself. She hadn't been fine for a long time: since Boxing Day. She felt so bitter and angry towards Edward Ellicot. She couldn't get the man, or what he had done, out of her mind, and she was taking her frustration out on everyone she came into contact with.

Keith smiled at her. 'It would be very difficult to do that. Hard or soft, you're a very noticeable lady.' He pushed himself up from the desk. 'What do I do about Ted and his girls?'

She thought for a moment. 'Let them stew until tomorrow. Send a memo to Colin stating that any rumours regarding closure of the factory do not apply to Coprell. And send one to Ted saying I want to speak to him and all the Morrell girls, in the workshop, at four o'clock tomorrow.'

'Four o'clock?' he questioned with surprise.

'Yes. Let them sweat until the last minute.'

Keith levelled his gaze at her. 'It could backfire on you!'

'It could,' she replied without much concern. But she didn't think it would. They were making excellent profits and the wages she paid were higher than anywhere in the local vicinity. Ted might be militant, but he wasn't stupid. She suddenly smiled, realizing her mind had returned to its first love and was once more contemplating the future without the doubts that had been plaguing her earlier.

Keith responded with a knowing grin. 'We still on for tonight?' he asked, as he went to the door.

'So long as I choose the restaurant!' she pointed out seriously. Then she flashed him a grin that matched his own. They had to take it in turns to choose the venue for their evenings out. Keith was very partial to foreign food and liked to frequent Chinese and Indian restaurants. Her own preference was good plain English.

At three o'clock, Rachel was in Kate's office. They were in the middle of discussing the action they were going to take over a large, very overdue account.

'What do you think about me going to see them personally?' Kate asked, removing her large red-framed glasses and rubbing the bridge of her nose.

Rachel watched her for a moment. Kate had a wardrobe full of spectacles, all the colours of the rainbow. A pair for each of the very chic outfits she wore. Today she was wearing a scarlet suit that reminded Rachel of the one she had worn on the evening David had proposed to her. But Kate's dark hair made the colour more vivid. She wondered if she had looked as good in hers.

'Are you with me?' Kate replaced the glasses on her nose and peered at her suspiciously.

Rachel smiled. 'I was just thinking. A personal visit might help us to see how they're really fixed. If they have a genuine problem, it wouldn't hurt us to defer payment for a little while longer. Or suggest they pay in instalments.' She knew they were only a small company and hadn't been going all that long. If they were struggling she was willing to help them. 'But . . . If they are just being awkward, then we'll start legal proceedings.' She might be a little soft, but not totally.

Kate never got time to reply.

Flo came bursting through the door. 'There's been an accident!' she gasped breathlessly.

'What!' Rachel and Kate echoed together.

'There's been an accident,' Flo repeated, leaning on the desk to get her breath. 'In the loading bay. It's Keith. He's had a fall. I think it's bad.'

Rachel was out of the chair and on her way to the door. 'What happened? How bad?' she demanded, grabbing Flo's arm and dragging her with her so she could find the answers as she went.

'I don't know,' Flo gasped, as even her bustling steps found it difficult to keep up with Rachel. 'Colin just phoned through to tell them to get an ambulance.'

Ambulance! Oh God! Rachel thought, her heart racing like an express train and her feet matching the rhythm.

Not slowing down, she turned to Kate, close on her heels. 'Make sure the ambulance has been sent for,' she ordered. Then she raced out of the main doors and crossed the yard so fast she had to grab the wall of the loading bay to stop herself and get round the corner.

'What's happened?' she demanded urgently, as she hurried down the side of the large lorry parked in the bay. She could see Colin and Bob bent over something on the floor and her heart stood still. A crowd of the factory girls were gathering round and she pushed through them. 'What is it?' she demanded, panic filling her voice and going hot and cold all at the same time.

When she got her first glimpse of Keith she fell to her knees by his side. He was lying on the cold concrete floor with Bob's coat beneath his head. One leg was straight, the other at a very peculiar angle.'What happened?' she asked, looking into his ashen face in search of the answer.

'We were loading up,' Colin said, speaking for him. 'There was only space for one more carton in the lorry and it was proving difficult to fit in.' His voice was flat and she turned to him anxiously. He gave a sigh of regret. 'He climbed up the hoist to try and manoeuvre it by hand.' he paused, reliving the error of the stupid action. 'He got the carton in,' he finally continued. 'But when he turned to jump down there must have been some oil or grease on the boom and his feet slipped. He came down with a crack, right across the edge of the bay.'

'Oh! You idiot!' She turned back to Keith with anxiety written all over her face. She regretted speaking the words, but they had just slipped out, fear speaking for her. He attempted a smile but it ended in a grimace of pain.

'We had to move him,' Bob said worriedly. 'He was lying with his bottom half dangling over the edge of the bay. We couldn't have left him like that.'

Rachel glanced at the sharp concrete edge and felt her

stomach churn. If he had come down on that, heaven only knew what he had done to himself. Then she glanced at Bob, and would have given anything to hear him begin whistling 'Puppet on a String' and tell her this was all a bad dream. But all Bob could do was stare at her with regret in his eyes. 'You did the right thing. You couldn't have left him there,' she said, realizing he was seeking confirmation that there had been some sense in their actions.

She looked back to Keith and took hold of his hand. His skin felt cool and clammy and his face looked even paler than only moments ago. She looked at his leg. She didn't need to be a medical expert to know it was broken. But what else had he done? She tried to give him a smile of encouragement, but it only resulted in a tight little action of her mouth and reached nowhere near her eyes. 'You'll be all right,' she reassured.

He attempted to lift his head and looked down at his leg. She pushed him gently back down and he groaned loudly in pain. 'Don't move,' she instructed. 'Just relax. You'll be all right,' she repeated, not knowing what else to say or do. 'The ambulance won't be long now.' She hoped she was right. She glanced at her watch and thanked heavens it was not the rush hour. Then she had a sudden, horrible thought. 'Did he hit his head?' She turned quickly to Colin, her voice demanding the answer.

He shook his head bleakly. 'I don't know.'

Rachel heard a whimper behind her and realized at least one of the girls was crying.

'Get them out of the way,' she insisted to Colin.

He looked at her numbly, obviously reluctant to leave Keith.

'Please, Colin,' she begged. The last thing Keith needed was to hear snivelling in the background.

'I'll do it.'

Rachel looked round to find Kate and Flo right behind her. Kate rested a hand on her shoulder. 'He'll be all right,' she said confidently, before going to move the girls along.

Rachel silently thanked her for her reassurance and turned her worried gaze back to Keith. 'Can you speak?' she questioned gently.

Something came from his mouth that sounded like a weak yes. 'Who am I?' she asked, and looked closely into his eyes. The pupils were dilated and her heart sank. 'Who am I?' she repeated, panic lifting her voice.

'Soph . . . Sophia Loren.' He attempted another smile and once more ended in a grimace of pain.

'Idiot,' she chided softly. His voice was slightly slurred, she realized. But if he could joke he wasn't so bad, she assured herself. 'Just keep your head still,' she said, taking no chances. 'Just keep everything still.'

He gave her hand a little squeeze of acknowledgement and she began to smile. Then she suddenly wiped it from her face, fearing he might try to respond and end up in pain again. In the next moment she was heaving a sigh of relief. An ambulance siren could be heard in the distance.

It was with them in seconds and soon had Keith on board and taking him to the Infirmary. Rachel's BMW kept right behind them, caring nothing for the speed limits or the one set of red traffic lights the ambulance went through. If they could do it, so could she, she told herself, as she became increasingly more frightened for Keith's safety by the speed with which the ambulance man and woman had reacted.

She drove right up to the accident and emergency department with the ambulance. The car park was too far away for her to get there and back before Keith was taken in, and she wanted to be with him to make sure he got the best treatment. She had the feeling he was too groggy to know what they were doing to him. She contemplated leaving the car right there. But she saw the attendant bearing down on her through the rear-view mirror and knew she had to do something quick. She glanced around and saw there was one space in the consultant's parking area, and was in it and running from the car before the attendant could catch her.

A nursing sister was already taking Keith's details, as Rachel rushed to his side. 'I want the best,' she insisted, her hands closing tightly round the end of the trolley he was lying on, in the same anxiety with which she had grasped the steering wheel of the car. 'Money is no object. I want you to get him the best doctors you have.'

The sister scowled at her. 'Do you belong to this gentleman?' she enquired stiffly.

'Of course I do!' Rachel's eyes flashed with fire. 'And I want the best for him. No juniors. No trainees. Do you understand?'

'Perfectly madam!' The sister took on a very superior stance. 'This is an emergency facility. *Everyone* gets the best treatment!'

Rachel lifted her chin. When it came to superiority no-one could match her. Her voice was very cool and calm, but with an edge that threatened Armageddon if she was crossed. 'This man will get your very best consultants. They are my orders. I don't care what golf course you have to drag them off. I've already told you money is of no concern. Now I think you'd better get on with it. In my opinion you are wasting time in getting him the treatment he needs.'

The sister gave a snort of disapproval. 'Very well,' she said stiffly, and hurried away.

'Watch . . . it,' Keith said from the trolley.

Rachel looked down on him, and all the anger left her face and was replaced by a gentleness that made him want to smile. He gritted his teeth to stop himself. 'You might . . . end . . . up in here . . . yourself . . . one day. If that sister gets near . . . you . . . you won't half . . . suffer.'

His voice was still slurred, but she didn't think it was as much as earlier. 'Don't try to talk.' She laid her hand on his arm and fell silent, wishing they would hurry up. They should be doing something, she thought, and began to doubt the wisdom of her own words. Keith needed seeing straight away and she had insisted on a consultant. If there wasn't one around and they were having to find one the delay was her own fault.

She was just on the verge of going to find the sister and backing down, when a nurse came along and Keith was whisked away. And the sister returned and forcefully escorted her to the waiting room. 'You'll have a long wait,' she said, her eyes lighting with glee. 'The consultant is on his way. But he'll attend to the patient first – before he sees you!'

Rachel sat down on the padded bench without comment. She was in no hurry now she realized the message had been understood and acted upon. She looked around the crowded room. Old people, young people, babies and children were everywhere. Some in obvious pain and waiting treatment. Some obviously getting fraught because of long waits. Some looking resigned to the fact that they could very well spend the rest of their days sitting there. She noticed the vending machine in the corner and fetched herself a cup of coffee. Then she picked up a pile of magazines and settled herself down for the long wait. After one hour she was becoming jumpy. Every time a door opened, a name was called or anyone moved, she looked up. It was almost two hours when she realized she was reading an article on bleach cleaners for the second time, and it hadn't been very riveting on the first occasion. She closed the magazine and slapped it down on the bench by her side. Then she folded her arms and stared at the wall. What was taking them so long? What were they doing to him? What had they found? The wall provided no answers, but her head came up with plenty, none very pleasing.

It was three hours twenty-five minutes, when the sister poked her head through a door, and called, 'Mrs Broadhurst.' Rachel looked around at the sister, then turned her gaze back to the wall. 'Mrs Broadhurst!' the sister repeated, more loudly. Rachel looked round the waiting room. No-one moved. *'Mrs Broadhurst!'* The angry insistence of the voice made Rachel look at her again. It was only when she saw the annoyed gaze she was receiving that the penny dropped. The sister was speaking to her. She suddenly realized she had never been asked to give her name and the sister had jumped to the conclusion that she was Keith's wife.

'Oh, sorry.' She leapt from the bench and hurried over.

'Thank you!' the sister stressed meaningfully. Her disapproval had not decreased, so Rachel kept silent and did not put her straight as she followed her hurried steps down the maze of corridors.

The sister held one of the many doors open, but did not enter. 'Mrs Broadhurst!' she announced, in a manner which perfectly displayed her feelings.

Rachel gave the sister a thin smile of acknowledgement. Then stepped inside.

'Rachel!'

'Oh!' She came up short, pinned to the spot by the surprised gaze she was receiving from the dark-suited man on the opposite side of the desk. She closed her eyes and took a deep breath, knowing her own surprise had been equally severe. But no! Damn! Damn! Damn! She kicked herself for not having had the sense to think. But she had been too concerned for Keith's safety to stop and remember Edward Ellicot was an orthopaedic consultant. What she had demanded! The best!

'Mrs Broadhurst?' he uttered in disbelief. He glanced down at the notes in front of him, then frowned at her with a question in his eyes.

'No.' She shook her head and went to the chair in front of the desk and sat down without waiting to be invited. 'No-one asked my name. They got the wrong end of the stick.'

She heard a gasp of annoyance behind her. Then the door closed and she realized the sister had been having a few interesting moments.

She looked into his face, not knowing what to say. He watched her silently, waiting for her explanation. And she suddenly recalled the feel of his lips on hers. She felt warmth creeping up her cheeks and, when she spoke, her voice was harsh, spurred by her own inner anger. 'Keith is my production manager. The accident happened at work. I felt someone should come with him.' She looked around the sterile room with the desk at one side and an examination couch at the other with sickly lavender curtains. The wall above the couch was covered with children's posters: Thomas the Tank Engine, the Care Bears, He Man, Ninja Turtles and Roland Rat all looked back at her. And she knew which one fitted best, she thought, dragging her eyes away from Roland to the man at the other side of the desk. 'So how is he?' she asked, suddenly recalling that was why she was there.

'Not as bad as we first thought.' He leaned forward on the table and looked very professional.

Relief swept through her and she smiled.

For a moment he fell silent. Then he dropped his gaze to the notes on the desk, and continued. 'Although there were no signs of any cerebrospinal fluids, we thought he might have a serious head injury. The concussion is quite severe . . .'

'Hold on.' She lifted her hand to him. 'Speak in English,' she insisted. She wanted to know the truth, not be blinded by science.

He smiled knowingly and she was reminded of the way he had looked at her on Boxing Day. She was also reminded that there had been nothing genuine about him on that day. 'I want the truth,' she said.

'Of course,' he replied, so easily that she had the feeling he had done it on purpose. 'The concussion is from the bump on the head. It will make him groggy for, perhaps, a couple of days, and he could sound as if he is drunk for a little while. But there is no fracture to his skull. The femur, er, the thigh bone,' he quickly amended with a tiny smile, 'is the worst injury. That is a bad break and I have had to pin it.'

She glanced at his hands, at the long fingers. Surgeon's hands, she thought. Concentrate on Keith, she told herself angrily, as he continued, 'But it should heal without much effect on him. There is a possibility of a slight limp. There's no telling at the moment. But if there is, I would not expect it to be very bad, and nothing to impair him in any way.' His eyes narrowed on her for a moment and she realized there was a question in them. Then she realized his last comment had been made in a way that suggested she might have some personal interest in Keith's continued performance. Well she did, she thought. She didn't want to see her production manager limping round the factory, knowing he had got the injury while doing his duty for her. She kept her expression blank and waited for him to continue. If he thought she was going to relay her personal life to him, he could think again.

'Other than those,' he finally said, 'there are two broken

ribs. But both are minor and no problem to his breathing – but don't make him laugh.' He smiled once more. 'Does that satisfy you enough to keep you off the nurses' backs?'

She looked sheepish. 'Old habits die hard.' She didn't explain that she had got so accustomed to biting people's heads off that she had forgotten you get things done just as well by being reasonable. After all, he was the cause of it.

He leaned back in the chair and sucked on his bottom lip and studied her for several intent moments. 'And just so you're absolutely convinced he did get the right treatment, a neuro-surgeon looked at his head. I didn't think it was necessary for the two of us to come and get grilled when there was no problem in that area. We are both busy people . . .' He paused significantly. 'And neither of us finds time to play golf.' His eyes looked right into hers and she felt two inches tall.

'Sorry,' she said. 'And thank you,' she added sincerely. 'Can I see him?' she asked, and smiled, feeling suddenly very grateful to him.

'I'd rather you didn't. He is very groggy and I'd rather he slept without any disturbance. You can come first thing tomorrow morning, if you like. Tell the nurse I said you could and they will let you in.' He paused and made a pyramid with his fingers and stared over the top at her. 'All you had to do was tell them who you were and ask for me by name,' he said.

'And you would have come running?' She couldn't keep the disbelief from her voice.

'Yes,' he replied very definitely. 'It is my job. If I had come to you for a dress would you have turned me away?'

'We don't make your size,' she said. It made him smile and she wished she had kept the thought to herself. She didn't like it when he smiled like that: as if there was some genuine feeling between them. She fell silent for a moment. Then had to ask, 'How's Rosemary?'

For a moment there was something in his eyes she could not explain: regret, she doubted, compassion, she couldn't believe. 'She is very unhappy,' he said quietly. 'And I know I'm the cause of it.'

443

She gave a gasp and swung her eyes to the wall, then back to fix on his with a resigned sigh. 'It had to be for Rosemary, didn't it.' Just ask for me and I'll come running! But not for her. For Rosemary, because he felt he had a way of getting round her to make his daughter happy again. The rest of the world could be drowning in their own tears, but that wouldn't matter a damn, so long as Rosemary was all right!

'Well, Rosemary knows where I am. *If* she wants to find me!' She stood up, having no wish to prolong the meeting, and suddenly wondered why it bothered her that he could do something for Rosemary, but not for herself. She didn't want him to do anything for her. She despised the man. Anger spiked her voice, as she went on. 'That has to be her decision. Unfortunately, I am not in a position to help her make it. *Am I?*' she stressed, to make her point clear. If he was unhappy about his daughter then it was time *he* did a bit of explaining. Without waiting for any reply, she turned and walked out the door. Then she hurried through the corridors and out of the hospital, only to find her car was blocked in by a black Jaguar – and she knew exactly who it belonged to.

With her tail between her legs she returned to the room where she had left him. He was no longer there. She wandered down the corridor that seemed suddenly to be devoid of activity. Hospital staff were like policemen, she thought. You could never find one when you wanted one. Then, just as she reached the corner, he came hurrying round in the opposite direction and almost knocked her flying.

'What are you doing!' she demanded irritably, as she grasped the wall to steady herself. 'Trying to make yourself a bit of business?'

'No. Trying to escape before anyone else decides to throw themselves off a crane.'

'Hoist,' she corrected.

'What's the difference?' he asked, as he began to walk down the corridor and leave her standing there.

'About twenty feet – I should imagine,' she called after him. She gave a despairing sigh and followed him, realizing if he was on his way out her car was about to be freed.

444

'Anyway, what are you doing still here?' He glanced at her suspiciously, as she caught up by his side. 'Or have you come back for round two?'

'I couldn't get out. You're blocking me in.'

He stopped in his tracks. 'So it was you!' He shook his head as if she was a naughty child and began walking again. 'I might have known.'

'I was worried,' she retaliated.

'Did it not occur to you that you could be hindering the progress of the very person who could ease your worry?'

'Point taken,' she replied humbly.

'Just think yourself lucky that I am not now on my way to theatre to perform a five-hour operation,' he continued as the electric doors slid open and they stepped out into fresh evening air.

Rachel didn't reply. She knew she had been wrong. They were halfway across the ambulance unloading area when she suddenly stopped. 'I'm sorry,' she gasped. 'I didn't mean to be nasty. I was so terrified.' The emotion she had been holding in check since Flo first came bustling into Kate's office and told her the news suddenly overwhelmed her. Before she knew what she was doing, she had dropped her face into her hand and begun to cry.

'Come on. He will be all right.' Edward's arms went round her and he pulled her to him. He held her close and continued to speak soft reassurances with a gentleness that made her cry more: for Keith, for Rosemary, and for herself. There was nothing threatening in the feel of his arms. She felt like one of his patients, cared for and protected by those strong arms and capable hands. And she felt safe in a way she hadn't felt since David's death. It was a frightening realization. She lifted her tear-stained face to his. The dark eyes were filled with a compassion that seemed to leave a trail of warmth over her skin. No! she thought. It couldn't be. It wasn't possible. She quickly pushed him away and fumbled in her handbag for a tissue.

'I'm sorry. What must you think of me?'

'It's a natural reaction,' he assured her. For several moments

445

he watched her profitless searching. Then he produced a cleanly folded handkerchief from his pocket and handed it to her.

'Thank you,' she mumbled, and wiped her eyes and blew her nose. Then stuffed the handkerchief into her bag, taking it for granted he didn't want it back now she had used it. 'I feel such a fool.' In more ways than one, she thought. But she couldn't explain to him how she had felt just now, when he had held her. It was just the situation, she told herself, trying to regain some of the self-respect she had lost in her own eyes.

'How do you feel now?'

Humiliated, she thought. She flashed him a thin smile. 'A bit shaky. I'll be all right in a minute.' She wondered why she was shaking. Because of Keith? Or because of him?

'You're in no fit state to drive home,' he pointed out seriously.

She gave a resigned shrug. 'I could get a taxi. But my car is in a position to get up one of the consultant's noses.'

He smiled dryly. 'You're getting better,' he proclaimed, stuck his hands in his trouser pockets and looked thoughtful. 'It will have to stay here until the morning. I'll get someone to run it to the factory for you. Come on. I'm taking you home.' He grasped her arm and steered her to the car.

'I can get a taxi!' she insisted. But he had the car door open and her inside before she could raise further objection.

She spent the entire journey telling herself that, whatever she did, she must keep control. She must not break down again, must not give him any reason to touch her again.

'Is there anyone I can fetch to stay with you?' he asked, as he pulled the car up by the side of her house.

'I'll be all right,' she insisted.

'Isn't there anyone?' He sounded and looked incredulous.

'My sister. She lives down . . .' She suddenly checked herself. Having him turn up on Sarah's doorstep was definitely not a good idea. 'I forgot, she's out tonight,' she quickly said.

'Then you'll just have to put up with me,' he informed her in a manner that brooked no refusal. Then he was out of the car, leaving her to stare woodenly at him as he rounded the car and opened the passenger door for her.

Resigned to her fate, she climbed out and remained silent as he followed her up the path. They were in the sitting room and she was having vivid memories of Boxing Day, before she finally spoke. 'You really are making a fuss,' she told him, and threw her bag on to a chair in frustration. He was doing nothing for her equilibrium. She felt far worse with him around. 'I wouldn't have thought you would have wanted to come here again,' she said, fixing a pointed gaze on his face. She had the feeling it would be safest to provoke him to return to the antagonistic man she was more acquainted with. He was still playing the doctor and the feeling of safety in his arms was still very strong in her, and it frightened her.

'Delayed shock can do some strange things. You shouldn't be on your own.'

'I'm not the one who had the accident!' she said frustratedly. He went from one extreme to the other. She looked at him and sighed. She wondered if there was a bit somewhere in the middle which she might like. She turned quickly away and walked to the window and gazed across the river to Mulberry Bush Lane. There didn't need to be a bit in the middle, she realized defeatedly. She had found the bit she liked. She had felt more in those few seconds in his arms, than she had felt in all the months with Keith. Ironic, wasn't it, she thought. She'd waited all these years and then found it right where she couldn't have it – and didn't want it.

She turned back to face him squarely. 'I think you should go,' she said, her voice clear and precise. 'I'm perfectly all right now.'

'I know you are. I'm the doctor, remember. But I don't want to go.'

For a moment she was stunned. It wasn't what she had expected and it certainly wasn't what she wanted to hear. If he thought she was going to allow another little farce like before . . . But Rosemary was not here to see she suddenly realized. 'What . . . what do you mean?' she asked, staring numbly at him. The dark-grey suit and startlingly white shirt showed him to be the same man who had been at the hospital. Yet suddenly he looked so different: uncertain, insecure. She tried to imagine all the things he must have done to Keith, and told herself it was impossible for someone so capable to look insecure.

'You told me once before that I was a fool, Rachel,' he said, speaking her name in the way he always spoke it, and coming towards her.

She didn't move. She told herself what she should be doing, but she didn't do it. She just stood very still and stared into his eyes, hearing the way he made her name sound like a caress, in a manner that no-one had ever done before.

'Well, I was a fool. But in more ways than one.' He reached her and stood right before her. She had to bend her neck to look up into his face. The dark eyes washed over her, as if taking in every contour of her face. And she was surprised to find they were blue, like darkest sapphires. The black hair looked so silky soft and she found herself wondering what it would feel like to run her fingers through it. His lips curved in a gentle smile and she blushed slightly, fearing she might have spoken her thoughts out loud. She suddenly recalled how she had thought he looked like the devil and was incredulous that she had been capable of such a thing. His face was beautiful.

'I was too terrified of losing one thing,' he continued, 'to see I was losing another.'

Rosemary! She had not given her a thought. She tried to step aside but it was too late. She was in his arms and his mouth was against hers. Rosemary went from her mind. All she could think was that if this was nothing more than a moment's madness, then it was a moment she wanted. Right or wrong, she had neither the will nor the desire to stop him. It felt so right being in his arms and his lips seemed to have been made for hers. As he pulled the pins from her hair and ran his fingers through it and let it fall, she had never felt so much like a woman before in her life. And she wanted to feel like a woman, all woman, for this man. As his kiss deepened and he pulled her so close she felt she would melt into him, she wrapped her arms around his neck and gave herself to him in a way she had never given herself before.

Rachel woke to the squeak of the garden gate and the sound of chinking milk bottles. For a moment it was just another day. Then it all came flooding back, like a tidal wave about to suck her away. Keith, the hospital, Edward Ellicot – and the rest. She turned her head and felt something very solid sink in the pit of her stomach. He was still there, sleeping peacefully by her side, and she was mortified. She couldn't imagine what had come over her to make her act so free. To allow herself to accept him with open arms. And her arms had been open wide. She couldn't push the blame on to him. She had wanted him as much as he had wanted her.

With cheeks hot from the memory, she crept from the bed. As if she was a thief in her own home, she thought, not taking her eyes from the silent form in the bed, and she grabbed some clothes and took them into the bathroom to dress.

She dropped her clothes on the stool and felt a little safer with the door closed behind her. She gazed at her reflection in the mirror and wondered what she had turned into. To go to bed with a man she hardly knew . . . And what she did know she didn't much like. A picture of the good doctor, the caring professional man, came to her mind. She cast it quickly aside and scraped her fingers through her tangled hair. He hadn't been very professional last night, she thought. She had been in shock. He knew that. She sighed and dropped her hands. She had been perfectly all right. And she knew that.

She wanted to bathe but there was no lock on the door: she had never found the necessity for one – before. She glanced bleakly at the closed door, then again at the bath. It was too risky, she decided. She wasn't having him walking in on her. She turned the shower on and jumped inside.

It was the quickest shower she had ever had. She strained her ears above the noise of the water for any signs of life in the bedroom. Then she jumped out, gave herself a quick rub down with the towel and threw her clothes on. Once she was dressed she felt slightly more confident, but no happier. She thought of Keith, of all the nights she had stopped him because she felt he was going too far. And now, when he was lying in a hospital bed, she had been cavorting round in another bed – with the doctor who was treating him!

She dropped her head into her hands and gave a shuddering moan, as the memories of the night came flooding back. She had never realized she was capable of such feelings. David's lovemaking had always been enjoyable, but he had never lifted her to the heights she had reached last night, over and over again.

She picked up her towel and began to rub furiously at her wet hair, trying to rub away the memories. She didn't know how she was going to face him. What could she say? It had been terrible. She stopped rubbing at her hair and looked at herself in the mirror. Be truthful, she told herself. There had been nothing terrible about it. It had been lovely. She almost expected to see horns sprout out of her head as she admitted her true feelings. She had enjoyed every minute of it. And that made it twice as sinful.

'Oh damn!' she cursed, and flung the towel angrily at the floor. 'Go away Daniel Cooper. You're dead!' she said fiercely. She tossed her damp hair behind her shoulders and straightened the magenta-pink blouse and matching skirt. Then she gave herself a very determined stare in the mirror. Her father had been dead for years, yet she still allowed his bigoted opinions to cloud her life. She had done nothing sinful, she reassured herself. A bit silly, perhaps. But definitely not sinful, and she wouldn't let her father, or anyone else tell her different.

'Rachel?'

Her heart stopped and her determination wilted. He was awake and she told herself what she had done had not been a bit silly, it had been the most stupid thing of her life. She checked herself. That wasn't correct. Going up the top with Micky had been the most stupid thing of her life, and last night had born no relation to that. She glanced back at the window. But if she hadn't gone up the top with Micky, Rosemary would never have been born. 'Oh!' she groaned and looked at the ceiling in despair. She was talking herself into one of Sarah's psychology lessons. She took a deep breath and went out of the bathroom.

He was sitting up in bed with his arms folded across his naked chest. She was grateful he hadn't got up and was wandering round waiting for her to get out of the bathroom. He smiled at her. 'I thought you'd run away,' he said, and held his hand out to her.

She tried to smile, but it was thin and awkward. Then she shook her head.

He dropped his hand and looked immediately concerned. 'What's wrong?'

'What's right?' She almost wanted to laugh. 'Rosemary hasn't spoken to me since Christmas and *I* did nothing then. Keith's lying in hospital and . . . and . . .' She gave up with a breathy sigh, folded her arms and looked defeated.

He frowned. 'You told me Keith was your production manager. Are you now telling me there is more to it?'

'We've been going out for a few months,' she said, feeling ashamed and dropping her gaze to the floor.

'Are you lovers?' he demanded.

Her head shot up and she glared at him. 'That's none of your damned business,' she snapped, feeling heat rushing to her cheeks with his directness. He should meet Sarah, she thought. They could see who could reach the highest score for the most personal question.

'Yes, it bloody well is!' he blasted back at her.

'Since when?' Anger took over from embarrassment and her eyes shot ice at him.

'Since last night. What the hell did you think that was all about?' he enquired coolly, and caused the blood to rush to her face again by getting out of bed without any consideration for his lack of clothing.

She quickly turned her back on him. He took her shoulders and forced her round to face him. 'Did you think it was all a game? Is that what you think of me?' His fingers tightened on her shoulders and she had the feeling he would have liked to shake her, as she stared fixedly at his face, not daring to

451

drop her gaze. 'Or is that the way you always conduct yourself. With anyone?' he finished angrily.

'No, it is not!' She was quick to defend her own pride. 'And I don't know what to think of you. I don't have much to make any judgement on, do I?' she added pointedly. She glared at him as his jaw tensed. Then she turned her head away, as regret overwhelmed her. 'After last night, I don't know what to think of myself, either. And, on top of everything else, we both seem to have forgotten *your* daughter is of the opinion she has squatter's right to you!'

'Forget Rosemary! I want to know about you!' His voice rose threateningly and she smiled grimly. This was the man she knew and remembered.

She pushed his hands from her shoulders and turned her back on him once more. She folded her arms protectively round herself. 'I can't forget Rosemary. I've spent a lifetime trying to do it – with no success.'

'I'll talk to her. It will be all right.'

She gave a dry laugh. 'Do you think I want to live the rest of my life knowing you twisted her arm?' She suddenly wondered what she was saying. Her words had almost been an admission that she wanted him. She didn't, she told herself. Last night had been madness. She wondered if there had been a full moon. 'Go and shower and get dressed,' she suddenly ordered him. 'We'll talk over breakfast,' she added, and walked out of the bedroom before he had time to object. Having him standing naked behind her was doing nothing for her self-confidence. He looked large in clothes. But in their natural state his shoulders and chest seemed immense and gave her the feeling he could have crushed her with one hand.

When he finally came downstairs, looking extremely respectable in the charcoal-grey suit, the expression in his eyes told her very clearly he was in no mood to talk. In a way it pleased her: she had the feeling the previous night would be best wiped from memory. She knew she was asking the impossible. It had been an unforgettable experience. But neither could she forget Rosemary or the look of horror that had been on her face when she caught him with his arms around her. She wanted her daughter back. But this was definitely the wrong way of going about it.

She placed a plate of scrambled eggs and toast in front of him. It was all she had to give him. She never had breakfast herself. He ate in silence and she busied herself around the house and kept out of his way. It wasn't until he had finished eating and stood up, that he said, 'Do you want a lift to work? Or do you want to come to the hospital and pick up your car? And see Keith?'

She didn't miss the tightening of his voice on the last. 'I'll come to the hospital,' she said. The last thing she needed was for him to drop her at work, where someone was bound to see them.

The silence continued as they left the house and got into his car. The car was moving down the hill before Rachel saw Sarah standing at the end of the yard. Her heart hit her throat. As they approached Sarah began to wave frantically for them to stop.

Rachel sighed in despair. 'You'll have to stop,' she said. 'It's my sister.' It was the last thing she wanted to do. She tried to relax, knowing the expression on her face would immediately give her away to Sarah.

He silently obliged and pushed a button and the electric window purred downwards.

Sarah stuck her head through the window. 'Hi,' she said, and gave Edward a very detailed inspection, and received the same in response.

If the situation hadn't been so ridiculous Rachel would have laughed.

'I heard about Keith,' Sarah said. 'How is he?' she turned her attention to Rachel.

'Haven't you heard of the telephone?' She gave her a warning glare. She knew Sarah was just using the excuse. She would not have missed the car standing outside her house all night. She gave an inward groan, having the vivid imagination of her sister jumping up and down like a jack-in-the-box throughout the night, to check if it was still there. 'He's got a broken leg, otherwise isn't too bad. I'm going to see him now.'

'Oh!' Sarah looked from her sister to Edward.

'Then we're going to the factory!' Rachel stated pointedly. 'So, if you don't mind, we are in a hurry!'

'All right.' Sarah backed away wearing an outrageous smile. 'I'll see you tonight,' she called, as the window slid upwards.

Yes, I imagine you will, Rachel thought dryly, as the car moved away. She had no doubts that Sarah would be waiting on the doorstep when she arrived home, with a list of questions a mile long and of a personal level that defied description.

'So that was your sister?'

'I'm afraid so.' She stared out of the window, unable to look at him, as she wondered how the devil she was going to explain him away.

'And you think she is more like Rosemary than yourself?'

'In some ways,' she said, then fell silent. She had thought Rosemary to be very like Sarah in her manner. But she had been wrong. Sarah was in love with love and was of the opinion everyone in the world should be in the same happily intoxicated state. She would never have stood in the way of anyone. She would have done everything within her power to push them together. She sighed inwardly and damned Edward Ellicot for making his daughter as possessive as himself. Then she damned Keith for being fool enough to climb up the hoist and nearly break his neck and get her into all this bother.

As they reached the hospital, she was wondering if there was a man alive who was as normal as David had been. Then she remembered the Jim Featherstone affair and realized he had also had his faults.

'You'll have to take it to the car park,' Edward said, as he pulled up behind her car, leaving her enough room to reverse out.

'Yes,' she replied simply, and got out of the car and went to her own without another word. The perfect ending to a perfect night, she thought bitterly, and drove away without a backward glance.

Chapter Thirty-five

Keith was propped up on a pile of pillows with his plastered leg hoisted in the air.

'How are you feeling?' Rachel asked as she sat down by the side of the bed and presented him with a bunch of wilting tulips she had found in a vending machine in the hospital's main corridor.

He looked at the flowers and gave half a grimace, the other half would still have been too painful.

'Better than these,' he said dryly.

Rachel laughed. 'They were all I could find at this time in the morning.' She had deliberated whether they were fit to give him. But there had been nothing else in the machine and her mind had been too tied up with her other problems to remember to bring something from home. She looked at the plaster cast concealing the length of his leg. 'How do you feel?' She levelled him an assessing gaze. He looked better than yesterday. His colour was back and he no longer looked as if he was in agony, and his words were not so slurred.

'Not too bad, for a bloody fool.'

She nodded her head. She had to agree with him. Climbing up the hoist had been a stupid and dangerous thing to do. 'If it had been anyone else you would have given them hell.'

'I know,' he agreed. Then gazed into her eyes for a long moment. 'Thanks for what you did,' he said, and reached for her hand and gave it a squeeze. 'Even though there was a moment when I felt if that sister got me alone, she'd put me out of my misery just to get you off her back.'

She gave a thin smile. 'Well, it worked,' she said.

She didn't admit that she did feel rather ashamed of the way she had reacted. In more ways than one, she thought, her mind turning to Edward Ellicot. And she quickly turned

455

her mind to work and began talking rapidly. Then, after spending half an hour with him, she went on her way to work.

Fortunately, with having Keith's work to do as well as her own, she found herself too busy to dwell for too long on the previous night. The day flew past and on the odd moments when she found her thoughts turning to Edward Ellicot, she immediately turned them to Rosemary. She felt guilty that Rosemary had not given her enough cause to make her see sense and stop her allowing things to go too far. She had still clung to the hope that, one day, Rosemary would realize there was nothing between herself and her father, and that she would be willing to take up the contact again.

Rosemary would never know about last night, she told herself. But she found no confidence in the thought. All her confidence seemed to have been washed away by the realization of how unreasonably she had acted last night. It had been so out of character and it was both worrying and frightening, and she threw herself into work with an extra zeal, hoping to make herself forget.

After work, Rachel went to see Keith again. This time she had a large bunch of grapes and a bottle of lemon barley water. He looked to have improved even from that morning and he was managing very ably to smile at a little red-haired nurse who was fussing round him.

'I see you're making the most of it,' Rachel teased, as she sat down and the nurse scurried away with a slightly pink face. She looked at the tulips standing on the bedside cabinet in a bright blue vase. They had picked up now they were in water and didn't look so forlorn. 'Here.' She plonked the grapes in his lap and put the lemon barley water by the flowers.

'I might get to like this.' He grinned at her and she felt a warm relief. He had managed it without a grimace of pain and that was a very definite improvement.

'They're not all for you,' she said, and leaned over and took a grape and popped it into her mouth. 'You might have been lying here enjoying yourself, but I didn't even get time for a sandwich at lunch.'

'How did the meeting go with Ted and his merry band?'

She pinched another grape. 'I told them straight,' she said, and smiled at the look of concern on his face. After talking to him yesterday she had been ready to back down and give in to them. But she had given in to them on too many occasions in the past and it gave them the impression she was a soft touch. But with all the worry about his accident and the anger at herself for last night, by the time the meeting had arrived, she had been ready for them. 'I told them Coprell got the work done as well as they did without all the whinging and groaning. And that if they were not satisfied with the conditions I offered they were free to go elsewhere.'

'What did Ted say to that?'

'Nothing,' she said, and Keith looked incredulous. 'He sat there as quiet as a mouse.'

'I don't believe it!'

'It's true. He never said a word. Maggie Cauldwell, of course, got up and began spouting about the union and their rights. So I pointed out that the union could do nothing if I decided to close down.'

'I imagine she had plenty to say about that?'

'She said I was bluffing. I said try me. Then Sue Cartwright pulled Maggie back on to her chair and a number of them told her to shut up.' She stared at him and shook her head. 'It was a relief, I'll tell you, to realize most of them were on my side.'

Keith dropped his head back against the pillow and laughed. Then he groaned and held his ribs. He looked at her with tears in his eyes. 'I don't know where you get it from,' he said. 'You always stick your neck on the line and manage to come up smelling of roses.'

She gave a shrug. She knew exactly where she got it from. Anger! Pure and simple. She allowed herself to get so frustrated about her personal life that she had to have an outlet. Fortunately, up to now, it had always paid off. But she wasn't stupid enough to realize that one day she could fall flat on her face. In fact it had already happened. Last night had hardly been a feather in her cap. But she hadn't been angry then, she

457

realized. It wasn't a very comforting thought. She pinched another grape and began relaying all the well-wishers' greetings from the factory.

It wasn't long before Kate and Flo arrived with more grapes and a pile of books. Close on their heels were Ted and Colin, and the ward sister began to give disapproving looks at the crowd around the bed. So Rachel made her farewells and left the others there.

As expected, when she arrived home, Sarah was close behind her. She was in the process of unpacking some fruit she had bought along with Keith's grapes, when Sarah came into the kitchen. She stood right behind her and folded her arms.

Rachel glanced round. Then continued to put the oranges and apples in the fruit bowl.

'Well!' Sarah said, when she realized Rachel wasn't going to be the first to speak.

'Well what?' she enquired casually.

'Who was he?'

'Who?' She continued to evade the issue. She kept her back to Sarah and gave an inward sigh and wished her sister could be more like herself. Then she took the wish back: she wouldn't have wished that on anybody.

'Rachel!' Sarah scolded. 'Sit down and tell me!'

'He's from a southern group of shops who want to start buying from us. He was up here to look at the merchandise.' She knew she didn't sound convincing.

'And did he see it?'

Rachel forgot the fruit and turned to Sarah with a cool glare. 'What exactly do you mean by that?'

'Come off it. He was here all night.'

'He was looking for a hotel. It seemed only polite . . .' Her voice drifted away. Why was she bothering? Sarah could see right through her and her excuse hardly seemed credible to anyone with two ha'porth of sense. Wasn't it time she stopped trying to live a lie? she asked herself. The answer came back as a very loud and clear yes.

'Sit down,' she said, and pulled two of the high breakfast stools out. Then she changed her mind. 'In the sitting room,' she instructed, having the feeling she needed to be sitting in a comfortable chair for what she had to say.

Sarah sat down in the chair opposite to her and her amazement grew wider and wider as Rachel began to unfold the story of her life: at least the part Sarah knew nothing about.

'A baby!' she gasped, a few minutes later, her disbelief enormous. Her puritanical sister had a secret baby. She couldn't believe she was hearing this. 'How could I have missed that?'

'You were very young.' Rachel smiled at her reaction. 'Only nine. And we'd both had a very sheltered life.'

Sarah shook her head, pushing back the years. 'Wait a minute!' She suddenly looked victorious. 'I do recall thinking you had got fat.'

'Then I got thin again,' Rachel put in dryly. Then she went on to relate the fictitious story of Michael Holden, except she didn't say he had worked at the mill, and she never mentioned the word rape. If it was all to come out in the open Micky would hear about it. But Micky had done well in the years and was now in a position, both personally and professionally, where any scandal could ruin him. He wouldn't open his mouth now. The only part she regretted about it was that the fictitious story would probably give him some peace of mind. He had avoided her like the plague since their little talk at Sarah and Alan's wedding. So her warning must have had some impression on him. She was throwing all that away now, releasing him, as well as herself.

'And that was the adoptive father?' Sarah said, still looking amazed. 'The man you were with this morning?'

Rachel nodded slowly. 'The very one.'

'And he stayed all night?' Sarah looked tremendously interested.

Rachel sighed. 'Yes,' she said flatly.

'And?' Sarah sat forward in the chair, obviously not wanting to miss a word.

Rachel sighed again. 'And nothing. He is a doctor. He treated Keith at the hospital. I bumped into him there.'

'How did he know who you were?'

Rachel told her how he had come to the house with Rosemary on Boxing Day. She didn't tell her how he had acted. 'So, he already knew me. And I got a bit upset about Keith and he didn't like the idea of me driving home.'

'So he brought you home. I can understand that bit. But why did he have to stay all night?'

'Sarah!' Rachel flopped her head back against the chair and looked to the ceiling in despair. 'Do I have to spell it out?'

Sarah grinned. There was hope for her sister yet. 'But if he's not married and you're not married . . . What's the problem? It isn't illegal, is it?'

'That is hardly the point.' She lifted her head and gazed wearily at her sister. 'Rosemary has had her father all to herself for so long. She is very possessive about him.' And she knew where she got it from, she thought. Then checked herself. She was doing it again. Speaking as if Rosemary was the only obstacle, as if she really wanted him.

'Don't be silly!' Sarah's voice displayed her disbelief. 'If you're her mother and he's her father, what better arrangement could she wish for?'

Rachel dropped her head back on the chair once more. Trust Sarah to see everything in black and white and miss all the vital points.

Sarah sighed, reading her sister's mind. 'You always look for complications. Why don't you just ask Rosemary out right what she thinks about it?'

She didn't need to, she thought. She already knew the answer. She had seen Rosemary's face. But she couldn't tell Sarah how she knew. She felt the whole incident on Boxing Day made her look very feeble. If she had made her feelings immediately known to Rosemary, instead of trying to cover up for him, she wouldn't be in this mess now. And if Rosemary had realized she was no threat to her, she might still be seeing her.

'Look!' Sarah spread her hands in front of her to emphasize her point. 'The girl is eighteen, almost nineteen. She knows what's what. She isn't a little girl who thinks her daddy is being stolen from her.'

'I'm not stealing him because I don't want him,' she returned sharply. This had gone too far and she wanted it ended right now.

Sarah sat back in the chair and levelled her eyes at her. 'Then why all this hassle?'

'There isn't any hassle. I just wanted you to know about Rosemary and explain exactly who he was.' She wondered why she had started the conversation; why she had thought telling her sister would help her in any way.

Sarah pursed her lips and looked thoughtful. 'But don't you think there's a reason why you wanted me to know?' She looked suddenly very knowing and, just as suddenly, Rachel wanted her to go.

'No,' she replied stiffly. 'What reasons could there be?'

'You're in love with the man,' she stated confidently.

For a moment Rachel was speechless. 'How can you love someone you hardly know?' She began to finger Polly's locket, hanging round her neck. Almost at the same time Polly's grandfather clock, standing in the hall, struck eight o'clock. Go away Polly, she thought, and dropped her hand into her lap. She wanted no messages, no omens. On this one she knew her own mind, and no-one was changing it.

'Very easily,' Sarah returned with the same confidence as before.

'You read too many books,' she replied dismissively. Then she changed the subject. 'How is Christopher getting on in the football team?' He had just got himself into the school's first team and was very proud of himself.

'Fine. So what are you going to do about Doctor Ellicot?' Sarah continued, refusing to be put off.

'Mr!' Rachel pointed out with a sigh of frustration. 'He is a consultant. And I'm not going to do anything because there is nothing to do.'

Sarah shook her head in despair. For a few minutes she had thought her sister was showing signs of normality. She wanted to get up and shake her. Fortunately the sound of running feet stopped her.

Christopher came bursting through the door, followed by a more sedate Alan.

'I swam fifteen lengths,' Christopher announced proudly. His shaggy blond curls were standing up in all directions. As usual he had gone mad with the towel at the swimming baths, but forgotten that a comb could be useful as well.

'I think that deserves a treat.' Rachel smiled fondly at her nephew and attempted to brush his hair down with her fingers. 'There's a bar of chocolate . . . you know where.'

Christopher dashed off to the kitchen, his hair showing no benefit from her attention.

'Don't I get anything?' Alan flopped on to the settee with exaggerated weariness. 'I had to keep up with him.'

'No,' Sarah put in determinedly. 'You'll get fat.' She went to sit by his side and prodded him in the waistline, which had recently begun to show signs of expansion.

'It makes me more cuddly,' he teased, wrapping his arms around her and pulling her tightly to him.

'Behave yourself,' Sarah warned, struggling free and giving him a playful tap on his hand.

Rachel smiled at the pair. And she thanked heaven that she had not got her way and kept them apart. She did not know any couple who were as happy as her sister and her husband. They seemed to grow closer with the passing years. She suddenly thought if only! Then asked herself if only what?

Fortunately Alan stopped her thoughts. 'Are you coming on holiday with us then?'

'Oh don't start again!' Rachel replied in frustration. They were going to Corfu in a couple of months and since booking they had continued to harangue her to go with them. 'I am not coming on holiday with you and I don't want to hear another word about it!'

Alan moved to speak again, but was cut off by a quick dig in the ribs from his wife. 'Rachel's worried about Keith,' she said. 'We'd better get going and give her some peace.'

Christopher appeared then, his mouth wrapped round a large bar of chocolate. 'Can I stay?' he mumbled, with his mouth full.

'No you can't!' Sarah spoke before Rachel had a chance. 'Come on, Alan.' She dragged her husband from the settee and pushed him towards the door. 'I'll catch you up,' she instructed. 'I want a word with Rachel.'

Alan departed with Christopher like the dutiful husband he was. Rachel looked bewilderedly at her sister, wondering what gem she was now going to come out with.

'What about Keith?' she asked seriously.

Rachel gave a shrug. 'He'll be all right.' He was in good hands, she thought dryly.

'I don't mean his health. I mean how do you feel about him?'

Rachel gave another shrug. 'I don't know. I like him.'

'Then you don't love him,' Sarah stated with blunt certainty. 'So, if you don't do something about it, you're a fool.'

'Thank you,' Rachel replied dryly. Why couldn't Sarah understand and leave it alone, she thought irritably. She wanted Rosemary back and she meant more to her than her father ever would.

'Forget about Rosemary,' Sarah said, with an insistence that made Rachel feel she could read her mind. '*If* she objects, she'll come round. Talk to him about it and get him to talk to her if you can't do it.'

She smiled grimly, recalling that had been his own suggestion. Then she recalled the cool parting a little later that morning. 'I don't think there will be any chance to talk to him . . . again!' she added pointedly, and felt relief that the problem had been taken from her hands. She had no illusions that he would be making any further calls. And that pleased her greatly. She just wished Sarah would understand that.

'You mean to tell me that you spent the night with him – then blew it this morning?' Sarah looked incredulous. Only her sister would be capable of it! she thought in despair. 'Well, if you're visiting Keith at the hospital, you're bound to bump into him.' Not if I can help it, Rachel thought. 'So take the chance to make him notice you,' she continued. 'Give him something to think about.'

Rachel gave a dry laugh. 'What do you suggest?' she

enquired. 'Fishnet stockings and a plunging neckline?' She tried to picture herself dressed as a lady of the night, accosting the sophisticated Edward Ellicot. The image wasn't even funny.

'If that's what it takes. Yes!' Sarah insisted, with a lack of concern only she was capable of attaining on the more personal subjects of life.

Rachel grimaced. 'Go home, Sarah. They'll be waiting outside for you.' She jerked her head towards the garden, where she knew Alan would be hanging around for his wife's appeareance.

'All right,' she reluctantly agreed. 'But if you mess this up you're more stupid than I ever believed. Stop meeting problems halfway and give yourself a chance.' She was at the door before she stopped and turned. 'I only want you to be happy. And, despite what you think, that blessed factory doesn't do it.'

She went after her husband and son, leaving Rachel feeling like a naughty schoolgirl who had just received a lecture from the headmaster. But it didn't change anything. She still knew she would be a whole lot better if Edward Ellicot stayed right out of her life.

Chapter Thirty-six

The little talk with Ted and his girls had done the trick and throughout the summer and autumn the factory did better than ever. Rachel came to realize her first love was to be her only love and turned once more into a fully oiled working machine, driving herself to the limits to get that little bit extra from all her staff.

It took until October for Sarah to drop the subject of Edward Ellicot. But after a final, very volatile argument, when Rachel had stated very plainly that she never wanted to hear his name again, she had finally given up.

The only good thing to come out of Sarah's constant lectures was to make Rachel see that Keith was no more than a friend. She broke it to him gently after he had been out of hospital for a while. That he seemed to be expecting it eased her guilt a little, and she was very relieved to find it didn't affect their working relationship in any way and that in the office he was still the same old Keith.

She had never seen or heard from Edward again, neither did she hear anything from Rosemary. She had hoped she might during the long summer holiday from university. But there had been nothing. It saddened her. But she clung to the hope that one day Rosemary would seek her out again. Perhaps at Christmas, she told herself as the festive season neared and the factory and office became a buzz with anticipated excitement.

'Oh good grief!' Flo muttered, as she struggled to erect the large Christmas tree in the reception.

Rachel leaned on the reception desk and smiled, knowing, despite all the mutterings, if she tried to interfere she would get told off. When Flo was in charge of something she suffered no help or hindrance. 'It's crooked,' she said, giving the tree

465

a critical eye. 'Twist it round. It's leaning towards the door as if it's trying to escape.'

Flo chuckled and moved the tree a quarter turn.

'Now it looks as if it's coming out to grab me.' Rachel said. 'Didn't you check it when you picked it up?'

Flo stood back and studied the tree. 'It looked a good one,' she insisted. 'I think we must have bent it getting it into the van.'

'Turn it so it leans towards the wall,' Rachel suggested, her smile broadening as she recalled the arrival of the tree. Bob had taken Flo to choose which one she wanted and the van had come back with its back doors wide open and the tree poking out. And a rousing chorus of 'Hark the Herald Angels' was coming from the cabin as the van swung into the yard.

Flo gave the tree another twist and it began to fall and she almost ended up on the floor with the six-foot spruce lying on top of her.

Rachel hurried forward and stopped the disaster in the nick of time and they were both laughing, as Jean, the receptionist, looked up from the switchboard and informed Rachel there was a call for her.

Leaving Flo supporting the tree, she went to the telephone on the reception desk and took the call there.

'Rachel?'

Her heart stopped. The voice was so familiar, yet one she had hoped she had forgotten. 'Yes,' she said carefully.

'It's Edward.'

He did not complete the name and she found it odd. And there was something in his tone that was also strange. She didn't know whether to feel angry that he had called her, or sad that she had to speak to him. 'Yes,' she repeated, just as carefully.

'Rosemary has had an accident.'

'What!' she gasped.

Flo and Jean looked round at her, but she didn't notice them. 'When? Where? How is she?'

'She is in intensive care. I thought you should know. If you . . . I think . . .' His voice cracked and she suddenly knew

466

the strangeness in his voice was tears. There was deathly silence. She wanted to shake the telephone to get some response from it. But she didn't move, she couldn't, she was fastened to the spot. 'Please,' she begged. 'What is it?'

'You should come quickly,' he finally managed to say.

Her heart was somewhere in the region of her feet. No, she thought. It couldn't be happening. 'Yes,' she said quickly, and was about to put the phone down. Then had a sudden thought. 'Where is she?' she screamed into the receiver, fearing he might already have gone.

'The Infirmary,' he said flatly, and then the line went dead.

'Whatever is it?' Flo had watched the blood drain from her face and had deposited the tree against the wall and come to her side. She placed her hand on her arm and looked anxiously into her face.

'An accident,' Rachel said, without looking at her. 'My daughter has had an accident. I have to go.'

'Your daughter!'

But Rachel did not hear or see Flo's surprise. She brushed her hand away and was in her office. She grabbed her handbag but did not stop to get her jacket. Then she raced out of the door, finding her car keys as she went.

She raced all the way through the hospital to the intensive care ward. Then, at the door, she stopped, fearing she was already too late. She took a deep breath and slowly walked through.

'Mrs Morrell?' the sister asked, with a gentleness that made her fear the worst and made her want to scream. She couldn't believe it, when the sister then said, 'This way. I'll take you to her.' She wondered if the sister knew who she was. What the hell did it matter? she thought, and silently followed.

When they reached the bed where Rosemary lay, the sister immediately left her standing there. She stood for a while looking on the bloodied and battered figure on the white sheet, connected to tubes and pipes that were all the more frightening because she did not know what they were. Then she turned her gaze to the silent figure sitting by the side of the bed with hands clasped and head bent. And the knowledge that he knew exactly what was happening inside Rosemary, and what her chances really were, froze the blood in her veins. He didn't look up, he didn't move a muscle, and the misery he emitted touched her skin and she trembled.

She didn't know what to do and stood there feeling there must be something. She felt so useless and impotent and silent rage grew inside her, born of fear and guilt and regret. Then, without totally realizing what she was doing, she fell to her knees and prayed to the God she had shunned, hoping that if He was as good as He was supposed to be, He would listen to her. Then she prayed to Polly, knowing, if it was within her powers, she would help her.

When she finally got up, it was to find a chair had been placed next to Edward. She hadn't been aware of it being put there and she sat down, assuming a nurse must have brought it. Edward was still in the same position and she had the feeling he was incapable of movement.

For a long time she matched his silent stupor. She stared frozenly at Rosemary's face, unable to take her eyes from the battered features. A large jagged gash ran along her forehead and up into her hair. The left side of her face was a mass of small cuts and grazes and the right side was swollen and discoloured. By some miracle her nose appeared to be completely untouched and stood out like a beacon in the midst of a battle field. Her beautiful daughter had been turned into a hideous monster and tears began to well up in her eyes.

'How . . . What . . . ?' she finally began. Then stopped, she didn't know what to say, or if he would answer her if she got the question out. She bit hard on her lip to stop herself breaking down in self-pity. She looked at Edward and he looked so distraught she knew she had to be strong, for Rosemary and for him: stronger than she had ever been in her life. 'Thank you for calling me,' she said, knowing it must have cost him something to give her a moment's consideration at this time.

He moved then. Reaching over, he took her hand in his and held it tightly. She didn't know if he was offering comfort, or seeking it. But she was grateful for the show of unity and clung fiercely to him.

'What happened?' she asked gently.

He didn't look at her, his gaze lifted numbly to his daughter's face. 'A lorry came out of a side road. Their car went underneath. It's a miracle they weren't both decapitated.'

'They?' she questioned, with a frown.

'She was with her boyfriend.' His face pivoted to her. 'She does have a boyfriend!' he added meaningfully, reminding her of her harsh words of the previous Christmas.

'I'm sorry,' she said. She wasn't sure of what she was apologizing for: the accident, her angry words, or all that had happened between them. 'Where is he?' she asked flatly.

He nodded in the direction of the door. She turned to look, but couldn't see. 'Is he . . . the same?'

He nodded his head but did not speak and Rachel also fell silent. They remained that way, clinging to each other, listening to the continual pips and beeps from the electronic wizardry that proved the inert form on the bed still contained some life. Every now and then Edward looked up and laid his free hand on Rosemary's arm. 'Rosemary,' he said. 'It's Dad.' But the sight seemed too painful for him to bear for more than a few seconds and he would turn his attention to all the machinery. Staring at each one in a way that made Rachel feel he was trying to will some more action from them. She wanted to ask what each machine was doing. Then she thought, perhaps it was better if she didn't know. His greater knowledge was obviously making it far worse for him and she felt her own emotions were too shaky to understand the blunt technicalities. So she kept quiet and clung to his hand and watched his head go up and down at regular intervals.

For three hours they sat that way, both too numb to realize the passing of time. Edward's head was down and he was staring at the floor when the first groan came from the bed and the electronic gadgets suddenly became erratic. His head cracked up like a whip. Rachel gasped. And simultaneously their grip on each other's hand tightened.

'Rosemary!' he said and, letting go of Rachel, grasped both of his daughter's hands. 'It's Dad,' he began. Then continued talking to her as she began to thrash around the bed. At first the jerky, almost fitful movements and the throaty gargling noises alarmed Rachel. She sat on the edge of her chair and grasped the bed. She wanted to grasp Rosemary and hold on to her as Edward was doing with such intensity, as if he was dragging her back to life. But she knew that was a line she could not cross. They were father and daughter and she had no right to come between. She sat back on the chair and felt her sadness overwhelm her.

The groaning and thrashing went on for several minutes, then she fell silent again. Edward returned to his chair, but he kept hold of her hand and began to rub it in a gentle massage, and he carried on talking; about things they had done and things they had planned.

Rachel sat very still and listened, learning about her daughter in a way she had not thought possible. All the lost years of her childhood, Edward recounted, and silly little things that would have been meaningless in other circumstances. Tears filled her eyes and she realized why he loved Rosemary so much. And she also realized why he had been so terrified of losing her. She felt like an interloper, a spy who had no right to know these secret intimacies, and she sent up a prayer of gratitude that he had sent for her. Because she could have understood if he had not. She had no rights to Rosemary. She had given them all away when she had given her away: a tiny defenceless baby, without any knowledge of what she was sending her to. She sent up a second prayer of thanks that it had been to Edward, who had given her all the love and care she hadn't been able to find in her own heart. She thought of the past year, how she had sat waiting and wallowing in her own self-pity because Rosemary had not contacted her. Rosemary owed her no obligations and she should have recognized that. She had contacted her once and she should have been grateful and accepted it for what it was: Rosemary's natural inquisitiveness in wanting to see this woman, this so-called mother, who could give her away. Was it any wonder she hadn't wanted her father to associate with someone with so little heart?

In the depths of despair, she got up silently from the chair and left them alone together. Father and daughter; the little family she had no part of. She walked up and down the corridor outside the ward several times. She had the feeling she should leave; walk out of their lives for ever. But she couldn't do it. Despite all she had done, she knew the love she felt for Rosemary was genuine and she could not have walked away not knowing if she would live or die.

'Are you all right?' a young nurse came out to ask.

'Yes,' she said simply. 'I . . . I wanted to leave them alone for a while.'

The nurse smiled at her with a compassion that tore at her heart because she didn't deserve it. 'Well, if you want anything, just come and ask,' she said, and went back into the ward.

For several moments Rachel leaned against the wall and stared numbly at the antiseptic floor. Then she looked at the ceiling. Help me, Polly! she begged silently. Remember your rainbow, lass. Just you trust old Polly, came back in reply.

She sighed and looked bleakly around the corridor. She couldn't see any rainbows in these plainly sterile walls. She gave another sigh, heaved herself off the wall and went back to sit by Edward's side and listen to him talking to his daughter.

For four days the pattern of life became the same. The factory was forgotten, except for one brief phone call to tell Keith he was in charge until further notice.

'How are things?' he asked with concern.

'Not too good,' she replied, and offered no further explanations. Then she stood for a while and stared at the telephone. It finally came to her: Edward's phone call, herself telling Flo and Jean that her daughter had had an accident. Strangely, she felt no shame or humiliation, just a great sense of relief that it was finally all out in the open.

The days were spent sitting with Edward at Rosemary's bedside. They took brief breaks to grab a drink and something to eat, though neither of them ate much. At night they went home to try and find a few hours sleep. But Rachel never managed more than a couple of hours and she knew from the dark circles under Edward's eyes that he was the same. And no matter how early in the morning she arrived at the hospital, he was always there before her.

'How long can this go on?' she asked, when he had a rest from speaking to Rosemary and leaned back looking exhausted.

He shook his head. 'Days, weeks, months, years!'

'Years?' She looked at him in despair.

He nodded his head and, for a moment, stared at her with a desolation that felt like a knife entering her heart. 'But however long it takes, I'll be here.'

She gave a tight little smile. 'So will I . . . if you want me to be.'

'I want you to be,' he confirmed. 'I *need* you to be!' he added with so much feeling that her heart contracted painfully inside her chest. Emotion clogged her throat and, in that one moment, she knew Sarah had been right all along. She did love him. She loved him as much as she loved the young woman lying in the bed.

'What have I done?' she asked despairingly. Suddenly she saw everything as her fault. She dropped her face into her hands and wanted to cry. If she had kept her mouth shut, if she had believed Edward. She thought of the night he had spent with her, the way he had made love to her. Sarah had been right again. She was stupid. She had to be: to have experienced that and still been capable of turning her back on her real feelings. If she had acted differently everything might have been different and Rosemary might not have been in the wrong car at the wrong time. Then she had an awful thought. She looked at Rosemary, then she turned to him with dull eyes. 'We're paying for our sins,' she told him woodenly.

'What sins? Good God!' For a moment he was filled with all the emotion that had evaded him for the past days. Then he dropped his head into his hands and gave a deep sigh.

Rachel bit her lip. It was true. She had committed one

472

of the seven deadly sins. And now she was receiving her justice.

He turned his head and stared at her. 'What sins?' he repeated.

'Fornication.' The word was little more than a whisper.

'Is that what it was to you?' he demanded angrily.

She dropped her head and could not reply.

'Fornication!' He shook his head in disbelief. 'I made love to you because it was what *I* wanted to do. And I thought it was what you wanted, as well. I knew I'd been a bloody fool. I admitted that and I was prepared to explain everything to Rosemary . . . If you had given me the chance.'

'Then why didn't you?' she asked tightly. He had had plenty of chance to put things right, but had obviously never done so.

'Because I didn't think there was much point.' He looked at her steadily for a long moment. 'Was there any point?' he finally asked. 'Would it have helped you get Rosemary back if I had told her I had fallen in love with you? Do you think she could have come back to you, knowing I felt that way, and knowing you wanted nothing to do with me?'

She shook her head in sadness and regret. He loved her and all the things he had done had been for her. Despite everything, he had wanted Rosemary to come back to her. 'It isn't true,' she said, looking right into his eyes. 'I didn't want nothing to do with you.' She had constantly told herself she hated him, that he was the last person she wanted to see. But she had only been protecting herself. Deep down she had known the truth. Fear had made her reject it and Edward. Fear that if she cared too much she would lose him, the way she had lost David. She was terrified of being hurt again and being left alone in her misery and pain. Yet she had almost allowed her own fear to do exactly that to her, depriving herself of Edward and leaving her to a lonely existence of incompleteness. 'I love you, Edward,' she said, and she knew she had never spoken those words and meant them in the way she was meaning them now. She had loved David, in a quiet and gentle way. But now she understood the euphoria that glowed from

Sarah's face when she looked at Alan. She smiled thinly, suddenly remembering the silent form on the bed. 'What about Rosemary?' she asked uncertainly.

'Oh Christ!' In the next moment she was swept off her feet and was being dragged down the ward. It wasn't until they were in the corridor that he stopped and explained his actions. 'She's probably just heard all that.'

'Oh no!' She covered her mouth with her hand and stared at him anxiously. All she could think was that she had said fornication. She was mortified.

Then suddenly Edward began to laugh. 'Well, if she did, we don't have any problems about how we're going to broach the subject.'

She tried to laugh with him, but she couldn't. Rosemary had hated her before, if she had heard what they had been saying she could only imagine she would hate her more.

'It isn't so bad,' he said, looking at her downcast face. 'She would have known sooner or later.'

But not everything, she thought. She looked up at him with shame all over her face. 'She might think I go to bed with everybody I meet.' After all, she herself was proof enough that her younger days had not been snow white. She dropped her gaze, then suddenly looked back into his face. 'You don't think that, do you?' she asked.

He gave her an ironic grimace. 'Someone who can use words like fornication? I hardly think so!' His smile was touched with amusement. Then he grabbed her hand and dragged her back to the ward. 'We should not be messing around out here,' he informed her sternly.

Although his words reminded her of Rosemary and that all her troubles were not yet over, she could only smile at him. And, for once in her life, she thanked her father for teaching her his own very bigoted outlook on life.

The moment they both sat down once more by the side of the bed, Edward said, 'Hello, Rosemary. It's Dad.' Rosemary immediately began to move and moan, though Rachel noticed the actions were not so jerky as before and the noises not so garbled. Edward stood up and leaned over her. 'Rosemary, it's Dad,' he said, in the way Rachel had heard him say so many times during the last few days. But he didn't continue. He suddenly fell very silent and her heart lurched violently in her chest and she leaped to her feet. Why wasn't he speaking? was all she could ask herself, and could only come to one terrifying conclusion.

She clung to the edge of the bed and tried to peer round him, but he was leaning right over Rosemary and she couldn't see a thing. 'What is it?' she demanded frantically.

He glanced round and moved aside. She didn't need to see Rosemary, with eyes open, to know she had returned to the land of the living. The expression in his eyes had told her everything she wanted to know.

'Dad,' Rosemary said, her voice weak but plain.

'It's all right, darling. You'll be fine,' he said, and Rachel felt the wave of relief that rushed through him, reach out and wash right through herself as well. Rosemary knew who he was and she had spoken the one little word coherently.

Tears misted Rachel's eyes and she sent up a grateful prayer to the God she had thought would have shunned her. Then she sent up a second thank you, to Polly, because she felt she must have had a bit of a hand in it too.

'I'm sorry, Dad.' Rosemary stared into his eyes with a look of remorse.

'There's nothing to be sorry for,' he said, and Rachel knew he was close to tears. She wanted to reach out and offer him comfort and support. But she stayed back, once more the outsider.

'I didn't . . .' Her voice trailed away in weakness. She glanced at Rachel, then turned her gaze back to her father with the same look of remorse.

'Did you hear . . . everything?' he asked carefully.

She gave the slightest nod of her head to indicate yes. Rachel bit her lip. 'I'm sorry,' Edward said meaningfully.

Rosemary made an attempt at a smile. Then she turned to Rachel. Rachel tried to smile, but she recalled the cool expression she had received last Christmas, and she knew the only thing she had managed to do was tighten her mouth into a thin line. Tears pressed harder at her eyes and she waited for the moment of rejection that would be twice as hard to bear, because she would be losing Edward, as well as her daughter.

But, as Rosemary's eyes gazed out of the battered face, there was something in their expression that told Rachel she was smiling at her. Then, for the very first time, she said, 'Hello, Mum.'

The words were very weak and feeble, but strong enough to send the tears she had been holding back flowing freely from Rachel's eyes.

Epilogue

The air was chilly though, strangely, there was not a great deal of wind to make Rachel's eyes water and spoil the view, as she stood at the top of the hill and counted her blessings.

She gazed out over the fields and over the golf links, and the memories came flooding back. She turned to look down the hill, to the cottage that had been her first home. She thought of her father and mother. And Joseph, who had never returned to England but, from what she could glean from the one letter he sent annually with a Christmas card, seemed to have made a good life for himself in Germany.

She recalled herself as the insecure young girl who had responsibilities heaped on her shoulders. How she had worked day and night to achieve her dreams.

She looked across the river to the house that had been David and Judith's. Her eyes rested briefly on the weir and she pictured a sad white bundle floating in moonlit water. She looked up to the scudding clouds and hoped they were together: that David and Judith had found each other again.

A noisy engine prompted her attention back to the hill. She smiled. Christopher and his precious sports car, she thought fondly. The engine came to a halt and she watched Christopher and his girlfriend emerge and walk into the house which had once been her own. Now it belonged to Sarah and Alan. Her smile broadened. She suspected there might be an engagement announced this afternoon, while the family were all congregated together for Christmas tea.

Her gaze wandered past the sports car, down the hill to another cottage. She sighed reflectively. 'I'd never have done it without you, Polly,' she said, speaking into the air, as the fond and grateful memories warmed her right through to the bones. She smiled once more, feeling sure she heard Polly denying the fact.

'It's been a good life, Polly,' she continued. The rewards had more than compensated for all the hardships and heartache and struggles. The factory was going from strength to strength. The past year had seen the completion of the third workshop and they now supplied throughout the country and into Europe. Europe had been Keith's idea. He was still with her, still single, and he enjoyed himself tremendously, gadding around foreign parts and bringing back the orders.

She shook her head in wonder. All from nothing, she thought. From a frightened girl who had just given away her baby.

She thought of that baby, now a paediatric registrar and married to another doctor. Rosemary had made an excellent recovery from the accident. Now, apart from one scar on her forehead, which was hidden beneath her fringe, there was nothing left to remind her of that terrible time. The boy she had been with had also survived, but they had not continued the friendship, and she had soon found the man she was eventually to marry and the accident had been forgotten.

Her thoughts moved on and, as if her mind had drummed him up, a tall figure came out of the house, paused to look up to where she stood, then came towards her.

As he approached, they shared the smile that was reserved just for themselves, filled with a secret promise, of hopes and dreams.

'Christopher is getting anxious,' he said. 'He wants you back so he can have everyone together. I think he has something he wants to tell us.'

'I think I already know what it is,' she replied, bathing in the eyes that smiled down at her.

He gave a laugh. 'So does everybody else. But he thinks it is a big surprise.' His eyes crinkled with amusement and Rachel felt her love for him expand inside her.

'Come on then.' She moved into his open arm and wound her own around his waist, and they walked down the hill, joined by the love that had surrounded them for all the years of their marriage.

As they reached the end of the cart track and came to the tarmac road, a second figure, much smaller, came dashing out of the house.

At the tender age of eight, Stephen Edward Ellicot was showing all the signs of being the image of his father. But he also had much of his mother in him. He was becoming more and more interested in copying her designs, and creating his own, with an ability that she found surprising in one so young. And she was now happily confident she had found her successor.

'Come on!' Stephen demanded, as he met them at the gate. 'We're waiting to open the presents.' He swung the gate wide with frantic urgency.

Rachel smiled and Edward stroked a consoling hand over the top of his son's dark head. 'We're coming,' he assured him, with a fatherly fondness that put a lump in Rachel's throat. Then he took the gate from out of Stephen's hand and the boy dashed off up the path.

Rachel paused and took one last look at Polly's cottage.

'Is something wrong?' Edward asked.

She smiled at the look of concern on his face. 'No. I was just remembering.'

'Good or bad?'

'Good,' she said with feeling, and looked up into his eyes and knew there was not another pair of eyes in the world she would rather be looking into. 'Edward Ellicot, I love you,' she declared.

And, right there in the road and in broad daylight, he pulled her against him and kissed her with the passion that came so easily to them.

Somewhere in Rachel's fuzzy mind she had the impression she could hear Polly's voice: There's a reason for everything, lass, it said.

It wasn't until Stephen's voice was heard, loudly proclaiming, 'Yuk . . . sloppy!' from the doorstep, that Edward released her.

They laughed together: at their son, at each other. Then, with hands and fingers tightly linked, they walked up the path together.

I found the rainbow and the gold, Polly, Rachel confirmed silently as they reached the door and went inside.

As Edward closed the door behind them, Rachel had the distinct feeling that Polly was chuckling.

THE END